Bodyguard by Night

A Grumpy Bodyguard Small Town Romance

Happy Acres
Book 2

Taryn Quinn

Bodyguard by Night
© 2022 Taryn Quinn
Rainbow Rage Publishing

Cover by LateNite Designs
Photograph by Lindee Robinson Photography
Models: Jake & Shayna

First print edition: September 2022
ISBN Print edition: 978-1-940346-80-9

Acknowledgments

Sometimes we make up fictional places that end up having the same names as actual places. These are our fictional interpretations only. Please grant us leeway if our creative vision isn't true to reality.

For the artists and the TikTok peeps that always keep us entertained.
We love you madly.

This one's for you.

Chapter 1

Willow

For Really Real

I blew my hair out of my face. I should have put it up, but my damn vanity always got me. My hair was my best feature. And it wasn't like I was cooking for anyone else.

Well, except the camera.

Which was where the vanity came in, but that was another day's therapy.

Anyway, I was used to finding long red hair everywhere in my apartment. Okay, the apartment I shared with four other girls. Which reminded me I only had another hour in the kitchen before my sworn enemy, Dennelle, came home from her shift.

She hated my "little project" as she called it.

"That little project had two hundred thousand views yesterday," I muttered as I cleaned off the counter. I rushed around the miniature island to check my camera. That last clip was going to be great for my bloopers' reel.

Here I was on my third try making pâte à choux. The baking shows made it look easy—though I'd watched more than one contestant melt down when the pastry was too runny. Not-so-pro tip—the little pastries didn't puff up into beautiful golden vehicles for filling when that happened. And now I knew their pain.

I was going to make a batch of these suckers that rose properly today if it killed me.

Or I ran out of time.

I played back my last take. Some of the footage was salvageable. Just not the last twenty minutes when the buttery sludge had spread across my Slipat sheet.

Hmm. I paused. Maybe I should use what I had. Show the not so pretty side of baking. People needed to know that shortcuts were great, but they couldn't be used for everything.

Especially something like cream puffs.

I set the camera to do another take. I had about thirty minutes left on my memory card, so I'd need to make them count. Then I'd see what I had and edit. I could probably get two posts out of this debacle.

I huffed out another breath, my frizzing curls fluttering around my face. I could do this. I was *good* at this, dammit.

Gingerly stepping around my tripod, I masterfully hopped over a box I used to prop my lights up just right and got myself situated around the kitchen island.

Social media apps were all about showing people the good parts. They definitely weren't supposed to see the jar of Skippy I used to make my tripod just a touch higher to get the full kitchen island in frame.

Then again, my particular fans liked to see the behind-the-scenes footage too. I didn't mind leaning into some comedic timing for the views. I'd learned long ago to laugh at myself. It staunched the tears.

Laughing through my stumbles was what my social media channel was all about. Making mistakes and finding the shortcuts to create the cool things people found on television or on the various video channels. Or even failing and ending up with a new lesson to add to my personal cooking arsenal.

Maybe I'd make a video about that, actually.

I glanced around in my chaos on the kitchen counter, then I spotted my phone on my last carton of eggs. I grabbed it and quickly opened my notes app to write down the idea. A notification popped up about yesterday's video, distracting me from said notes app.

Maybe I'd just check my replies really quick.

I scrolled as I wound my way around the couch that bisected the kitchen from the shoebox-sized living room. Living in the city—even if it was in the more generous apartments located in Brooklyn—meant space was a premium. I was pretty sure our lovely landlord had sliced up the living room space to add another bedroom.

My bedroom. Or coffin as I called it lovingly.

I smiled at a few of my regular commenters, quickly scrolling past the trolls telling me I sucked and the bots telling me I should DM them for more followers. I'd learned a long time ago to ignore the noise. Reading that crap was the road to a depressive spiral that made me question everything, followed directly by searching job sites for a regular job that included a steady paycheck.

But then I remembered I really sucked at regular jobs and I got my ass up to make another video. I wasn't so good at the whole being to work on time. The number of times I'd been fired for that reason alone made my resumé look like swiss cheese. Nine times out of ten, they hated to fire me too but there were rules.

Rules were the bane of my existence.

And here I was getting paid to actually *break* them. After the last firing, Wil's Way began.

I soaked in the sweet replies about being excited for another video. Answered another one asking a question about doing a collaboration. And deleted another one that was obviously a spam reply.

My heart stalled as the *willowsheart611* screenname jumped out at me.

"Dammit."

My first instinct was to delete the reply, but that only made them post again. And then their making a big deal about me deleting their replies had turned into a witch hunt in the comments. People loved adding their two cents when it came to internet outrage until my post had a thread one hundred replies deep with people raging about perceived slights.

Soon, it had been a mindless stream of hateful diatribes that got so twisted I had to hide or delete them. I'd lost count of how many times I'd blocked this particular person. I had a feeling it was a dude, but I couldn't be sure. Regardless, they always came back with a new screenname.

One that was suspiciously close to the last one.

They probably had made a bunch of them at once to have them on hand. Okay, perhaps I was being paranoid, but I'd been through the fixation game a time or two.

Once in person.

I wiped my suddenly clammy palm against my thigh. No, we weren't going to go there. That had happened a damn long time ago and he couldn't hurt me anymore.

Couldn't *find* me anymore.

I slammed the box closed on that little trip into my past.

This was a totally different thing. Just a minor annoyance. I wasn't special in this regard. Anyone with a successful channel had these problems. Just one of the downsides of fame.

Or perceived fame. The internet helped make people hot and just as quickly, fall into the not column. I was focused on staying in the former category.

"You can do it. Just get it over with," I muttered to myself. My heart rate slowed. Okay, that one wasn't bad.

---

willowsheart611: *Your beauty is only second to your amazing culinary genius.*

Much like the replies they'd first made. Back when I'd thought that person had been harmless, if a little odd.

I scrolled on by it and dropped a heart on a few other ones. Replied with a few links to previous videos for people asking questions. In a perfect world, people would look at my feed, but then again, I'd learned neon arrows were the preferred path.

People were fucking lazy.

I glanced at the time and swore. Now I only had forty-five minutes to get my video done. Quickly, I checked my makeup and hair in the skinny mirror we'd crammed in the corner of the living room. I'd let my hair do the curly thing today, but it was getting hot with the lights.

"Screw it." I twisted up the long, thick strands and secured it into a messy bun. Vanity only worked when the effect was actually cute.

After rushing back to the kitchen, I found my remote under my recipe notebook and turned on the camera.

I flashed a grin directly into the lens. "Ready to do this choux thing? I think you are. No, you know what? I *know* you are. We can totally do this." I pulled the eggs in front of me. "Handily, I don't have Paul Hollywood staring at me as I figure this out." I nibbled my lip and let the smile spread. "He really is a silver fox, isn't he? Whew! Do you have a favorite chef—other than me, hello! Throw your thoughts in the comments."

I went through the steps of making the pastry. This time, it actually looked as it should.

"Okay, I know this seems like a lot of eggs, but trust me...when you stuff one of these suckers in your mouth hole, you won't care."

I was my usual chatty self as I made the half dollar-sized circles on the baking sheet.

"And that's it. Time to cook. Now if it looks too runny and you don't get these little peak thingies, then you gotta start over. I know, I know. It sucks, but that's part of baking." I snorted. "Wait until you guys see the blooper reel for this one. I have failed no less than five times."

I shrugged with a good-natured smile and straightened up, making sure my *Wil's Way* apron was in the frame.

"You know I want to give you shortcuts for dang near everything —can't do it here." I grinned into the camera. "However, I do have some tips to make the filling. Guess that means there's a part two for this one! Hit that plus sign to follow for more."

I let the camera roll for an extra few seconds, and then I grabbed my remote. I was about to check the video when I heard swearing outside the door.

I glanced at the clock on the microwave. Why did Dennelle have to be so damn punctual?

Wiping my hands on my apron, I quickly scooped all my tools and wrappers into the big garbage bowl I used to keep things semi-controlled.

"Dammit, Willow. What the hell did you order this time? This box is as big as our television."

I frowned as I dumped everything into the sink. I hadn't ordered anything. Sometimes I got items from companies looking for reviews, but I wasn't sponsored.

Yet.

It was one of my secret goals.

Also, I also had a PO Box for anything that was sent to me unsolicited. I didn't give out my address to *anyone*.

I rushed to the front vestibule. Dennelle wasn't kidding.

"Well, don't give me those stupid big eyes. It only works on idiot men. Help me."

She was such a delight.

Hurriedly, I lifted the other end of the box. We shuffled our way into the living room before she dropped her end.

Something inside shifted and made a loud clunk.

Dennelle stepped over the box, her icepick heels landing an inch away from my foot. "That better not take up more room in the kitchen. It's already full to the brim with all your shit."

"I didn't order anything."

"Yeah, well, it says your name, doesn't it?" She shook her platinum blond hair out of her face so it fell in the severe straight lines that framed her glacial cheekbones and pointy chin. Elsa had nothing on her ice queen look.

Self-consciously, I pushed at my sagging bun. I always felt extra frumpy around her. My hair was about as tamable as my mouth. Most of the time, I liked that it was wild, but the minute this woman was in my space, I couldn't help but notice our extreme differences.

Her flawless, pale skin—my endless freckles. Her suit, my embroidered jeans and bare feet.

I must have been extra bohemian today since her forehead dared to wrinkle with her sneer. "Are you ever going to grow up?"

My eyebrows rose. "Excuse me?"

"You look like a twelve-year-old who got her clothes from the thrift shop."

My jeans were actually hand-stitched by an artist and probably cost as much as one of her Louboutins. Not the pair—I wasn't *that* extra with my clothes. Though I was pretty extra if you asked my sister.

I frowned. Speaking of my sister, maybe she sent the box. "What's today's date?"

Dennelle rolled her eyes. "I rest my case."

"I work for myself. Days have no meaning."

Dennelle snorted.

"But I still pay my rent and utilities, unlike you did for a few months last year."

She flushed. "I was deciding between firms."

I gave her a flat smile. And okay, it had been a very shaky thing to make rent before I'd discovered the joys of social media creator funds. Happy hail Mary pass for the win.

Not that I really knew what a hail Mary pass was, but it sounded good. And there had been many prayers, tears, and deals made with various deities as I learned the online ropes.

Dennelle gave an exasperated sigh. "You're having one of those conversations in your head again, aren't you?"

I resisted the urge to roll my eyes—barely. "Look, I'll make sure to take care of the box, okay?"

"Whatever." She glanced into the kitchen. "And clean that up," she added as she flounced.

Well, in my overactive imagination it was a flounce. It was more like a stalking click of heels down the hardwood hallway that led to her bedroom.

I plopped onto the couch and dragged the box closer to me. I didn't recognize the company on the address label, but I did love presents. Who didn't? My sister was famous for sending me odd little unexpected gifts.

At least she used to. Now it was all things wedding with a side of honeymoon and the occasional discussion about the CocoaBus craze she'd created in Happy Acres.

Guess we were more alike than I'd thought.

I dug out the old guitar pick I kept in my pocket for opening boxes. My ex...three exes back? Maybe it had been four. Bobby had been a long time ago. The only good thing I'd kept from our *very* short-lived romance was the pick. One would think a guitarist could find his way around a clit.

Alas, no.

Unfortunately, he also thought it was okay to spread his lack of knowledge around. Evidently, a guitar could make panties disappear. And I'd been blind to it for a few weeks before catching a clue, followed by getting tested because *ugh*. Gross.

But damn if the sharp end of a pick wasn't the perfect thing to pierce packing tape. I ripped the box open and my stomach flipped.

"No way." I flung the thick brown packing paper over my shoulder. "No actual way." I dug into the box to find sturdy shelves and heavy black iron connectors.

No cheap *Wish* knockoffs here, thank you very much.

I set aside assembly instructions and a huge brown bag of parts stuffed down inside the box.

Reverently, I smoothed my hand over the varnished shelves. How had my sister known? If it wasn't her...

I couldn't remember talking to the company, but maybe I'd sent an email begging for a review package in a late night fugue state. I definitely would have had it sent to my PO Box though. Some companies wouldn't use PO Boxes, but there was an option with my post office to have a physical address for just those exceptions. I was damn careful.

Even if there was an off chance I was allowed into the inner sanctum of RID Inc., I would probably only rate a small basket. Nothing like this.

I hauled the shelves out and carefully set them on the floor. I would not be eligible for a top of the line storage unit, which I knew cost well into the three digits.

I was doing well for myself, but I was still basically a newbie. But oh my gosh, I had wanted this cart so very badly. I must've saved and liked advertising videos for this cart a dozen times.

Before I could think any harder about where the box came from, I decided it was a gift from the gods and I was taking it.

I spent the next hour ignoring the kitchen, breaking two nails, but finally managing to get all three shelves secured together.

It was even straight according to the tiny level in the box. I mean, who actually included that in the box? RID Inc. did. They thought of everything and that was exactly what made them top of the line.

I pushed the cart away from me and would you look at that? The wheels were smooth as freaking Kerry butter. I spun it around in the small space with a happy little laugh.

The front door slammed, and I looked up to see my favorite roommate struggling through the hallway. "Hey, Merry." I went to help her. She was a nursing student and had a pile of books on her at all times.

"Oh, thanks." She offloaded her notebooks and a textbook that looked like it could be a weapon. She shrugged out of coat and tugged off her hat so her lemon blond hair exploded in every direction. New pink streaks fluttered around her triangular face. At my wide grin, she threaded her fingers through her short cap of hair and wrinkled her nose. "My sister needed to try out something for her certification."

"It's cute."

Merry rolled her eyes. "Can't I ever be called sexy?"

I pointed to my own red curls. "Girl."

She laughed in her bubbly Merry way, which reached into my chest and warmed me right up, before dragging me into a spontaneous hug. "What are you up to?" She leaned around me. "Oh, man, what is that? Den is going to lose her damn mind."

I sighed. "Yeah, she already ripped into me. But look at it!" I pulled her over to show off the cart. It was full of little slots for my tools and had three tall shelves that would perfectly stack all my cooking supplies, all done in the most amazing industrial vibe. It was my heart in a cart.

"Oh, well, *that's* pretty. I'd love one for my bedroom." She nudged me. "You know, just saying. Hook a girl up."

"I wish. I can't believe I was gifted this bad boy. It retails for like three hundred bucks."

"What? Is there gold in the wheels?" She placed her palm on the top shelf and spun it. "Okay, so that's pretty cool. It's like that super expensive luggage that twirls like a ballerina."

I hugged myself. "I know. It's just perfect."

Merry frowned. "You sure you got it as one of those promo things you get by being internet famous?"

My self hug became a little more guarded. "It has to be, right?"

"But don't they usually send you a packet to make sure you do all the—oh my God, this is the coolest thing ever, you know you want one too—kind of things?"

A twinge hit my stomach and twisted. She was right. A promotional packet was pretty standard. "Yeah. I didn't get one of those."

Nothing was free in this life.

I slid my phone out and opened my email. Nothing with RID Inc in my emails. I did a quick search for the name of the item to see if it was gifted from another company doing a collaboration. Internet marketing lived for a good collab.

Nada.

My heart started racing. A quick sheen of sweat prickled at the nape of my neck. *Relax, Wil. It's not like before.* "It could just be a gift."

But I could hear the reticence in my own freaking voice.

"It came here or your PO Box?"

Now my head was pounding in time with my heart, the excitement fading in the cold slap of reality. "It could be from my sister."

"How would she know you wanted this specific thing?"

"Dammit, Merry, stop being logical."

She gave me a sad smile. "Honey, who has your—*our*—address?"

"I..." My phone looked watery all of a sudden. I blinked and my vision cleared, but that of course flooded my stupid eyeballs with tears. I dashed them away with the back of my hand. "I never give it out. I swear." I turned to Merry. "You believe me, right?"

"I know you get really excited and sometimes you don't think things through."

My heart climbed into my throat. I couldn't refute that. Before I'd found my footing in Wil's Way Kitchen, I had tried my hand at a ton of different jobs. Heck, I'd even accidentally done one of those multi-level marketing things.

I still had protein smoothie pouches stacked in one of my closets.

On this one thing, I was very careful. Especially since I had roommates.

And... No, I was not even thinking *his* name ever again. It had been years and that part of my life wasn't a factor anymore. Regardless, I'd always had a PO Box because of privacy. I wouldn't ever put anyone in danger, let alone my roommates.

I scrubbed my palm against my jeans. "You know what? I'll talk to my sister about it."

"Are you kidding me?"

Dennelle's shrill voice made me flinch.

Her long crimson dagger of a nail was pointed at my new cart. "We do not have room for more stupid Willow show crap."

"It's not crap," I shot back.

And it wasn't the Willow show. It was Wil's Way, thank you very much. Not that I'd remind her. I might lose an eye.

"All of your things are crap. I'm sick of it all cluttering up our place. For God's sake, our kitchen is barely made for one person and it's *not* you."

"I don't hear you complaining when I serve food."

Her eyes went bright with temper. Actually, maybe there was a little crazy in there too. "Your stupid corner-cutting food is gross."

My chest tightened. It wasn't gross. I thought I was helping when I used my video leftovers to feed the house. My eyes burned, but I wouldn't let her see a tear fall.

Merry stepped forward. "Who the hell pissed in your Cheerios?"

She'd changed out of her suit into skintight work out clothes that accentuated just how overly skinny she was. "You all do. Every one of you brings chaos into this place. There's no fucking peace."

"Then find another place to stay," I snapped.

"Why don't you? I bet if we took a vote, you would be the one who was asked to leave."

"Dennelle!" Merry's voice raised.

"What? Am I lying?"

Merry crossed her arms. "We all love Willow."

My breath stalled. Her voice did not sound confident in any way. "Merry?"

She turned to me. "We love you. A few minor inconveniences would never override that, sweetie."

"I'm sorry." My voice was barely more than a whisper. "I never wanted to be an inconvenience."

I thought I'd found a place that accepted me. All of us in this apartment were on various career tracks. Some of us passed each other in the hallway with tired waves, some of us chilled in the living room together when we had the time, but in the end, we just tried to be mindful of everyone.

Had I really been the awful roommate no one wanted to deal with?

Merry tried to grab my hand, but I twisted away. "No. I get it. I'll just get out of everyone's way."

"Wait. No, Willow, we don't want you to go."

"Speak for yourself." Dennelle's snide voice made my shoulders bunch up tighter to my head.

"It's fine. I can go to my sister's early. I'm supposed to go in a few weeks anyway." Tears started choking me, but I wouldn't let Dennelle see them. I swallowed them down ruthlessly. "I'll just get out of everyone's hair for a bit."

Merry grabbed my hand. "Honey, that's not—"

"It's okay." I didn't look at Dennelle, just met Merry's gaze. "It'll be good for everyone."

Merry let out a sad sigh, which only made me feel worse. But she gave up arguing quickly.

Far too quickly.

Shame and guilt rose up in an ugly stew of acid in my gut. My gaze darted around the room. It wasn't like my job required me to be in any particular place. I could crash at my sister's place.

My aunt Laverne was forever telling me I should come visit more.

At least they would want me.

Probably.

I stalked down the hall and grabbed boxes out of the closet. We had no shortage of them with all the moving in and out that had happened over the years. I grabbed the tape gun from the top shelf and returned to the kitchen.

"Come on, Willow."

Dennelle rolled her eyes. "Good riddance."

"You are not helping things," Merry hissed.

"Ask me if I care?" Dennelle plopped down on the couch and turned on the television, cranking the volume.

Merry took the tape gun from me. "You don't have to pack things up."

"I don't want to take up space."

Merry winced. "It's not like that."

"Oh, but I think it is." I swung open doors, pulling out my pans. I stacked all my baking sheets, bowls, measuring cups, gadgets, and silicone molds on the island. Everything started sliding, and Den turned up the volume even more.

In a daze, I washed dishes, scrubbed the sink, and then cleaned the counters. I tried my best to erase my very existence from the kitchen. I stuffed down the sadness. The first kernel of what I was meant to be had started right here on this faded Formica counter. Late night brownies had become brookies—a cookies and brownies mashup.

I'd tried to crack the recipe from a bakery in Manhattan. Just for fun.

For people who didn't live in New York City.

For me, because I was a poor idiot who didn't have anything better to do than to rip apart a recipe in the dead of night. And that night had changed everything for me.

I dashed away a tear and dumped the perfect choux pastries in the garbage. They wouldn't survive a trip in my SUV. I definitely wouldn't be bringing my inferior pastries to my Aunt Laverne's place. Not when I was going to be begging for a place to stay.

I climbed onto my step stool to make sure I didn't miss anything in the higher cabinets. Every once in awhile, I sniffed back an onslaught of tears. Merry stared up at me, her eyes equally watery.

Shaking my head, I gave her a hard stare. I wouldn't get through this if she tried to placate me or make excuses. I didn't want to stay where I wasn't wanted.

Merry put together another box and I filled it. Again and again, until I was literally deleted from our—*their*—cramped kitchen. I moved on to my room, dumping piles of laundry into any bag I could get my hands on.

It took five trips to load everything into my old Santa Fe SUV.

And I damn well took the cart—I just wouldn't think about its origin story.

My evil villain cart named...Loki.

I swallowed down a laugh. Dammit, the cart was so freaking pretty. Just like his namesake.

Merry came out with a large suitcase. "I really don't want you driving while you're so upset, especially since it's dark. Can't you wait until tomorrow?"

"It's fine. I like driving at night." I took the suitcase and crammed it into the passenger side. Loki took up most of the back. I'd packed around him.

Flashbacks of doing the same when I left college threatened to strangle me. Everything was too much the same. The memories of the fear and loss crowding up my throat ready to bubble into a sob.

"You're really not leaving, are you? Like not for really real."

I gave her a tight smile, but it *felt* for real. I swallowed hard against the wash of anxiety. I needed to focus on the now.

Besides, packing up the kitchen stuff was all that was important beyond my clothes. Kinda put a serious stamp on the finality of it. I'd lived there for three years. But the only thing that truly mattered was what I'd done in the kitchen.

I pulled her into a hug. "I'll pay rent until I figure it out."

"That's not what I meant and you know it." She gripped me harder.

"I know." I swayed with her for an extra minute before pulling back. "Maybe it'll be better in a few weeks."

But I knew it wouldn't. And Merry knew it too.

"Tell the girls I said goodbye. I'll come back for the rest of my stuff...soon."

"Dammit, Wil." Her navy-blue eyes filled.

"A change will do everyone some good."

Merry dabbed at her eyes with her sleeve. "I didn't think today would go this way."

"You and me both." I glanced back at the old two-story house that wasn't sure if it wanted to be a brownstone or a concrete slab. When I'd first moved in, I thought it was charming in its uncertainty—kind of like me.

Now I just saw how much it didn't fit me anymore.

I gave Merry one more hug. "I'll send pictures of the beautiful bride."

"You better."

"See ya."

I climbed into Lola, my SUV and headed north.

I wasn't sure Happy Acres would be a good fit either, but anything was better than here right now.

Chapter 2

Ransom

Lucky Shot

The familiar twenty-foot neon green shamrock seared my eyeballs as I pulled up to Lucky's.

Small towns, man, didn't really go for the whole low-key vibe. Bonus points—the bar served a decent draft and had a professional dart board.

I also was pretty sure I'd been added to some sort of hitlist when it came to this place. People pounced on me the minute I walked through the damn door. Which was also fucking weird. I wasn't used to being noticed.

My whole adult life had been about being in the shadows.

I wasn't sure there was a shadow to be had here in Turnbull. Even in the bitch ass winter that was perpetually gray. But the days were getting longer and spring was finally breaking through the lingering frost, yet another reminder that Clay's wedding was approaching.

April was zipping along faster than I'd realized.

Dammit, I'd forgotten to go to my fitting—again. Clay Winslow, my best friend and pain in the ass, would be on my case. Maybe after a beer or three, he'd forget.

I swung the door open, and a few shouts of my name reminded me of the old *Cheers* reruns. Was I the new Norm?

Now that was fucking depressing.

I nodded to the regulars and headed to where my preferred beer waited for me on the shiny bartop. "Hey, Ruby."

"Hey, Surly. How's tricks?"

"Firmly in the hat."

Her lips quirked. She was a stunner in that she-might-beat-me-up-or-she-might-make-out-with-me kind of way. "Was that a joke?"

"Probably not." I leaned on the bar and did a quick scan of the room. It was one thing I'd never be able to quit. Knowing my exits and keeping track of my surroundings meant I wouldn't end up dead. Most likely.

A couple of rowdy townies were too many beers deep in the far corner. I noticed Ruby also focused on them as she scrubbed the already gleaming cherry wood.

Her biceps were almost big enough to rival mine. Her black tank echoed the green shamrock logo from outside, except there was one on each tit with Lucky's scrawled between them. Skintight jeans showed off the rest of her assets.

She was exactly the kind of woman I usually found appealing. So much so that I'd almost hooked up with her my first week as an official Turnbull resident. Emphasis on the *almost*. Shitting where you eat—or drink, as it were—was not smart.

Clay was busy with his new fiancée, Rachel, and I had far too much time on my hands. Especially since my security job had been effectively squashed when Clay turned his winter residence into a permanent one. I wasn't overly mad about it either.

Manhattan had never felt like home to me though I'd grown up there. Alternately, Turnbull was quiet, remote, and people left me alone—mostly.

I sighed as one of the townies made a beeline for me. His staggered gate put me on alert enough that I automatically braced against the edge of the bar. Nelson Taggert liked to take offense to a westward breeze. I wasn't really in the mood to bloody up my knuckles today.

Something about my face made people eager to start shit.

I took a long drink and gave him a bored look.

"I want a rematch."

Gently, I set down my beer. I'd crushed his ass in pool last weekend. It wasn't even my game, but I'd been bored and annoyed enough by his constant begging to take him on. "No, you don't."

He jabbed a stubby finger into my shoulder. "You owe me fifty bucks."

I arched a brow at him. "I can't help it if you can't keep the eight ball on the table."

Nelson swayed once then stepped directly in front of me.

Ruby snapped her towel on the bar. "Time to pay your tab, Nelson."

He stumbled to the left, gripping the bar to steady himself. "I'm good for it, Ruby."

"Didn't say you weren't. But it's time for you to close out and go home. And, dammit, leave Ransom alone. He's tired of paying for the chairs he throws you into."

"That's a true statement." Nelson kept bouncing off my fist, but I knew the jackass couldn't afford to pay for damages and I wouldn't leave Ruby to pay for it instead.

I should probably stop coming in since something about my scent made people want to either punch me or challenge me. I lifted my glass again. The beer was damn good though.

The door opened and late spring air swept in. I kept my gaze on Nelson since he was probably two beers past intelligent.

"Then maybe you should pay for another," he snarled.

The right hook came for my face, and I dodged it easily. My fingers curled tighter around my glass. Wouldn't want to spill a perfectly good IPA.

"That's it. You're out, Nelson." Ruby's voice was sharp and no-nonsense.

"What? I didn't even hit him."

"Because you have piss-poor aim."

For fuck's sake, this mouth of mine would never learn. Or the brain that went with it.

Though his next swing was wide, he managed to clip my chin with his bulky class ring. Who the hell wore a class ring past senior year?

I thumbed away a bit of blood. Damn stone had sliced through my heavy stubble. "Nelson, don't make me toss you out of here. I'm pretty sure the chair place Ruby buys from has them on backorder."

"You son of a—"

"I'm five minutes late, and you're already starting a fight?"

My best friend's smooth, cultured voice came from behind Nelson.

Nelson reared back to swing again, and his elbow caught Clay in the gut. Clay let out a *whoosh* and grabbed the shorter man by the neck of his jacket and shoved him into the bar. The stool skittered into the next one down, causing a chain reaction. The scrape of chairs and stools combined with the commotion from the drunk jackals across the bar rushing our way created the perfect clusterfuck.

With sincere regret, I took another drink of my beer before handing it to Ruby.

"Crap." Ruby released a resigned sigh. "You weren't even here five minutes!"

"I didn't do it." I ducked as a drunken arm came at me. What did I do to this guy?

Ruby threw down her towel and finished off my beer.

"Hey." I frowned at her, feigning left as another fist came my way.

She pulled out her bat from under the cash register. "Don't make me use this, people!"

I caught one of Nelson's buddies' fists as it came for my face. I squeezed until I heard knuckles pop and the guy yelped.

The heavy clomp of steel-toed work boots heading my way made me roll my eyes. Great, even more reinforcements.

I glanced over at Clay, who was holding his own. That was interesting. I didn't think he remembered how to get his hands dirty.

Boarding school was a long time ago. Then again, much had changed since he'd swapped his daily suits for plaid and denim.

Some enterprising fool came up behind me and tried to grab my arms. His pal threw a punch. I dodged left and he landed a shot to the guy behind me. I shook him loose while he was stunned and spun to use it to my advantage. He was a blond with thinning hair and blood flooded from his nose and between his fingers as he clutched his face.

I probably didn't need to add insult to that injury.

Before I could move out of the way, the guy who'd thrown the punch attempted to grab me. I was tempted to hurl him over my shoulder, but we lived in a litigious world. A quick Google search would show I came from money.

Instead, I used his momentum to swing him into the bar and Ruby rapped his fingers with her bat. The bald dude howled, and then he cradled his hand against his chest.

Ruby wasn't afraid of being sued. No one here had balls big enough to try it.

I shuffled and dodged my way over to Clay, so we were back to back. He was a few inches taller than me, the damn mutant. Now that I knew he actually knew how to fight, I was hedging my bets his way.

"This wasn't what I was thinking when I said let's go for a beer," he muttered as he threw out a jab.

"They keep wanting to start shit with me."

"Then why do you keep coming back in?" He grunted as he used one of his long legs to kick a third guy spinning through the brawlers.

The guy went down with a howl. A knee shot always worked.

I hooked my arm through another idiot's arm and sling-shotted him back toward the pool tables and out of the confined space around the bar. "Really good beer," I said with a grunt.

"I have good beer."

"You have a girl." I put the thinning blond into a headlock. Jackass had come back for more even with blood staining his teeth.

"What? Why? Rach likes you."

"Three's a crowd, man. Besides, no one wants to watch you play kissyface all the damn time."

"Kissyface?" He glanced over his shoulder at me. "Who the hell says that?"

A flush climbed up my neck. I was hanging out with Laverne too much lately. I was rehabbing one of her old roll-top desks for the lodge. The woman lived to hover.

I shoved the blond toward the now open door. Another arctic breeze signaled new blood. I only hoped they weren't looking for trouble.

Why would I get that lucky? "Shit."

"What?" Clay followed my gaze. "Eh, crap."

Two of the Manning brothers were standing, legs spread, their weight on the balls of their feet. Justin Manning was rubbing his hands together. Hayes, the older, usually more responsible brother, mirrored his stance.

"Hey. Looks like we got here just in time," Hayes said with a wide grin.

"Fuck." I growled as someone got a rib shot in while I was distracted. Forgetting the earlier responsible Ransom, I cold cocked the asshole and watched him go down.

Clay turned. "Damn."

I shrugged. "I'm tired. I just wanted a beer and to play darts, man."

"I'd kick your ass."

"You'd try," I said genially and ducked, knocking out the blond dude when he came back for more.

"Hell," Ruby shouted from behind the bar.

I winced. "Sorry, Ruby."

"Yeah, yeah." She had the bat up, ready to swing.

Justin, the lankier of the two brothers, put some burly bearded dude in a headlock and waved at us. Pure joy lit his face. He was a damn troublemaker. "Hey, guys."

I gave him a quick nod then grunted when Nelson came swinging through once more. I deflected a punch. The wiry bastard had a cannon of a fist when he planted it right. I twisted Nelson's arm behind his back and shoved him into the corner of the bartop. His ribs took a good shot, but he was feeling no pain.

Adrenaline had made him even more of an asshole.

He came back for more, giving me a trifecta of knocked out men. My hand throbbed as Nelson hit the floor with a thud.

"How do you do that?" Clay shook his hand.

"I'll show you later."

Finally, there were only six people feeling rowdy. Once they saw the people laid out flat on the beer-splattered floor, three of them wisely made tracks for the front door.

"Aww." Hayes put his hands on his hips and leaned forward to take a deep breath. "I was just getting started."

Justin slapped his back. "You did pretty good, old man."

"Fuck you." Hayes shoved him back. "I'm only eighteen months older than you."

Justin dabbed at a bit of blood in the corner of his mouth. "Still slower than me."

Hayes stood up straight. "I'm not the one bleeding, now am I?"

"No, but you're winded—that's the old part." Justin stepped over one of the men on the floor and leaned on the bar. "Heya, Ruby."

"Send that charm over to the table of ladies watching from over there, baby Manning."

Justin looked over at the quartet of girls giggling, then he turned back to the bartender, his teeth a slash of white in his scruffy face. "Aww, why won't you give me a chance, Ruby Rose?"

"You couldn't handle me." Ruby set a beer in front of him. "Free beer if you drag John off the floor there and put him outside."

"Deal." He bent down and hauled up the man he'd just stepped over.

The man swayed a little before shaking his head. "What happened?"

"Time to go, my man." Justin gripped him by the upper arm and helped him across the room.

I braced as one of the last of the feisty ones stood in front of me.

He looked around and saw most of his friends were either unconscious or nursing wounds. He held up his hands. "I'm good, man."

Finally.

I rubbed my aching rib, but when he started to walk away, I hauled him back by the neck of his jacket. "Put something in the tip jar for the trouble your friends caused."

The man's eyes went wide, but then he pulled out a crumpled bill and stuck it in the big green jar on the bar. "Right. Sure." Then he practically ran for the door.

Just like that, the conversations started back up. People sat down and returned to their pub grub and drinks.

I picked up a stool and sat down on it, then I kicked Nelson who was still on the floor in front of me.

"Don't give him any more brain damage." Ruby set a draft of beer in front of me.

"Too late." I lifted my glass and took a long swallow.

Clay sat next to me. He smiled at Ruby, then he winced. "That lumberjack looking one has a hell of a left hook." He wiggled his jaw.

"Glass jaw."

"Shut up." He nodded gratefully at the bartender as she set another draft in front of him. "Thanks."

Hayes collapsed next to him. "Hey, Clay."

"Hayes."

Hayes folded his arms on the bar. "You guys sure know how to have fun."

Ruby rolled her eyes. "Beer or whiskey?"

"Beer, thanks." Hayes shoved his mop of hair off his forehead, leaving sweaty spikes.

I propped my elbows on the bar as I curled my hands around the cool glass to ease my abused fingers. "I didn't do a damn thing."

Ruby grinned as she pulled a draft. "Good thing you're too pretty to ban."

"Stop. I'm gonna blush." I grinned from the rim of my glass.

"Dimples and everything." Ruby fanned herself as she set Hayes' glass in front of him.

Hayes grinned. "Think she likes you, Ransom."

Ruby gave me a sly smile. "He's afraid of me."

I lifted my glass in salute. "I am."

Clay threw back his head with a laugh. "Since when are you afraid of anyone?"

"I know when I'm outta my league."

Ruby's grin spread into a wolfish smile.

I wouldn't even have to chase her. And while the stress relief would be awesome, I didn't want to screw up my welcome in my favorite bar. Somehow things with me never ended well.

Finally, she went to the other end of the bar where customers were waiting.

Clay finished half his beer. "So, did you get that fitting yet?"

"Goddammit."

"Guess that's a no. I'm gonna keep asking 'til you do it, man. Rach has blazed past lists at this point. She's got a whiteboard in the kitchen." Clay twisted his glass in the condensation around the bottom of his glass.

"That's what you get with a ring." Hayes passed his glass from one hand to the other.

Sounded like there was a story there, but I made it a point not to ask questions. That way I didn't have to answer any of my own.

"I don't mind it much. She's just very particular with her check-lists. She even made me download an app on my phone. I can hear the checkmark tones in my dreams."

Hayes snorted. "Taylor probably told her about it."

"I wouldn't doubt it."

Taylor was the super organized manager at the Happy Acres gift shop. I was almost certain she and Rachel fed off each other's need to control all the things.

Actually, I didn't want to know these things about so many people. I kept to myself, but somehow I was always getting volunteered to help at the orchard or the tree farm.

I blamed Clay. He was blinded by the fresh insanity of love and access to sex on the regular.

Thankfully, things had quieted down once Christmas passed. We'd spent most of the winter shoveling or planning to shovel. The snow was no joke around this part of New York.

I slapped Clay's shoulder. "Let's go play a round now that the idiots have dispersed."

Hayes gave us a salute and got up. "I'll go see if I can steal a girl away from my brother. I suck at darts."

Clay followed me through the maze of chairs and tables to the upper part of the bar where the darts area was set up away from the tables. TVs were bolted the walls showing various sports from US soccer to football in the UK since football season here was over. The other wall of screens had on various baseball games.

It was a Friday night and the mood had lightened considerably since Nelson and his crowd were no longer taking up space. Well, Nelson was still out cold, but he wasn't causing any trouble for now. I glanced back down to the main bar and saw he'd been propped in the corner near the bathrooms.

We played a few warmup rounds and caught up on mundane life shit. Rachel's dress had come in, the bachelorette party was coming up, and Clay had bought a small gaming startup that had been floundering.

He was far more involved in his family's business than I was. My mother was still head of Douglas International and not looking to change things anytime soon. She was as odd as an Andy Warhol

26

painting and worth about two hundred of them. Good thing since my worthless father just liked to spend the money, not actually work for it.

I wasn't going there. I'd left home so I didn't have to think about how my family put the fun in dysfunctional.

"Ready to get your ass kicked, Winslow?"

"Bring it, Dougie."

"Fuck off." I gathered my darts. He hadn't called me that since we were kids. Before I could throw a blue dart at the board, a husky laugh floated across the bar.

My chest tightened and my gaze swung to the door. I knew that laugh.

Fuck.

Not her.

Willow Doyle.

I'd been actively planning to hide in my cabin when *she* came into town. Which was not supposed to be until the end of the month.

"Aw, hell."

Clay peered around me and his face split into a grin when he caught sight of Rachel and Willow giggling and bouncing against one another as if they had pregamed before they got here.

"Hey, Almost Wife," he shouted over the bar noise.

Rachel's huge eyes glinted with happiness even across the damn bar. "Hello, Almost Husband."

"Shoot me," I muttered.

Chapter 3

Willow

Got Fifty On It

I'd rolled in an hour ago—on fumes because I'm the dimwit who should've stopped for gas—and somehow got wrangled into going to a bar with my sister.

Firstly, that was new. I couldn't count the number of times I'd had a drink with my big sister. Secondly, she was adorable. I'd never seen heart bubbles popping around someone's head in real life, but there they were, coming off her like love perfume.

Her target, the tall drink of billionaire up on the second level. Since I was currently holding her hand, I got dragged along behind.

My chest tightened as I spotted the moody best friend of the groom standing beside Clay. Ransom—hot guy name, and boy, was he aptly named—stood just behind him, arms folded broodingly. He was wearing an ancient leather jacket that had molded to his shoulders and arms over the years until the leather showed off every delicious line.

Whoosh.

Calm down, nipples.

My job was to support my sister in all ways for her wedding. Okay, and to hide out at the orchard for awhile, but none of that included lusting after the bestie of the groom. I could lust quietly in my head—just a little bit. It wouldn't hurt anyone.

And the more miles I put between me and my old apartment, the more I'd evened out. I'd rather focus on my sister's wedding than my dumpster fire of a living situation. Some harmless lusting was far more enjoyable.

My sister picked up the pace and dragged me deep into the crush of bar patrons and made a beeline for the stairs to get to her man.

Wait, what was that on Clay's white shirt?

My height was an advantage in many ways—reaching high shelves, when painting, and picking on my sister, to name just a few. But the best part was being able to see over a crowd. Add in my awesome vision, and I was a force. Mostly in my own mind, but in this case, it was very helpful.

"What did he do now?"

I still had a bit of side-eye going when it came to Clay. In my opinion, my sister forgave him too easily from the drama this winter. He should have groveled with extra jewelry and maybe another one of those cool buses before she forgave him.

They obviously loved each other, but still.

I muttered apologies as we weaved our way around tables and chairs. The scent of nachos made my stomach roar. Luckily, it couldn't be heard over the cheers from the people on the top level crowded around the baseball game.

After narrowly missing the corner of a table, I spotted a guy in all black with a green shamrock over his pectoral muscle. Since it wasn't St. Pat's anymore, that meant only one thing—waitstaff. "Oh, hey. Could we have an extra large order of those nachos up there near the blissfully happy idiot on the second level there?"

The guy gave me a quick once over and his smile powered up a few dozen watts. He glanced up at where I pointed. "Sure. What's your name?"

I raised an eyebrow. "Why do you care?"

His smile widened. "For the ticket for the kitchen."

"Oh." *Getting ahead of yourself, Wil.*

"But I wouldn't mind your digits to go with it."

My cheeks pinked up. "We'll see how you do with the nachos."

He was cute and way safer than Sir Grumpsalot.

My sister tugged on my hand. "Okay, okay." I waved over my shoulder. "Biggest nachos."

Mr. Shamrock laughed and nodded.

"You know, you could just let go of my hand."

"Nope." Rachel's face was practically glowing. She pulled my hand tighter to her chest. "I'm so glad you came early."

I plastered on a smile. "Couldn't stay away."

Her blue eyes were so damn bright and happy. Little crinkles had formed at the corners from her perpetual smiles and her new outdoor lifestyle. At the very least Clay had definitely put a light inside my sister.

I was pretty sure it was more than a light based on her giddy laughter.

Orgasm glow was like perfect makeup—you shouldn't know it was there, but it showed off the best parts of you—and mine was expired. Probably because most of the men I'd been with didn't know a clitoris from a thumb. The way my sister was dragging me up to see her fiancé, I was pretty sure he was all good on that front.

Sure, it could be love, but probably not *just* love.

As we got closer, my sister's glow dimmed. She dropped my hand as we got to the top of the stairs.

"What happened?"

Yep, that was blood on Clay's collar. And Ransom was sporting a few busted knuckles and an angry gash on his chin.

I stuffed my hands into my denim jacket pockets. "Hey, Weirdo."

Ransom gave me a quick jerk of his chin. "Chaos."

I wrinkled my nose at him. "Bar fight? Really?"

Ransom shrugged. "Wasn't my fault."

Rachel rushed to Clay and touched his bruised cheek. "What happened?" she repeated.

31

"He didn't duck," Ransom said as he leaned back on the chair rail beside the dart board.

His relaxed pose didn't fool me. His storm-colored eyes were far too intense as he scanned the half dozen people who filtered in and out of our section. Especially a pair of guys getting progressively louder in the corner.

Clay lifted his beer to rest against his cheekbone. "It's nothing. Little bar fight is all."

"Little—" Rachel sputtered.

He set his beer down, then he brought her hands down to lay against his chest. "It's over."

"Except for that shiner."

Clay glanced at Ransom. "Not helping."

"I was actually surprised you remembered how to fight at all. Desk jockey."

"Web jockey these days," Clay shot back.

"Still includes a desk."

My gaze bounced from Clay to Ransom and back again. "Are we still measuring dicks at this age?"

"And you're...what? Twenty?" Ransom smirked.

"Twenty-six, thanks."

He shook his head. "Infant."

I flipped a middle finger at him.

"I rest my case." He reached for a glass on the table.

"And how old are you, hotshot?"

"Thirty-six."

"Ancient."

"Hey," Clay interjected as he sat down at the table, dragging Rachel onto his lap.

"Aww, you're not old, honey." Rachel looped an arm around his shoulders. "You're just right for me."

My eyes lit up as I saw Shamrock guy come up the stairs with a platter of nachos. "Because you're almost thirty."

"Hush," Rachel hissed. She straightened up and her eyes got wide. "Oh, hey, are those for us?"

"Mostly me." I waved to the waiter. "You definitely delivered on the big."

He grinned at me. "I do love to exceed expectations."

Clay grabbed his glass to make way for the food. "Those look great, man."

Shamrock's smile brightened. "Can I get you any drinks, ladies?"

Rachel nibbled on her lower lip and scanned the platter for the perfect chip. "Well, if we're having nachos..."

"Margaritas," I said happily.

"I'll need to see your IDs."

I handed mine over. He took it and scanned the details. "Willow. Finally got your name."

"You only need to check the particulars, not memorize her address, creeper." Ransom snatched my license back from him.

The guy's face went to stone.

"If that's the way you talk to people, no wonder someone threw a punch." I tried to pluck my ID out of Ransom's fingers. My alternate PO Box address was on my license, so it didn't give any details anyway. He held it tighter and we played tug of war for a few seconds. "Excuse his rudeness. What's the best margarita on the menu?"

"Ruby's got a special blend," Shamrock said tightly.

I glanced at the logo on his shirt again and saw there was a name stitched in the middle. "Well, Kyle. We'll have two of those on the rocks."

"Sounds good." His smile was a bit less friendly as he quickly typed something on a clunky-looking tablet.

I elbowed Ransom beside me. "Apologize."

"No."

"He's sorry."

"No, I'm not."

Kyle tucked his mini tablet into his apron. "I was just checking her name, man."

"If she didn't give it, then you don't need it."

"Oh my God. Did you forget how to flirt? Or just never knew how?" When Ransom just flared his nostrils at me, I nudged him behind me. "I mean, if it *was* flirting. Probably not now," I muttered. Dammit, Kyle was cute too. "Thanks, Kyle. We really appreciate the quick nachos. And can't wait to try out Ruby's margaritas."

"Right." He glanced at Ransom one more time with a shake of his head before he headed down the stairs.

Ransom's breath was warm on my neck as he stood right behind me. *Don't react. Don't react.*

Would it be wrong to check my jacket to make sure it hid all the things reacting?

"Thanks for being an asshole."

"Probably does that twenty times a night, sweetheart."

And now I wanted to rip out his tonsils.

I turned around and stabbed his chest with my finger. Wow, nothing moved under there. *Focus.* "Thanks. Now you're just being an asshole to *me*. I'm cute, dammit. Maybe he was flirting."

"A girl like you doesn't need some player waiter looking to get under your skirt."

"I'm not wearing a skirt. It's a dress."

"Same difference. But hey, if that's what you're into."

I swiveled my head toward Rachel and Clay, who were plowing their way through my nachos and watching us as if we were a sitcom. "Why is this your best friend?"

Clay shrugged as he scooped up another load of jalapeños and guacamole. "Can't get rid of him."

Ransom finished his beer in two long gulps. "I'll get out of here and let you three have some time."

"You don't need to do that." Rachel grabbed a napkin and came around the table. "We want you to stay. Get to know my sister since you guys will be doing a lot of best man and maid of honor stuff together for the wedding."

I literally watched Ransom's face go stony.

"Is it so abhorrent to walk me down the aisle?"

Well, *that* came out wrong.

His eyebrow arched into the rafters. Arctic gray eyes stared at me unblinkingly.

"You know what I mean."

"Speaking of walking down the aisle, did you get your fitting done yet?" Rachel chirped.

Ransom's head dropped back. "No."

"Told you, man," Clay mumbled around some chips.

Rach twirled around. "Told him what?"

Clay stuffed a loaded chip in his mouth.

Taking pity on him, I swiped a trio of discarded darts off the table. "How about one game? If you still want to go, then we'll endeavor to survive without you."

He narrowed his eyes at me. "You play?"

"A bit." I sort of was the queen of darts at the bar near my apartment—*ex*-apartment.

He took the darts from me. "I'm blue."

I wrinkled my nose at his retreating back, but I grabbed the red darts.

Clay hooked an arm around the back of his chair, interest lighting his patrician face. The two men couldn't have been more different. Clay looked like a suit even when he wasn't wearing one and Ransom screamed some sort of military or security with his watchful gaze.

Well, except when it came to me. His eyes barely grazed over me —he actually seemed to be actively *not* looking at me. I resisted the urge to check my armpit. It had been a lot of driving, but I'd washed up and changed before I left Clay's cabin-slash-mansion.

Whatever. I didn't care.

I shrugged out of my denim jacket and tossed it at my sister. Ransom's jawline tightened as I turned back around to him. My navy maxidress floated around my ankles. The sleeves were long and flowy and the whole thing was dotted with sparkly navy stars on a matching sheer background. It had a few layers so there was nothing revealing about it, but it was loose and comfortable—and hid the fact that I was more leggy than curvy.

"Problem?"

His nostrils flared.

"Why are you so weird?"

"He can't help it," Clay said helpfully. "Think his personality was permanently starched into his uniform."

I tipped my head. "Army?"

His flat gaze didn't waver.

"Suit yourself. 501?"

He nodded curtly and stepped aside.

I wasn't sure why his military time was a sticking point. Most of the guys I knew who served shouted it from the rooftops. Of course those guys also had small dick energy. Not so much with Ransom.

Pushing *any* dick energy to the back of my mind, I rolled my neck and shook out my fingers.

Darts was an easy game, but it was more about accuracy than brains. Well, besides doing some simple math. We'd shoot for highest points for who started the game. My first throw was...not good. He smirked when he went to the board to pull out my red dart on the outer ring of the seventeen space.

He handed me the dart, and without looking at the board, he threw an outer bullseye.

I studied the narrow green space around the bullseye. "Gonna be like that?"

"Scared?"

I dipped my hand into the pocket of my dress, pulled out my emergency fifty, and flashed it. "You?"

"I don't mind taking your money." He rescued his dart and moved back to the line. "Do you need me to move back a bit for an advantage?" He stepped back another four feet.

"Shut up and play."

The first player to zero won. Each round included three darts.

He smirked and set himself right behind the line. His first throw of three darts killed a good chunk of his total. Freaking double points. Lucky shots. Or he was showing off.

Once I learned the weight of the darts and settled into my new surroundings, I chased him hard. It only took five rounds for him to get down to double digits from five hundred. His focus was a bit preternatural, if you asked me.

Like there was this bubble of calm around him.

I stepped closer, watching the fierceness of his angular face as he consistently shredded my score. To win, you had to hit a double on the board to create part of your score—two darts in the same number. He needed forty-five and he could do that with this last round.

I still needed one hundred and seventeen. Ugh.

I was tempted to blow in his ear a-la Kevin Costner's *Robin Hood* movie, but I'd probably be wasting a good distraction on him.

He was a damn robot.

"Do you mind?"

I tucked my hair behind my ear. "Do I make you nervous?"

"You annoy me."

"Why, because I play so well?"

He gave me some side-eye without turning my way. "Do you have questionable math skills? I'm about to win."

"Right." I linked my hands in front of me and swayed. "Sorry. By all means, go ahead."

"I am."

"More action, less talking," I said with a smile.

I heard my sister snort from the table. "Bet that's the first time you've heard that one."

Ohh, there went another nostril flare. Maybe I could use my sister to distract him instead of my female prowess. "Bet he'll choke," I answered her.

"Can I put fifty on it too?" Clay called.

"Where is the loyalty?" Ransom muttered as he stripped off his jacket.

I'd thought the jacket showed off his arms. I was misinformed. The worn green Henley under it hugged all the good parts. Chest, arms, the hint of muscular midsection—all of it was so wrong.

"You did take me for two hundred last weekend," Clay shot back.

I blinked out of Lustland. I was pretty sure my jaw wasn't on the floor. I glanced at my sister, but she was too busy staring at her fiancé with a sappy lovesick smile. At least no one else had noticed how Ransom affected me.

"That's because you have no aim." Ransom let the dart fly and it hit the twenty mark on the board.

I would not be deterred. He still had to get another twenty. I still had a chance.

The thunk of the dart sitting right next to the first one in the double ring section of the twenty segment made me throw my head back. "For fuck's sake."

"Language!" Rachel said without any bite in her tone.

Ransom's face was stony again when I looked at him. "What?"

"Are you always this dramatic?"

"Yes."

He threw the last dart, then he swore.

"What?" I ran for the board. He'd aimed for the five which would put his score at zero—aka winner, winner, chicken dinner. But it was just over the metal line that made up each pie slice of the board. "Yes!" I whirled around. "Boo-ya!"

His face was emotionless.

I did a shimmy shake and twirled back to him at the line. "Move, sucker."

"What was that about you being an adult?"

I nudged him aside with my hip and got hit with a blast of dryer sheets and mint. His scent immediately made my rebellious nipples tighten again.

Hopefully, he wouldn't notice.

Now we were almost even with a possibility of me winning. It was a long shot in every way, but I was going for it.

Dear God, I was going for it.

I shook my fingers out and hopped up and down. "Okay. You can do this."

He frowned. "Right. You're going to win this?"

"Yep. Two bullseyes. Totally easy."

He barked out a half laugh and folded his arms. "All right, Katniss."

"What if I want to be Hawkeye? Sexist much?"

His lips twitched. "Less talk, more action, Willow."

Okay, now my nipples were really excited. Him saying my name should not have done all of that. In fact, there were tingles all over. His voice was like smoke and gravel had a baby.

Concentrate!

"Cake," I muttered under my breath. "You are competent and amazing."

He cocked his hip. "Thanks."

"Not you—me. Affirmations are good for the soul, jerkface."

He grunted instead of replying, which actually relaxed me. Grumpy Ransom was his baseline. And not at all sexy.

Mostly.

I threw my first dart and it hit the center of the seventeen with a firm *thwack.*

Instead of celebrating, I let out a slow breath and aimed again, hitting the bullseye.

"Unbelievable," he muttered.

My lips slid into a sly smile. I threw my last dart and it smacked into the thin metal ring around the bullseye and fell to the scarred wooden floor. "Balls."

I was expecting the glee in his eyes since I'd been a bit of a shit when he missed his throw. Instead surprise lined his expression.

"What? Ready to show me up now?"

He went over to where my dart was and picked it up, then he pulled out the two in the board.

I stalked up behind him. "Gonna show me how it's done?"

He turned and we were chest to chest, the heat radiating off his Henley burning through the thin dress I was wearing. I stepped back quickly. His stormy gray eyes swirled with something, but then they were back to that misty flat gray. I'd probably imagined it. "Think you're doing just fine, Chaos."

"Rude."

"Kinda accurate," my sister said from the table.

Cripes, I'd nearly forgotten she was there. I snatched the darts from him. "Then let's do this again."

"Nah. I'm good with a tie." He handed me his darts too.

"There's no tie." I juggled them together in one hand. Thank goodness for my long fingers. "You're way ahead of me."

He jammed his hands into his pockets. "Not meant to finish this one."

I put my free hand on my hip. "That doesn't make sense."

"You should appreciate the chaos aspect...Chaos."

I almost stomped my foot. Then realized just how insanely childish I was being. Why did this guy bring out the crazy in me?

Because there wasn't going to be anything between us but a walk down the aisle together.

For my sister. Not like for really real.

"Fine, your loss."

His lips twitched, but he didn't say anything else. Then he crossed to the ooey-gooey love table and dropped a bill in front of them. "Think that's it for me tonight."

Clay sat up, sliding his arm away from Rachel. "Nah, man, it's early."

"It's cool. Catch up with your guest. I have some shit to finish up tonight anyway."

Clay's eyebrow rose. "And what would that be?"

"None of your business anymore, pal. You fired me, remember?"

What did that mean? I knew Ransom had a security background, but not that his job ended.

Then again, I'd made myself scarce after the big holiday engagement. My Aunt Laverne had been giving me the matchmaker side-eye. I definitely didn't need that in my life right now.

I set the darts back in the holder beside the board.

A couple of guys sauntered over. The lighter-haired one smiled widely, full of asshole peacockery as he sipped from a bottle of Bud. "You can play with us."

A glass thudded as it hit the table. My head swiveled to see Ransom's shoulders tightening. His long, blunt fingers gripped the top of his glass, but then he released it and hustled down the stairs and through the bar without looking back.

I gave the blond a tight smile. "I'll sit this one out."

"Aww, c'mon. We were watching you with grandpa. Kicking ass."

"And I'm sure I'd kick yours too, but I'm going to go visit with my sister."

He glanced at the table with a whistle. "Cherry and a bit of chocolate. Maybe both of you want to play."

Clay started to stand, but I waved him off. "Do you think that kind of line works with women?"

He gave a harsh chuckle then looked at his buddy. "Sure. Sometimes."

"No times." I strode to the darts holder and grabbed two darts—one red and one blue. I came back to the guy. "Let's throw for it. You beat me, then I'll play."

"You're on." He took the red one.

I swung my arm open. "You first."

Of course he went right to the line. The guy didn't have a chivalrous bone in his body. He took another swig of his beer and tossed the dart. *Thwack!* Then he lifted his beer into a salute. "Beat that."

Of course he threw it into the secondary bullseye.

Maybe some of Ransom's sharpshooting was still in the dart. I tried not to think about the last dart I threw falling to the floor. I blew out a slow breath as I threw and smiled when it hit the direct center.

"Aww, sorry."

The guy's eyes narrowed and the meanness he'd been hiding bracketed his mouth. "I didn't want to play with a chick anyway."

I rolled my eyes and went to the board to put away the darts as the assholes went off to troll elsewhere.

"Since when do you play darts like that?"

I slid into the chair beside my sister. "Me and Merry—one of my roommates—get bored during the week sometimes."

A pang from my sudden departure from the house hit me out of nowhere. I took a deep drink from my margarita to wash away the bitterness. The mix of fruits and tequila did its job. "We go to a dive bar near the apartment to kill time and fleece executive dudes who think we're poor little college coeds who don't know what we're doing."

Rachel laughed and slid her arm through mine. "I miss having you around."

"I missed you too." I rested my head on her shoulder. "So much."

"Everything okay?"

"Getting better now." I stabbed my straw into the melted ice. "So, what's with the grumpy best friend?"

"Ransom is...Ransom."

Clay leaned back and laced his fingers over his middle. "He's figuring stuff out. I assumed he would go back to the private sector when I moved back to Turnbull, but he seems to like it here."

"Private sector?"

"Yeah. He's done a few bodyguard details since he got out of the Army. A few diplomats in DC, the mayor for a while in Manhattan, but he didn't really like him. Didn't last long."

"I'm shocked."

Clay laughed. "He's a good guy. When he gets bored with Turnbull, he's got options or he can work for his family. Don't think he's about that life though. He'd rather wear Kevlar than a suit."

I stared down at my pink margarita. "Wow."

So, did that mean he was rich like Clay? Not that I was asking, but holy shit. The stoic forcefield made a lot more sense.

Then I noticed the fifty on the table.

He was still a jerk.

Chapter 4

Ransom

And Then Chaos Walked In

I parked my Jeep Gladiator under the makeshift carpark. I'd done a skeleton build this winter just to have something against the ridiculous level of snow, but it definitely needed more. I was pretty sure those were the words that should be bolted to the front of my house.

Needs more.

For now, the two-car garage around the side was my workshop. Brushing some snow off my Jeep was a small price to pay.

I was tempted to go into the garage and lose a few hours to woodworking. I was building a desk for Rachel for a wedding present from Clay—not that he knew it yet. She needed space for all her shit. How I knew this? My best friend bitched to me about her taking over his office every day.

What she *didn't* know is we were making over one of the bedrooms into an office for her. Clay figured he was going to just order a desk unit and be done with it. I didn't know Rachel like he did, but I understood her.

She needed something more personalized. And Clay would get some extra bonus points. He deserved them. I was glad he'd finally gotten his head out of his ass about making a future for himself, instead of what his grandfather thought he should have.

A hard lesson all of us had to learn. Some of us were still learning.

And that was enough of that.

I slammed the Jeep's door and crossed the lawn. It was a sad excuse for one, but I'd been lectured about planting grass seed too early by the resident plant lady, Sarah Manning. Central New York could have snow into May.

That was heinous, but as it was April and we'd just had seven inches a week ago, I believed her.

Sarah was Laverne's sister, but she was a bit more persnickety. Like a cat who might slash or purr depending on a change of wind. I liked her.

She was as mercurial as her sons were affable. Unless there was a bar fight to be had. The Manning boys like to play as hard as they worked. I was getting to know a whole lot more people since I'd planted my flag in Turnbull.

I still wasn't sure if that was a good thing or not.

I wiggled my fingers against the inevitable swelling in my knuckles before I grabbed the banister. I hoped I had a bag of peas in the freezer.

It was the only thing they were good for.

My porch light was on, highlighting a snoozing dog. I'd sort of inherited him when I bought the old house. Not that he'd come inside, but he looked intimidating and kept most people away.

Win-win and worth the dog food.

I clomped up the stairs, bouncing on the top one when it squeaked. Dammit, another addition to the list. This place was a fucking money pit.

I dug out my phone and added a note to the house app that Clay had asked me to beta for him.

Now that he was Mister Marriage, his work was starting to skew toward families. We were actually working on a safe home setup that had better security than the ones on the market—at least when he could pull himself away from his soon-to-be bride.

I opened the lid on the bucket of kibble I kept on the deck and Midnight's ears perked, though he didn't lift his head. Just a big ass satellite ear twitched to listen for the metal dish getting filled.

He was a massive mutt of a dog who was probably part Malamute and part German Shepherd. Someday I'd get a swab in his mouth and do one of those DNA things.

Not that he was my dog, but he was a question. And I hated questions.

I dumped two scoops of food into his dish and checked his water bowl. He must have been playing frisbee with it again. It was covered in dirt and slobber.

Midnight grunted a little while getting up. I knew how that was. I ruffled the fur around his scruff, then brought the water dish in with me and cleaned it along with my mug from this morning. My house was tidy. Rachel called it spartan, but I just didn't like clutter.

Nor did I like company, so she didn't have to look at it.

I filled the dish with water, then brought it back out. As usual, the dog hoovered his kibble down as if I didn't feed him three times a day. I set the water down, but he was only interested in food. He flopped back onto the deck with a disgruntled moan and stretched out on his side.

Nice life if you could get it.

I went back inside, added wood to the fireplace, then went upstairs to wash off the bar fight and the hint of lemons that I couldn't get out of my senses. Spring was supposedly here according to the calendar, but there was still a chill to the upstairs. I was still renovating the second level, but downstairs was insulated to the hilt and the fireplace kept it warm.

Instead of getting dressed again, I dragged on a pair of sweatpants and padded down the circular stone staircase. I was hungry and cooking evened me out. And because I'd been denied the pub food I'd been looking forward to, that would be on the menu.

"Hey Siri, play my cooking playlist."

The watery tones of Hozier filled the downstairs. Because my best friend was who he was, I was privy to all the toys in his arsenal. Including a sweet speaker set up that was built into the two sheetrocked walls. The rest was stone that I'd salvaged from the original house and from a few local quarries.

With the fire crackling and steak searing in the perfectly seasoned cast iron pan, I pushed away thoughts of chaos—both situational and a certain redhead.

She'd been a surprise tonight and I wasn't fond of those either. In fact, it was more of a full-on hate kind of deal. Instead of letting thoughts of Willow Doyle in my head again, I smashed garlic on my cutting board with the side of my knife.

I made a paste with a few more herbs then dumped it all into my miniature processor with some butter. Once the steak was seared, I threw it under the broiler to cook and set my phone's timer. As I was scrubbing a potato, there was a knock at my door.

I grabbed a towel. Dammit, if Clay was stopping by to give me shit about fittings again, I'd punch him. And double dammit, I forgot to use a bag of frozen peas on my knuckles.

Slowing, I frowned. Clay wouldn't knock—or if he did, it would be directly followed by him walking in.

Nor did he make kissy noises at Midnight.

I opened the door and my whole body tightened. The golden glow of my porch light made Willow's auburn hair into a fiery cloud around her slim shoulders. She was draped over Midnight, her wild curls mixing with his dense black and gray fur.

"Who's the sweetest boy? Are *you* the sweetest boy? How are you owned by Mr. No Personality?"

"What are you doing here, Chaos?"

She looked up with her cheek next to Midnight's blunt snout, his big spotted tongue lolling out in pure euphoria. "Hello to you too."

"No dart boards here. Go home."

She straightened and the dog leaned on her hard enough to knock

48

her sideways a step. She giggled and dropped her hand on his massive head. "At least he likes me."

"He also thinks his water dish is a Frisbee."

She dug her long fingers into his thick fur. My dick thought about twitching, but I remembered I was going commando and breathed through the thought. Sweatpants hid nothing.

She rubbed his ears until the dog gave another joyful moan. "He doesn't even get you a toy?"

Midnight's jet eyes looked up at her adoringly.

Of course I didn't get him a toy. He wasn't my damn dog.

My fingers gripped the edge of my heavy door. "What. Are. You. Doing. Here?"

"Your place is hard to find."

Her gaze tracked to my chest, but it immediately bounced back up to my face. Was that a bit of pink under all those freckles?

"On purpose." My tone was flat and harsh, but I didn't want her in my space. I didn't want *anyone* in my space, but she was top of the list.

She pushed by me, her denim jacket brushing against my belly as she let herself in, her lemon scent now back in my head again.

"Luckily for me, Beckett told me where you lived. And helped me when I got lost—twice."

"Remind me to rip Beckett's tongue out."

She threw a quick grin over her shoulder. "What smells so good?"

"My dinner."

"You cook?"

"I cook."

"Hey, me too."

I knew she did. Though she cut corners I never would think of doing, but she was entertaining enough. The few videos I'd watched anyway.

Rachel was very proud of her sister and wouldn't stop texting the videos to everyone she knew. And okay, maybe Willow was the only person I followed on the stupid social media app. I could only get the link so many times before I had to actually watch one.

Willow tossed her coat and purse on my leather chair. I picked them up and hung both by the door. The one that I'd be pushing her out of momentarily.

I found her peering into the sink. "What kind of potatoes are you making?" She also opened the processor with the butter. "Oh, is that garlic butter?" She pushed her sleeves up, moved the potatoes, then washed her hands.

"Help yourself."

She grinned at me. "Thanks." She dabbed her pinky into the butter and licked it off. "Wow. That's good. Recipe?"

"No."

"Huh." She glanced around my kitchen. Herbs growing under a special lamp crawled up the wall of my fridge. She drew a finger down a spiky basil leaf. Her hazel eyes shifted toward the hanging rack of pans, the bins of vegetables, and the massive cabinets before she met my gaze gain. "You really can cook. Based on the smell, that's not the tasteless man-leather kind of steak."

I crossed my arms.

She shrugged. "Most guys I know don't know the difference between a Pop Tart and a croissant."

"Stop hanging out with children."

"That's true. But then again, you guys don't grow out of that, do you?"

"Don't lump me in with anyone you know."

"So grumpy." She turned to the oven and turned on the light instead of opening the door. At least I wouldn't have to bury her body for ruining my steak.

I sighed and nudged her away. "If I feed you, will you tell me why you're here?"

"I can help."

"It's almost done. I just have to do the potato." Well, now potatoes since I had a guest. I grabbed another from my root vegetable storage in the corner of my stone kitchen. It was a reclaimed chicken coop that I'd modified. I liked the old look of the piece and it was more interesting than a boring pantry.

I returned to the sink and scrubbed the potato, setting it onto the cutting board with the first one.

She moved down a step—the girl did not believe in personal space—and leaned back on the counter, bracing her elbows behind her and pushing out her tits. The stupid filmy dress had been enough for me to deal with at the bar, but in my space? *Fuck.*

"Should have done the potato first."

I pulled out a fresh knife. "I know you enjoy the whole shortcut thing, but the steak requires a resting period that will cover the potatoes." I sliced each one a little more than three quarters through in thin, even sections and brushed them with butter and added some Parmesan cheese before wrapping them up in foil. I had the convection oven set for a quick cook.

I looked up and she'd tipped her head, watching me closely.

"Now we have some time to kill. Why are you here?"

She sighed. "It's not like I want to be."

"That makes two of us."

"Why are you so miserable anyway?"

"Why are you so annoying?"

She messed with the ruffle thing around the wrist of her sleeve, pulling it down then shoving it back up. "Do you have any wine or something?"

She was obviously stalling. I didn't have any idea what she would want with me. Well, beyond something of the naked variety, but I didn't think she was into mindless sex.

Nor did I need that kind of grief with the familial hooks in both of us.

"What am I saying? You probably only drink beer."

"I have wine." I opened the wine fridge I'd hidden with a facing that matched my cabinets.

She peeked around my shoulder. "Oh, do you have a Shiraz?"

I grabbed a bottle she requested. I wasn't sure if she liked the sweeter wine or actually knew it paired well with steak. Regardless, it worked out. I uncorked and poured us both a glass.

"Now talk."

"I don't want to ruin my—"

"Willow."

Her name felt foreign on my tongue. I'd called her anything but since we'd met that first day at the Christmas tree lot.

She took the glass and took a large gulp.

I arched a brow at her. If she kept that up, she'd be crashing on my couch.

"It's good." Her voice echoed in the wide rim of the glass.

My phone trilled out the chime for my alarm. I opened the oven. "By the time I tent this steak, you better be talking."

"Fine." I heard her take another fortifying gulp. "I like this song."

I ripped a sheet of foil off the roll in my drawer. "You have about five seconds."

"Right. I'm only acquiescing because that smells really good and I'm starving. Rachel and Clay ate my damn nachos." She tapped her nail against the glass. "Why does the dog stay outsi—"

I gave her a hard stare.

"It's a good question."

"If you don't want to eat your steak out of Midnight's bowl, you better start talking."

"Ohh, is that his name?"

The name had come to me soon after he started hanging around and it was better than continuing to call him dog. I zipped the tips of my fingers down the foil to make a triangle and laid it over the steak before turning around to lean a hip on the counter.

"Could you put a shirt on?"

"My house." I flipped my towel over my shoulder.

"It's distracting."

"Sounds like a *you* problem."

She wrinkled her nose.

I checked my watch. I really didn't want her in my house. Even having her this close made my skin too tight. Nothing about her was quiet or calming. "Ten minutes. Talk."

She held up a finger and took another sip. "I know this is going to sound crazy. I'm probably overreacting. You know what? I have to be."

"Not sure your lip gloss matches your bridesmaid's dress?"

"You know, you're a real dick. Like I'd come to you for that kind of problem."

"Best man gets the shit duty usually."

"Since when were you a best man before?"

I gritted my teeth and did not answer. Only one other time and that had ended in disaster. For so many people.

"You're very unhelpful."

"Then why are you here?"

She swirled the wine. "Look, I wouldn't be here unless I had to be."

Fuck.

My eyes narrowed as I took in her posture. She was trying to play it cool, but there was a lot of nervous energy vibrating around her slim shoulders. She tapped her foot, swaying from one hip to the other as if she wasn't sure where to put herself.

The woman from the bar had been more of a ball-buster. Comfortable in her own skin and her appeal. Now not so much.

If my head hadn't been in my ass, I'd have picked up on it. Damn town was sucking the instincts out of me.

I folded my arms. "All right. I'm listening."

"I don't want to worry Rachel."

I waited for her to continue. Patience used to be my finest feature. I fisted my hand under my arm as the seconds turned into a minute. This could be a sister thing, but I wasn't the guy she'd go to if it was something simple.

That was Laverne's station. She was the one who dealt with the sibling crap and the maze of chick emotions that was so far beyond me, it might as well be Saturn.

"Okay, why didn't you go to your aunt?"

"I don't want to worry *anyone*." Her voice was tight, exasperation warring with whatever was going on in that beautiful head of hers.

"Is this a guy thing?"

When her body language changed, I knew I was on the right path.

"No. Well, I don't know."

I frowned. "You don't know?"

She set the glass down and scraped her fingers through her hair. "I'm getting ahead of myself. But it happened twice, so I'm freaking out here."

"You're not making sense."

She stalked back and forth in the narrow space between my kitchen island and counter. "It's because I can't believe it. Who would do this? How would they do this? Why—"

I stepped in front of her, but instead of making her slow down, she crashed into me. I grabbed her upper arms. Fucking mistake. Her lemon scent made my head buzz. I wasn't expecting it. The sharpness of the lemons, the softness of her dress, and her wide wild eyes staring at me were a punch. I had an irrational urge to put my face into all those curls.

Fucking get a grip, man.

"I get it. You're freaked. I can't help you until you give me some information here."

Looking at me mutinously, she didn't say a damn thing.

Dammit. Why the hell did I have to deal with this shit? "If you're not going to tell me, then scram."

"You're a dick."

"You came to me."

"Obviously, I'm am idiot." She tried to shake free. I would have let her if I didn't see the fear there under the bravado.

"Instincts were called paranoia first, Chaos."

She stiffened.

"Too many people ignore them until it's too late." Myself included. Especially right now. All my instincts were screaming for me to push her out the door.

There was trouble swirling in those hazel eyes. Defiance, fear, pride—but the only one that tugged at me was the fear.

Goddammit.

She let out a gusty sigh and twisted free. This time, I let her go. "Something happened today. Twice. It doesn't make sense."

"If you don't get to the point..."

"Right. You're right. Okay, so I should probably start at the beginning."

This was going to be a long night. I pinched the bridge of my nose and prayed for deliverance.

"So, you know I have the whole channel thing, right? Not really a YouTube channel, but that's in my future plans. Anyway, that's not the point. I have a lot of followers. Some are the troll types. They're easy to ignore. Well, not easy, but I've grown a slightly thicker skin."

Her fair, freckled skin was anything but thick. The internet was a cesspool, so I was sure she got some interesting comments on her videos. I'd read a few and had to exit out of the app.

Fucking pigs out there.

"Right. I know how the comment section works."

"So, I have some people that are a little too familiar. I mean, I don't know for sure and I can't really know because there was no note, but..."

I frowned. "Slow down."

She blew out a controlled breath. It was a miracle. I didn't think she had it in her. "Okay, right. I got this box at my apartment. Something I really wanted."

Her eyes sparkled suddenly and the excitement I usually saw in her videos was right there in front of me, only far more intensely. I suddenly wished for a hoodie or an apron.

Shit.

"It was this really cool, *really* expensive kitchen storage setup. Like whoa, top of the line, and while I have lots of collaboration opportunities thanks to my channel—not something like this."

"You don't give out your address to people, right?" I interrupted her as the thought flashed.

"No." She shook her head vehemently. "No. I have a PO Box. I'm not stupid."

The space between my shoulder blades started to itch. It wasn't unheard of for people to give out their address as easily as they breathed. Not many people thought about security the way I did— exactly why so many got their identities stolen.

"Look. I'm careful. Very few people have my physical address. Not even utilities. I just pay my share to one of the girls in my apartment. Or I did, but that's not what this is about."

I frowned. "We'll get back to that one."

She did that nose wrinkle thing. "Anyway, I know it wasn't Rachel. She's all wedding all the time right now. And while it's kind of a Rachel gift..." She twisted her fingers together. "Maybe it was a Rachel gift. Maybe I'm just being crazy."

"Did you ask her?"

"No."

I arched my brow.

She rolled her eyes. "When I got to the orchard, Rach was so excited to see me, it didn't come up. And besides, I hadn't been to the cabin yet. Not that you can call it a cabin, it's a freaking mansion." At my flat stare, she sighed. "Sorry. It didn't get weird until we got back from the bar and I found another box addressed to me at Rachel's and Clay's place."

My instincts locked my muscles down. "Was it another one of your type of gifts?"

"Same company. No note. Not even a packing slip inside. This one was more personal. Not something for the kitchen." Her fingers trembled before she clenched them together. "How would anyone know I would be there?"

"You weren't supposed to be here for a few weeks, right?"

"Exactly." She fussed with the sleeve of her dress. "I've mentioned my sister's wedding. People like to know stuff about me. And I knew my videos would be different while I was away. I was trying to pre-film to put them up while I was busy with Rach."

"Makes sense."

"But I don't understand why he—they—whoever, would send me these things. How do they know I wanted them?"

"Is this the first time you've gotten gifts?"

"Unsolicited? Yeah. Sometimes I do collaborations with other influencers, but again, I always use my PO Box."

"Always?"

Her hazel eyes flashed. "I told you I'm not stupid."

"Didn't say you were, but did you ever use your home address before the... What do I even call your thing? A business?"

"Before I went viral? Yes, I've had the box for years even before I started making videos." She paused, looking down at her feet. Then she looked up. "I'm careful."

"Okay. Fair." There seemed to be more to that one. The space between my shoulder blades was damn near on fire.

"My name only blew up in the last two years. My content is pretty narrowly focused on food."

"Maybe this person picked up some clues from videos. I've only seen a few of your posts."

"You saw my stuff?" Her eyes softened.

I cleared my throat. "Rachel's pretty proud of you."

Her eyes went from soft to shiny and my hackles rose. Dude, no tears. "Have you made any off the cuff videos? Something that would give someone a clue as to who you are? Your bedroom, living room? Anything that would give something about you away."

"I shot videos at the Christmas Tree Farm, so I guess they could figure out that at least. Make inferences to Clay and find his address maybe?"

"It's a leap to go from gifts to something more sinister."

Her spine snapped straight, changing her defensive pose to offensive. I preferred it to the wounded bird. And there I saw the flicker of fear again.

"Are you not telling me something?"

She reached for the wine. "There are a few people who make some comments that make me uncomfortable. There's a block function in the app so they can't see my content or comment. But it doesn't stop them from making another account." She tipped her head back. "God, I sound insane."

"What did I say about paranoia?"

"It's just instinct."

"Right."

She was trying to make excuses for shitty behavior. And while there was no reason to think this person was being anything other than inappropriate, it was enough to make *me* unsettled, let alone a woman.

"Stalking laws haven't caught up to the internet."

"This can't be happening." She put her face in her hands.

"It's a wide definition, but people can get fixated on famous people. You're in their phone all the time, right?"

Her brain was working overtime. The fear and instinct were battling it out. I fucking hated it. I saw it with women far too often.

"Look, I have two sisters."

Her eyes went wide. "You do?"

"I do have a family."

"The lone wolf thing is strong with you, sir."

And I didn't mind cultivating that fact. People were goddamn exhausting. "Guys are creeps and women should lean into their instinct instead of being nice."

"Do I look like I care about being nice?"

"Yes."

Disgruntled, she dropped her arms. "Fine. I can't be too much of an asshole because I want people to like me, dammit. You know, so they'll watch my content and then I can make a damn living."

"Is that how it works? Views equals money?"

"Pretty much. Viral videos make more money of course. Then it leads to other opportunities."

"I get it. I mean, I don't get wanting to put your face on the internet, but I understand in theory."

She rolled her eyes. "Thanks."

While Willow fought her instincts, I'd learned to lean into mine. "But I know you aren't telling me something."

She nibbled her lower lip. "It's not like I have proof."

"Proof is for cops, but if you're here looking for some help, then give me what you've got."

"I can give you a few usernames that have creeped me out."

"It's a start. I have some contacts from working in Manhattan and D.C.. And my own family has some helpful people I can ask." After my sister disappeared all those years ago, I'd lost count of the number of private investigators I'd gone through in order to find her.

While Marigold was frustratingly adept at staying missing, I'd discovered a few of the companies were actually good at their job, Roth Defense being one of them.

I pulled out my phone. It would probably be a dead end. Most companies wouldn't share information easily. "Which company were the gifts from?"

"RID Inc.. I've been dying to work with them. They don't do much in the way of collaborations. Not that they need to."

My ears buzzed. Un-fucking-believable.

That was *my* goddamn company.

Chapter 5

Willow

Distractions & Deceptions

"What's that face for?"

"Nothing."

"It's definitely something." As soon as I said the name of the company he'd gone all stoic and glacial. I was beginning to figure him out. Sort of. Rachel told me he was fairly self contained. I'd go with vault. The kind that Hans Gruber had to use a laser to crack.

And Grumpasaurus wasn't going to tell me because I definitely didn't have a laser in my purse or a John McClane. Also, now that my mini freak out had a release valve, I was starving.

I was trying to be adult and everything, but this hot dude cooking thing was killing me. The bar Ransom had been distracting in a distant and annoying way, but who cooked without a shirt on?

Not to mention I hadn't known all those muscles existed on a male body outside of the model or bodybuilder types. Then of course an errant image of him doing a bench press tripped through my brain.

Muscles quivering, concentration maxed out.

Remember the asshole part, Wil.

Even if I drop-kicked the attraction part out of my brain, the fact that I'd immediately sprinted out of Clay's and Rachel's place when I spotted that second box was what really freaked me out. Like I didn't even pass go and discuss it with my sister.

Full-on Olympic gold sprinting.

Oh, and I'd never sprinted a day in my life. These coltish legs were God-given, not maintained.

And who had I run to? Right to Ransom.

My sister obviously hadn't sent the first box. Her huge bluebell eyes had been so confused when the RID Inc. box had been waiting for us after we'd gotten back from Lucky's. She'd assumed it was a wedding gift, but when she saw my name on it, things went sideways.

Had it been delivered at the same time as the box at the apartment?

I still didn't understand why or how someone knew I was going to be at Clay's place. It wasn't as if I mentioned the date of the wedding.

Some Google-fu could obviously be at play. Clay was fairly famous thanks to the whole billionaire thing, but he tended to keep things on the downlow about his Turnbull and Happy Acres ventures.

The wedding was going to be intimate instead of the three-ring circus of a Manhattan socialite situation.

I wrapped my arms around my middle. I wasn't even supposed to be at the orchard for another two weeks at a minimum. Had someone been watching me pack today?

"Your head is going to spin off your shoulders."

I blinked. "I'm trying to figure out where I fucked up, if you must know."

"You probably didn't."

"Does Clay keep his name off of his properties?"

Ransom frowned at me.

"You know, like unlisted or under a company name?"

"Interesting question." Something flickered in his eyes, but then it was gone. Okay, so maybe I wasn't figuring him out. Or he was a master at keeping his thoughts in check.

"And the answer?"

"I'm more on the security side of things, but I'll check into it." He moved over to the counter where the steak was resting, tucking the towel in the front of his sweats as he went.

Sweet heaven, his back was just as impressive as the front.

Distraction station, party of one, here's your ticket.

There wasn't an inch of ink on his whole upper body. These days that was more of a rarity. It was actually refreshing to see all the dips and...scars.

I crossed to him to get a better look. Not that I needed to, but I couldn't stop my stupid feet. It was a theme today, evidently.

A large silvery-pink scar slashed along his side, followed by two smaller ones.

"Knife."

Startled, I took two steps back. "Sorry."

"No you're not." He didn't turn around to talk to me, and his voice was so damn matter-of-fact.

"How did you get them?"

He reached for a knife stuck to a magnetic strip bolted into the stone backsplash. The edge looked damn sharp. Quietly and competently, he cut the meat on a bias and my stomach roared at the perfect medium rare color.

Was he not going to answer me?

Just as I was going to ask again, he turned with two plates with a perfect fan of steak on each. "Bad guys wanted me dead. Almost got their wish. Go sit down, I can hear your stomach from here."

Happy to get off my feet, I took the bottle of wine and our glasses with me to the cozy nook in the far corner of his kitchen. Most of the downstairs was made up of the warm-toned stone walls. I was pretty sure they were the real deal too, not just some fancy faux finish.

The house had an older feel. It wasn't terribly large and had the odd angles of a place that had been added onto over the years.

During the day, I'd bet there was a gorgeous wash of daylight across the whole space. "I like your place."

"Your sister doesn't." He added the potatoes to our plates, then he stacked them down one arm like a waiter with silverware in his other hand along with undyed cotton napkins.

At my arched brow, he shrugged. "I don't like waste."

I snapped out the napkin and set it on my lap. His whole house had a bespoke quality to it. Nothing trendy, more like everything had a specific purpose and was probably one of a kind. From the fireplace, to the heavy beams overhead, to the scarred and ancient floors—everything was built to stand long after he was gone. "I gathered that from the lack of a picture on your walls."

"Decorator got fired."

"I just bet."

"So, I'm going to need your log-ins," he said without preamble.

I sat up straighter, my fork hovering over my plate. "Can't I just tell you about the screen names that freak me out?"

"Doesn't work like that. Especially if this asshat has been switching his profiles."

"Could be a her." At his steady look, I sighed. "It feels like a guy."

"Agreed. Also, there are protections in place for the social media accounts." He finished off another bite of steak. "I know a guy. He can do a search and see if there's anything to see in your history."

I took a swig of my wine. "History?"

My social media history was...*eclectic* to say the least.

"It's not my specialty, but I know a guy who knows what to look for." He stabbed at his potatoes, the tines of the fork clicking on the plate as he efficiently plowed through his food.

Did he even enjoy it?

He hunched forward and the medallion he wore glinted in the low light. I figured it was a patron saint or some such thing, but it looked more like a coin.

Interesting.

He gave me a hard look, and I lifted my gaze to his face. I couldn't help it if I was curious. Which was why I was uneasy about him looking at my history.

It was easy to go down rabbit holes on social media. From true crime to fashion, to make-up, to haunted places. It was a time suck, but it was also fascinating for someone like me.

Everything seemed interesting. Cooking was just on top of the pile.

"Look, I don't care if you're watching thirst traps. Aidan Roth won't care either."

My neck heated and I was pretty sure my face was scarlet. There were probably a few too many Loki and Winter Soldier videos in my history too. "He doesn't work for Clay, does he? Rachel said he does some security things."

Ransom shook his head. "Different circle. He's more personal security, where Clay is cyber and game."

I relaxed a bit. I didn't know much about the security world, but I'd figured they might've been in each other's circles. I really didn't want to worry Clay or Rachel right now. The wedding was right around the corner and then they were going on a nice long honeymoon.

My odd gifts were not cause for holding any of that up. And I knew my sister, she'd cancel everything. Especially with what had happened before.

I set my fork down and tucked my hands under the table. I really didn't want to stumble down memory lane there. Nor did I want to rehash it with Ransom.

He gave me a long look, but he didn't say anything. I was almost certain he had some secret mind-reading talent. He didn't want in this melon. My Gemini brain would give him apoplexy.

I cleared my throat and picked up my fork again. "Roth is who you mentioned earlier?"

Ransom nodded as he broke open the second half of his potato. "Aidan will probably try to recruit me again." He pointed at me with his fork. "I blame you."

"I do appreciate it." I nearly moaned as I took a bite of my steak. "Really. I know it's a huge inconvenience."

He stared again and I tried for an innocent look. It was tough since my mouth was having a foodgasm.

Finally, he resumed chewing. "I can handle it. If it turns out to be something more than a nuisance, we're going to tell Clay and Rachel."

"After the wedding."

He paused between shovels. "Fine. It'll take some time to get Roth to dig in there. I'll also have him do a web crawl on you."

I frowned. "That doesn't sound good." I forked up some buttery cheesy potatoes and let out the moan I'd been holding back. "Dear God."

He glanced at me, his storm-cloud eyes flat, but then he did the whole jaw clench thing and I had to swallow twice. The man was a menace.

"It's good."

"I know."

I rolled my eyes. Then he said shit like that to remind me that an annoying attraction would be easy to ignore. Unless I went for more of a hate bang.

No hate banging, Willow Renee Doyle.

We ate the rest of our meal without conversation. I was tempted to fill the space, but he seemed to be working something out in his head. After we were finished, we cleaned up in companionable silence.

When the last dish was put away, he wiped down the counters. I tried really hard not to watch all his muscles flex and bunch. I was very unsuccessful.

"Does your sister know you're here?"

"No."

"Think maybe you should check in?"

"Probably." I draped myself over the clean kitchen island. *Ugh.* "I suck at lying though."

"Yeah, you do."

"Thanks." I straightened and flipped back my hair.

"Don't make it all convoluted. Tell her we are working on a surprise for them." He gathered the towels we'd used. Then sprayed the counter down again after my face-plant.

Evidently, he was a bit of a germaphobe. More interesting.

Then he opened a skinny drawer and tossed the armful inside. I peered over his shoulder. He really was into the whole carbon foot-print deal.

Stop being interested.

"I'll be right back." He loped up the winding stairs.

I hoped he put on a shirt. He was very distracting.

But now I had to figure out what I was going to tell my sister. Probably texting was best. Less chance for error.

I looked around. I'd thrown my stuff on his chair when I came in. Then I spotted my belongings hung up neatly by the door.

Boy, was he particular.

I pulled out my phone and found a zillion notifications.

"Focus, Wil." I forced myself not to click on them. Those were the hazards of an online work life..

When I opened my text messages, I found three from my sister.

Rach: Where did you go?

Rach: Hello?

Rach: Could you check in please? What is this box? Can I open it?

I quickly replied back.

Me: No. Hello, wedding is coming. It's a present.

Lies. It definitely wasn't a present. Well, not for her. I hadn't even checked what it was before I hoofed it out of there. Just seeing it was from RID Inc. was enough to send me spinning into a freefall. Which super sucked since I loved that damn company.

Not that there was much about it out there. Just a simple logo and the shortest bio in the history of companies. Didn't stop them from being one of the most sought out furniture makers on the market.

My phone vibrated.

Rach: Where did you go?

Me: Nunya.

Rach: <side eye> I hate when you say that. Everything should be my business.

Me: This is why we can't have nice things. Also, Ransom is helping me with something.

Rach: Willingly? Did you blackmail him?

That was a little too close to the truth. He didn't want to get involved. I wasn't dumb enough to believe he was doing any of this altruistically. I'd dumped it on him and practically cried like a little girl.

Ugh.

Then I'd pulled the 'don't tell Rachel' card. I was lucky he hadn't tossed me out the damn door. I really hoped I was just letting out my dramatic side. At the very least I could get some pointers about dealing with some of the more problematic aspects of my business.

That wasn't a bad deal.

Then I'd get out of his hair and we could go back to growling at one another. And maybe I'd have some fantasy fodder. His chest really was a masterpiece.

Me: Hey, you're the one who made us have to work together being the MOH and BM.

Rach: That's true. Hint?

Me: Nope. I'll be home soon though.

Rach: Can I look in the box?

Me: What did I say?

Rach: Lame.

Me: Your shower is coming up. Tons of things to open.

Rach: That's true. Okay. See you in a bit.
Me: K.

That wasn't so bad. Distracting her with presents was definitely going to be my go-to.

"Okay, let me just get some details."

I turned at his voice, and thankfully, he had on a shirt this time. I ignored the disappointment at the hoodie. The little vee things at the top of his low slung sweatpants would be missed most of all.

He held a slim laptop, nodding at the living room with the fireplace.

I followed him in and sat next to him on the couch.

"All your log-ins."

"All?" My...well, *everything* lurched.

"All."

I pulled out my phone. "It's a lot."

"Aidan will need them all. Even personal ones."

I tapped the side of my phone. Everything seemed very invasive. I wasn't the one who had done anything wrong.

"I can't help you if you hold out on me."

"Are you a mind reader or something?"

"Your tells are like neon arrows, Chaos."

I blew out a breath. I did have a separate account that I used to follow other influencers that I didn't want to show up on my list of people I followed. It wasn't sneaky exactly.

Okay, maybe a little bit.

I pulled his laptop over to me and started typing away.

He watched me silently. Probably judging the fact that I had so many damn social media accounts. I did exceptionally well on two of them, but I never knew when things would change.

Apps went in and out of vogue in the space of a heartbeat.

I skimmed through my passwords app to make sure I had them all.

"You don't use the same password everywhere, do you?"

I glanced at him. "No. Too easy to get hacked and cloned that way. I have a password app that changes my passwords every two weeks."

He grunted.

"What?"

"Smart. But Aidan will probably have you use his software. The Apple version doesn't have his level of encryption."

"I'm not a spy."

"Personal information is floating around out there at an alarming rate. And there are far too many people who get too attached to public figures."

I slipped off my shoes and pulled my feet under me. "I understand that, but I'm still pretty much a nobody in the grand scheme."

He plucked my phone out of my hand, his blunt fingers swiping through the bevy of apps I had on my phone. I instantly wanted to snatch it back.

Privacy, hello?

He made a few noises as he opened and closed applications. Then he met my gaze. "Nobody? Three of these apps show you have well over eight million followers." His eyes narrowed. "Each."

I laced my fingers together to stop myself from yanking my phone back. "Yeah, well check out a Kardashian and then get back to me."

"That's something different. And they have a security detail to cover any issues they have. Crazy is a Tuesday for famous people. That's why Aidan has so many clients."

I pressed my lips together.

"Look, even if this amounts to nothing, it's good to start worrying about privacy when it comes to your company. That starts with me looking through your posts and sussing out how much info is out there."

"I'm not stupid."

"No one said you were. To be honest, you're more careful than I was expecting."

I leaned into the couch cushion, surprised that it was so comfortable. It was on the tip of my tongue to talk to him about Jason.

He was the reason I had always been more private than the average person online. But this wasn't Jason Grafton's type of stalking. Besides, he'd lost interest in me a damn long time ago.

Even if I never could quite forget about him.

"This is everything?"

"Everything."

He searched my face. Those shrewd eyes reminded me of Aunt Laverne in the middle of an interrogation. She had nothing on Ransom.

"Well, except the screen names I have on my watch list. Do you want those?"

"No. I'd rather figure them out for myself."

Nerves bounced around with my exceptional meal, making me feel nauseated.

"Don't delete anything either. Leave all your posts as they are, including the comments section."

"Sure you don't read minds?"

"Definitely. If I got in yours, I'd probably run screaming."

"Har-har."

His lips twitched into an almost smile. "Now go home. And don't open that box until I see you tomorrow. If I came over now, Rachel would get too curious."

"I told her it was a wedding gift."

"Still. It'll hold until tomorrow."

I huffed out a breath. How was I not going to open it?

"I'm sure Rachel can keep you occupied."

That was the truth.

I slipped my shoes back on and he followed me to the door. Silence was heavy between us, but I did feel relieved. This could have been a bad idea, but now I thought I might be able to sleep tonight.

He opened the door and Midnight scrambled to his feet.

"Why don't you let him inside?"

"He won't come in."

The massive dog came right to my side as I stepped out onto the porch. "Maybe he can tell he's not welcome." I slipped my fingers into his dense fur along his neck. The dog leaned on me, knocking me over a step until I brushed into Ransom.

Fabric softener and mint swirled around me with a blast of chilly spring air.

He righted me with a hand to my elbow. I was tall enough that my eyes lined up with his lips. They were firm and flat as if he was perpetually holding his words behind another shield.

I wished I wasn't curious. Then maybe he wouldn't be so damn interesting.

I shuffled the dog over and crouched in front of him. "Pleased to meet you, Midnight. Hope I see you again soon."

Ransom didn't say anything.

Not that I was shocked. Every part of him said *stay away*, from his hands stuffed into his hoodie pocket, to his closed-off expression and his furrowed brow.

I laughed as Midnight swiped his big spotted tongue up the side of my face. I kissed his nose and stood.

"So, I'll just wait until you call me? Do you have my number?"

"I'll find you."

"Right."

Hurrying down the stairs, I glanced over my shoulder to find him watching after me with his huge dog standing right beside him.

I ignored the pang in my chest at just how solitary he seemed. By design, or because he was just too stubborn to be anything else?

I opened my door and climbed in.

"Not your problem," I said to the cold, dark SUV dash. And because now I couldn't quite help myself, I checked the backseat.

Handily, my four totes of clothes and kitchen items crowded out the chance for an intruder. It also reminded me I had to have a longer talk with my sister.

That would be a future Willow problem.

Right now, I just needed to face-plant on the nearest flat surface.

Chapter 6

Ransom

She's Safe From Me

I sat back, my eyes as dry as sand. I'd been poring over Willow's social media accounts for hours. I'd sent all of her logins over to Aidan and his resident cybersleuth, Poe. She was a wonder, and I was positive she'd come up with more in-depth details than I would, but I was curious.

I really didn't like questions.

Willow's online persona wasn't much different than the woman I knew. A little manic, a lot friendly, and she could toss a zinger like a natural. She was good with people and her mind was a helluva lot more interesting than I'd initially given her credit for.

Mostly because I wanted to slot her into a safe box where she didn't scratch at my brain. I didn't want to be fascinated by her. At all.

Regardless of my ill-timed interest, I would do this for her.

Because of Clay and Rachel. She was theirs and indirectly, that made Willow mine.

The fact that my chest tightened at the thought made me dig deeper and harder into the swimming torrent of words in her comment areas. Poe would have some fancy way to sift through the data and I was all for it. I'd go out of my mind if I had to do this sort of thing every day.

I'd been at it for five hours and I had a new appreciation for the former hacker, now white hat. Was that still a term? Whatever. I was more of a gun and Taser sort of guy. My prowess with a keyboard was limited at best.

Instead I focused on the overall feel of the reactions to Willow's social media. I'd gone way back to the beginning, watching her clips and videos with the most hits first. It was a lesson in the iterations of Wil's Way. Her earlier videos were all over the map, but even then, she'd been remarkably comfortable in front of the camera. She flirted with creating meals and do-it-yourself hacks, but it was pretty obvious what themes got her excited.

I could see why people were drawn to her.

In the end, she'd found her niche—figuring out how to break down a recipe into layman's terms. Sometimes she broke up her videos into a few parts. It was surprising what she could jam into three minutes.

Her groupies were impressive. There were a few different levels there as well. When it came to the more friendly types who replied again and again, she happily interacted with then as if they were her friends. Maybe even some of them had become a bit more than acquaintances.

Then there were the troll types—and there were an alarming number of them. Most were harmless, but some had me reaching for the legal pad I kept beside me on the couch. I'd flag them to dive into their accounts and find out if they were just jackasses in general, or if they were more fixated.

I swung my legs up onto the couch and stretched out my back. My old knife wound twinged a little from hunching over my laptop. Instead of stretching out the muscles, it just made me want to shut my eyes. I rolled off and crossed to the corner of my living room. I'd installed gymnast rings into the stone when doing the renos.

My physical therapist had pushed me to use them after my last injury. It had taken me longer to heal from my last mission with my team. I'd caught a stray bullet while carrying Jones out of a warehouse we'd been sent to blow up.

The whole assignment had gone to hell. Just like the last five missions we'd been on in five weeks. Each one more dangerous and inching into the gray area I couldn't live with.

Being a Night Stalker wasn't as glamorous as the SEALs. Hell, we were the ones who pulled SEALs out of the shit more times than I could count. But my last mission had been such a clusterfuck that if I hadn't been injured, I'd have filed my papers to get out of the Army anyway. I'd given more than ten years to them.

I'd been disconnected from my family, flown in and out of sinkholes of depravity, and spent more hours in a Blackhawk than anyone in my unit. For years, I'd allowed myself to be used for any op my unit chief asked of me.

Until Jones.

Until he'd died while slung over my shoulder.

Most people didn't even know we existed. We were the last defense in the ugliest rescues. But when I couldn't even rescue my own partner, I'd had enough.

As I was jumping into the chopper, a bullet had shredded through my ribcage and scraped close enough to my spine to nearly put me in a chair for the rest of my life. And that had put a period on my career.

No one besides my unit knew I'd been hurt.

The Army had dumped me in a off-site health center in Chicago. Even the staff hadn't known who I was. I'd just gone by my initials, RID. The clinic was well-versed in secrets and happily used the government money for their research and advancements. When I'd healed up enough to go home, my charts had been classified, then redacted and put in a hole as deep as the shitholes I'd rescued people from. No one in the Army wanted to own up to the shitshow we'd walked into.

I'd been done.

The only good thing that had come out of my injury was learning how to rebuild the muscles in my back. Goddamn gymnast rings had saved me. I'd hung them in my house to remind me what I'd had to do to come back to my family.

Not my mother and father, but to Clay and my sisters. I'd run away just like Marigold. If I'd stayed with the Army, I might have ghosted everyone just as effectively as my sister had.

I wrapped my fingers around the warm wood and just hung there, letting all the tension slide up and out of me.

I did a few halfhearted pull-ups, but I didn't really want to get my blood pumping. I needed some downtime. I knew Chaos enough to expect a visit tomorrow, regardless of my instructions.

I dropped to the floor, stretching my arms out and rolling my shoulders as the last of the tension fell away. Then I returned to the couch and spent another hour reviewing the list of profiles I'd flagged. Most of them were just assholes, leaving me with three names that worried me enough for a deeper check.

Eventually, I stretched out on the couch watching her latest video. I fell asleep with her husky voice following me into dreams.

My phone vibrated on my chest, dragging me out of a restless sleep. Chaos's hazel eyes and full lips dissipating with each pulse of my heart.

I swung my legs to the floor. "Yeah."

"Morning to you too." Aidan Roth's clipped voice put me on alert.

I pinched the bridge of my nose. "It's barely eight. You can't have details yet."

"Poe started working on it last night as soon as you sent it over. She actually follows Doyle's channel. I didn't know she cared about cooking since she lives off energy drinks."

"She has that effect."

"Is that right?"

I blamed lack of sleep on that stupid comment. "Must be something good if you're calling me so early."

"Poe flagged me at five this morning."

"And you're just calling me now?"

"I did some digging on my own."

"And?" It wasn't like Aidan to drag shit out.

"Think you guys can make a trip into the city?"

I stood up. "What the fuck did you find?"

"A lot to get into on the phone. I'd rather have you come in."

"Jesus, Roth. This better not be a recruitment."

Aidan barked out a laugh. "I'm always recruiting. I'd pay you well for your talents."

"I told you I'm not interested in the private sector."

He sighed. "Doesn't hurt to ask. But no, this isn't just to lure you into my very top notch building with all the toys you could ever want."

"I don't believe you."

The cajoling dropped from his voice. "Today if you can."

"Is this serious enough that I should get her sister involved?"

The line was silent for a full thirty seconds. "You can make the decision after we show you what we have."

"We can teleconference, you know."

"Just get here." The line went dead.

I stared at my phone then swore and ran upstairs for a shower.

Twenty minutes later, after I gave Midnight some kibble, I was in my Jeep. I debated texting Chaos to let her know I was coming, but I decided it was easier to just show up.

Clay was used to me dropping in for morning coffee. His fiancée knew how to brew a damn good cup. I parked behind an ancient red SUV that had to be Willow's. As I got out and headed for the door, I spotted a helluva lot more totes in her vehicle than a quick visit would require. Even someone as over the top as Chaos.

As I let myself in, the scent of bacon and coffee nearly made me groan.

"Hey, Ransom. Do you have a bacon sensor in our house or something?" Rachel's quick grin made me smile back automatically. She was wearing an old denim shirt over a pair of stretchy pants that every woman seemed to have in their arsenal. Her dark hair was gathered on top of her head with a heavy sweep of bangs framing her heart-shaped face.

Sometimes it was hard to believe this woman was related to the aptly named Willow who was all long limbs and freckles, where her sister was petite and dark-haired.

I really did like Clay's woman. That helped strengthen my resolve to make sure Chaos wasn't into something that would worry them both.

"More like a sensor for your coffee."

Her blue eyes sparkled with happiness. "Well, have a seat. Wil is on her way down. She wanted a shower."

I glanced at the couch made up with blankets and a pillow.

Rachel blushed. "I wasn't ready for her to drop in. Our spare bedroom is full of wedding gifts."

"Ah. I can, uh, help move stuff." I sat at the counter and warmed my hands around the mug as she filled it. "Thanks."

"Sure." She held the pot, waiting for me to take a few gulps for her to refill. She knew me well. Turning to put the pot down and check on the bacon, she sidestepped her cat to get to the fridge. "We'll have to figure out where to put everything."

"She can stay at my place."

Rachel paused with the door open and her arm full of eggs and cheese. "What?"

I swallowed down another scalding gulp of coffee. "She can stay at my place. The attic space is done."

"Since when?"

I sighed. I didn't share my space with anyone, let alone the details of what I was doing in renovations. "Last month. I was bored when we got snowed in—again."

Rachel put down the food and came back to the counter. "You don't have to do that."

It would be easier to watch over Chaos if she was under my roof.

Even if the thought of her in my space had my skin tightening. The relief on Rachel's face had me swallowing down any protests. All the wedding planning had been stressing her out.

The actual ceremony was a small affair at the orchard's chapel, but I knew juggling all those details would make anyone insane, let alone a type-A perfectionist like Rachel Doyle.

"I guess she can help you with that surprise you guys are cooking up. I had no idea you guys were up to something." She pulled out a whisk then attacked a huge bowl of eggs she'd already cracked.

"I'm not telling you what I'm—*we're*—working on."

"I didn't ask."

I lifted my cup. "Mmm-hmm."

She set the whisk down. "C'mon. Just a hint."

"Nope."

"Bah." She blew her bangs out of her eyes. "Damn vault."

Clay came in next. He was half dressed for the office. A shirt and tie over a pair of sweatpants told me he'd been in teleconferences already. Considering he had business dealings all over the globe, it wasn't surprising. I couldn't say I missed the hours he kept.

"Hey." He dropped a quick kiss on top of Rachel's head before snagging a strip of bacon. "I didn't know you were coming over today."

I held up my mug. "Can't beat Rachel's brew."

She hip-checked him away from the food. "Ransom offered to put up Willow."

Clay's eyebrows shot up. "Really?"

I shrugged. "I finished the attic renovations. Easy enough to stick a bed in there."

He popped the last of the bacon in his mouth. "It would help us out a lot. If another damn box comes for the wedding, I'm going to need to rent a freaking storage unit."

"We didn't even put much on the registry."

Clay gave her sidelong look, but he didn't comment.

I grinned behind the lip of my mug.

Clay made a lot of concessions for his woman. It was interesting to see my formerly uptight best friend bend like a damn reed for her. But he did—gladly. Which was even more of a surprise.

Another reason I'd made sure I had my own space from them. I didn't like to bend. And while I was willing to do a lot for them, it gave me a place for peace.

There was nothing peaceful about Rachel and the schemes she was always dragging Clay into.

However, she did have a particularly amazing talent with coffee. I took another long swallow of the brew that only seemed to come from her magic pot. Even when she sent me home with the same beans, mine never tasted the same.

Rachel set a shallow bowl full of eggs, bacon, and perfectly fried sausage in front of me.

Her culinary skills had also improved.

I lifted a fork and dug in as the natural flow of their morning rituals went on around me. Teasing, laughter, the lingering touches and looks that I tried to ignore.

Clay was happy and if part of me attempted to long for the same, I locked it down. I liked my quiet. Access to a warm and willing female body had its moments, but in the end, I got itchy to be alone.

"Rach, you're killing me with the bacon. I barely managed to make myself get dressed before running down here...oh. Hi."

Chaos, with freshly washed hair and a pair of tight black jeans that showed every line of her mile-long legs, entered the kitchen like a breath of summer.

The sun streaming through their kitchen highlighted the gold threaded in the dark red of her wet hair. She wore a black tank which was dotted with water from her heavy, still dripping hair.

"I didn't know you were coming by so soon."

I finished chewing and managed to swallow the once delicious breakfast that now tasted like sawdust. Maybe I needed to go down to see Roth on my own.

I wasn't sure I could manage a trip into the city with her.

"Soon?" Rachel turned with a pair of tongs in her hand.

Willow shot a panicked look at me.

While it would probably kill me to have her in my house, subterfuge was definitely not one of Chaos's talents.

"We worked on your surprise late. I told Chaos it would take some time to dry."

"Oh." Rachel's eyes brightened. "Still no hints?"

"Nope."

She pointed the tongs at me. "You suck."

I picked up a piece of bacon and popped it in my mouth. Thankfully, it was back to delicious.

Willow peeked over her sister's shoulder. They did this little dance that told me it was a common occurrence as she crowded into Rachel, reaching around for a piece of bacon. "Hey, I just want one."

Rach elbowed her back. "Go sit down. I'll feed you for once."

Chaos managed to filch one out of my bowl instead before going around the counter. Her fresh lemon scent hit me, making my mouth water.

She bumped her arm with mine as she climbed on the stool, using it to distract as she went for another bit of bacon.

Sneaky minx. "Do you mind?"

She shrugged. "You can have one of mine when my slowpoke sister gives me some." She crunched through the end. "Maybe."

I hunched around my bowl, blocking her from more thievery.

"What are you doing here? Did you find something out?" she asked in a Willow whisper—meaning not at all.

"After breakfast," I muttered.

She nodded.

"Find something out about what?"

Willow's head whipped toward her sister. Rach stood in front of her with a bowl.

"Surprise." Willow took it with a cheery grin.

Okay, maybe she wasn't so bad at it.

Rachel wrinkled her nose at her sister and for the first time, I was struck by something they did alike. The two women were very different, but in that moment, they were mirrors.

Willow held up a single piece of bacon. "Here."

I leaned forward and snapped it out of her grip with my teeth.

Startled, she locked those big hazel eyes on me. I didn't know what had gotten into me. Must've been sleep deprivation.

I went back to my breakfast as conversation hummed around me. I'd been forming a plan on how to get her out of Turnbull to see Roth, but the longer I sat next to her, the more I wondered if I should make it a solo visit.

"Ransom offered up his attic for your stay."

Willow looked up at Clay, then toward me. "Really?"

I shrugged. "It's only a few weeks."

"About that."

My fork stilled over the remnants of my eggs.

Rachel slapped her hands on the counter, a wide smile in place. "Are you moving back?"

Willow put her fork down and twisted her hands in her lap. "Things have gotten a little tense with my roommates."

My shoulders tightened. *How* tense?

"Oh, Wil. I don't know how you did that whole sorority house setup for so long."

Willow looked at her hands. "I like being in the city."

"But you're so busy, you hardly go out exploring down there anymore anyway."

"I know." She flattened her hands on her thighs, rubbing up and down before digging the tips of her fingers into the denim.

Without thought, I covered her hand. She froze for a moment before flipping over one of her hands to grip mine before she released it and went back to her bowl.

Clay was staring at me when I looked away from her.

I cleared my throat. "I saw a lot of bins in your Santa Fe."

She hunched her shoulders. "Yeah. I took as much as I could with me."

And like a puzzle piece found on the floor, I knew how we could go down to the city. I'd been planning on taking the plane, but a road trip would be just as easy.

"I can help you pick up the rest."

Willow shot me a look. "You would?"

I nodded. "I need to go into the city anyway to talk to someone about a job."

Clay rinsed his bowl and tucked it into the dishwasher. "A job?"

"A one and done with Aidan Roth."

Willow stiffened.

Lying to Clay wasn't something I did easily. There had been far too many lies between us once and it had torn apart our friendship. This way, I could just circumvent the truth.

"Careful, Aidan will snap you up before you could get a *no* out of your mouth."

"Believe me, I know." I glanced at Chaos. "You're in Brooklyn, right?"

She nodded.

"My meeting shouldn't take much longer than an hour. Then we can pick up your stuff and head back north."

"Sounds like a plan. You know, if you're sure."

"I'm sure."

Clay was still looking at me with far too many thoughts going on in that brilliant brain of his. "I was going to take the plane, why I stopped in." I lifted my mug. "Ulterior motive for coffee."

Rachel laughed. "I'll make up a Thermos for you guys."

"Thanks."

Chaos slid out of her chair, taking both of our bowls with her. "I was afraid to tell you guys. Impulsive Willow strikes again."

"I know I've given you grief about it before, but I'm embracing a bit of that myself. Maybe we can even do some videos on the CocoaBus for your show."

Willow put her bowls back down and ran around the counter to hug her sister. "I'd love that."

She hugged her so tight that Rachel gave Clay a startled look before she hugged her back. "Hey, it's okay." She patted her back. "We'd love to have you around."

"Thanks," Chaos whispered.

Her gaze crashed into mine before she squeezed her eyes shut. "I'm going to go get ready."

"Is something going on?" Rachel looked at me.

"Isn't something always going on with her?"

Clay came up behind her. "With you two?" He lightly cupped his hands over Rachel's shoulders. "You're usually looking for the exit when it comes to Willow."

Rachel folded her arms, tipping her head.

Damn that hundred-yard stare she had. She could go toe-to-toe with any drill sergeant in the Army. And they were right that I'd prefer to be far away from Chaos and her exceptional talent at making messes.

However, she was theirs, which meant I had to deal with this problem and make sure it wasn't more serious, even if every instinct told me it was.

But right now, it was easier to misdirect and get more details before I needed to put fear into their eyes.

"Don't worry, she's safe from me."

Clay frowned. "That's not what I meant."

"Isn't it?" I slid off the stool. "Tell her I'll be outside."

Chapter 7

Willow

Roadtrip

I quickly rubbed my lotion in on my arms before pulling on a cloud-soft black sweater one of my fans had sent me. Hand-knit abilities escaped me. My Gemini brain wouldn't allow me too sit that long in one spot to make something so beautiful.

I ran my hand over the texture, calming myself. Or trying to.

Why was he here?

Had the news been bad?

My hand shook as I put in my gold hoops. Curling my fingers into my palm, the sting of my nails cut the blooming nerves. I'd learned the quick prick of pain could distract me enough to calm myself when I'd first started making videos.

It really wasn't working at the moment.

But it was enough to let me put in both earrings. I tucked a strand of hair behind my ear. I'd straightened my hair and tried to cover my freckles up with some makeup.

The bane of my existence was looking far younger than I was. A little professional armor would go a long way in showing Ransom and this Aidan person that I wasn't a complete trainwreck.

At least that was how I saw it.

"Fake it til you make it," I said to the mirror before grabbing my messenger bag from the bathroom counter. My laptop and iPad were inside. I could probably get some work done on the drive. I had a feeling my chauffeur wasn't going to be a great conversationalist.

My sister was waiting in the hallway. "Is something going on?"

I pressed my lips together.

She narrowed her eyes. "It feels like more than just this surprise you're working on."

I shrugged. "He's kinda a jerk, but I can deal with him for a few hours. Don't worry."

"That's not what I meant. Don't be obtuse."

I folded my arms over my chest. I really sucked at this lying thing. Maybe I should just come clean with her.

Just as I was about to open my mouth and probably blurt out the whole damn thing, her phone blared from her pocket. "Well, get it."

"It's fine." She came forward and pulled my hand free to grip it in hers. "You can talk to me."

"I know."

Her phone started up again and Rachel huffed out a breath. "One sec."

"It's okay. We'll talk tonight."

I could see the indecision in her eyes, but whomever was on the phone put a whole different kind of anxiety in her eyes. "What's up, Nat?" Her mouth dropped open. "No. We can't have a reception without music."

I winced and rubbed her arm quickly. Rach gave me a apologetic smile and I just waved her off and mouthed that I'd see her later.

Saved by the drama.

It would be much better if I found out what Ransom knew before I worried her anyway.

I rushed down the stairs, only taking a minute to pull on boots. April often came with sudden rain showers. I grabbed my hip-length rain slicker from the closet and grinned at the thermos of coffee waiting by the door with two travel mugs. Rachel never missed a trick.

As I opened the door, I kicked a box on the porch. My hand shook until I noticed it was actually addressed to my sister.

"Get it together, Wil." I shoved the box through the door, meeting Ransom's gaze as I stood.

We matched—indirectly. He wore black jeans as well, but his were worn in all sorts of interesting places. His hands were fisted in his front pockets and heavier scruff made his jawline look even more sharp. There was also a tiredness around his eyes.

He wore layers of cotton and his necklace peeked from his neckline, drawing my gaze to his corded neck.

Why oh why did he have to be so damn attractive?

His grumpy attitude should have made him ugly, and yet...nope.

Dammit.

"We can unload my..." I trailed off when I saw his vehicle. It was a mammoth Jeep that seemed to have merged with a truck.

He opened the passenger door. "Unless you have a king-sized bed, we should be good." He took the thermos from me.

"Definitely not. Who needs that?"

His eyebrow arched.

"What do you need one of those for?" I nodded toward the truck.

"I like space." He leaned in. "For many things."

I had no reply for that piece of information. Except that suddenly, the crisp April day felt too warm.

"Get in."

"Are you going to tell me what Aidan said." I stashed my gear and the mugs before I grabbed the handle and hoisted myself up. I twisted to face him.

His eyes were definitely not on my face.

Well, that was interesting.

His gaze snapped to mine and his nostrils flared. Instead of answering me he slammed my door and went around the back. He stowed the thermos in the backseat in a cooler.

Yeah, I was definitely glad I brought work with me. This was going to be so fun.

He climbed in and started the engine. Instead of the loud rumble I expected, it was a low hum. Guess the whole carbon footprint thing included his hybrid truck. He looked over his shoulder even though he had a backup camera and a waft of mint hit me.

His jaw worked with a piece of gum a bit aggressively.

More interesting.

Then again, I seemed to bring out the growly parts of him for some reason. Even that first time I met him at the Christmas Tree Farm, he'd been awfully intense.

In the beginning, he'd seemed delighted with the way I'd gone at Clay. I couldn't help it. I was protective of my sister.

She was my older sister, but the updates from Aunt Laverne had left me itchy to come up and make sure she was okay. I wasn't used to hearing that Rachel was anything less than Wonder Woman. Then I saw the articles both online and in the actual newspaper about Clay and some chick and I'd shot up to Turnbull, seeing red the entire time.

In the end, Clay had been a stand-up guy, but I'd been ready to skin him alive.

And as far as I was concerned, she should have made him grovel way more. CocoaBus II was pretty amazing, but still.

As I'd feared, it was silent in the car as he maneuvered the winding road Clay lived on. I let him play mister quiet as I concentrated on answering a few comments on my last video. Thankfully, I had a couple videos in the queue to be uploaded over the next few days.

"Well? What did he say?"

"Why didn't you tell me you were staying in Turnbull indefinitely?"

I huffed out a breath and set my iPad on my lap. "I was still trying to figure it out, that's why."

"You just up and packed your SUV?"

"Yes. It wasn't exactly the best exit strategy, but one of my room-mates freaked about the package and I didn't handle it correctly."

Flashes of Dennelle's icy blue eyes flashing indignation made my stomach twist again.

He tapped his finger on the steering wheel, but he said nothing.

"I was scared and it made *them* scared. One of my former room-mates wasn't exactly the easiest to live with, and we...well, let's just say I hope she's not there when we stop in."

"It was the first time you got something there?"

I nodded, hugging my iPad. "I tried not to overreact, but I'm really careful about keeping my privacy."

He glanced at me, his eyes shark-flat before he returned his gaze to the road.

I tightened my hold on my tablet. The worst part of all of what was happening was that it brought up a lot of memories from college. I'd worked long and hard to have a safe life after Jason.

"What did Aidan say?"

"He didn't."

I twisted in my seat. "What do you mean, he didn't?"

"He didn't tell me jack. Just asked me to bring you in."

I tucked my iPad away, grabbed my mug, and then I leaned against the door. I took a fortifying sip of the still hot coffee. "Is that usual for him?"

"I haven't worked with him that often, but I do know he likes to keep things close to the vest."

My vise grip on the mug eased. "So, maybe he's just the cautious sort."

He glanced at me again. "Maybe."

"But you don't think so." It wasn't even a question. While Ransom was a vault, even I could tell Aidan's reaction made him tense.

"I can't say what Aidan did on the initial search would hold up in court, but he and Poe are thorough. And if she found something, then it's probably important."

I bit my lower lip. I was well-versed in the proof game. One of the reasons why I'd left college had been because nothing Jason did could be construed as overly aggressive.

Getting an order of protection had done exactly nothing. He hadn't been able to come within one-hundred yards of me. He'd been able to do plenty from afar.

Orders of protection hadn't exactly caught up with the digital age.

"No questions about that?"

"I'm a true crime girl, Ransom. I get that stalking laws are about as gray as an April sky."

"This isn't a podcast."

"I know that," I snapped out. "I'm also a woman. We're well-aware just how little power we have when it comes to an asshole who wants to come at us."

His fingers tightened on the wheel. "I'm not letting anything happen to you. We don't even know what this guy wants yet. It might just be a super fan thing."

"I know."

But I really didn't think so.

The next ninety miles passed in silence. I finished my coffee and nibbled through my stash of Swedish Fish. I didn't even want them, but they kept my mouth occupied. We fought over the radio a little, but in the end, I just let him listen to what he wanted.

His musical taste was close to mine, but I wanted some mindless pop right now. I put in my headphones and listened to my happy playlist and did a little research on Roth Defense. I was fairly certain if there wasn't a price package on the website, I couldn't afford them.

Just what kind of friends did Ransom have? I knew Clay came from money, but did that mean Ransom did too?

Everything inside me wanted to research Ransom's name too, but something held me back. I could've done it without guilt since he now knew far too much about *me,* but the wall around him gave me pause.

So, I played my puzzle game to even me out for a few minutes, but even that wasn't cutting it.

Finally, I couldn't wait any longer for a break. My butt was asleep and my bladder was crying. When I saw the sign for a rest stop, I pulled out my ear bud.

"Can we stop?"

"We still have three hours to go."

"Yeah, well, it was a big coffee."

He sighed, but he signaled to move over. With the way he was driving, we were definitely going to make it into the city in less than four hours. Well, depending on traffic when we got closer to Manhattan anyway.

He pulled into the rest stop and I went to hop out.

"Hang on." He climbed out and came around the truck to open my door.

"I'd like to think you're being a gentleman, but I doubt it."

He took my hand, helping me down. "My grandmother taught me well, Chaos."

I narrowed my eyes. "Hmm."

His gaze swept the parking lot as we headed for the food court where the bathrooms were.

"I can go to the bathroom myself, you know."

"I had just as much coffee."

Somehow I doubted he'd have stopped if I hadn't asked him, but I decided to keep my mouth shut for once. If he wanted to play mister protective, who was I to dissuade him?

Too bad his protection didn't make for a clean bathroom. *Ugh.* Quickly, I did my business and washed my hands.

He was leaning on one of the vending machines when I came out. At first glance, he looked like any other guy waiting for his partner to finish with the toilets, but he wasn't on his phone like most people these days. Instead, his intense eyes were taking in everyone and checking the exits. I couldn't imagine living that way—being on guard at all times.

Finally, his wintery gaze drifted to me. He straightened and I noticed he had a bag in his hand.

When I got to him, he held it out. I took it and peered in, surprised to find more Swedish Fish, the soda I preferred—Coke Zero, not diet—and two 100 Grand Bars. I frowned at him.

He shrugged. "You seem to like snacks."

"How did you know about this?" I held up the candy bar.

"Rach put some in your stocking at Christmas."

"And you remembered?"

"I like them too."

"Oh."

His eyebrow arched.

"I thought you got two for me."

He rolled his eyes. "Let's go, Chaos. I want to get into the city before gridlock."

"Good luck there."

True to his word, we were over the bridge in record time. His beast of a truck practically mowed through traffic. It was obvious he knew his way around the city. He took shortcuts and streets I didn't even know were actual roads.

Then again, some of them seemed more like suspicious alleyways.

Eventually, we arrived at a huge, towering building, jet black from the outside. The windows seemed to be opaque, making it look even more like a monolith in the middle of downtown.

We didn't have to worry about parking since Roth Defense had its own underground garage. If I hadn't known Aidan and his brother were so impressive before today, the building would have done the job. It was a rare feat to have parking in Manhattan without stacking vehicles like Legos.

A guard let us into the well-lit parking garage and gave us a special tag that he put on the dash. There were rows of black cars and luxury SUVs that seemed deceptively stylish, but I could tell they were also personal protection vehicles.

Roth Defense was leagues above what my kind of case would require. At least I hoped.

"Are you sure we should waste Aidan's time with my *maybe* stalker. This place seems like guarding Lindsey York level."

He parked. "First of all, you're just as important as some musician."

"Impressed you know who Brooklyn Dawn is, Grumpasaurus."

He gave me that flat stare.

I shrugged. "I am. Regardless, I'm not *this* kind of important."

His nostrils flared. "Get out of the car."

I sighed and grabbed my bag. Evidently, I wouldn't need my coat. Before I could open the door, he was already there waiting for me. "I don't know why you're so grumpy. You're Ransom and your default is snarly, but jeez."

He invaded my space so thoroughly that his minty breath fanned my lips. "You matter. Whether there's a million dollars in the bank or not, you matter. Especially to my best friend's soon-to-be wife."

Right. Just to his best friend. Mustn't forget that.

His eyes were more blue than gray now, like the rolling sea just before a storm comes in. Pretty sure I needed to remind my nipples this was all business because they were as hard as diamonds.

"We don't know what my situation is. I just mean this is very high tech for something so random as a guy—or girl—finding my address."

"Lucky for you, I know good people. And if it wasn't serious, he wouldn't have called us in." He took a step back.

I swallowed hard and nerves swarmed up my spine. "And I appreciate it." I touched his arm. His muscles were hard as steel under the two layers of cotton. "I do."

He nodded curtly and stepped aside for me to start walking. I hooked my messenger bag over my shoulder and we went to the elevator without speaking.

Ransom pulled his phone out of his pocket and fired off a text. As we got to the doors, it buzzed in his hand. He looked down and then punched a code in to the elevator panel.

Holy crap. Just what kind of place was this?

The doors slid open soundlessly. Inside was as jet-colored as the outside of the building. Shale-colored carpeting added to the sound-proofing as we stepped inside.

Whatever code he'd put in programmed the car to go to a partic-ular floor. When the doors opened again, the hum of people and machines was jarring. Four large cubicles sectioned off the space. Inside each were massive computer screens with two people manning surveillance of some sort.

One of them was a blond woman with quick fingers. She barked orders into a headset as her partner rolled around on a chair checking a laptop, then some sort of radio, then back to the intricate board that reminded me of a studio with levels and knobs.

Ransom hustled me along down a hallway. I craned my neck to keep watching as he curled his hand around my arm. "Nosy," he muttered.

"What? I can't help it. It's right there. It's not like there's a door around them."

"Still none of your business."

I huffed out a breath. "Spoilsport."

The farther we got down the hall, the less the cacophony of noise seemed to penetrate. There was a set of double doors with one open.

"I want to do a deeper dive, but I need you to okay a dip into the dark web." A husky yet hyper voice drifted out of the room.

"As if you have ever asked before," a man answered drily.

"I said deep, didn't I?"

Were they talking about me? Surely not.

Ransom walked a little faster in front of me and went through the door first. "Roth."

"Ransom, good to see you."

He strode forward, his hand outstretched to the large, muscular man built like a damn wall. His inky dark hair swept back from a strong face, and his heavy dark brows knitted together over intelligent dark eyes.

Eyes that seemed to see the most minute detail of everything, including me.

The room was large and floor-to-ceiling windows showed off a busy Manhattan outside. The rest of the room was more of the same deep gray carpeting with black leather chairs and a long black table that seemed to suck up all the light.

I didn't realize I was hovering in the doorway until the man smiled at me. "You must be Miss Doyle."

"Willow," I replied and crossed to him, holding out my hand as well. His grip was firm without being a bone-cruncher.

"I'm Aidan and this is Poe, our internet intelligence specialist."

Poe nodded, the movement showing off her improbably black hair tipped with an ultraviolet hue. Her clothing was all black with the same violet peeking from slashes in the material at her arms and midsection. "I don't do touching," she said, dipping her hands in her pockets.

"Oh. That's cool." I smiled brightly, but the woman just tipped her head slightly and stared at me.

Suddenly, she shot forward. "Maybe I'll make an exception. I really liked your brookie recipe." She held out a hand.

Delighted, my smile relaxed into a regular one. "Thanks." I shook hers. "Thanks for helping me with...whatever is going on."

"When Aidan told me it was you, I jumped in."

"Really?"

Poe nodded sharply and an array of silver hoops jingled from her ears. Tattoos climbed her neck and disappeared under the collar of her shirt. "I really like your stuff. Helps to watch your vids when I'm coming down after work."

A flush climbed up my neck and my freckles were probably now glowing. "I'm glad."

Aidan pulled out a chair at the head of the conference table. "Why don't you sit down so we can have a chat?"

Ransom pulled out a chair for me, then he took the one beside me closest to Aidan.

Poe went around to the other side of the expansive table and sat at a laptop near her boss. Screens I hadn't noticed before flicked to life behind Aidan.

Dozens of windows full of my face, black boxes with code, and two other live feeds popped up, one by one. There was too much information for me to focus on.

The code was like a different language and I immediately discounted that to focus on the two larger boxes filled with a grainy feed from a security camera.

"When Ransom came to me with your problem, I initially thought it was a simple case of cyberstalking. Maybe some bullying."

I laced my fingers together on the table to stop the shaking. That word still brought me to places I didn't want to go.

"Then again, you're well versed in stalking aren't you, Willow?"

Ransom's head snapped toward me. "Is there something you forgot to tell me?"

Chapter 8

Ransom

Dark Secrets

Watching the color drop out of her face ramped up the anger clawing my chest. I knew she'd been holding something back, but I figured it would be something inconsequential. The embarrassment young women dealt with on the internet.

Not this.

She lifted her chin, even if it wobbled a bit. "That was a long time ago."

"It's a detail we should have known about, so we could discount it. Now we wasted time combing through records from when you were nineteen."

I turned my attention to Aidan. "You're discounting it?"

Aidan's gaze drifted to Poe. "Want to show them?"

Poe's fingers flew over her keys and something on the screen bounced in my periphery. I twisted to take in the screen.

"Jason Grafton, twenty-eight, twenty at the time of offense, UC Berkley graduate, CFO of Grafton Enterprises in California. Your typical dirtbag rich boy. I dug up a series of accusations from women through his college years, but nothing ever stuck. Things got a little quieter once he graduated. Pretty sure because Daddy got him a better lawyer. I did some digging and found a few payoffs."

Chaos's head lowered and her fingers spread on the table, the tips whitening as she pressed them harder into the surface.

I listened to Poe stream off all his offenses, particularly women who came forward and then abruptly dropped charges. My blood pressure spiked with each new bit of information.

Her shoulders hunched as another list of women hit the screen. She didn't look up, but I did. Twenty names—all females.

A small sniffle dragged my attention back to Chaos. I shifted as she delicately dabbed at her nose.

"It's not your fault, Willow." Aidan's voice dragged me out of the redlining anger.

"I could have done more," she said quietly. "I just ran."

"You were nineteen." Poe's voice was a gunshot. Sharp enough that Chaos looked up at her.

"I should have done more," she whispered.

"Tell us in your words so we can tie it up." Aidan's tone was quietly firm.

"I went out with Jason a few times. He was charming and boy, did he come for me as if I had a bullseye on my forehead. And maybe I did." She shook back her hair, the mix of gold and amber making her face seem even paler.

I fisted my hand on my thigh under the table.

"It was my first year. I got in on a partial scholarship and was so excited to get out of New York. I saw him on campus a few times—parties, a coffee shop, movie nights, that kind of thing. He was really good." She laughed but it was a brittle sound. "He was flirty with all the compliments, then he started to press for a date."

Poe pushed a box of tissues across the table.

"Thanks." She plucked one out and wiped her eyes then her nose. "I only went out with him a few times before I got a bad feeling.

He was hitting me pretty hard with the love deal. We went out twice before he began telling me he thought I was the one."

I clenched my jaw so hard my head started to throb.

"Most women wouldn't have figured it out so fast," Aidan said quietly.

"I didn't," Poe added.

Chaos looked up.

Poe's face was devoid of emotion.

Chaos gave her a sad smile. "I'm sorry."

"He was when I was done with him," Poe said without remorse.

Chaos gave a watery laugh. "I wish I could say the same. Anyway, I tried to tell him I wasn't interested in anything too serious. I was a freshman, majoring in New Media and Business. To say I was buried in classes and projects was an understatement. At first, he was good with it and played the understanding card, but then he started showing up at all of my classes to see me before and after. Just a nice guy who wanted to make sure I got to all my classes safely, yada yada. Then he showed up at the library and the coffee shop when I went out with my friends." She paused, opening her fist. The tissue she held was shredded. "Then he locked me in a classroom."

My heartbeat was so loud in my head I could barely hear her voice.

"I was there late doing some group work and was the last to leave." She didn't seem to be in the room anymore. Her eyes had a faraway look to them. "He started yelling at me. Telling me how much he liked me. That I should be happy a girl like me had his attention." Rough laughter tore from her chest. "That I should appreciate it."

I dragged her chair toward me. Her hazel eyes were bloodshot with tears as she stared at me. She laid her hand over mine where it was clamped on her chair. "I'm okay."

I nodded because I wasn't sure I could speak right at that moment.

"I got lucky that time. My classmate came back to make sure I wasn't alone. Jason cornered me a few more times and scared me enough that I finally ended up calling the campus police. That was useless. That's when I found out just how rich Jason Grafton was." She took a deep, shaky breath. "After that, my semester was hell. I got an order of protection, but it didn't do any good. He was always watching, even if it was from across the quad."

I glanced at Poe, then at Aidan. His jaw was clenched.

"He trashed my dorm room and my roommate asked for a room change." She laughed. "A freshman with a room to herself, you would have thought it was a dream. Except he managed to get a key."

"All right, that's enough." My voice was raw.

She reached over to grip my hand.

"It's okay. I didn't get hurt. He scared me, but I couldn't get anyone to take me seriously. Even the cops couldn't do anything because he didn't physically harm me. Just liked to scare me. My parents were a wreck, and my sister was so scared for me. They wanted me to come home. There were tons of colleges in New York I could go to, but UC Berkley had always been a dream for me."

"And then it was nightmare," Poe said quietly.

"In Jason's mind, I'd just give up and go out with him. In the end, he won anyway. I was flunking out because I couldn't concentrate. The day I got the letter that I lost my scholarship, I just gave up. He won. I packed up all my things and rented a van when he was at one of his games and drove across country. I never saw him again."

She pressed her lips together. "So, there you go. That's everything."

Aidan glanced at me and narrowed his eyes on our linked hands before zeroing in on Willow. "Thanks. I'm sure that was difficult, but your details filled in a few things we couldn't pin down. You're right, there was a lot of covering up because of his name. The Graftons give a lot of money to Berkley."

"I guess that's not shocking." Chaos sighed.

"You have good instincts. You're sure there's nothing else?"

"I didn't say anything because I knew Jason wasn't doing this. I'm just sorry I didn't fight harder, so all those women didn't have to go through what I did."

Poe's fingers flew over the keys again. "I double-checked Jason's whereabouts just to be sure. He's too busy getting married to some bread princess." She rolled her eyes as she did whatever it was that she did on her laptop. "The future missus has a sterling prenup, so I guess that's as good as we're getting with that."

"What's with the live feeds?" I needed to redirect the conversation before I lost my goddamn mind.

"That's why I called you in."

Chaos's grip tightened.

Aidan swung around in his chair toward the screens. The smaller boxes grew larger, splitting the screen. "We found this in a dark web forum."

"*We?*" Poe chimed in.

Aidan glanced over his shoulder. "Royal we."

Poe did a little royal wave, but there was no laughter.

"That's my apartment," Chaos whispered.

"And the goddamn farm." I got up out of my chair and started pacing. "Where did you find that? What kind of forum?"

"Evidently, it's not just Willow they're after. We've found a nest of people who look for inventive ways to stalk celebrities."

"I'm not a—"

I whipped around to face her. "I've read your feed. Eight million people are watching your videos on a consistent basis. That's celebrity status."

"Her following has boomed, actually. More like eleven," Poe corrected.

"Great."

Chaos snapped her mouth shut and folded her arms. She looked so damn small and defenseless in the executive chair, but I shoved that dark thought aside.

"So, what did you find? It has to be more if you called me in without any details."

Aidan leaned back in his chair. "You're right. More than one person has paid for this information. Six that I've found so far."

"Six." Willow sat forward. *"What?"*

"Apparently, watching a celebrity's every move is a hot commodity. I was tempted to check out the Jason Momoa cam I found, but I resisted." Poe's attention stayed on her screen. "Most of the details are of the photo variety."

A startling number of photos came up with Willow at a cafe, on the farm, outside of her apartment, and some in a park. A bunch were from the Christmas Tree Farm during the insanity from Clay's own viral video.

And this was why I was barely on social media. Everyone wanted a piece of you, and they weren't happy with what you shared, they wanted invasive, intimate moments.

"I found the standard fare—fan videos, remixes, and fangirl accounts. Wil's Way keeps growing exponentially, with the public interest to match." Poe rattled off the details as if it was a shopping list.

"I didn't know about even half of these." Chaos seemed oddly fascinated by the screens.

Frame after frame of accounts and photos made my chest tighten until the urge to flee had me bristling with anger.

"People are clever and mostly harmless. A bit more fixated than I like, but the world we live in allows for such things. Fandoms are easily found if you have a bit of knowledge. Add in social media accounts and hashtags to find one another and well, it's a lot. There are also accounts who just literally rip off work for their own uses. Makes our jobs more difficult every day." Aidan stood. "But the video cameras are concerning. Photos, there isn't much you can do."

"How did I not know they were taking the photos though?" Chaos was hugging herself again.

"Telephoto lenses, long ranges even on our cell phones these days —take your pick. Hell, if you're good enough with a drone, you can get some serious video feeds. Which is what worries me. Small cameras are affordable and can be rigged up with a Bluetooth connection if you're savvy enough."

"And they're definitely savvy," I muttered.

More than one.

I was already on edge at one or two people who looked hinky on her socials, but an underground network of people? *Fuck.*

"We'll keep digging. But you're right to be worried about someone knowing your home address and Clay's address." Aidan glanced at Chaos's bag lying on the table. "Did you happen to bring your electronics?"

She nodded. "Laptop and iPad. Of course, my phone too. That's all I usually use. My camera wirelessly uploads to my cloud accounts for my videos."

"Poe will rig your devices with some proprietary software she's designed, so it's not on the market. Should make it harder for people to hack."

Gritting her teeth, Chaos curled her fingers around the strap of her bag.

"I found some of your unpublished videos online too." Grimly, Poe looked at Chaos. "Someone got into your cloud account. I'd bet money on it."

"Dear God."

I stood behind Chaos's chair. "You'll fix it?"

Poe nodded. "Give me an hour and I'll have you all buttoned up. Then I'll show you how to use it."

Chaos pushed her bag across the table, then she rattled off her passcode.

"We have some new software that will make it harder to get into your devices as well. Thumbprint and facial recognition." Aidan glanced at me. "Can we talk a minute?"

Chaos craned her neck to look up at me. "Shouldn't I be included?"

I swiped my hand down her hair. "I won't keep anything from you."

She stared hard at me, then she nodded. "All right."

I followed Aidan into another room. He closed the door behind us, engaging the lock.

I arched a brow at him. "State secrets?"

"No ears."

I folded my arms. "What didn't you say in there?"

"Dark web stuff makes me itchy. It's not my forte, though Poe is familiar with it and works well in those dark fucking corridors. I don't like that there's a goddamn network of people that can get this kind of detail. Not just on Willow. I found an ugly amount of shit in those forums. Some things on my other clients as well. Now I've got to handle all of that."

"Guess we opened a can of worms."

"And then some." Aidan rubbed the back of his neck. "When Poe came to me with this, my bullet wound got twitchy."

Aidan's brother Marcus discounted his brother's spidey senses, but I didn't. My own had saved my life on more than one occasion.

"I'm going to send one of my people to the farm to find any other cameras. The one that's directed at Willow's apartment, I'm not sure I can handle. Might be in a personal residence or in a goddamn tree. She's close to the park."

"That won't be an issue. She's moved out. If the jackass has been watching her, he probably knows that too. She packed up her car yesterday."

"So, she's relocating to Turnbull with her sister?"

"With me."

Aidan's eyes narrowed. "I see."

"Clay and Rachel's wedding is coming up. No room at the inn with them."

"Hmm."

I raked my fingers through my hair. "It's not ideal, but I can keep track of her easier if she lives with me. And no one will be getting a camera near her."

"Will you be keeping track of her with your dick?"

"Fuck off."

His lips kicked up at the corner. "Yeah. You don't work for me, so I can't say anything about it. Emotions make shit messy. Even if you're not getting naked with her, I know she's Clay's sister-in-law. Makes her important."

"You never miss a trick."

He snorted. "You'd think so."

I frowned at him.

"Never mind."

I wasn't one to pry because I hated when people did it to me, so I let it go. "I don't want to scare Rachel, but I will if I have to."

"For now, let me keep digging. Poe found six different people who want the details, but I don't know if it's six people or six personas right now. Digital trails are getting harder to track, especially on the murkier dark forums that want to stay anonymous."

"Yeah. *Fuck.*"

"We'll figure it out, it just will take some time. Until then, we'll safeguard her as much as possible."

"I could tell her not to post."

Aidan barked out a laugh. "Right. It's her career. Unlikely. And that might make this guy more dangerous, anyway. Right now, he's just probably jerking it to videos of her."

"Jesus Christ, Aidan."

"Sorry."

I crossed my arms. "You're just telling me straight. I appreciate it."

"If Poe finds anything else—or something new—I'll be in contact. Otherwise, I'll send you updates every other day on what we find."

He opened the door and I followed him out. "Set up a billing cycle. You have my details."

"I'm sorry I couldn't find your sister. Her skills are impressive."

"That's Marigold, definitely made to be a spy." I glanced down the hallway and found Chaos standing just inside the doorway to the conference room. She was gnawing on her lower lip, her eyes on that damn screen.

She turned and spotted me.

"We have an eatery on the third floor. Why don't you take her down for a coffee or something to eat? I'll tag you when Poe's done."

"Good plan." We shook hands. "Poe is gonna give me nightmares, isn't she?"

"Probably."

I blew out a breath. "Want to get some food, Chaos?"

Aidan's eyebrow shot up. "Chaos?"

Her long legs ate up the carpet as she came toward us. "An unfortunate nickname he's come up with. He thinks he's clever."

Aidan laughed. "We'll be in touch. It was nice to meet you, Willow. I'm sorry it's under these circumstances."

"Me too." She waited for Aidan to walk away before she turned toward me. "Want to explain what that was about?"

"Let's get some food. It's been a while since we had those eggs."

"Okay. Are we going somewhere?"

"Just downstairs. Marcus and Aidan are nothing if not efficient when it comes to options."

"I'm not really hungry."

"We both need fuel."

"All right." She chewed on the corner of her lip. "I'm sorry I didn't tell you about Jason."

"I can't help you if you keep things from me."

Her gaze lowered. "I'm not proud of it."

I tipped up her chin. "You didn't do anything wrong." Her eyes were still red-rimmed, but thank God, the tears were gone. Her gaze bounced from my eyes to my lips.

I stepped back and let her go.

She tucked her hair behind her ear. "Okay, feed me, Seymour."

I jerked my head toward the hallway. "Get moving."

She gave me that brilliant smile that millions of people fell in love with—and fuck me, I wanted to smile back.

But I didn't. Not that she noticed.

Maybe I could work on doing the same. Then I wouldn't notice her spectacular ass swinging its way down the hallway to the main part of the floor.

"Shit."

Chapter 9

Willow

Phone Thief

I resisted the urge to go into the cubicles and ask questions. Curiosity was the bane of my existence.

Instead I went right to the elevators. I could feel Ransom behind me. His gaze felt as heavy as the wool blanket my Aunt Laverne had made me.

What had they been talking about in that room?

Could it truly be any scarier than the details I'd stared at on that massive screen in the conference room? My entire life had been rolled out as if some cosmic god had stuck his damn finger on me. Like a bug.

The involuntary shiver hit me just as Ransom came up to meet me.

"Cold?"

I shrugged. "More like the heebs."

"Aidan and Marcus will figure out how this asshat is getting his information."

"And you?"

I didn't look at him as I asked. Would he run far and fast? Leave me to figure it out on my own? Rescind his offer for his attic space?

Dump me at my apartment with a pair of deuces to the sky?

I tunneled my fingers into the sleeves of my sweater, hiding my trembling hands from his prying eyes.

"I'm not letting you out of my sight."

My gaze swung up to crash into his flat gray eyes. "I couldn't impose like that."

"There's no imposing. You're not staying alone. Anywhere."

"Anywhere?" I stepped in front of him, staring up at him. "What's that supposed to mean?"

"It means until we know what we're dealing with, you've got yourself a new roommate. Or rather, I do. Any shopping you need to do, we'll do it together. Luckily, the wedding stuff we both need to do, anyway. I'll just be more hands on until the big day."

That was probably the most words I'd ever heard tumble out from his firm, very distracting lips. Right now, his mouth was mostly just an annoying pie-hole.

"It's not that serious."

He leaned down until our noses practically touched. "What part of that video feed did you not catch?"

"He was a creep and hacked into someone's security cameras. It won't happen at your place."

"It won't happen because I'll be on the lookout. And I'll be on your ass like a fucking barnacle. Where you go, I go."

The elevator doors opened behind me, startling me forward. My chest brushed his, making me stumble back into the car. "What did you and Aidan talk about? Was there more?"

"Wasn't all that enough?" He stalked forward, matching my steps like we were doing some choreographed dance.

My back bumped into the rail along the perimeter of the elevator. He didn't stop. He invaded my space until his thigh slid between my legs.

"This is how easy it is for someone to get into your space. Do you get that? You are fucking defenseless. Your big eyes widening, your breath catching. Absolutely no protective instincts."

I pushed at him, but he didn't budge. "Because I trust you."

"Why?"

The flatness of his tone made my heart kick hard against my chest. "Because you're Clay's friend."

"So? You think that makes me less dangerous?"

His chest crowded into me until the rail dug into my back. He clamped his hands on either side of me, his breath hot against my ear. My fear response was getting crossed with an attraction I didn't have any defenses against.

"Ransom."

"I could kill you right here. Do you get that?"

"I get it," I whispered.

He stepped back. "This isn't a game. You're Rachel's family which makes you Clay's family, so that makes you my responsibility."

"Is that all I am?" I met his arctic eyes.

"That's it."

I crossed my arms over my middle. My kneejerk reaction was to tell him to fuck off, but that wasn't an option. "I'll stay out of your way, don't worry about that."

His jaw flexed, but he didn't say anything else.

When the doors opened behind him, I brushed by him and out into the brightness of the eatery. Upstairs, I'd told myself I wasn't hungry, but with all the delicious smells assaulting me, I didn't stand a chance. I was a nervous eater, anyway.

Ransom was true to his word. He stayed at my side. When there were too many people around us, he held me by the arm, making sure I was tight to his side.

That itch to learn and know everything pushed back the fear and the anger. I wanted to try everything. One of the best things about New York City was the varied food trucks and eateries. Roth Defense had a rotating selection of food truck-worthy popups along with a few quick staples like pizza, sandwiches, vegetarian fare, and Asian.

"We aren't here for research."

I ignored him and chitchatted with two of the food trucks I recognized from Twitter. I pulled out my phone to do a quick video to upload for content.

Ransom plucked my phone out of my hand. "I thought Poe had all your devices?"

I tried to snatch it back, but he stuffed it in his pocket. Before I could do something stupid like dig into his pocket, I put my hands on my hips. "She set up my phone first."

"You do realize this guy can probably still track where you are?"

Instinctively, I wanted to share my experience, but if someone was watching my every move, this kind of share would be like a beacon to exactly where I was.

No privacy. No anonymity.

No spontaneity, which was basically my personality in a nutshell. Now what made me *me* was a risk.

I dropped my hands to my sides. The smells and excitement were overwhelming me now. There were far too many people surrounding us. When I looked over my shoulder, someone was staring at me.

Was it because they knew who I was? Or because I was acting like a freak?

Ransom grabbed my hands, shaking them out. "Chaos. Willow— it's okay." His voice sounded as if it was under water. "Hey, c'mon."

I pulled back my hands as I backed away, inadvertently bumping into someone with a tray. I automatically apologized and swerved as if I was drunk.

There were so many people here all of a sudden.

It was too hot. My wool sweater was too warm, the cloud-soft material clinging to my skin instead of comforting me. I rushed to the windows and then to the door to the outdoor patio, currently unoccupied due to the rain.

An arm came around me from behind and pulled me back. I struggled and Ransom's voice finally dented the panic.

"Chaos, you're okay. You're fine. Breathe."

He pushed us forward out the doors onto the wet stone. I tipped my head up to let the rain coat my face. It was probably steaming from my flushed skin.

Ransom kept his arm around me, his long fingers flat against my midsection. "Two quick breaths in through your nose. Don't exhale. Just twice in then out through your mouth."

The haze around my vision cleared. The misty rain beaded up on my sweater and on his wide hand then dripped down my cheeks as I rested my head against his chest.

"Again."

I followed his orders because it was easy.

Because it worked.

I relaxed against him by degrees. Slowly, the sounds of the city cut through the white noise in my head. I was staggeringly thankful for the tiny bit of privacy the patio afforded us.

Panic attack.

I hadn't had one of them in a damn long time. They'd been a gift that kept on giving after Jason had locked me in that classroom. I hadn't been able to go back in there. Even if three-hundred people were in the atrium, it didn't matter. I looked for him at every exit.

When I shuddered, his hold tightened again, his fingers flexing against my belly. I covered his hand. "I'm okay. I guess a panic attack was bound to happen after that meeting."

His nose bumped against my ear. "I don't want to scare you, but you have to start thinking."

I stiffened.

He held me tight. "I know you're not stupid. Not that kind of thinking, but you have to realize things need to change."

"I just wanted to share." I hated how watery my voice sounded. "That's all I ever wanted my channel to be. Sharing my excitement with people. I won't let him take that."

"You don't have to." He stepped back and turned me around to face him. He swiped at the rain on my cheeks with his thumb. "You just can't do it instantaneously."

"You said that he'd be suspicious if I didn't share things."

"And I believe that. But you should be careful like any other woman. You share after you're out of the area. Even if it was just a fan, what if he or she ambushed you?"

I looked down at his chest. The light rain was turning his gray Henley to a graphite color and the navy T-shirt under it was wet along his neck.

Every muscle was defined under the damp fabric.

Pay attention, Wil.

I didn't even realize my hands were resting on his belly. Talk about crappy timing with this reaction. God.

He cupped my cheeks, drawing my attention up to his face. "You think I like scaring you?"

"I don't know. Do you?"

His jaw flexed. His fingers slipped into my hair to grip the back of my head. I was tall enough that we lined up as if we were made for one another. All I had to do was lift my mouth and we'd be kissing.

Did I want that?

Did he?

The doors banged behind him. Instantly, he pushed me back a step so he was blocking me from whatever perceived threat was coming through the door.

"There you are. Aidan's been texting you."

I peeked around him to see Poe's curvy, tattooed body filling the doorway.

She glanced from him to me then back to him as her lips kicked into a smile. "Well, well."

"Just a little panic attack. He was helping me."

"I bet he was."

I rolled my eyes and pushed Ransom forward. "C'mon. I didn't get any food, dammit."

"We'll stop somewhere on the way to your apartment."

"Deal."

And we'd be discussing exactly what he and Aidan had been talking about in their little huddle.

Poe and Ransom discussed tech things I didn't understand. Something about a sweeper that would check for unknown signals on the farm.

Not even the farm was safe from this...whatever it was. I didn't even know if it was a *he*. The names seemed to be dead-ends from what I could gather.

Why would anyone build a network like this? To watch people? I understood if someone wanted to watch Harry Styles, but me? I wasn't even a blip on the radar of life, no matter what Ransom said.

Then again, fixations didn't have to be famous—I'd learned that lesson far too well.

What was it about me that made people go way off the deep end? That was what I didn't understand.

As the doors opened, I realized Poe had brought us to a different floor. There seemed to be an extra hum to the entire space. A massive locked room took up most of the floor.

"That's our resident geek's lab."

"You're not the geek?" I asked as I hustled to keep up with them.

"Nope. I'm the mastermind." She flashed a smile over her shoulder as she unlocked a door that didn't really fit the vibe of the building.

The room was so her, it didn't need a name placard on the door. Even the door had a goth flavor to it, with a heavy doorknob that didn't match the rest of the hardware I'd seen. And she literally used a massive skeleton key to open it along with a keypad and retina scan.

Holy shit.

Inside, it was all dark colors and retro-styled furniture with a skinny fridge tucked in the corner. Her computer station was gigantic, with three screens as large as televisions. Keyboards—plural— were scattered around the table. Some television show was playing on an iPad on a stand.

Was that *Supernatural*? Yep. Hello, Dean Winchester.

"Okay, I have your laptop all set. I set you up on a different server than the regular iCloud. So, it'll be encrypted and I have decent firewalls set up. If anything or anyone tries to hack in, I'll get an alert."

"Wow."

"We don't mess around with cybersecurity."

"Do I have to do anything special?"

"Nope." She handed me my messenger bag. "Just work as usual."

"And you can see everything?"

"I won't go looking." Poe dropped into her chair and spun around.

The chair was black with hot pink racing stripes. I was nearly certain it was custom-made for her body. I really needed to ask her who had outfitted her space.

"Sexy selfies can be put into a shielded folder if you're worried about it."

I flushed. "I think we're good. I was thinking more along the lines of my stupid outtake videos."

"Sure you were."

She glanced past me to Ransom. "How about you, handsome? Want me to beef up your tech?"

"Clay's toys suffice."

Poe blew out raspberries. "Winslow's stuff is child's play compared to my gear."

Ransom gave her one of his rare smiles. "I'll let him know."

"You do that." She spun around to her keyboard and tapped something. "He tried to steal me away from Aidan last winter. He still can't afford me."

Ransom pressed his lips together, but he didn't comment.

I stepped up to Poe's setup. "Is any of that about me?"

She closed a few windows and expanded a few more. "I found this while I was running diagnostics on your laptop. I expanded your RAM while I was in there. Should make your video editing easier."

"Oh. Thanks."

"No problem. I've got parts all over the place. Marcus is always breaking his laptops. I just steal the memory chips out of them."

I laughed. "Box of scraps."

"Box of scraps!" she parroted back in a deep, annoyed voice. "*Iron Man* is the best."

"Rich RDJ, yes, please."

"Right?" She grinned up at me. "I knew I liked you."

"Back to the part where you found something?" Ransom asked flatly.

"Right." Her fingers flew over the keys. "I was able to dive deeper on one of the names who requested a workup on you."

I shivered.

"Poe," Ransom said in warning.

"Sorry. I'm in work mode. I don't usually let anyone in here except Aidan. Anyway, this dude or chick was actually online while I was checking. I chased them around for a bit, but he or she must've gotten spooked."

Her fingers got louder on her keyboard. I could just imagine she didn't like that anyone was better than her. It had to be rare. She seemed spookily efficient at what she did.

"I'll find him. Or her. Or it." She turned back to us. "Until I do, just do what you usually do."

I licked my suddenly dry lips. "Do you think he knows I'm onto him—*them?* Whatever."

"Not sure. Might get him off that we are, to be honest. Regardless, we'll figure it out. I'm on it now."

I hooked my thumb along the strap of my messenger bag. "Thanks for helping me."

"I have a vested interest. I want you to keep making videos. Hey, think you could do some snack stuff? I'm not much for huge meals. But I like fun foods that fuel me up."

"Hmm." I turned to Ransom. "Can I have my phone back?"

He sighed and handed it back to me.

I opened my notes app and jotted down a few thoughts. It would be a good series. Lots of people ate at weird times these days.

Ransom rolled his eyes and slid his fingers around my arm. "All right, let's get moving. You can brainstorm in the truck."

"Right." I glanced at Poe, still occupied with the ideas lighting up my brain. "Thanks."

Poe waved me off. "I get it. I put an encrypted chat on there too. If you feel something is off, just tag me there. I'll look into it."

"Perfect."

Ransom turned me back toward the door. "I'll be in touch."

"Ta."

I was already typing away on my phone. I searched snacks, foods that boosted productivity, or even ones that would help relax someone if they were having a late-night snack.

"Put your phone away."

"Just another—*hey!*"

He opened my messenger bag and tucked away my phone. "You need to be aware of your surroundings. Your face aimed down at the screen ain't it, Chaos."

I blew out a breath. "We're just going down to the parking garage, and you're right there."

"Start learning now, and maybe it'll dent that beautiful head of yours someday."

I glanced over at him. "You think I'm beautiful?"

He didn't reply, just hustled me into the elevator.

Well, *that* was interesting.

Chapter 10

Ransom

Do I Look Like a Churro Guy?

I deserved a beer after this shitshow of a day.

I'd been expecting bad news when we got to Roth Defense, but Poe had unearthed things I hadn't fathomed. Which was pretty shocking since I'd been in the bodyguard game for years. Also, learning Willow had been through this before twisted something inside of me on a fundamental level.

Protective instincts were just a baseline for me. They were what made me join the Army after seeing my family implode. I needed that stability, that order—and now I was smack in the middle of a never-ending hurricane named Willow.

I just wasn't sure how it had happened. Or why I didn't want to detangle myself.

Maybe one too many trips up in a Blackhawk. Obviously, there had to be some residual brain scramble.

Now here I was watching her run around happily in a forgotten parking lot where food trucks liked to congregate for secret tastings. I was shocked how many of them still used this space. People never really knew when they'd show up, or how many—but the rhythms hadn't changed much since I'd left.

Clay used to have an affinity for finding hidden gems even though the bazillion dollar Winslow campus had eateries to cover just about everyone. Before Rachel, he'd just used checking them out as an excuse to get away from his office.

And lo and behold, now his wandering ways had disappeared. He finally knew where he belonged.

Hell, I'd marry Rachel just for her coffee skills.

Now I was getting rained on to make another Doyle happy. The greasy scent of a grill and eye-searing spices floated over to me in the misty rain. Vanilla and buttery confections chased the sharp aroma of peppers, making me glad I was a few hundred feet away.

I flipped up the collar of my pea coat. It was a little warm for the wool, but it kept me dry. Chaos was bouncing between a taco truck and a churro specialty truck. She'd agreed not to post any videos while we were in the abandoned warehouse parking lot, so I was letting her do her thing. The employees were thrilled to speak to her since the rain had kept people away.

Not exactly shocking. A leggy redhead with a huge smile made damn near everyone take notice—male or female. She'd pulled on her raincoat, making it easy to spot her bright pink hood as she delighted damn near everyone with selfies, videos, and taste tests galore. She kept trying to bring me over samples.

I didn't want to like her. I definitely didn't want to be charmed by her. And here I was fighting a smile as I leaned against my Jeep.

Knowing we would hit gridlock traffic into Brooklyn should have been a factor and yet here I was, almost as at ease as she was. We were safe enough that I didn't invade her space. She was relaxed and happy. She kept looking back to make sure I was still there and my gut ached from bracing for each of those smiles.

Damn her.

I glanced at my watch. Fun time needed to be over. We'd be rolling into her neighborhood in the dark if we didn't get moving.

"Chaos, let's go."

She spun around, a churro in each hand. "One more—"

"Losing light. Nope."

She said something to the girl leaning out of the truck. The older woman with a ball cap cackled and shot a look my way.

"Want some to go, handsome?" came her heavily accented voice.

I shook my head. I was still full from the tray of tacos we'd plowed through. I wasn't sure where Chaos put all the food she ingested. It certainly didn't show on any part of her.

She waved at the woman and accepted a to-go box before crossing the pitted gravel parking lot. She skipped around puddles, laughing as she played some sort of game of hopscotch only she could see.

"This was great. I can't wait to edit the footage. I think I got some really great stuff." She pushed back her hood enough so she could grin up at me. Her ginger lashes were starred with water and her makeup had long since washed away. She looked impossibly young with all her freckles and her cheeks flushed with excitement.

She popped open the box and held up a bite-sized version of a churro. "Sure you don't want anything?"

I narrowed my eyes. "Do I look like a churro guy?"

"You look like a guy who *needs* a churro." She held it up to my mouth. "Come on, Grumpasaurus. How can you not want something as perfectly cinnamony as a fresh churro?"

My mouth opened and her delighted laugh made me far bolder than I should have been. I nipped at her fingers as she popped it into my mouth. I chewed slowly, watching her hazel eyes go from playful to dilated with awareness.

Slowly, I licked away the sugary cinnamon that clung to my lips.

I should have straightened up and put her in the damn Jeep. Instead I widened my stance. "I'll take another one."

Her tongue flicked out to wet her lips. "I knew you'd like it."

"I don't hate it."

Her gaze dropped to my booted feet before she stepped closer. "I have one that's dipped in chocolate, or dulce de leche."

"Caramel always wins."

"Yeah?" She tapped her lip as she peered into the box.

I waited patiently. My abs tightened as I forced myself not to drag her closer. Stupid. This was so stupid. We'd be living under the same roof for what could be weeks.

I had no right to turn up the heat on whatever was simmering between us. And yet the fresh rain and lemon scent of her was damn near killing me.

She held up the iced piece. I wrapped my fingers around her cool wrist. "You taste it first."

"I'm full."

"Is that right?"

She licked her lips. "Maybe a little taste."

A little taste was not going to be enough. I forced my body to relax even if everything wanted to tighten. She looked at me as if I was the caramel snack, not the bit of buttery confection dripping between us.

I slid my finger into the belt loop of her jeans and tugged her closer. The churro fell into the box. I closed the top and set it on the hood of the truck behind me.

"I thought you wanted a taste?"

"I do."

Her bright pink coat flapped open in the wind kicking up around us. "Is this a good idea?"

"Nope." I lifted her hand and wrapped my lips around her thumb. Smoky caramel and butter tasted way better off her skin than any churro.

"Isn't this going to get messy?"

"Why I took the box away."

She snaked a hand into my coat. "You know that's not what I mean."

"You can say no, Chaos. I can control myself." I was reasonably sure, anyway.

She nibbled on the corner of her lip and never stopped staring at my mouth. Her nails bit into my belly and no amount of training could make me play the relaxed card. And still, I let her make the choice.

"You don't even like me."

I pulled her closer. "Is that what you think?"

She sucked in a quick breath at the very hard, very active participant behind my zipper. "That's biological. Men can get hard from a stiff breeze."

"Not all men."

Finally, her gaze lifted to mine. She rocked against me and I had to grit my teeth against the need to drag her in and take over. I could change her mind and take away any doubts she had on the attraction end of this, but she was right about one thing. I didn't have to like a woman to kiss her.

That wasn't the case here—and it was the number one reason I should ease her back, and be smart about this.

Evidently, I wasn't.

"An experiment then."

"Experiment. Sure, whatever you want to call it, Chaos."

She wrinkled her nose. "I really hate when you call me that."

"No, you don't."

And then there were no more words. I straightened up and raked my fingers through her damp curls, pushing off the hood so I could get to all of her.

Her chin lifted to meet me and there was only rain and lemons and heat between us. I hovered just a breath away from her mouth. Yeah, one taste wasn't going to be enough. I brushed her nose with mine and licked my lips.

But there was only one first kiss with a woman.

The air steamed between us as I brushed her lips lightly. Sugar and cinnamon clung to the little divot at the bow of her lips. I licked at the soft skin. Her huge hazel eyes were still open, swirling with questions. Ones I damn sure didn't have answers to.

The buzz in my chest roared into my head then went dead silent as I covered her mouth. I gripped the back of her head and tilted her for better access. Lemons and rain blended together and reached into my chest and squeezed tight. She tasted like spring. Cool with a sneaky heat that knocked me flat.

My other arm slid around her back until she was flush against me. Her hands were trapped between us and she pushed at my shirt, her cold fingers tunneling under for warmth or to get to me, I wasn't sure.

She scraped her teeth over my lower lip. "More."

"Definitely."

The kiss went deeper, our tongues tangling and searching. Where I'd been expecting sweet, she gave me heat and aggression. Her nails dug into the skin at the top of my jeans and I groaned into her mouth.

I fisted her hair and she panted against my lips. "Didn't think this was in you, Grumpasaurus."

"Same."

And then I took her under again. I sucked at her tongue, wishing desperately we were on my king-sized bed with nothing between us. Even knowing the danger it would bring on my head, I took more. Demanded more.

She gave it.

The rain started to beat down on us, but instead of it chasing us into the truck, I sipped the rain off her lips, her chin, and finally, her neck. My tongue swirled along the softness, searching out the lemon tang even as I explored another patch of salty, wet skin.

She tipped her head back, giving me all the access I could stand until her heated shudders turned into chattering.

I eased up on the taste, dragging my bristled chin along a trio of freckles.

"No, don't stop."

"You're freezing."

"I'll live."

"We're putting on one helluva show for the trucks, Chaos."

"I don't care." But another shiver ripped through her. Not the good kind.

I bit down on her shoulder. Somehow I'd pushed her coat aside and that soft sweater teased my nose. I nipped at the skin between her shoulder and neck before pulling her coat closed and her hood up. "Get in the Jeep."

She'd reached around my torso and now she smoothed her fingers along the scars that mapped out my back. Normally, I'd flinch away or reroute the touch. But she already knew a little about those stories, and her gentle strokes left me shaken enough that I needed to shut this down.

"I don't want to stop. You'll get in your head, and then we won't do this again."

She was right, but that was a problem for later. For now, I needed to get her inside and warm.

And to rein in the lust I hadn't been prepared for.

Chapter 11

Willow

Winter Soldier Hot

The ride into Brooklyn was silent. Not even the radio broke the quiet.

I stared out the window and couldn't stop touching my lips. They were abraded from his beard and I was probably pink from the...*whoa.*

Kiss didn't cover it.

I'd been kissed plenty. That wasn't kissing. That was more.

Jesus, Wil, be a bit more fanciful.

And that was why he probably wouldn't do it again. How was I supposed to go back to our regularly scheduled programming after *that?*

I glanced over at him. His jaw was still doing that flex-y thing, telling me he was gnashing the hell out of his molars. TMJ, anyone?

I forced myself to relax my own tight jaw. Kissing wasn't supposed to have this kind of effect.

Sure, you could get all fluttery and want to make sure it happened again. Half the time, the second kiss wasn't nearly as exciting. First contact was where the rush was at.

That was probably how this was going to be.

Surely.

There. I could handle that. I mean, not that I wanted to kiss him again. I usually wanted to toss flour at his face, not get a hold of those hard slashes of lips with a ridiculous softness that I wasn't expecting.

Oh, yeah. We're so cool. Except not.

He turned onto a quieter street, and I finally realized we were in my neighborhood. Dusk was fast approaching, and the misty rain made the park across from my apartment seem ominous.

The vintage lights on the path flickered like fireflies on the damp evening. I'd always loved the park. I'd done more than a few videos there on the wrought iron and wood bench, usually ideas for picnics and easy to fix romantic lunch dates.

One of my biggest videos had been for my mustardy potato salad and toasty club sandwiches. It felt like a million years ago.

Knowing that I'd been out there, making my silly little videos and someone might have been watching me...

I pulled my jacket tighter around my body.

"Cold?" Ransom reached for the heater.

I shook my head. "We're just about there."

He dropped his hand to his lap, his fingers drumming lightly. I only noticed because he always seemed so damn still. So relaxed in every situation while I was freaking out.

"You must be ready to drop me off and run for the hills, huh?"

He gave me a side-eyed glance.

"After all that from Poe and Aidan, I mean. I'm just a hot mess of a situation."

He gripped the steering wheel harder.

See? He was totally rethinking his deal with me. He'd gotten out of the bodyguard game, and I was way too much of a problem.

"I can move into one of the lodge rooms. I'm sure Aunt Laverne can find me something until the wedding. Then it'll be all packed, so I'll have to figure out something else, but until then, I can just stay over there. Easy peasy. There will be tons of people around."

His jaw suddenly eased.

There. I was totally making the right call. So much easier to get out of his hair. Poe would do her thing and find out why someone was watching me.

If I was in the orchard, I'd definitely be out of the way.

Maybe he could do a few of those perimeter checks that Rachel told me he used to do when Clay was on the tree farm. He was a careful guy and that would be more than enough.

It wasn't as if this dude—probably a dude, right? —was doing anything overt. I was perfectly safe. So, he'd sent me a few packages. It wasn't a huge deal.

Ransom pulled up in front of my apartment and expertly parallel parked his tank of a truck. I couldn't park mine if I had two spaces available, but whatever.

"Are you done?"

I stuffed my hand in the opposite sleeve of my coat to hold in heat for my frigid fingers. "I'm just making things easier."

He unclipped his belt and the metal tab smacked on the glass as he turned toward me. "Let's get one thing straight. You will never be alone again. I don't care if you're in the middle of fifty people. I'm going to be right next to you for the duration."

I plastered my back to the door as he reached for me.

"I don't know what conversation you just had with yourself in your pretty little head but get used to the fact that I'll be taking care of you until we get this settled."

I narrowed my eyes. *Taking care of me?* "Pretty little head?"

"That's what you focus on?"

The far safer question. I still couldn't get over the *taking care of me* statement. "I'm not some idiot woman."

"You're sure acting like one." His fingers dug into my thigh as he leaned in. "You were there when Poe and Aidan showed us the slide show from hell, right?"

I swallowed, my heart rate kicking into overdrive. "Yes."

"This isn't some rich kid having a power trip."

I stiffened. Jason had been a bit more than that.

"And I'm not negating what you went through when you were younger, but this is someone with a lot more knowhow and some fucking scary tech knowledge."

I flinched.

He slid his hand away and raised it to cup my face. "I don't want to frighten you again, but you have to know this isn't just a regular stalker. This guy is focused—and yeah, I think it's probably a guy. Maybe it was just a job at first."

I frowned at him, but I found myself leaning into his touch. His thumb gently glided along my cheek.

Was that us too?

Just a job, just a responsibility at first, and now it was becoming more? Should it? The tangled strings between us were a lot to navigate. My sister, his best friend, my family—it was worse than Rachel's yarn after her mischievous cat Gary got ahold of it.

"Is that how you think it started?"

"I don't know." His eyes were hard as flint and those lips that had kissed me stupid earlier were thin slashes of anger.

I was sure he hated fessing up to not knowing for certain. I lifted my hand to cover his. "I'm used to doing things alone. After Jason, I told myself I'd never be in a position to be afraid like that again."

"Maybe this guy really is just doing it for a payday. Cryptocurrency is big on the dark web, and I'm sure he's getting paid in some way or another. But sending you gifts makes it different. I just don't know."

A shiver racked my system. I was used to being watched. I literally put my face out there every day and wanted to be seen.

This was different. So very different.

I broke our locked gaze.

"Chaos, look at me."

I closed my eyes, gripping his hand.

"Look at me."

I opened my eyes and could see nothing other than his stormy gray gaze locked on my face. "I'm good at this. I protect what's mine."

His brow furrowed. "You're part of Clay's and Rachel's family. That makes you mine."

"Right." I shuttered the foolish part of my heart that perked up when he said that, and then I pushed his hand away and slipped out the door.

Obviously, this heightened danger thing was making me an idiot.

He swung open his door and came around to me. "Chaos." He grabbed my hand.

"Can we not do this? I get that I'm a responsibility. You don't need to literally shove it down my throat. You know, where your tongue was an hour ago—quite happily, I might add."

He blew out a breath and stared at his feet. "Look—"

"I knew right after you kissed me you were gonna become the 'I gotta be stoic' dude." I dropped my voice to mimic his gruff one. "And shocker, it happened."

"That's not what this is. I can't protect you if I'm—"

"What?" I crowded into him until he looked at me. "You're what? Human. Attracted to someone? We've already established you don't have to like me to want to fuck me, Ransom."

He curled his arm around my back and slammed me into his body. His firm chest, his insanely tight belly, and his rapidly stiffening cock made my breath stall. "If it was just about scratching an itch, we would have gotten that out of our system a long fucking time ago."

I pushed at his chest because I wanted to do the exact opposite. Wrapping myself around him like a freaking octopus was *not* an option.

His gray eyes were far more blue than usual right now. The kind of dangerous glacier blue that meant I should be running into my old apartment ASAP.

Suddenly, his gaze wasn't on me anymore. It shifted to the street and then toward my apartment. His hold gentled, but he kept me close. Almost as if he couldn't let me go.

More fanciful thinking there, Wil.

"What?"

He glanced over his shoulder at the park.

"Ransom." I gripped his shirt. "Hello?"

Finally, he looked down at me and bent to cover my mouth with his. Shock and annoyance slid away under the onslaught of his ridiculously talented mouth. My hand slid up to his shoulder, then to his short, thick hair.

The rasp of his bristly beard buzzed against my chin and lips, leaving tingles everywhere. He slanted his head to open me up for a deeper exploration. One I was there for in every way, damn him. Our tongues tangling and chasing as my other arm came up to circle his neck. I could taste the misty rain on his lips, the bite of mint, and the heat.

Dear God, the heat.

Finally, he pulled back, nipping my lower lip before he looked around again.

I frowned.

My mouth felt raw, and my blood had been replaced with CO_2 bubbles. Everything was jangling inside of me. We weren't going to discuss the rest of my body, which was very ready to take these kisses to a different zip code that included a mattress.

Yet Ransom was scanning the road as if he hadn't just rocked my damn world.

Again.

"What are you looking for?"

"Nothing."

Stubborn man. Was he afraid someone would notice we were... what? Making out? I didn't even know what to call that kiss. It was far too intense for a sidewalk.

"And what exactly was that all about?"

"I wanted to kiss you. It's the only thing that keeps you quiet."

My mouth dropped open. Why that asinine piece of—

Then he grinned at me. The last time I'd seen him actually smile was way back during Christmas.

He pulled one of my hands down to lace with his and instead of lambasting him for what he'd said, I frowned. This guy had me so off-balance, I couldn't catch up.

Since when did we hold hands? Tonsil hockey was one thing, but this was just weird.

The front door to my apartment building burst open and Merry came flying out down the steps. Ransom immediately pushed me behind him.

Merry stopped on the patchy wet grass. "Willow?"

I tried to twist my fingers out of his hold, but he'd somehow replaced his skin with Velcro. "It's just my roommate. Well, old roommate." I peeked around Ransom. "Hey, Merry."

"Don't 'hey, Merry' me. Who is that and why was his tongue in your mouth?"

"Christ," he muttered and led me toward the crumbling cement steps.

I brushed my fingers over my very puffy mouth. "Merry, this is Ransom."

"*The* Ransom?"

He glanced at me, the corner of his mouth kicking up. "*The?*"

"Shut up." I tried to dislodge his hand, but he still wasn't having it. "Ransom, Merry."

He nodded curtly.

I rolled my eyes. "Can I hug my friend?"

He sighed and let my hand go, but he started looking over his shoulder again.

Merry frowned as she pulled me in for a tight hug. "I was so worried. You haven't been replying to my texts."

"I know, I'm sorry. It's been a little crazy."

"I was hoping you'd change your mind and come home." She looped her arm around my waist as we walked up the steps.

"C'mon, Dennelle probably has five applicants to replace me already."

Merry sighed. "Four."

I laughed. I'd only been gone a few days, but it felt like a million lifetimes. "It's okay, Mer. I know it's time to move on."

"With *him?*" she asked out of the side of her mouth. "You didn't mention he was like Winter Soldier-intense-I-could-kill-you-hot."

"He's literally behind us."

Merry looked back and waved. "I mean, you *are* hot. You must know it."

Ransom gave her a bland stare.

I pushed Merry through the door. The familiar squeak of the old hinges and hint of beeswax mixed with pine made me just a bit homesick. So much of my life had been spent here in this oddly cut apart old house. "We're just here to get my stuff."

Merry hugged my arm. Her familiar powder scent made my eyes sting. "I really don't want you to go."

"Hey, look at it this way—you can come out to the orchard after your boards."

Even as I said it, I knew she would probably never come visit. Maybe if I wished for it hard enough, she would come upstate.

"Yeah?"

I leaned into her. "My Aunt Laverne will pamper you and my cousins are pretty hot."

"Hotter than *him?*"

"You're going to swell his head."

"Which one?" she asked without bothering to whisper.

Ransom slid his hand along my hip, his fingers twisting in the beltloop of my jeans. His breath teased my ear. "As much as I enjoy you talking about how hot I am, can we move this along?"

"You're an ass."

"You like my ass."

I glanced back at him. "What is going on with you?" He wasn't wrong, but I didn't say that kind of thing out loud. My inside-my-head voice was loud enough for three people.

Merry looked from me to Ransom and then back again. "Can we

talk?" She gave Ransom a bright smile. "I'm just going to steal her for a minute."

He shoved his hands into his pockets "What do you want me to start moving?"

"Well, you did get three more boxes." Merry pointed to the large boxes in the corner of the living room.

I froze.

Ransom's jaw tightened. "When?"

"Every day since you left. Actually, we got one that night from FedEx."

He stalked to the pile. The boxers were oversized and the bottom one looked similar to the flat pack box that had started all of this drama.

Bending at the waist, he lifted them all at once and muscled his way to the door.

I met him at the door, opening it for him. "Ransom."

"Not here," he said through gritted teeth.

I noticed the familiar logo on the box. "Why?"

"I don't know, but I'll be figuring it out." He pressed a quick, but firm kiss on my shocked mouth.

"I'm so confused, but I'm equally jealous," Merry said from behind me.

I watched him run down the stairs then navigate the crumbling walkway as if it was even blacktop on his way to his truck. He lifted the boxes up and over the side of the truck as if they didn't probably weigh over eighty-damn-pounds.

Yes, it was hot, but I wasn't sure how I felt about him taking over, even if a small part of me was relieved.

And why did he keep kissing me all of a sudden?

I looked out into the misty gray and shivered. I'd taken my slicker off during the drive, not that it would have kept me warm, anyway.

I half expected him to notice I was cold, but he wasn't paying attention to me any longer. He had his phone out, calling someone. Poe? Aidan?

Feeling exposed, I shut the door and faced Merry. "So, that happened."

"Yeah. Why is he kissing you? And why didn't I get a text about this new development?"

"Because that new development happened about three hours ago."

Merry's eyes sparkled. "Ohh, so this is fresh?" She suddenly frowned at me. "Do you need a sweatshirt? I found a box of your clothes as I was cleaning out the crawlspace."

"Yes." I followed her down the hall to my old room. The mattress was stripped, and my sheets were folded neatly on the corner with two boxes beside the small pile.

I'd cleared out my rickety end table when I packed up. No one needed to see what was in there, thanks.

I should probably leave the end table behind, even though it had so many war wounds from the various filming setups I'd put it through when I first started out.

Nope. I just couldn't leave it behind.

I picked it up and set it by the door.

"Why aren't you talking?" Merry pulled one of the flaps open from the largest box. She unearthed my favorite orange sweatshirt with the ratty sleeves and thug life written in yellow retro bubble letters.

She really did know me so well.

Now I felt even worse about believing she'd never visit me. Maybe she would. Or maybe I needed to make more of an effort to keep people in my life.

I took it from her and quickly changed out of my wet sweater. I squeezed Merry's hand briefly before going into the hallway closet to get the tape gun.

What was I supposed to tell her?

Oh, hey, I really left to make sure everyone here is safe. Also, I'm going to live with a guy who probably could kill fifteen men without breaking a sweat. I love you, see you soon?

Dear God.

Returning, I found her perched on the edge of my bed with her arms crossed. Her excitement had been replaced with worry. I set the tape gun on the box and sat beside her.

"I'm safe."

"Starting like that is not relieving my worry."

I laughed softly. "There's a situation. More than some creep finding out our address."

Merry turned to face me and gripped both my hands. "No. Not like..."

She was one of the few people who knew about Jason. Mostly because she'd been the one to deal with my first panic attack when someone recognized me on the street. That had been a treat, but I'd learned to cope over the years.

"Not like Jason. Different. Evidently, a lot of people like to keep tabs on famous people. Not exactly the sort of thing I thought about when I started Wil's Way."

She tucked a lock of pink hair around her ear. "Tabs? I don't understand."

You and me both. I chewed on the corner of my mouth. "I didn't really see myself as famous per se. Internet famous? I mean, is that really a thing?"

"Yes. That's *the* thing these days."

"Yeah, well, it comes with some more advanced creepers." It wasn't exactly the right definition, but I didn't want to scare Merry the way Aidan and Poe had scared me.

No one needed that living inside them.

"That doesn't sound good."

"No. But Ransom used to be a bodyguard."

"Now that doesn't shock me." She looked up and gave him a wiggling finger wave as he marched into the room. I supposed his sort of phone calls didn't take long. "He looks dangerous."

I rolled my eyes. I opened my mouth to ask him something and he shook his head. He was right. We didn't need to discuss *this* in front of Merry.

"That end table, the bed, duffel, and a few boxes. That's it."

He gave me a slight frown, then he lifted the rickety table, arching a brow at me.

"I know. It has sentimental value."

He tucked it under his arm and grabbed the duffel bag on his way out.

"So, he doesn't really speak? Just kisses you stupid?"

"That's a new thing."

"I feel there's a story there. But let's go back to the dangerous creepers."

"Not much else to talk about. He has a friend who's helping us figure it out."

"So, you're an us?"

"For now." And that was the part I needed to remember.

He wasn't forever material. This whole situation screamed temporary—most of all, my temporary bodyguard.

Chapter 12

Ransom

Two Truths and a Lie

I was surprised this was all she had, but her lack of possessions made the stop even quicker.

I resisted the urge to bundle her up and stick her in one of Roth's safehouses in the city. I even knew of one right here in Brooklyn that I could break into—or call Aidan for a code to get in if I wasn't feeling adventurous.

Unfortunately, that wouldn't help anyone. Rachel would lose her damn mind and then Clay would kill me.

So, that was out.

I'd already planned on checking in with Roth before we left Brooklyn, but the minute we pulled up to her apartment, I'd realized we were in the exact spot that matched the feed Poe had found in her search.

Was it bright to kiss her on camera?

Nope.

Would it move this along? That was a good question.

I'd always been impatient when it came to recon. Why I hadn't lasted long in the bodyguard game. That and I didn't like people.

Too bad that didn't seem to apply to Chaos. The urge to get her in my arms was getting harder to deny. But I'd told myself giving in to my impulses had a two-pronged benefit in this case—keeping her close and also possibly pissing off this idiot.

Add in the fact that she would be under my roof for the foreseeable future, and I might be able to use this...whatever it was between us to my advantage.

I rubbed my chest at the idea of using her, but the end result would be as good for her as it would be for me.

Maybe the guy watching her would get bored when she wasn't as available. It would be easier to keep tabs on her at my house and at the orchard and handing the wedding details would provide a distraction for her from her usual videos.

Would that cause him to escalate? Or lose interest? Or he could be patient enough to just wait us out/ I didn't have enough details on the man behind the keyboards and drones.

Instinct told me this was a guy.

The power trips felt more like what a man would do, including the control aspect to the videos and gifts. His moves were designed to put her on edge.

I could almost guarantee the shithead was watching to see her reaction to his little game. But what he'd do when he got me as a buffer was still a wildcard.

Right now, I just needed to get her back to Turnbull. Oh, and convince her that us getting together would be a good thing.

Doing a one-eighty in my reactions to her was pretty suspicious and she wasn't stupid. But maybe it would put the focus on me instead of her.

I gripped the edge of her mattress. We'd wrapped it in a tarp, but it was small enough to fit under my truck bed cover. The rain had let up long enough to get us packed and let the girls do the hug it out thing with a bonus batch of tears.

I didn't know if I was itchy because I knew we were on camera— yes, I'd gotten a confirmation text from Poe—or due to all the emotions flowing between the two women.

Probably both.

Merry grabbed Chaos in another hug. The two of them swayed back and forth as if they'd never see one another again. "I'll be there for the wedding."

"Oh, you will?" Chaos shrieked and the hugging intensified into another round of giggles and tears.

I jammed my fists into my pockets, wishing I was anywhere but here.

"C'mon, Chaos, it's going to be a long drive home."

"Right." She brushed away tears with the cuffs of her obnoxiously bright sweatshirt. "I'll see you in a few weeks then."

Merry nodded before she pinned me with a surprisingly scary look. "You make sure my girl is safe."

I wasn't sure what Chaos had told her, but I saved myself a conversation by nodding. "You don't have to worry."

"I know. I can tell."

I looked down at my scarred boots. She didn't know me, nor did she know how many times I'd fucked up over the years, but I'd make sure Clay's future sister-in-law would be safe. I had very little family left that I cared about. I wouldn't let him or Rachel down.

Chaos finally got into the truck, and we started the arduous journey north. Full dark was upon us, and the rain had come back with a vengeance by the time we got out of Brooklyn. I really wished we'd taken Clay's plane.

"Thanks for today."

I glanced at her. She was curled up with her hands tucked in the sleeves of her sweatshirt. It seemed as if she was always cold. I reached for the heater, and she waved me off. "Sure?"

She nodded. "I already have a headache brewing. The heater will make it worse."

I reached behind my seat and snagged one of the bottles of water tucked in the pocket. "There's Advil in the glovebox."

"Really?" She let out a half laugh. "You think of everything." She leaned forward and found the travel bottle of meds, then she took the water from me.

"It's my job to be prepared."

"And you're good at your job, I know." She took a few deep swallows, closing her eyes wearily.

"Why don't you push the seat back and get some Zs? The rain is going to make it a long drive."

"The passenger is supposed to make conversation and man the radio."

"I'm not listening to any more Harry Styles."

"C'mon. You know you secretly love 'Watermelon Sugar'."

I certainly did not. I also wouldn't admit the weird "She" had been a pretty good song. If I did, she would put it on repeat.

Chaos fit her for music as well. Songs on repeat, then fast forwarding through dozens to find something, then hopping genres for another before the song ended. She was exhausting.

"I'll just do some edits. You can listen to what you want."

Luckily, all the emotions of the day seemed to have been too much for her busy brain. She pulled out her iPad, but she nodded off before doing much of anything.

The rhythmic sound of the wipers and rain eased my mind as well. I left my favorite Hozier album on repeat and battled my way over the bridge. Chaos slept on, leaving me to plan for how we'd deal with Clay and Rachel.

Wedding details would keep the three of them busy. And since I needed to keep my eye on Chaos, I'd be in the thick of it as well. But that would give Poe time to analyze the data she was combing through. Maybe she'd even find a few more digital footprints. If anyone could, it would be Aidan's people.

I had to trust in the process and that wasn't my strength. I also didn't like that the digital angles were outside my wheelhouse.

By the time we were on the Thruway, my bladder was begging for a stop. I'd managed to hold out until we were about an hour outside of Turnbull. I really needed to check in with Clay too. I pulled off at one of the toll rest stops and parked.

I texted Clay to let him know we'd run late and I'd just take Willow back to my place.

She was pretty knocked out, but I wasn't comfortable with leaving her alone. And I needed a burger or something for some fuel. I pushed a wild curl out of her face. The rain had turned her fussy straight hair back to curls.

She turned toward me, her eyes fluttering in that hazy world between sleep and waking. The soft smile that followed kicked me in the chest. "Are we home?"

The idea of her calling my place *home* was far too enticing. I wanted to lash out. My usual replies to make sure she didn't get too close burned like lemon juice on the tip of my tongue. Instincts I'd honed over the last ten years urged me to retreat, but I leaned down and accepted her softness instead.

She hummed into my mouth and a lazy sigh drifted between us. Instead of breaking things apart, she lifted to meet my mouth again, her nails scoring my scalp as what should have been a quick kiss turned into hot flashes of tongue and panting breaths. My earlier hunger for food faded and was replaced with the urge to take her under.

To taste whatever she'd allow.

To turn her whimpers into moans.

To let someone in.

The last thought was enough to have me break the kiss. Her eyes shone in the dim light of the parking lot.

"Well then. Who cares if we're home with a kiss like that?" Her nails gentled along the nape of my neck, then she toyed with the chain I wore under my shirt. "What exactly are we doing, Ransom?"

"I don't know." Seemed like a safe answer. I sure as fuck had no clue, so that part wasn't a lie.

Her lashes hid her gaze as she stared at my mouth. She touched my lower lip with her other hand. Her short nail brushed my teeth as

I opened and nipped at the pad of her forefinger. "I'm pretty sure I'm not in your league."

I laughed. "Think that's the other way around."

A slow grin with a quick flash of her tongue behind her teeth made me go instantly hard. "A very inadequate one-night stand with a lawyer is about all I've got to show for my romantic entanglements in the last year."

My fingers dug into the beltloops of her jeans. The idea of her with anyone else, inadequate or not, made me insane. My knuckles brushed the soft skin of her stomach. I tunneled under the warm sweatshirt to the quivering concave of her belly. The need to stamp out the idea of someone else made me bolder than I should have been in my truck.

She hissed as my fingers cupped lace and cotton. I sucked her finger deeper into my mouth as an apology for my cool fingers. I watched her pupils flare as I pinched her rigid nipple between two knuckles then lightly soothed and returned for another languid tug.

Her sly grin dissolved and she drew in a shaky breath.

"There's no before, just now."

She swallowed hard, then she tipped her head back as I slid under the bra from the top, flicking the tight tip again and again until she was lifting her hips in time to some internal rhythm. One I wanted to learn and master.

There were too many people around for me to really do what I wanted. To dive under the ancient cotton and get my mouth on her. To peel all of the layers away until I could wrap those long legs around my neck and make her scream.

But for now, I could give her a little something to take the edge off. She was primed and sleep had left her walls down enough for me to sneak behind her defenses. I slipped my hand between her thighs, the friction from the denim making her jerk.

She gripped my shirt. "Ransom."

Fuck, the sound of my name on her lips would chase me into dreams tonight, no matter what came next. I knew it and still tugged at one nipple then the other, pushing her bra up to her neck so I could get to each of them. All the while, she writhed against my hand.

The spacious Jeep suddenly seemed too small, the windows fogging from her panting breaths.

I didn't stop. I rubbed harder at the seam of her jeans, imagining how slick she was under there. I could get into her pants. Her zipper wasn't much of a barrier, but once I got her silky heat on my fingers, I'd want more.

I wouldn't be happy until she was in the backseat with her ankles in the air.

Until my mouth was on her, drinking from her until my name bounced off the roof.

My aching cock wanted inside of her, wanted the release I didn't ever think would be possible. But that wasn't happening now. Not in this dingy parking lot in my goddamn truck with my console trying to rip a hole into my ribcage.

Her hips lifted, erratic now that my attention had scattered. Her soft moans were all the direction I could handle right now. I buried my face in her neck, finding that spot I'd discovered this afternoon in the rain.

Her pulse thrummed against my mouth as I sucked harder then eased her with a swirl of my tongue. Lemons filled my senses, salt burned my tongue, and her cashmere-soft skin filled my palm.

I dug a knuckle deeper along the seam of her jeans and she arched her back.

I covered her mouth just as she screamed. I swallowed her moans, held her down in the seat as she shook under me. As she clamped her legs over my hand and I swore I could feel her heat through the denim.

The kiss went from nuclear to soft as water. Her moans melted to sighs as she relaxed. I stroked her breast gently before shifting the twisted lace back into place. She opened sated eyes and released my hand.

Words couldn't cover what that was. And for once, I was almost sure she thought so too. She pulled my hand from under her sweatshirt and up to her cheek. She kissed my palm then my mouth.

There was not a damn thing left to say. Far more shaken than I wanted to admit, I leaned back onto my side of the truck and opened the door. I stood in the cool rain, letting it lash over my face. It was probably steaming off my goddamn skin.

She came around the front of the truck and stood in front of me in the rain. I looked down at her, blinking against the fat drops.

"I don't think it's fair my best orgasm of the last decade was in a truck."

I couldn't stop the laugh. "Decade, huh?"

She hit me in the stomach. "Teen hormones can't be beat."

She bounced back unlike anyone I knew. Far better than I did.

"We'll see about that. That was over clothes. Just wait until I get you naked, Chaos."

"Smug bastard."

I curled my arm around her shoulders and dragged her close. "I think there's a cheap cheeseburger with your name on it inside."

"Oh my God, yes."

"Don't sound too excited."

"I'm starving."

"You ate a dozen tacos."

"That was hours ago." She wrapped her arm around my waist and we drunkenly hopped around puddles. It felt good to laugh.

To pretend for a little while that this was real.

Chapter 13

Willow

Queen of Bad Ideas

The pop of gravel under the tires of his truck dragged me out of a light doze. A belly full of deliciously crappy burgers had put me right out again. Damn rain always made me sleepy too.

And maybe some denial about the fact that my best orgasm in recent memory came from some over the clothes action in a truck as if I was a damn teenager.

Knowing Ransom was intense wasn't the same as being in the same space as he was for an extended time. Clearly, that intensity also included sexual sports because *holy crap.*

I was definitely the novice there. I wasn't sure how he knew every place to touch on the first—okay, second try. One kiss in the rain shouldn't have given him that many details about what I liked.

Or maybe he was just that experienced in hooking up.

Nope, I wasn't going to think about that. Besides, I didn't know what the hell was going on between us, anyway. He'd gone from 'this isn't a good idea' to 'maybe we should get naked' within a span of hours.

Unfortunately, my starving libido had been waylaid—quickly.

149

But I wouldn't be so easily distracted now that I was a bit more satisfied. At least I was pretty sure.

I opened my eyes and frowned. "This isn't Clay's house."

"We went over this. You're staying with me."

"Yeah, but I have to figure out how to tell my sister that."

"We already told her you were taking over the attic loft, remember?" He parked under his half-finished car port and got out.

I hurried to get out, but I got tangled in my belt. Swearing, I pushed open my door. The rain had stopped, but the air was still frigid. "I don't have any of my stuff."

"You have a box of clothes in the back."

"Yeah, stuff for winter."

He went around the back and flipped up the truck bed cover to grab my box of clothes.

"But what about my mattress? We haven't even fixed up the room yet. It's like one in the morning."

"I know." He kept walking toward his house.

"Dammit." I ran after him, sliding a bit on his patchy grass that was mostly mud, thanks to a thorough April soaking.

On the porch, Midnight leaned against Ransom's thigh as he gave not-his-dog a good scrub before dumping food in his bowl. The man moved as fast as a ninja and just as quietly.

Midnight saw me and let out a happy bark, his gaze going from his food to me with his tail wagging manically. I jogged up the stairs with a laugh and gave him a quick scratch. His dark eyes were adoring in the dim light of the porch light.

"Eat," Ransom said curtly.

Midnight happily stuffed his face in the bowl and hoovered his food.

"I can stay on the couch."

Ransom gave me a bland stare before muscling the large box of my clothes through the narrow doorway.

I huffed out a breath. "We haven't really discussed what —Ransom!"

He dropped the box and hiked me over his shoulder. "Chaos, I'm tired. I've been driving for close to ten hours today. I don't want to put your bed together."

I tried to wiggle my way down. "This is your solution? I'm not a sack of feed you can carry around."

He clamped his hand on my ass. "Stop wiggling."

Midnight whined on the porch.

Ransom turned around at the sound.

"Well, let him in."

"He never wants to come in."

A whine turned to a keening yip, then a sharp bark.

"He obviously wants to come in."

"No, he doesn't."

"Open the door, dummy. And put me down."

He only complied with half of my request and cracked open the door. Midnight shoved his big head through the opening, shouldering his way through.

Ransom gave a long sigh and closed the door after him, locking it and typing something on a keypad I hadn't noticed last time I was here.

"Stair lights ten percent," he said as he stalked through the dark kitchen to the stone stairs and followed the slight curve of the staircase. The wrought iron sconces threw a soft glow against the earthy stone that made up the walls and stairs.

I scratched the smooth stones, trying to slow his trajectory, but he was a man on a mission. Apparently, it included his bed.

With me.

Midnight happily bounded up the stairs next to him. There was a bit of curiosity in the tilt of his head, but he seemed happier to be with us as a unit.

Me and Ransom as a unit. I mean, what?

I was so very confused.

At the top of the stairs, he went down a narrow hallway. It was dark, but I could tell there were framed things on the walls—and not in a straight line from some decorator. No, the wall hangings were in varying sizes and covered the walls in a far more creative way than I expected from someone so rigid.

Before I could ask for him to turn on the lights so I could see more of his space, he went through a doorway. "Lights twenty percent."

"Is this *Star Trek?* What's going on? You don't even have to ask Alexa?"

"Amazon isn't everything."

"Since when?" Then my brain went offline.

His bedroom was stunning. Sage green walls and a vaulted ceiling that definitely hadn't come standard in a house as old as his were the first things I noticed, followed by a massive stone hearth that dominated the room.

He swung around and I gripped his arm. "Would you put me down? You're making me dizzy."

Okay, wow. The equally impressive king-sized bed now took center stage in my spinning brain. The frame was in a gorgeous ash wood—which I only knew because I secretly coveted a bookcase made from the same wood, thanks to late night Pinterest scrolling. The headboard and the footboard had a simple half-moon shape with no-nonsense lines.

No intricate scrollwork for Ransom's bedroom.

The effect was far warmer than I was expecting after the spartan decorating downstairs. But he didn't disappoint with his choice of bedding. The corners were crisply tucked in, and two pillows lay unadorned at the top of the bed. The muslin blanket was a surprise, but the other colors were practical browns and neutrals.

He set me down next to the bed. Midnight trotted in behind us and hopped right on the bottom of the bed.

"No way." Ransom snapped his fingers. "This is not your bed."

Midnight just put his huge head on his man-sized paws and closed his eyes.

"Unbelievable."

I would have laughed if I wasn't supposed to be so outraged.

Except I wasn't. And I really didn't know what to do with that fact. "What are we doing?"

He invaded my space. "We're going to sleep. And then we're going to figure out what to tell Clay and Rachel. Then we're going to do all the wedding crap."

"I meant about sleeping arrangements, but thanks for the other details." I tipped my head back to look him in the eye. "You want me sleeping here?"

"Yep."

"Have you ever slept with a woman?"

When he frowned at me, the sharp furrows between his brows made me want to smooth them away. Gah, what the heck was wrong with me?

"I'm not a monk."

I rolled my eyes. "You know what I mean. We haven't even done the all the way naked thing—"

"Yet."

I huffed out a breath. "There's a difference between getting our groove on and actually sleeping with someone. Especially when you barely know them."

"It's a big bed." He glanced at the dog taking up the bottom third. "Mostly."

I couldn't resist giving Midnight's ears a quick rub. The dog gave a low moan and leaned into me for a heavier touch.

"Lucky dog."

I glanced back at Ransom. "You like your ears rubbed, tough guy?"

"I like something rubbed, anyway."

I rested the top of my head against his chest with a laugh, my hands resting on his belly.

He rubbed my arms. "Why don't you go take a shower? Everything seems better after you're clean. Then we'll see if we dirty you back up."

I didn't know how to deal with that idea, so I escaped to the en suite bathroom. My breath stalled at the shower with the stone walls much like the rest of the house. That was the only thing primitive about it. Pristine glass encased a huge portion of the room with multiple shower heads hiding in the crevices as well as a bench to sit in the steam.

The rest of the space was painted in a soothing caramel tone. Towels and washcloths were rolled up and tucked in a wooden alcove built into the wall across from the shower. The top shelf held some back-up soaps, both shower and hand. I turned to the sink and mirror and gasped. No wonder he'd sent me in for a shower. My face was a smatter of freckles over pale skin and my hair was...well, I wasn't going there.

I was a bedraggled mess.

After stripping out of my damp clothes, I folded them neatly onto the reclaimed wood vanity. The piece had been hollowed out, so the bottom was just a trio of wood baskets made in the same ash as the bedroom. Something about the style itched at my brain, but I was just too tired to figure it out.

I peeked into one of the baskets and found a few female products. Maybe he did have women over more often than I realized. I imagined his soap was of the Ivory variety, so I snagged the pricey French stuff at the back of the bin.

I probably should have felt guilty, but the moment I got into the shower, I didn't care. The heat and water pressure were magnificent. The rain hood and the lower back sprayer were officially the new loves of my life.

"Don't steal all the hot water," he yelled through the door.

With a sigh, I finished washing my hair. Surprisingly, Ransom appreciated good hair products. Or the same female who had the fancy body washes had left those provisions, as well.

Not that it mattered to me.

Okay, it mattered, but everyone had a past. It was stupid to over-think it. It was heading for two in the morning and nothing good came of late night spirals.

I wrapped the largest of the towels around myself, then I put up my hair turban-style and opened the door. I should have slipped my damp clothes back on, but hopefully, I could steal something from Ransom.

Steam bellowed out after me. I was prepared to freeze my butt off, but the fire was crackling and Ransom was laying on the end of the bed beside the dog, his feet still on the floor.

His hands were folded on his belly and his breathing was even.

Had he really passed out? He'd just yelled at me ten minutes ago. Okay, maybe it had been more than ten. That shower was a bit of heaven on Earth.

Midnight's tail thumped once. I went around to the other side of the bed to give his nose a few kisses. His tail thumped harder, and Ransom startled awake, sitting up.

He stretched his arms over his head, leaving my tongue as dry as stale oat flakes. I gave Midnight one last kiss and padded over to the fireplace.

Ransom stood and kept his back to me.

I appreciated the gentlemanly gesture, but a tiny part of me wished he would just take the reins again. Like in the truck where he'd dissolved every nerve and replaced it with heat and blissfully fuzzy lust.

It wouldn't take much to convince me to lose the rest of the night between those crisp cotton sheets. To forget the fears and changes coming at me like a lake effect storm.

"I'll be right back. I left one of my shirts and found a pair of my sister's yoga pants from her last visit."

"Sister?"

His hands fisted at his sides. "Yeah. Maple."

I smiled at the name. Very incongruous when compared to his own. "Ransom—"

"You're killing me here."

"I'm covered."

"You're in a damn towel in my bedroom." His voice was little more than a growl.

"Didn't seem to be a bad idea in the truck."

"This time, I won't stop."

Even with the fire at my back, I still shivered. "You're the one who brought me to your room."

He looked over his shoulder. "I want you more than I've wanted anyone in a fucking long time. But today has been a lot to digest. Doing what I want to you—*with* you—is not a good idea."

"Because you said so?"

"Yeah." Then he disappeared into the bathroom.

Maybe the couch was a better idea. I was sure he probably had a bunch of blankets in the closet. I tucked the towel around my chest a little tighter and went to the door. There was a large safe inside with a fist-sized turning lock as well as something smaller that looked big enough for...a fingerprint?

I shivered. It seemed a bit big for just money and valuables. More like it was sized for weapons.

I shut the door. The reality of who he was and just what I was involved in had me gripping the doorknob like a lifeline. "What are you doing, Wil?" I asked myself softly.

Midnight hopped off the bed, padded over to me, and bumped his nose against my leg.

I dropped my hand on his big head. "I'm okay. I think."

He whined and leaned on me.

"I'm okay, for real." I went to the chair beside the fire and stepped into the soft black pants. He'd left an old gray sweatshirt with it. The bold font simply said *Army* across the front. *His* sweatshirt. I touched the frayed collar. I imagined it had rubbed against his stubbly throat for years.

"You are officially in trouble." I pulled on the sweatshirt and hustled to the bed. Midnight jumped up and did the dog twirl until he found the perfect spot then curled into an extra-large shrimp.

This would be fine. There was plenty of room between his side and mine. But was this normally his side? I glanced at the bedside table and found a book, a much thumbed through copy of *Into the Wild*.

Leaving everything behind to get lost in the wilderness—how very Ransom.

I set down the book and went to the other side of the bed. I shouldn't be surprised since he'd probably want to be closer to the door. Mr. Protector until the end.

I peeled back the tightly made bed enough to shimmy under the covers. It smelled of fresh laundry and...something else. Ransom didn't seem to wear any cologne, but mint always seemed to be in the air around him.

As a taller than average woman, I had to admit the leg room was lovely. Even with a dog who could have starred in *Game of Thrones* taking up a chunk of the bed. I tucked my feet under his big body and stared at the crackling fire.

No gas fireplace for Ransom's bedroom.

The snaps and pops of the wood and the warmth seeped into me. Usually, I had a hard time sleeping anywhere but in my own bed, but a day of too many surprises apparently was like a sleeping pill for my exhausted brain.

I wasn't sure how long I nodded off, but I woke to darkness, save for the flickering firelight. I rolled over to find Ransom beside me, his arm draped over his face.

There was a good three feet of space between us, but it seemed like miles and no space at the same time.

"Ransom?"

"Go to sleep, Chaos." His voice was rusty with weariness, not from being awakened.

"I just wanted to say thanks. I know I'm asking a lot of you."

He dropped his arm, and the firelight accentuated his strong browline and slightly bent nose. Even in the shadows, I could see the furrow between his brows. As usual, I wanted to smooth it away. His gaze remained firmly on the ceiling while his arms were outside the blankets, his fingers laced on his belly again. So much muscle and skin.

He wore a tank, and I was hoping some pants, but I was too chicken to look. I didn't want to think about all that hard muscle and his more than impressive...goods.

If you can't say cock, you don't get to play with one, Wil.

It was a really nice one. At least it had seemed like it from all our close contact today.

Don't think about his cock.

My nipples tightened under his sweatshirt. It wasn't as if he could see them, but I tugged the bedding higher to cover me.

"Did you hear me?"

"I did."

"How about saying 'you're welcome, Willow'?"

"You're welcome, Chaos," he said quietly, then he rolled over, showing me his wide shoulders. I had the strongest urge to snuggle against his back. I knew he'd be warm and solid.

He was reminding me of all the things I hadn't believed I wanted. My life had been my career for so long. I just assumed someday in the future I'd make room for someone.

The fact that the hazy someday man now wore his face was probably a very bad idea.

Then again, I was the queen of them. Maybe he'd just be one more in a long list.

Or maybe he'd be something else entirely.

Chapter 14

Ransom

Pretty Woman, Give Your Smile To Me

I gave up sleeping around dawn.

There had been no cuddling in the night like a damn romance movie. In fact, I'd ended up checking on her a few times since she didn't move at all. If anyone had bet me she wasn't just as chaotic in sleep, I'd have lost a million dollars.

And here we were in my massive bed, and we hadn't even mussed up the sheets once.

Pathetic.

I shut my eyes for a few more minutes, hoping I'd doze off. Restless energy hummed under my skin. When I started distinguishing between the types of birds chirping outside, it was definitely a sign to give up.

I got ready quickly and left her to sleep.

Midnight gave me some side-eye. Instead of following me, he spread out next to Chaos and draped his big head over her legs.

I couldn't blame him, since her legs were one of my favorite parts of her too. Before I crawled back into that bed and woke her up to burn off whatever was jangling through my system, I stalked out of the room.

I was too wired for food, but an extra large thermos of coffee was in order. As I was locking the front door, I doubled back to leave a note about my whereabouts in case she got freaked out.

It was weird to worry about someone else, but there were going to be some growing pains in this new arrangement.

I checked my emails and found a few new tidbits from Poe, as well as a tracking number for some new surveillance equipment Aidan had sent for my network. He'd included a few small cameras that rivaled Clay's technology. I had a feeling some of them were a benefit of his military connections. They were encrypted and hard to to hack, according to Poe.

I could set them up at my house and a few at the orchard for an added layer of protection. I didn't think this guy was into anything other than watching Willow right now, but I preferred to be over-prepared when I didn't know my enemy.

By the time I finished my perimeter walk, the sun was bleeding through the trees and taking the edge off the morning chill. I unloaded my truck and put her boxes and her mattress in the garage. We'd figure out that whole mess later.

I should set her up in the attic. A smart man would remove the temptation from the equation. But I'd made my bed and now I had to lie in it, even if it included a redhead who made me insane.

Putting one problem aside for now, I concentrated on my new collection for RID since production took months of prep work.

My family focused mostly on manufacturing and real estate. When I'd gotten out of the Army, I hadn't been interested in jumping into the family business, which had suited my mother. She wasn't ready to groom a successor just yet. According to Jean Douglas, she was in the prime of her life. My father certainly believed he was. Too bad his idea of prime included younger and younger mistresses.

After my sister Marigold had disappeared, my mother had become even more driven. My younger sister Maple had escaped into the modeling world as soon as she turned eighteen, effectively scattering all the Douglas children across the world.

At this point, I pretty much only worked when I was drawn to. RID turned enough profit to keep my mother happy and leave me alone. I'd invested well and my work with Clay had netted me more money than I'd be able to spend in three lifetimes. My father was enough of a drain on the family fortune. Besides, I preferred to make my own way.

I wasn't sure how long I'd been at the lathe when the chime of my phone finally dented all the noise. I'd been working on spindles for a prototype sideboard. Dining room pieces weren't generally my focus, but I'd been itching to add on to the small nook in my kitchen. I didn't have a lot of storage in the old house, requiring built-ins or structural changes. Unique pieces always won in my book.

When my phone started blaring a second time, I picked it up and saw Clay's name. "Yeah."

"Open the damn door. I've been out here forever."

"Then why didn't you just walk in?" I clicked off the phone and shoved it in my pocket, then I opened the garage door. "What are you doing here?"

"Rachel is losing her damn mind."

"So, Chaos is in the house. Go talk to her." I went back to my bench and checked the spindle. It was crooked as fuck. I tossed it in the kindling pile for upstairs and pulled out another piece of wood to start again.

"Why didn't you guys come over this morning?"

"It's still morning."

"Barely. It's after ten."

"Really? Shit." I stood up again and cut the power to my tools. "I was supposed to check in with..." Jesus, I really was sleep deprived.

"With who?"

"Chaos. I told her I'd put her bed together for the attic."

Clay raised his eyebrow as he folded his arms. "So, where did she sleep last night?"

"None of your business, Dad." I went to the little shop vac I used to get the shavings off me before tracking sawdust in the house.

"Is there something going on between you two?"

I hit my jeans a extra few times before I answered him. We were heading into a sticky area with family and I hadn't checked with Chaos about how much we wanted to share. I was officially a cluster-fuck of idiocy.

I turned off the machine. "We're just working on your wedding gift. Not a big deal."

"Why don't I believe you?"

"Not my problem."

"She wouldn't put up with your shit anyway." He shoved his hands into his pockets. "Can you bring her over to the house? And for the love of God, get your fitting done before Rachel takes another strip out of my hide."

I hung my head. "Yeah. I'll do it today."

"Promise?"

I rolled my eyes. "Now you sound like Rachel."

"Happy wife, happy life. You'll see."

Unlikely. "Are you coming in?"

"Nah. I have a meeting in less than an hour."

"Why didn't you just go check with her?"

"Because you've got this place outfitted like the White House, man. And you changed the locks again, so I don't have a key."

My fail column was getting lots of checkmarks. "Sorry. I forgot. I'll get one made."

I'd put in a new door last month. Part of the house overhaul had included upgrading locks and security. Now I was glad I had gone through the trouble since I had a precious houseguest.

"It's fine. The wedding has gotten us all a little fried."

"You mean you guys."

Clay transferred his hands to his pockets, rocking back on his heels. "I just want to make sure it's perfect for her."

"It will be. Rachel will make sure of it."

He laughed. "That's the truth. All right, I'm gonna head out."

I leaned against my work bench. "You could have just called. Checking on us?"

"If I am?"

I crossed my arms. "She's a big girl."

Clay stared at me for a beat. "It feels like there's more to this."

I was tempted to share about what Chaos was into, but then his worried frown made me hold my tongue. There was nothing they could do yet except worry.

"There are some growing pains with her career. Not to mention learning that she was a burden to her roommates threw her a bit. She's just licking her wounds. Turnbull's the perfect place for her."

Clay narrowed his eyes. "That's rather intuitive for a guy who hates to get involved with people. And who says it needs to be your house that she stays at? Laverne would put her up in a heartbeat."

"She stays here—for now."

He whistled softly. "Careful, buddy. The Doyle women know how to get under a man's skin."

If that wasn't the truth.

"I'll take that under advisement." I straightened and followed him to the door, pulling down the heavy door behind us. The April air had a bite to it, but the sun was high and bright, cutting some of the cold. Maybe spring had actually come to stay.

"She might be what you need, man."

"You were warning me off her yesterday."

He slapped my arm. "I've had time to think on it."

"You need new hobbies."

He barked out a quick laugh. "Maybe. Better than dealing with seating charts, that's for sure. I'll see you in a few hours." His long-legged gate slowed as he got to my driveway. "Don't forget the fit—"

"I got it," I called after him.

He waved before he got into his SUV and backed out.

Midnight met me on the stairs, lifting his head in the eternal hope for another scoop of food. The dog was always hungry. Maybe I'd pick him up a big bone from the butcher while we were out. Now that I had a houseguest, I'd need some provisions.

Especially when said houseguest was always cooking or baking something.

I unlocked the door, but Midnight decided his sunny patch on the porch was preferable to coming indoors this time.

When music punched me in the face, I almost agreed with him. Apparently, she'd figured out how to hook herself up to my speakers.

Then I spotted Chaos dancing around my kitchen. She must have raided her box of clothes because my sister sure as hell never wore anything like that. At least not off the runway.

Christ, her legs went on for fucking forever. She was wearing some sort of black skintight material that climbed up to criss-cross along her lower belly. Then some lacy half tank cupped her perfect mouthful-sized breasts.

The sun filled my kitchen, streaming across the floor as she twirled around. She wore an oversized sweater in a dark yellow that made her skin glow. It fanned out as she spun, making her look like a crazy mix of hot and bohemian.

I realized the song was Hozier, but instead of the usual watery tones I was used to, it belonged in a club. And she knew every word.

She danced with more heart than style, but it was all Willow. Chaotic and sexy as sin.

The song changed and her eyes opened. She blew away a stray hair that had come out of her braids. "Oh, hey. There you are." She grinned at me. "Hope you don't mind. I figured out how to get into your iPad."

"Music level three," I said. When the volume lowered, I folded my arms. "And how did you manage that?"

"I saw you punch in your numbers on your phone. Figured it was the same."

"Evidently, I need to change that."

"I didn't snoop." Her eyes sparkled. "Much."

I shook my head, then I tore my gaze away from her enough to see what she'd been up to. "What happened to my kitchen?"

"Oh." She toyed with the end of one braid. "I tried this bougie French toast recipe I found on TikTok. Simplified it." She ran over to the pile of bread that had lost the war with eggs and milk then she shifted to a smaller plate that was more camera-ready. "It's really good. I can make you some."

"No, thanks."

"Don't knock it." She gathered the empty egg carton that probably would have been my breakfast and split things into my various trash receptacles. The fact she remembered I recycled and composted should not have impressed me.

She popped a strawberry in her mouth as she put the tops on my stash of powdered sugar and cinnamon. "So, what's in the workshop?"

"Our cover for secrets."

She grinned at me. "Is that right?"

"I've been working on a desk for the office remodel Clay is setting up for Rachel at the house. He's got a crew coming in while they're on their honeymoon."

"Like literally working on it?"

I snagged a strawberry and a couple blueberries from the pile of berries in disarray. "Yeah, I dabble."

"Dabble?"

"I was under the impression your vocabulary was better than this, Chaos."

"Well, if you spoke in complete sentences, I wouldn't sound like an idiot."

I leaned on the counter. "Sleep isn't always my friend. A buddy in the Army taught me some stuff when I bunked with him between missions." A flash of memory hit me like a slap—Jones's wide grin when we finished the armoire for his mama.

The even bigger smile when the two of us installed it in her old farmhouse kitchen. Tears and lemonade had been the reward for all the hard work. It had felt better than any stack of bills in my life.

Until those tears had turned to sobs at his funeral.

"Where did you go?"

I blinked out of the memory to find Willow in front of me, her hands on my middle. "Nowhere. I'm right here."

"Liar."

Because it was easier to kiss her than to explain that level of shit in my past, I lowered my mouth to hers. She tasted of strawberries and sugar with just a hint of maple syrup. I slid my arm around her back, splaying my fingers along her spine under the sweater. Her skin was soft and warm from dancing.

She smoothed her hands up my chest to my shoulders as she went on her toes for more. The kiss careened through hot and heavy and back to a dreamier, relaxed pace. "You know, I am onto you with the kiss thing."

I tangled my fingers in the weird straps of her pants, pulling her closer. "Is that right?"

"Whenever you don't want to answer me, you distract me."

"Does it work?"

She shrugged. "Maybe." Her hazel eyes shone gold in the sunlight. "For now. But it doesn't make you less of a rugged, tough guy to share some of your past."

My hands slid lower to cup her ass with an extra squeeze. "Who says it was my past?"

"Those sad gray eyes."

I drew her arms down from around my neck, brushing a quick kiss on her sugar-dusted knuckles. "We all have things we don't want to talk about. You proved that to me."

She looked away. "Jason is different."

"Not so different. We all carry our demons." I stepped away from her. "We have a few things to do today. Why don't you finish cleaning up? You get to come with me to my tux fitting."

"Lucky me."

"Do you need to change?"

She looked down at herself, her eyes full of laughter. "What, too much?"

I resisted the urge to touch her exposed expanse of belly. And more importantly, to find out if those straps came undone easily. "Only if you want everyone distracted today."

Her laugh filled the kitchen. *"You?* That's new."

I wasn't a big fan of the realization, but I damn well wasn't walking into that conversation. "I'm going to go shower off the sawdust."

"Okey doke. I'll see what I can find in the box of crazy."

I stopped at the bottom of the stairs. "So, that outfit was in the giveaway pile or what?"

"The out of my comfort zone pile. Now that I know it makes you all growly, I'll try a few more on."

I groaned. "Good thing we're going to get your stuff from Clay's."

"Yeah, good thing." But she was smiling way too widely.

Yep, I was officially in trouble.

I took a quick shower and changed into jeans and a Henley. Spring might have arrived, but the heat part was still on hiatus.

I found her waiting for me downstairs. The kitchen was sparkling, and the music had changed over to a moody Halsey track. She'd swapped the dick-killer pants for jeans and a Ramones shirt layered over a button-down white shirt with a pair of well loved Vans.

Just when I thought I had her figured out, she changed lanes on me.

She'd done something to her eyes to make them look huge and mysterious. She looked up and smiled at me before glossing her lips with a killer red shade, turning her from sweet to...

Something I didn't want to examine any further.

All I knew was that my jeans were too fucking tight, and I had to spend the day with her. Bonus points for me if I didn't do something stupid like drag her back upstairs and find out what her lips looked like when they were smudged.

"Ready?"

"Definitely." She shoved her makeup in her bag and hooked it over her shoulder. Where the hell she'd found that massive bag, I didn't want to know.

"What exactly do you need to haul around with you?"

Her lips quirked up. "You probably don't want to know."

"You're right. I don't."

I held the door open for her, and she ducked under my arm, trailing the scent of lemons in her wake. Midnight had disappeared into the woods along the back of my property as per usual.

Her long legs perfectly matched my pace, and we got into the Jeep without conversation. She was checking something on her phone, then she shoved it into her bag.

"Not putting your day on the internet?"

She wrinkled her nose. "No. I'll do that later just for you. The joys of an online life mean I have to answer some comments. I'll get some footage in town though. Where's the tux place?"

"There's a place in Crescent Cove."

"Oh. I haven't been there for a long time. Imagine the tuxedos in Turnbull? Clay's family would faint."

My family too. I had a tux from working with Clay, but I was pretty sure the Kevlar-layered black on black wouldn't work for a wedding.

I'd been out of the loop with using my family tailor. If I'd been more on the ball, that was what I should have done.

The Cove was a quick trip from Turnbull. We stopped at the coffee shop Brewed Awakening for a jolt of caffeine. Chaos lit up like a Christmas tree at the eclectic café. She couldn't stay put long enough to do her order, so I just got her an iced coffee from the specials board.

She was off taking videos, chatting with people, and making waves without even trying. People were naturally drawn to her. They couldn't help but do anything she asked.

The fact that I was included in that group left me disconcerted and even more annoyed.

I lost sight of her while paying. My heart galloped for a moment before I caught her in the merchandise section with her phone in hand. She was probably making some sort of short video.

"Do I need to worry about her?"

I looked back at the person ringing me out. Her husky voice was as no-nonsense as her all-black attire.

"No. I'm sure she's already figured out all your social media accounts to tag or whatever she does. She's an online...person." I didn't even know how to describe what Chaos did.

The woman laughed. "Now you sound like my husband. Our kid is forever talking about social media stuff, and he gets this glazed look on his face. But we appreciate any free bumps online. I'm Macy, the owner of this place and the restaurant next door."

"Chaos—Willow—is an—"

"Wil's Way?" Came another voice. The woman had jet black hair and dark eyes. "I thought that was her." She nudged Macy excitedly. "I'm going to go give her some swag."

Macy rolled her eyes. "She's *my* social media person. I just smile and nod, it stops the chatter."

"You're a smart woman." I stuffed a ten in the tip jar and took our drinks. By the time I got to Chaos, she was chatting with the dark-haired woman as if they were long lost friends.

A few selfies later, she finally noticed me. "Hey, Grumpasaurus. Did you meet Rylee?"

I held out the iced coffee. "Briefly."

"We're going to meet next week for a collab." She took the iced drink as she shoved stuff in her bag with her other hand. "Halfway to Halloween is soon. We're going to do some summer bats!"

I had no idea what that all meant, but my life was not going to be my own for the next few weeks—or months. I already knew that for sure. "Guess we need to set up a calendar."

She rushed at me, looping an arm around my neck. I immediately curled my arm around her lower back. "I thought I was going to have to convince you with all of my wiles." Her voice was soft at my ear.

"Oh, we'll be doing some trading, Chaos. Don't worry about that."

She pulled back enough to give me a breathless look. "Quid pro quo then?"

Rylee's eyes went huge. "Are you guys a thing?"

Chaos spun around, sliding her delectable backside against my zipper. I twisted my fingers in her beltloops to keep her in front of me. No need to show off my not-so-small problem. "Uh, we're under the radar."

Rylee looked up at me then down at Chaos before she clapped. Then she mimed zipping her lips. "I won't say a word."

I had my doubts about that.

"C'mon, Chaos. The tux awaits."

Rylee's eyes went huge.

"Not us." Chaos shook her head vigorously. "My sister is getting hitched."

I could tell she was on the verge of oversharing and lightly squeezed her side.

"Soon." She glanced up at me, her gaze dropping to my mouth for a moment before she returned her attention to Rylee. "But I'll email you about coming back."

"Sounds great."

After a few more pleasantries, we finally managed to get out of the café.

"Can we walk to the tux place? I want to get a little more footage."

I nodded and let her do her thing. She twirled around on the sidewalk as she took in all the shops. The bakery with a line out the door —and a duck statue in the window with a large pastry in its mouth— an art store, a baby clothing store, and finally. the funky sign with Vintage December etched into a slab of beachy driftwood.

"Here?"

"Yeah. Evidently, she is a satellite shop for a place in New York City."

"We should have done the tux thing while we were out there yesterday."

"We had enough going on." And truthfully, I'd forgotten—again. The minute I'd found out how much was going on behind the scenes in Willow's life, nothing else had mattered.

Her wide smile faded. "I forgot about it for a minute." She sipped the last of her coffee and tossed it in the trash can.

I wished I could.

I did the same then opened the door for her. The space was airy and painted a neutral gray, leaving the clothing to provide all the color. Bright dresses in wild shades, a rack of vintage T-shirts and denim, and a dais chock full of Doc Martens in a rainbow of colors filled the front of the store.

Chaos dropped her purse by her feet and whipped out her phone.

I rolled my eyes and picked up her bag, letting her wander. Knowing she'd be distracted for awhile, I went to the counter.

An older woman in a tailored blue suit smiled at me. "Can I help you?"

"I called about a fitting for a tux. Ransom Douglas."

"Ahh, yes." She opened a ledger and flipped pages. It appeared vintage wasn't just the name of the shop. "Em is in the back. Give us just a second. We'll get you set up."

"Thanks."

I leaned against the driftwood counter. It had a poly veneer to protect it from the human element, but it had the same vibe as the sign outside. Old meets new with a bit of artistic flair.

Chaos held her phone over her shoulder as she flicked through a rack of T-shirts, then like a drunken bee, she moved to the dresses, boots, and back to the shirts. Within the time it took for the woman to summon the tailor, she collected an armful.

"Mr. Douglas, you finally came in to see me."

I turned toward the musical voice. The woman had pink hair that reminded me of cotton candy from the fair. It swooped over one eye and over her shoulder in waves. She wore a loose dress that moved with her. She held out her hand, shaking firmly before letting mine go. "I'm December, but you can call me Em." She peered around me. "I see your friend is doing okay with shopping."

Chaos turned with a big smile. Another half-dozen shirts had landed on her pile. "This place is amazing. I'm going to bust my clothing budget and then some."

"Anything can be altered to fit. I do them on premises."

"Oh, really?" Chaos's eyes lit up. "Nothing ever fits me." She laughed. "I'm all legs and no chest."

She was a bit more than a mouthful and that suited me just fine.

"We'll take care of you both. Why don't we go get you set up?"

Chaos hugged her pile tight. "This is going to be amazing."

Amazing and *not* quick. Fast was not a word in Chaos's vocabulary.

Or mine anymore, apparently.

Chapter 15

Willow

No Going Back

I wanted to marry Em.

I swayed in front of the triple mirror as the rosebud-pink dress settled perfectly at my waist. She'd created curves on me, for God's sake. "You're a magician."

Em grinned up at me. She'd tied her to-die-for pink hair back before she got to work letting out the hem on the dress to play up my legs. I usually looked best in short or a little long. Anything else made me look like I was playing dress-up in my mother's closet.

Ransom was in the fitting room, putting on his tux.

"It's amazing what a good fit can do for a woman."

I put my hands on my hips and stared at myself. "You aren't kidding."

"Now that I have your measurements, I can fix your jeans too, if you like."

"I like." I pressed the dress against my almost-a-B breasts. "Do you have boobs in that bag of tricks beside you?"

Her laughter was musical and husky at the same time. "No, but I can showcase the best parts. And really, that's all a woman needs in this life."

"I'm here for it. I actually have some more bespoke things that could use your touch."

"We can set something up."

"I'd be happy to talk up your shop if that's something you're interested in." I'd learned that people were usually open to some mutually beneficial collaborations. "Everyone should feel as amazing as I do right now."

She tipped her head questioningly.

"I'm an influencer of sorts. But I'm not looking for anything free. Just want people to know about your place. If you're interested."

I understood the online influencer culture led to some expectations of free stuff with the assumption that visibility was the main value. It had taken me a long time to realize that exposure didn't necessarily pay the bills.

She was quiet enough that I could feel the babble building in my chest. "It's okay if you don't want to."

"I'm just trying to figure out your angle. And it's okay to just want to do something for yourself, you know."

Honestly, I couldn't remember the last time I'd done *anything* just for myself.

Em finished pinning the hem. "I know what it's like to be hyperfixated on being financially independent, and I'm just letting you know that it can just be about you and your wants."

"But people should know about you." I looked at myself in the mirror. The way she'd made me feel so much better about myself with just a few fixes was a gift.

"Then maybe we can do something together. A project."

Maybe Wil's Way could be more than just cooking shortcuts. Ideas wheeled through my brain so fast I had to shut them down or I'd spin out. "Once I finish up with my sister's wedding, I'd really like that."

"It's a plan."

As the door opened, my breath backed up in my chest. Ransom stepped out wearing unrelieved black over a crisp white shirt. He'd left one button open at the neck, revealing his tanned skin and bitable neck. The jet-black lapel held a slight sheen and accentuated the breadth of his chest. "Holy wow," I whispered.

Em turned on her heel. "Well, he was made for a Tom Ford tux, huh?"

"Mercy."

She laughed. "Wait until I tailor it."

I was a dead woman.

Ransom walked in front of us, lifting his arms with a wince. "It's a bit tight."

His biceps looked as if they were going to bust the seams. I knew firsthand how impressive they were when flexed.

Roll up your tongue, girl.

His stormy gaze drifted over me from neck to ankle. Heat suffused my skin, leaving a flush in its wake. "You're gorgeous."

Suddenly, I wished I hadn't put my hair into pigtail braids. They'd been cute when I dressed up my jeans and shirt, but now I felt silly. Definitely not gorgeous. "Em is a magician." I cleared my throat. "Good choice on the tux."

"Classic seemed best. Better than the shiny one Clay wanted me to wear. Trendy asshole." He glanced at December. "Sorry."

Em stood. "Trendy has its place, but I'm sure you can tell my preference is old school finery." She smiled over her shoulder at me. "Why don't you get down and try on a few of the other things? Just don't mess with the pins."

I started to hop down, but Ransom held a hand up to me. I changed course to the two steps off the fitting stage. His hand was warm, his fingers blunt. A quick memory of them on my body made me wish I'd worn a better bra. This one didn't hide anything.

The flowy skirt of the dress swung around my calves as I stepped down and my breast brushed his chest. He stared me down, his gaze never breaking. His hold unbreakable on my hand.

Em was barely six feet away and I couldn't move. The air between us charged with awareness as my skin buzzed in reaction.

This would be us in a few weeks time, walking down the aisle together—for my sister. For his best friend. Maybe a slow dance or two for formality.

Or was that just me making a wish because I liked when he had his arms around me. All I could do was marvel how well we fit together. Generally, I felt gangly and too tall for most men. He was only a few inches taller than I was, but in all the right ways.

Too right.

Finally, I backed away. "I'm just going to try on a few more things."

He nodded, his gaze drifting to my mouth before he stepped onto the fitting stage.

I escaped to the dressing room, my heart racing as if I'd just run a mile.

Carefully, I slipped out of the dress, only poking myself a half dozen times. My skin was too tight and flushed to boot.

I collapsed on the bench and got my bearings. Surely all these overwhelming feelings would dissipate once we got this whole sex thing over with.

That had to be why I couldn't think about anything else. I liked sex. I missed sex. It was a great way to get rid of stress. But with Ransom? No, his kind of naked shenanigans weren't in the same league. I couldn't imagine laughing with him over a pint of ice cream post-orgasm.

Passing out face-first on the mattress and hoping for mercy, maybe.

"Get a grip," I mumbled to myself. "He's just a man."

Grumpy and intense with a side of asshole. I needed to remember that part. Not the fact that my knees stopped working when he looked at me as if I was his next meal.

I blew out a breath and threw myself into trying on the pile of clothes. I discarded a few pairs of jeans. Obviously, some things couldn't be fixed.

Like being four inches too short.

One of the many problems with my long legs and narrow waist. Beanpoles had just as much trouble as any other woman. Sleeves were much the same.

As usual, my reject pile outnumbered the ones to keep.

But the peacock blue dress was a dream. I left it for last because I didn't want to be too disappointed when it didn't fit. Before I could get too wired about it, I unclipped my bra and stepped into the cocktail dress.

The straps were thin and criss-crossed down my back in an intricate pattern. I spun around to check out how it looked and marveled how it made my freckles seem interesting rather than as if they belonged on a perpetual twelve-year-old girl's body.

The material hugged my chest, showing off my slight curves in a way that made me feel feminine and maybe even sexy. My neck looked long and elegant and the dress hit me at mid-thigh, showing off my long legs.

Now I just needed a pair of heels.

I opened the door and found Ransom looming in the doorway. His eyes were hooded as he took me in then his hot gaze blazed over every inch. His hands fisted at his sides.

"Where's Em?"

"Had to call her connection for a different jacket." His gaze dipped to my breasts and his jaw flexed.

My lips twitched. "Is that right?" I drew my fingertip down the line of buttons on his dress shirt. "What do you think of the dress?"

He pushed me into the room. "I think I need to help you with the zipper."

I laughed. "No zipper, pal."

His gaze skimmed up and over my shoulder to the mirror. "Christ." His long fingers inched over my waist to my hip to hold me in a firm grip.

"Not exactly easy to get me out of it."

His hand snaked down to my ass. "I'll make it work." His mouth crashed on mine as he kicked the door shut behind him.

"How long do we have?" I asked against his mouth between kisses. His tongue slid along mine with long, hot strokes.

He stroked his thumb over my jaw to open me wider before he circled my neck lightly to push my head back. "I don't care."

His teeth raked down my neck and over to the slice of skin showing above the neckline. His teeth clicked over the necklace I'd put on before we left. It didn't exactly go with the dress, so I'd tucked it underneath, but now it teased the skin between my breasts.

He slid his thigh between mine and the dress rose a few inches. I could only imagine the view behind me, but he seemed into it.

The bristles of his shadowed jaw scraped over the skin between my shoulder and neck, making me shiver. His hand slid lower, dragging me closer to ride his thigh.

The tips of his fingers went even lower, digging into the back of my thigh as he ground me against his leg. I groaned into his mouth. "You're not seriously going to do this in here."

"I seriously am."

He dragged one strap down and I quickly detangled my arm so he could get to my breast. I wanted to *finally* feel his mouth where he'd driven me mad last night with only touches of those deliciously calloused fingertips.

My head fell back as he licked the tight tip. He scored my skin with his rough chin, then he looked up at me as he lightly tugged on my nipple.

"Holy..." My hips shifted restlessly. "Yeah, I guess we are."

"How fast can you come, Chaos?"

I blew out a slow breath as he circled my nipple with his tongue then sucked hard. I gripped his shoulder and fought the need to shout out how good it felt. "Pretty fast if you keep that up."

He wrenched up the skirt of the dress and dropped to his knees. "Fast is good."

I stared down at him. "Wait, what—" He dragged one leg up and over his shoulder and tipped me back against the mirror. I gripped his hair and held him tight. "You..."

And then words were absolutely dust.

His hot breath fanned over the scrap of panties I was wearing, then he nuzzled along the inside of my thigh. "Hold on, Chaos."

With his other hand, he dragged the material aside, flicking a finger along my slit from the back as his tongue lashed and stroked from the front. He learned every blessed line and crease.

When he filled me with two fingers and teased my clit until the lights above the mirror flared like fireworks, I could only hold onto his head. Somehow I managed to slap a hand over my mouth as the first orgasm ripped through me.

There wasn't time to recover before he demanded more. He stretched me open and licked and sucked with a voracious appetite I'd never experienced before in my life.

As I grabbed at the breast he'd freed before, he growled against my thigh. "Yes."

I rode his tongue and let myself go, allowed myself the moment and swallowed every shout that I'd normally have let rip free. Hiding in this little room full of vintage clothes while desperately trying to be quiet only made the moment larger and more intense.

He used both hands to grip my ass and hold me still to hammer at every last wall I had. He drove me up and over one more time. The room went dark as I quaked around his mouth, my leg shaking as I tried to keep my balance. He dragged in a deep breath against my inner thigh before a sharp nip of the fragile skin there made me jump. Immediately after, he offered a soothing swirl of his tongue as he stared up at me.

He'd marked me.

Good grief, that shouldn't be hot. But my inner walls clenched with the truth.

He rose and then his mouth was on mine again, taking each scream still trapped in my throat. My taste, his taste, the maelstrom of emotions trying to break through the pleasure and make it something more—all of it was too much.

"Breathe, Chaos," he murmured, following the command with a quick nip of my lower lip.

I twisted my fingers in his shirt. Two buttons popped above his belt. I got my fingers into the weird hook clasp that was forever a nuisance in dress pants. "Inside me, Ransom."

"Not here. I don't—" He tried to stop me.

"Now." I pushed aside his hands and went for his zipper.

Our fingers were a tangle of wills while his eyes were a silver flash as he stared me down. "I don't have anything with me."

"That hobo bag is good for more than carrying my phone."

He shook his head. "I need hours."

"We have now."

His jaw clenched. "Now isn't enough for what I need." Chest heaving, he went for my neck again, kissing the spot behind my ear much more softly than before. Bringing me down instead of driving me up. "I want you too much to get interrupted. The next time we start this, we're both finishing."

I held onto his shoulder, then I dragged his mouth back up to mine with my other hand. "You won't change your mind?"

"I won't."

I pressed my forehead to his. "I'll hold you to that."

He rocked his hard dick against my still swollen center. "I can't wait to be inside you. Now that I know your taste," he nipped my chin, "there's no going back."

Chapter 16

Ransom

Sunshine, Wine and Ducks?

I closed the dressing room door behind me, leaving her to get her street clothes back on.

Not one of my finer moments.

For once, I didn't regret any of it. That dress had put me over the top. The sweet one on the stage had taken my breath, but in the dressing room...

Yeah, I'd been toast.

Wanting her was a constant low hum in my blood. I could mostly put it out of my mind if I concentrated. The Army had trained me well. Focus was one of my biggest strengths.

Then Chaos had arrived to show me that training could only take me so far. I couldn't even lie to myself that having her would take the edge off.

The need was growing, not waning. I was doubly fucked.

Yet so far, not fucked at all. Story of my life.

"Find everything you need, Mr. Douglas?" The older woman came over with a knowing expression in her eyes.

I hoped my shirttails covered the worst of my sins. It was going to take me more than a minute to get myself under control. "December is taking good care of us."

Her lips twitched. "Not as good as you are, dear."

I felt the flush creep up my neck. I cleared my throat. "Chaos—um, Willow—has quite a few things she'd like to get altered. Put it on my account, would you?"

Her eyebrow arched. "That's how it is?"

"She had fun today. I'd rather leave it as fun instead of looking at how much she spent."

"Hmm. I'll take care of it." She nodded toward me. "Em found a suit jacket to suit you. She'll have it ready for next week."

"Thanks." I slipped into the other changing room and gingerly removed my own pinned clothing. December had mostly used a chalkline to get my measurements as most tailors did, but there were a few lines that had gotten messed up due to Chaos.

Quickly, I tugged on my jeans and swapped out the dress shirt for my worn Henley, and then I glanced into the mirror. Dark circles bruised under my eyes.

I needed to find a way to get some damn sleep, or I was going to make mistakes. Chaos already had me on edge in more than one way.

And she was the biggest reason I needed to get it together.

I gathered my things and hung them on the rack December had left for us. Chaos was still doing whatever she did in the dressing room.

I definitely was *not* going in for another visit. I'd end up finding out if her purse did indeed have a condom in it.

Em met me at the counter. "Did she find what she needed?"

I wasn't one to preen, but she certainly had. I was the one with blue balls for the second day running. "If she tries to put that blue dress back, make sure it's in the buy pile." I slid over my Black Amex. "And whatever else she wants."

If December was surprised to see the somewhat rare credit card, her poker face didn't reveal it. She slipped it off the counter and rang up everything.

"I'd like to order an extra few shirts too. I don't dress up much, but they were comfortable."

"I started carrying them for the more...athletic men that seem so plentiful in this town."

"Is that what they call them?" Chaos asked from behind me.

I glanced back to find her with an armful of clothes.

December grinned at Chaos. "You should have seen me fitting the rather large construction worker who is getting married soon. Lucky nearly required two suits sewn together."

Chaos came up beside me, bumping me lightly. "I didn't know they grew Jason Momoa-types in this town. Should you relocate?"

I rolled my eyes. As if I'd ever grow my hair like his.

You might if Chaos suggested it.

Still no.

"I just need to set up an account and we can go."

"I took care of it." My voice was just this side of brusque. And not because severe orgasm denial was affecting my normally winsome personality.

She narrowed her eyes. "Pardon me?"

I snatched back my card from the counter. "I told her to put it on my bill."

"I'm not your arm candy, pal."

"No one said you were, Chaos."

She pointed a finger at me. "Don't 'Chaos' me right now."

I cupped her finger and lowered her hand. "It's a gift."

A growl came out of her chest. "Dirty pool."

I laughed. "I think we like darts more."

She drilled her finger into my side. "Fine. I'll let you—this time." Her attention went to December. "I'll be back for that project we talked about. Can I have this dress today? The rest you can sprinkle your magic on."

My gut clenched at the familiar slinky dress.

"Does it need any alterations?"

"No," I said gruffly.

Chaos brightened. "Fits great. Oh, and this sweater. I couldn't take it off."

December's lips twitched. "We'll get you all rung up."

Twenty minutes later, Chaos left the shop swinging a bag with the same beachy tone as the driftwood accents in the store. She wore a wine-colored sweater that dipped off her shoulders, accentuating the fact that she probably wasn't wearing a damn bra.

She'd taken her braids out while in the dressing room, leaving her hair a little wavy and wild around her shoulders. Once we stepped out on the sidewalk, the spring breeze lifted it and tossed it everywhere.

Christ, she was beautiful.

She turned back to me and grabbed my hand, dragging me across the road. "I need a drink. Shopping is thirsty work."

There was a small wine bar on the corner with a sandwich board outside suggesting wine slushies were on sale.

While they didn't interest me, I had a sneaking suspicion who just might be onboard for those.

"Chaos, we gotta get to Clay's."

"We can do two things at once."

"Pretty sure wine is not on the to-do list."

"No. But wine slushies are a great idea for the bachelorette party next weekend. And that definitely is on our to-do list this week."

"That's on *your* list. I don't have to worry about a girls' night." Thank fuck. But I had to worry about a guys' night. Good Christ.

"No, because the bachelor party is just whiskey and beer."

"Damn right."

Reluctantly, I followed her across to the brick building. Once there, I passed on a wine snow cone and got a regular lemonade.

It was late afternoon, and the sun peeked out between the trees near the water. With a sigh, I let her drag me down to the pass-through to the lake and then along the walkway that looped around it. There were a few people out with strollers and kids on bikes, the warm weather finally teasing people out of their houses. Especially

184

since sunny days were hard to come by in a lakeside town in the spring.

"I didn't realize how beautiful this town was." She hip-bumped me lightly. "My sister was warned away from it."

"Why's that?"

"Something about baby-crazy water."

I arched a brow. "That's not a thing."

She wrapped her lips around her snow cone and nodded toward the plethora of strollers. "Maybe a thing."

Now I was doubly glad I'd managed to resist her. I drew her off the path and in front of me, then swiped at her lower lip where the wine had stained her lips. "Enjoying that?"

"Nothing bad about a merlot." She dragged her tongue over the rapidly melting snow cone before holding it up to me. "Try?"

I lowered her hand and dipped my head. "I'd rather taste it this way."

I kept the kiss light. This wasn't the place to get carried away. But it was nice to have her sway into me, her lips curving under mine in a smile. The bold, red wine clung to her tongue as I lightly sipped from her.

When I pulled back, I couldn't help returning her smile.

She scraped her teeth over her lower lip. "I don't get to see that often."

I laced my fingers at her back. "See what?"

"A smile." She lifted her dripping cone to her lips and quickly swallowed down the wine. "You have dimples." Her eyes went golden in the sun and made my chest ache.

I tried to stop smiling but fighting how she made me feel always made it worse.

"This is a banner day, Grumpasaurus."

"Shut up."

She finished up with the little paper cone and crushed it as she looked around. I took it from her and tucked it into my back pocket.

"Stop being cute."

"I'm not cute." I took her hand and led her back up to Main Street.

She tugged me back. "Just a few more minutes?"

As if I could tell her no when she smiled at me like that. I dropped onto one of the empty benches. She set her bag down and sat down next to me, pulling my arm over her shoulder so she could curl against me. She even hooked one of her legs over mine.

I lightly stroked her bare shoulder with my thumb and accepted the fact that we could both use a pause. Neither of us felt the need to fill the gaps with conversation. A dog barking in the distance reminded me we weren't alone, but at that moment, it felt like it.

There was a lone sailboat in the middle of the lake taking advantage of the warm weather, and the lapping water added another layer of calm. Something I usually only felt when I was alone.

She rested her cheek against my chest. "It feels like I've been on the max setting of a record player for days."

I rested my chin on top of her head. "You've been amazing."

"Ha. Not so much."

"You could have ignored your gut. Many people do."

She straightened enough that our mouths were mere inches apart. "I'm only okay because I know you're in my corner."

Don't put that on me.

The voice inside of me practically screamed it. But there was another louder part of me that accepted the weight of responsibility and pushed down the shrill fear.

I brushed my nose along hers before kissing her gently. I didn't know what else to say. All I could do was show her that I wasn't going anywhere.

She lifted her hand to my cheek and those flecked green and gold eyes gutted me.

I knew right then I'd do anything to keep her safe. I wasn't pretending to want her by my side. Nor could I pretend—even to myself—that this thing between us was for the cameras.

I hooked my arm around her, holding her tight for a moment

before I let her go. "We better get back before your sister sends out the SWAT team."

"Imagine?" Her laugh was as light as the spring air coming off the water. She got up and jumped back, almost landing in my lap as a duck quacked at her. "Hey, little guy."

I eased her forward again and grabbed her bag. "Looks like we're in his spot."

"Or he was looking for this." She toed a little metal canister soldered to the bench. The top flipped up and the duck rushed over again.

Delighted, she used the little scooper inside to throw some corn. Chaos took out her phone and crouched to take a quick video.

I stuffed my hands in my pockets and waited for her to have her moment. "For the channel?"

She peered up at me. "Nope. For me."

I held out my hand to her and she popped up, waving at the duck. We skipped the winding path this time and climbed up the patchy grass to Main Street, our hands still clasped.

She checked her phone. "Can we stop at the bakery at the orchard? Rachel is requesting sandwiches for dinner."

"Sure."

The trip back to Turnbull and Happy Acres was a quick one. We were in the sweet spot between afterschool buses and people leaving work.

She ordered ahead, but instead of that making our stop quicker, we pulled up to find Laverne waiting at the entrance with two bags.

"Man, I'm gonna get reamed."

I parked. "You haven't seen her yet?"

"Nope. We've kinda been busy."

Guess it was time to face the music. Another *not* quick trip to add to my day. Laverne was very protective of her chicks.

Chaos slipped out of the Jeep and rushed over to the older woman. By the time I got to them, they were doing a similar sway thing to the one she'd done with Merry.

What was it with women and the sway?

Laverne cupped the back of Willow's head. "Why didn't you come to see me?"

"Today's the first day I've been home. When I got in the other day, you were in a meeting. A bunch of weddings happening here besides Rach's, huh?"

"We're overrun." She looped an arm around Chaos. "Nice to see you too, Ransom."

"Laverne." I tucked my hands in pockets, but she came for me, anyway. I patted her back awkwardly while Chaos gleefully grinned at me.

"Now what's this I hear you're staying with Ransom?"

Saying nothing, I leaned down to collect the bags at Willow's feet before turning to head back to my Jeep.

"Now don't think you can just run off—"

That was exactly what I thought. I held up one hand and continued walking.

"Coward," Chaos called after me.

She could call me all the names she wanted. A wise man knew when to retreat.

Chapter 17

Willow

When You Find Your Person

I couldn't believe he'd left me like that.

Hell, who was I fooling? I totally could. He was Ransom, after all.

I smiled brightly at my aunt. "He's a bit..."

"Ransom?"

I laughed. See? "Yes, exactly."

"He looks at you like you're his last meal."

"What? No, he doesn't." I glanced over my shoulder, and he was looking at me from the Jeep. Smoldering at me through the glass.

Damn, girl.

Okay, maybe he did. But that was just residual from the dressing room from... What? Hours ago? It felt like just minutes.

"You two suit each other."

I slipped my arm through my aunt's crooked arm. "Let's not talk about stinky boys. How's the orchard?"

"Busy as ever. What's this I hear you're moving back?"

I shrugged and walked with her over to the picnic tables in the outside eating area. "I've outgrown my tiny space in my apartment building."

She sat across from me. "I don't believe you."

My aunt was too intuitive for her own good—and mine. "My roommates hate me."

"I don't believe that either." She reached across the bleached wood to cover my hand. "Maybe they just don't understand you. Many people don't know how to deal with creative people. So many people go to their jobs and clock in and leave it all behind at the end of the workday. That doesn't apply to people like us. Especially those of us who own our own business." She propped her head on her hand, the familiar lines of her face calming me just by being there in front of me. "I can't remember a time when I actually clocked out."

"Me neither." My gaze swung to Ransom. He was leaning on his Jeep, scrolling on his phone. He'd probably Googled "how to avoid messy family interactions" to look busy. "I'm not used to people understanding that part of me."

"And he does?"

"Not really, but he doesn't hold it against me. Most people get very annoyed with me." One of the main things I'd taken with me from living in Brooklyn. Even Merry, who loved me, was often unsure how to handle me and my lifestyle.

"When you find your person, that's how it works."

I sat up straight. "It's not like that."

"Isn't it?" She followed my sight line. "He keeps checking to see you're over here."

That was because he was on bodyguard duty. Not that anyone knew that part. "He's just helping me with my move."

"Speaking of your move, we can set you up in the lodge. I have a cute little corner room that would be perfect for you."

I reached over to grip her hand. "This is your busy season. I couldn't take a room."

She straightened, dropping her other hand on top of mine. "Nonsense. I'd love to have you around. We can adjust the books. You can keep Rachel from going crazy with wedding plans. She's running herself ragged."

"I'll definitely be helping her. But I'm working on something with Ransom for the wedding."

Aunt Laverne arched a brow. "What kind of something?"

"A surprise he's building for them."

"Now you're a woodworker? At least I'm assuming that's what it is."

"No, but I have something in mind for Rach too." I picked at a stray splinter on the table.

"Or you found a more exciting bed."

The flush started at my shoulders and rushed up my neck. "Maybe."

She laughed. "Don't be embarrassed. I was young once too. And he's quite attractive. Just be careful."

"He wouldn't hurt me."

She gave me a long look. "I didn't mean that, but interesting you went right to that line of thinking. I meant that you're in the middle of a change. It's easy to lean on someone else when you're uncertain."

"Oh." She was right. And things had been zooming along at one hundred miles an hour. Was that why I was so wrapped up in him? Just to put the other things I had to figure out in the distance?

"You've been on your own for so long. You don't even come to visit us much, save for Christmas."

"I know. I'll try to be better about that."

"I'm not saying this to make you feel bad. Just that there are a lot of moving parts in your life right now. When you have attraction jumping into the mix, it makes things even more overwhelming." She peered down her nose at me. "And whatever else you aren't talking about."

How the heck did she know these things? Was there a flickering billboard above my head?

"Well, I'm home now. I always felt I needed to stay in the city because of what I did—that all the important things were there. I'm starting to see that it's all inside of me."

"Growing up includes lots of growing pains." She patted my

hand. "I'm just glad to see your smiling face again. In person, that is. I make sure to watch all your videos. And I've found a few other fun people on that app of yours."

Delighted, I slid out of the bench to go around and hug her. "You're the best, Aunt Laverne."

"Chaos, your sister is blowing up my damn phone," Ransom called out to me.

My aunt's eyebrows shot up. "What did he call you?"

"Yeah, he's a jerk."

"Did he say chaos?"

"He sure did."

Her smile got even wider.

"Don't get excited."

"Pet names are a sign of love, you know."

The fact that we'd had nicknames for one another since the day we met did not mean a damn thing, no matter what she said.

I pecked her on the cheek. "You see love everywhere. Must be all those weddings at the chapel and orchard."

"Must be." She rose. "Oh, I forgot to mention. You got a box today."

I stilled. "I did?"

She nodded. "I was surprised since I never get mail for you, which is what made me take notice of it. I was going to send the box to Rachel's house with one of the boys, but since you're here, I'll go grab it."

"No!"

Aunt Laverne frowned. "No?"

My heart raced. "I just mean Ransom can go get it."

"Okay. It is a pretty big box."

Ransom came forward, his brow furrowed. "What?"

He always seemed to know when I needed him. I wrapped my arms around my middle. "There's a box for me."

Every line of his face hardened in an instant. "Where?"

My aunt wrapped her arm around my shoulders. "Is there something wrong?"

"Just dealing with a mail problem. My packages are getting sent all over."

She frowned, but she didn't say anything else. "I'll show you where it is."

We went into the lodge located just beyond the bakery. The sweet scent of apple blossoms drifted through the lobby. A large arrangement of urns filled with clippings flanked the sign-in desk.

Ransom touched my lower back, letting me know he was right beside me. As always. "Relax."

Like that was going to happen.

Why did this person keep sending me packages? We hadn't even opened the other two. We'd been so tired and then distracted that they were still sitting in the back of the truck.

It wasn't a game and I'd been ignoring everything for far too long. And it wasn't stopping. If anything, the number of deliveries was increasing.

Aunt Laverne led us to the storage room and pointed to the second shelf. The box was wide and shallow. Not nearly as bulky as the ones from before.

I didn't see the usual logo. Ransom stepped in front of me and lifted the box. It was obviously lighter than the ones I'd gotten before.

"Should I expect more until you get a regular address?"

I tried not to shudder. God, I hoped not. But if the recent past was any indication...

I nodded. "If you get more, let me know. I usually get things from my PO Box. So, hopefully, that shouldn't be a problem in the future. I'll have to get a new one now that I'm not in Brooklyn."

Suddenly, a list of mundane business tasks unfurled. I'd need to update my address with my lawyer and find a new PO Box that could handle all the mail I had to deal with. Let alone the forwarding addresses. And to where.

I didn't actually *have* my own place. I couldn't crash with people indefinitely.

Especially people I'd been halfway naked with.

"It's fine, sweetheart. We don't mind." My aunt touched my arm, dragging me back to the present.

I nodded. "Thanks. Let me know if anything else shows up. We're going to head up to Clay and Rachel's."

"Give them a hug for me." Aunt Laverne gathered me close into a hard hug. "Just like this one."

I hugged her back, taking an extra minute to draw in her vanilla scent.

Reluctantly letting me go, she rubbed my arms. "It's really good to have you home."

I hadn't realized just how much I needed to be back until then. "I missed you guys."

"Then I expect to see you every day."

"You'll be so annoyed with me and my camera. You sure you want to open that door?"

"Very sure."

Ransom backed out of the storage room, and I followed him. The lobby was full of people and the sun was shining through the large stained-glass window over the doors. The noises of life—children's laughter and chatter and the happy barks of a scruffy dog on a leash.

It all sounded so far away. Now that I didn't have to pretend for my aunt, the shakes started.

Another package that shouldn't be here. How could this person even know about the lodge?

How much more did he know about me and my family? Did he know my sister was getting married?

Sucking in air, I quickened my step to keep up with Ransom. He pulled down the truck bed door and lightly set down the box. I stepped around him and he blocked me, pushing me behind him.

I couldn't keep letting him shelter me. Not when I was beginning to wonder what—and who—I'd unintentionally brought home to my family's doorstep.

"I need to see."

He squeezed my hand. "I don't know what's in there."

I pointed to the other two boxes. "That's three in the space of two days.'"And for the first time, I noticed only one was RID. So, this was the second one without a recognizable label.

Pissed, I sliced through the tape with my fingernail.

"Dammit, Chaos."

He nudged me back before I could open the cardboard flaps. But we didn't need to worry about that. The moment one was pried free, a machine lifted out.

Ransom shoved me back as a wide drone rose out of the box. The huge, eight-legged spider-like device hovered just above us for a moment. As it whirred, I froze in place.

What the hell was happening?

He dragged me behind him and stared down the drone. Then I realized the whir was a camera lens. The drone lifted over the parking lot and people began to notice, pointing and asking questions.

This was no tiny personal toy. The drone was professional grade and someone was behind the controls. All of a sudden, it went up even higher and the legs opened.

"What's it doing?"

"I don't know."

Slowly, the drone floated over the area and my heart stalled. "Is it taking video? I saw a camera."

Just as quickly, it shot upward over the trees in the distance and was gone.

Ransom pulled me in front of him and wrapped his arms around me. "It's okay."

"It's not okay." I gripped his shoulder. "There are so many people here. What if it hadn't been just a camera? What if it was a weapon?" I pressed my cheek against his chest. "Why is he doing this?"

"I don't know."

I could tell admitting that killed him. I wasn't the only one out of my element here, and he'd seen so much more than I had.

Which scared the shit out of me. Just what were we dealing with here? And what if it touched my family?

Gently, he eased me back. "Let's get out of here. There are way too many people looking at us."

They weren't just looking. People were holding up their phones to take video of the drone. To them, it was probably a novelty. Something funny. A prank even.

They had no idea I was quietly freaking out. And I really wanted to keep it that way.

"What about the other boxes?"

"Later." He pulled the truck bed cover closed, then slammed the tailgate door shut and hustled me to the passenger side door.

As I climbed up, he stopped me.

"We're going to figure this out, I promise."

I nodded and slid into the seat, reaching for my seatbelt as he closed the door.

He rounded the car and hopped in, backing out of the dusty parking lot before he bothered to put on his seatbelt.

The trip to Clay and Rachel's place was quiet, almost as if neither of us wanted to voice what that drone meant. Not that we even knew.

Escalation?

Messing with me?

Worse?

With shaking fingers, I pulled out my phone and opened the chat software Poe had given me.

"What are you doing?"

"Checking in with Poe."

"Good." He tightened his fingers on the steering wheel. "I don't like being surprised like that."

"And you think I do?"

"No." His jaw went stony.

All the fun from earlier in the day dissolved like sugar in water.

Wil: Hey. We had a weird thing happen today.

Poe: Drone perhaps? You're all over the damn social channels. And the forums.

Wil: Can we call? So Ransom can hear?

Poe: Yep. Incoming.

I found the iPhone charger cord that connected to his dash and plugged in.

Ransom frowned at me.

"Poe is calling."

His jaw tightened even more.

"You know, if you keep grinding your molars like that, we'll be at the dentist."

He gave me a hard stare, but the phone rang in my hand before he could say anything.

I accepted the call. "Hey. We're in the car."

"You guys just like to keep me hopping."

"We'd prefer quiet over this." Ransom's voice was tight.

"I was going to contact you, but your girl beat me to it." Manic typing in the background let us know she was pulling something up. "Okay, check it. That freaking behemoth of a drone was military grade."

"So, he's military?" Ransom frowned as he maneuvered through traffic.

"Nope. But he stole it from them. I did some digging and Aidan checked in with a buddy from the Navy. Looks like there's been a lot of theft. Sometimes off the container ships before they make it to port, sometimes rerouting them via the post office. Naughty, naughty getting into the federal fines now. These guys are super bold. I'd be impressed if they weren't so stupid."

I didn't know what exactly to say to that.

"So, you think it's part of the bigger problem Aidan was worried about?"

"Mmm-hmm." Poe punched some keys. "I sent something to your email. You can check when you guys land somewhere. But beyond the actual drone set-up, this guy has a feed. Posted it to the forums like a freaking hat trick. Hey, look what I can do!"

I hugged myself. "So, is it about me? Or just showing off?"

"Bit of both, I'd say. The footage was only a second, but then there was a link for people to buy in for future footage. Unfortunately, or fortunately—not sure which—he has these drones on a few people."

I leaned forward. "I really don't mind not being special."

"So, we'll be in touch when I know more. I'm off to dig into the ooey gooey dark web. Hang tight, kids. Catch ya later."

And then she was gone.

"What did you mean about Aidan?"

He sighed. "When he took me aside, he mentioned that it wasn't just you. Why he didn't include you in the conversation. A few of his other clients were also mentioned in those forums he found."

"I don't get why anyone would care about me." I didn't *want* to get it.

He pulled off the shoulder on the access road for Clay's house, then he slammed the Jeep into Park. "You should get it better than most. People get fixated for reasons only in their own minds."

"I know." The old feelings of helplessness wanted to lunge to the forefront but tamping them down was the only shot I had of keeping a clear head. And it was vital we keep thinking straight to make sure my family was safe.

They were my number one priority.

"And I had another thought." He turned toward me. "He's showing off. Is it to get your attention or is he working toward something bigger?"

A chill raced over my skin, raising goosebumps. "Well, that's comforting."

"In this instance, I mean showing off to get people to spend money."

"Oh." I relaxed in the seat. "I didn't think about that."

"I only thought about it from the forum stuff. Dark web stuff is murky for me. I don't understand what's going on there." He tapped his finger on the steering wheel. "But I don't get the drone angle. I don't know if he's trying to get attention to impress you or the people he wants to hire him."

I knew he was just talking it out, but it was disconcerting to hear him talk about my would-be stalker as if I wasn't a part of this.

He glanced at me. "Jesus. I'm sorry, Chaos, I—" He gripped the wheel and his arms flexed with frustration.

"Hey." I undid my belt and stroked his rippling muscles. "I'm not gonna start rocking in the corner. And I prefer it when you talk to me rather than playing that stoic, silent card you default to."

Slowly, he relaxed. "I'm not used to discussing things."

"Oh, I know. Truth be told, neither am I." At his sharp look, I shrugged. "I take care of myself."

"You don't have to anymore."

Now it was my turn to whip my head toward him sharply.

"Regarding this situation."

Of course. Right. Not that I'd assume he meant anything otherwise. Even if that smoldering look in his wolfish eyes said something more.

He hooked his arm around my shoulders and crushed me close. "I'm sorry this ruined an otherwise good day. We're going to figure it out."

The embrace was awkward in the truck, but I was sort of getting used to these heart-to-hearts in his vehicle. "I really appreciate the hug, but I think your console is trying to shove my rib into a vital organ."

His rumbling laugh made me rethink moving back on my side.

"Try getting a certain someone off with the same console, babe."

My heart kicked hard. Normally, a babe would make go for a

knee to the balls. Then again, Ransom seemed to have a whole check-list of things that usually pissed me off when it came to other men and somehow didn't with him.

I eased back into my seat. "I appreciate your service to the cause, soldier."

He threw his head back and laughed.

I couldn't help but join in. Tension broken, he put the Jeep back in Drive and we made our way up the winding road to Clay's place.

Rachel and Clay met us outside, Clay's arm tight around my sister's shoulders. They looked so at ease with one another. As if they were puzzle pieces that had finally found their match.

"Hey, guys." I slid from the truck and opened the back door.

"Finally." Clay came forward to take one of the bags. "We're starving."

"Aunt Laverne reminded me I hadn't checked in with her. Had to do a little catching up."

Clay peeked into the bag. "Her mac salad is enough for forgive-ness." He gave me a peck on the cheek and took the other bag. His voice pitched a little lower. "Everything okay?"

I pasted a smile on my face. "Of course."

"Hmm."

I patted his chest. "Guess what? Ransom even did his fitting today."

"Hallelujah!" My sister called.

I grabbed the bottle of wine my aunt had thoughtfully provided. Very necessary to get through this dinner without tipping my hand.

Or getting in any deeper with the man so determined to protect me he forgot one vital part.

I might be physically safer with him around, but what about my heart?

Chapter 18

Ransom

Knives Out

While the girls chattered on about colors, flowers, and the dreaded seating chart, I helped Clay clean up.

Clay paused while drying one of the plates, his attention on the women huddled together in front of the fireplace with a large book in front of them. "I'm glad she's home, whatever the reason."

"Chaos is a little out of sorts, but when I saw the apartment, I can see why she wanted to leave. She was probably hanging on for loyalty's sake."

"Wouldn't know what that's about, would you?"

I took the plate. "I didn't mind working for you."

"You were bored as fuck."

I shrugged. "Maybe. But I'd prefer to watch out for your ass than to work for my mother."

"Roth would keep you busy."

Stacking plates gave me a minute to formulate a reply. Because he was right. It would be easy to slide back into that world. I might not love bodyguard work, but I was good at it. "I'm tired of working for other people."

Clay flipped a towel over his shoulder. "Is that right?"

"Not like I need the money."

"You'll get bored."

"No. I'm not like you, man." I crossed my arms. "I like building shit when I'm in the mood."

"So, what, you're going to be a house husband?"

"Who says I need a wife?"

Clay glanced over his shoulder. "Who says you don't?"

I rolled my eyes. "Don't start with that shit again."

"I see the signs. Hell, I know the signs. I tried to ignore Rach and you see how that went."

"I'm not ignoring Chaos." Far from it. Would I be as wound up if I didn't have to have her in my life?

"I'll remind you about that later. How would you like me to deliver the 'I told you so'? Singing telegram? Skywriter?"

"You're a jackass." I picked up my beer and went into the living room.

Rachel popped up from the floor with her big book in her arms. "Oh, good you're back." She pushed me onto the couch and plopped the book on my lap. It was big enough to cover hers as well when she sat beside me.

"You're at the head table with us." She pointed one glossy pink-tipped finger on the diagram.

"Okay..."

"So, we have Helena coming with Reid."

I stiffened. "Reid is coming to the wedding?"

"I know, a little awkward. But Helena asked for a plus one. I didn't realize it would be him."

I wasn't sure what to say on that one. Helena Danbury had been Clay's social plus one for most of his adult life. Their families had been enmeshed since we were young.

"I can't believe you're cool with this." Chaos was sitting cross-legged with her arms folded. Her bare shoulders were backlit by the fire, distracting me from the soap opera on my lap.

"It's not Helena's fault Clay was an idiot."

"Thanks, Rach." Clay dropped into a chair and slumped down to rest his beer on his buckle.

"Well, you were. Handy for you I'm a forgiving woman."

Clay's lips twitched with a suppressed laugh. "Handy."

Rachel tapped on the chart again. "My problem is I don't know where to put them. I was thinking they could sit with Clay's grandfather, but I already have your sister at the table."

"Maple is coming?" My sister was usually jet-setting around Italy or Paris this time of year.

"Clay sent her an invite thinking you might like to see her. I'm excited to meet her. But I need to know if the Reid thing is going to be weird."

I hadn't seen my little sister in years. She'd also been pretty young when Marigold left. I was half-convinced Maple had gone into modeling to find our sister.

"My sister is well-versed in dealing with people she doesn't like. I doubt she'll be sitting at the table long enough for it to matter."

"I was hoping you'd say that." Rach bumped my arm. "I don't know a lot about that time."

"Clay told you." I didn't really want to go back down that road. It had broken me on more than one level.

The relationship between my best friends in the world had imploded, forcing me to take sides. Instead of facing the fallout, I'd just fucking run.

"Everyone was hurt that night." Clay's voice was husky and tight.

I glanced over at him. We'd never really talked about it. It was easier to just bury the whole damn thing and start over. And I sure as fuck wasn't going to talk about it now.

I slid the book over to Rachel and stood.

"Ransom." Clay stood up.

"Not now, man." I turned to Chaos. "Do you want me to come back and pick you up?"

"We're leaving?" She scrambled to her knees.

"I gotta go."

"You don't need to leave." Rachel sighed. "I'm sorry. I shouldn't have brought it up. It was thoughtless."

"It's fine. It's just been a damn long day."

Clay collapsed back against the chair. Part of me wanted to just gloss over the situation again. We'd been doing that for too many freaking years.

Don't talk about it and pretend it never happened.

It wasn't Clay's fault Marigold had blown everything to hell. At least I knew that in my head.

When Chaos held out a hand to me, I gripped it and pulled her up. "Rachel, I'll come here for lunch. And to get my stuff."

That was what we were supposed to be doing—getting her SUV so she could have some independence from me. Again, it was easier to tuck her under my arm and just take over. To make sure she was safe and...

To make sure she was *with me.*

She laced her fingers with mine. "Tomorrow is good enough."

Rachel closed the book and hugged it to her chest. "I didn't think." Her big blue eyes were swimming.

Dammit, I could not deal with her tears. Not now. I shifted back and tugged on the coiled curl of Rachel's ponytail. "It's not you, Rach. I promise."

Clay moved to her side, his hand on her shoulder. "We have to talk about this someday."

"Not today."

I should have shaken off Chaos's supportive grip, but I so rarely had someone to hold on to.

She hadn't bothered to bring in anything other than the food and I was more than grateful to make a hasty exit. The minute the door closed behind us, I dragged Chaos in for a hard kiss.

She tried to gentle me, her long fingers cupping my face with compassion in both her touch and in those golden eyes of hers.

"Maybe you should stay," I said softly, hoping like hell she didn't listen to me.

"I'm with you."

"It's not a good idea." All the ragged edges I was usually good at keeping tucked away were exposed like knives right now. What if I cut her?

She pulled one of my arms around her back then looped her arms around my neck. "I'm the queen of bad ideas, remember?"

"This isn't a game." But my fingers dug into her jeans, holding her tighter. Evidently, I was a bastard enough to keep her. I couldn't protect her from the asshole who was stalking her and I sure as fuck couldn't protect her from me.

"No, Ransom. We aren't a game. But I'm not letting you go home alone like this."

"And what exactly are you going to do?"

She went onto her toes and closed her mouth over mine. The slide of her tongue was aggressive and rough enough to activate all the frustrations living inside me. I gripped the back of her head and slanted my lips across hers for more.

Deeper, harder. I wasn't going to be happy until her taste replaced all my anger and pain.

I groaned as her hand slid down to cup my dick. "Chaos," I said against her mouth. "You sure you want to go down this road?"

She nipped my lower lip. "What road have *you* been on? We've been heading to your king-sized bed for days."

I gripped her ass. "Wanting you is obvious. The bigger question is if this is a good idea."

"I don't hear a question in your voice. Because you know you want this too." She increased the tension around my cock. "I definitely want this."

I pressed my forehead to hers. "You deserve anyone but me. But fuck if I care right now." I stepped away from her, clasping her hand before I stalked down the steps.

For God's sake, we were probably on Rachel's and Clay's security cameras. That was a problem for another day.

I stalked to my Jeep and opened the passenger door. Crowding her into the space between me and the seat, I buried my face in her lemon-scented neck. Her hair smelled clean and expensive, but lemons lived in my head when it came to her.

Hell, they were waiting for me in dreams.

"Put your seatbelt on, Chaos. I'm going to be driving like I'm trying out for *The Fast and the Furious.*"

She climbed up into the vehicle, making sure to drag her hip along my aching cock. "Just call me Letty."

I slammed the door with a wide smile. Leave it to Chaos to pick the biggest risktaker in that series of movies. I pulled out of the drive and skidded on the gravel as we sped down the winding road.

The sun was coasting along the edges of the trees. I chased sunset to my house. It was a mere five miles away, but it felt like a million.

Her smile was as wild as a summer breeze as she held onto the oh-shit handle. She kept shifting in her seat as if she couldn't stand the wait either.

"You're killing me."

She aimed that fierce smile at me. "Probably bad form to reach into these jeans and take the edge off, right?"

"Don't you fucking dare."

I slammed my foot on the accelerator and switched my engine from electric to gas. It kicked forward as she lowered the window. The wind whipped her auburn hair around her.

She turned on the radio and for once, I didn't care that she'd put on one of her shitty pop playlists. The driving beat echoed the heart-beat that was throbbing behind my zipper.

Her laugh was pure joy and sutured some of the cracks that had tried to open against my will. Since they were too damn close to the surface, I'd take the break she offered me.

Gratefully.

I turned off on my road. It wasn't as winding as Clay's, but it was barely paved. I fishtailed once and her eyes widened with excitement. I parked and before I could come around to open her door, she was already out and running toward me.

I braced for her, and she wrapped those ridiculously long legs around me. I gripped her ass and lifted her higher onto my waist, making a beeline for the porch.

Midnight was still out hunting in the woods, thank fuck. I leaned her into the doorjamb as I fished out my keys. She wiggled against me, doing her damnedest to drive me mad with her mouth on my neck.

I kicked open the door.

"Wait."

I held her against me, my breathing already fast and chaotic. Of course, she'd changed her mind. This madness was too much for her.

"Midnight."

I narrowed my eyes. "He's off playing in the woods."

She nudged the bin of food with her foot. "I don't plan on letting you up for air any time soon."

I juggled her enough for me to dip down and dump a huge scoop of food into his bowl. "Happy?"

"Happy." She linked her arms around my neck. "Take me to bed or lose me forever."

I closed my mouth over hers and swallowed her sunshine. I didn't have an answer to that one. I would probably lose her forever before I was ready, but for now, I was keeping her.

And the sunshine.

I slammed the door with my foot and stalked through the kitchen to the stairs. There was just enough sun left to light my way up the stairs.

She tipped her head and looked down at me, playing with the short hairs at the nape of my neck. I slowed my steps as I got to the top.

She lowered her mouth to mine and the kiss was no less wild, but this time, it was a slow burn. The kind that could last for days.

I pressed her into the wall at the top of the stairs and sunk into her flavors and textures. The warmth of her skin and the softness of her lips, the slow slide of her tongue along mine.

I skated my way down her chin to her neck as she arched back for me. Her collarbone looked so damn delicate. No straps, no jewelry, just endless freckles. I blazed my way across to her shoulder and scraped my teeth over the roundness there before lifting her again.

My gait was slow down the dark hallway. More of the late day sun streamed through the windows of my room. There wasn't much of it left, but maybe this first time, I could take her here in the shafts of sun.

Her soft, golden skin and long, supple arms and legs spread out on my bed.

I hardened again at the thought as I set her on her feet and drew the sweater over her head. I was right.

There was nothing underneath it. Just her softness and the cinnamon tips of her breasts. I pulled off my shirt and tossed it behind me.

She reached for me, her fingertips trailing over the coin at my neck to the ridges of each muscle along my belly to the patch of hair hair above my jeans. Her gaze never left mine as she flicked open the button then slowly drew the zipper down.

I hissed as my aching shaft finally was given a little relief from the pressure. She pushed at my jeans, and I tried to step away, but she held me still.

She crouched before me and tore at my boot laces, freeing one foot then the other, and then she tugged my jeans the rest of the way off.

I dragged in a breath as she nuzzled her cheek over my boxers, her smile wicked as she shoved at her own jeans until they pooled at her feet. A scrap of bronze-colored panties clung high on her hips, showing off every blessed inch of her—starting at the slight curve of her hips to the endless legs I would be exploring for hours. My gaze tracked up to her belly then to the upturned nipples on her breasts.

I ran the back of my knuckle along her thigh up to follow the line of her panties and on up to her middle. Even as she shivered, she leaned into my touch. When I got to the heavy underside of her breast, I coasted lightly around the curve to the tip.

I watched her eyes dilate as I flicked her nipple then pinched. The cinnamon color went dark in the low light. I lowered my mouth to taste her, swirling my tongue around the tip before I sucked strongly.

She cupped the back of my head and arched her back. I wrapped my other arm around her waist to make sure she didn't fall, but I took advantage of her surrender.

I took my time, sipping the sunshine off her skin. Her softness and fragility weren't lost on me. I didn't deserve to be touching her, but I'd worship her for as long as she allowed it.

I slid my leg between hers and felt my mattress against my knee. I lifted her, holding her tight to me as I crawled up the bed. Her uncontainable curls spread across my sheets as she rose under me, my name barely more than breath on her lips.

Reversing course, I dragged my mouth down her neck to her chest and over her ribs. She stared down at me. No shrinking violet here. She was an active and full participant.

She lifted her leg to drag her heel down my calf. "Where do you think you're going?"

I grinned up at her as I lifted the material of her panties away from her hip with my teeth. "They're in the way."

I dragged them down and tossed them over my shoulder as I opened her wide.

She scratched at my shoulders. "Oh, no, you don't. Up here, buddy."

"Never had anyone say no to this direction."

"Second round. Maybe third." She pulled my hair. "I need you up here. On me. Inside me."

I didn't need to be told twice.

I caged her with my arms, hissing as her fingers explored my back before following a meandering path around to my belly. Finally, she cupped me through my shorts. My necklace swung between us, glinting in the fading sun.

I lowered my hips to rub along her center. She lifted her legs, and I shook my head. "Open for me."

She let her legs fall open wider and I undulated against her from center to chest. My tongue swirled along her collarbone to her neck.

Her hands roamed down my back to cup my ass so she could hold me tighter against her slit.

"You sure you don't want me to have a little taste down there?"

She shook her head and angled her head to catch my mouth. "Inside me," she said against my lips. "You've been teasing me for days."

I kissed my way down her neck and lower to tease her breasts.

"Ransom." She gripped my hip with her leg.

"I need a little something first."

"Bet that little something is in the drawer over there."

I laughed against her bellybutton and flicked my tongue into the little divot.

As her hips rose, I dragged my bearded chin along the skin just above her pussy. "Nope."

"No?" She lifted her head to stare down at me. Her expression was on the verge of crazed. I liked her desperate.

Knowing she wanted me as much as I wanted her was a heady experience. And I'd damn sure need to have it more than just this once.

I lowered my mouth to her warmth. She was swollen and so goddamn wet for me, I couldn't resist a taste.

She levered upward off the bed, spurring me on. I had to have more. I slid my hands under her ass and held her tight to my mouth. She was sweet and salty and tasted better than she had any right to.

Already, I knew her tells.

She lifted against my mouth as I ground my chin against her and sucked her tight clit between my lips. She drenched my mouth, my chin, and I chased her soft groans until they were choked sobs.

I left her there on the edge and pushed off the bed.

She jerked up with murder in her eyes. If she'd had a weapon, I would've feared for my dick.

Thankfully, her only weapon was her glare, as formidable as it was.

"Be right back."

Chapter 19

Willow

Guarded Hearts

He did not just leave me like that.

No freaking way.

I slapped the mattress beside me. "If you try to tell me there are no condoms in that bathroom... Sir! You will be walking that fine ass to get my purse in the car!"

He stood in the bathroom doorway, the light silhouetting every delicious inch of him. And that jerk had a smile on his face. He turned the light off and tossed the box at me. "I'm always prepared, Chaos. You should know that."

I caught it and shook it. "Should get us through tonight."

His eyebrow arched. "Bet?"

"No way. It's been a while. But should last us the week." I dug inside and took one out. "C'mere."

He put his hands on his hips. "Just like that?"

"Just like that."

"Such a romantic." But he sauntered toward me, his eyes glittering in the waning sun. I much preferred the teasing glint than the banked pain from earlier.

Saying nothing, he tucked a lock of my hair behind my ear and waited for me to make my move.

I rolled to my knees in front of him and took my time checking him out. The peaks and valleys of his chest were staggering. He was so hard everywhere, but today I'd finally figured out there was a bit of marshmallow in there.

That big heart of his was what he guarded more closely than anything in his life.

I traced the coin that laid on his chest and continued down the ridges of his pectoral muscles to the arrow of his eight-pack. Over-achiever Ransom wouldn't have a simple six pack. Oh, no.

His gaze stayed steady on my hands while I discovered just what would make this stoic man crack. He shivered as I reached the elastic of his boxes. I lifted my gaze to meet his as I drew them over his hips, letting them drop to the floor.

Nothing left between us now.

I inched forward, pressing the silky hardness of his shaft against my belly. His nostrils flared as I curled my fingers around him. Right at that moment, I was glad for my long fingers.

God, he was impressive.

My thumb drifted along the underside of his flared head.

He dragged in a hiss of a breath, but he didn't move. He let me have the control. And I was grateful. It gave me a few minutes to learn him before I got pulled under by his intensity.

Once he got his mouth on me, I lost myself.

I reached beside me for the condom on the bed. His eyes went shark-flat as I released him, but he didn't inch back to give me any space.

Tension practically emanated from his pores. His muscles locked and his jaw was so close to granite, I'd bet his molars were dust.

But he waited. He didn't rush me.

Slowly, I rolled the condom over him, watching his face the entire time. The last rays of sun left turned his cheekbones golden and gilded all the hard lines of him, making him just a bit softer.

I slipped my hands behind his neck to draw him close. He didn't shut his eyes as I nibbled at the corner of his mouth. "I'm so ready for this."

"Good thing one of us is." He looped his arm around me before he dragged me out diagonally on his lake-sized bed. Then he shifted over me, bracing his arm beside my head.

I touched his lip. "I figured we'd be on the stairs, barely able to resist one another."

His lips kicked up in the corner in that endearing smirk I was beginning to crave. "Next time."

"Gonna plan my ravishment?" I dragged my leg along his hip and groaned at how close he was to sliding inside of me.

He rolled his hips and there he was. Watchful. Purposeful. *Mine.* At least for this moment. And finally, inside of me.

I arched up to meet him in a long, languorous meeting of bodies.

He took my hand away from his mouth and laced our fingers above my head as he drove into me harder with each stroke. Rising over me in the last winks of light.

The sun didn't allow me to see the winding wildness of us now, but I felt it. I embraced it, winding my legs around him as I took everything he offered. Opening for him, softening for all his jagged edges.

I bowed up under him as he crushed me closer with his other arm, his teeth scraping down my neck as he gritted out my name.

Not Chaos.

Willow.

He let my hand go and I dug my nails into his shoulder, hanging on as he braced himself against the mattress and lost himself in me as I lost myself in him.

The night closed in on us, cocooning us in only the sounds of our bodies coming together.

We rolled and I rose above him, the sudden coolness of the air a shock. He sat up, lifting his hips to get back inside me again and again. Holding me in a vise grip as if he couldn't believe I was there.

As if he thought I might vanish.

I twined myself around him and accepted the savageness between us was just part of what we were. A clash of wills that knew no boundaries. The friction was too much for me to resist. I shook around him, unsure of how I'd ever live without this even as I shattered and was rebuilt stronger to take more.

He held me tight and the once controlled glide of his cock inside me turned frantic. He was chasing something, but I wouldn't allow him to outrun this.

Not now.

I gripped the back of his head and dragged his mouth to mine. "Ransom. Ransom. Ransom."

His guttural groan slashed against my mouth, and he let go. I rode his pleasure and took more, demanding for him to stay with me. Our kisses went from clashes of lips and teeth to lazy sweetness.

I was fairly certain my legs were noodles and muscles I hadn't known I had access to screamed in revolt, but I didn't let go.

Finally, he dropped back onto the mattress, his chest heaving as he actually laughed.

I collapsed on top of him, our legs a tangle as we both groaned from whatever *that* had been. Tornado? Twister? Hurricane?

Perfection.

I rested my cheek against his stomach and turned to kiss his sweat-soaked skin. "Sir..."

He lifted his head. "Sir?"

"Sir." I lengthened the *r* until it was a sigh. "That was well worth the wait."

His head fell back on the bed. "I thought you were trying to kill me."

I wiggled my way up to rest against his chest. He toyed with my hair as we just laid there for a few minutes. So many words tried to bubble up in my throat, but I waited them out.

The endorphin rush of sex made pillow talk dangerous. And I really didn't want to fuck this up.

With my nail, I outlined the coin resting on his cooling skin. "This must be pretty important. You don't seem like a jewelry guy."

He pressed his lips to my forehead. "Was my great grandfather's. When he escaped Russia, he took a single coin to remember his homeland before he started over."

I lifted my head. "Wait, you came from sentimental people?"

"Imagine that?" He kissed me gently.

I touched his face, cherishing the afterglow for another minute. This kiss was unhurried and sweet, making me so very glad of the dark since my stupid eyes wouldn't stop stinging.

Suddenly, he got to his feet and tossed me over his shoulder again.

"You gotta stop this."

He slapped my ass. "We need a shower. And then I'm starting over at the beginning."

I went limp over his shoulder so I could reach his ass to give him an answering smack. "Your shower is glorious. I am a fan of this plan."

My heart tumbled and broke right open at his laugh. I was so screwed. But maybe I wasn't meant to guard my heart against him.

Maybe this was where I was supposed to be.

Clearly, his masterful control of my body included all the hand-held sprayers in his posh shower. Steam and orgasms were a perfect balm to the long, stressful days we'd endured lately.

This time, when he lifted me into his arms wrapped in one of his plush towels, I was happy to snuggle into his chest. I decided romantic Ransom was a wonder and if I talked too much, maybe he'd disappear.

He rolled me into his bed and followed me, curling around me from the back.

"What about Midnight?"

"He's used to sleeping outside." He nuzzled my ear. "Sleep, Chaos."

"It's early," I mumbled.

"Shh."

"Ransom?"

He sighed. "Yeah?"

I nuzzled into the pillow and pulled his arm more securely around my waist. "I wasn't expecting you."

"Look at that. We can agree on something. Now shut off."

I smiled into the darkness. "Yes, sir."

He bit my shoulder lightly and I drifted into dreams with a laugh.

Chapter 20

Ransom

Gone

I woke to banging and music.

Startled, I sat up. How the hell had she gotten out of bed without me noticing?

Especially since I'd been wrapped around her like a lovesick teenager. I scrubbed my hands over my face then rolled off the bed.

Dragging on a pair of sweats against the cool morning air, I took the time to wash my face and brush my teeth before heading downstairs.

The noise level seemed to indicate she was fine. Unless she was weirded out and had needed to get out of bed.

Christ. I wasn't used to worrying about the morning after. Namely because I didn't bring women into my house.

One and dones were usually easier to handle at the woman's place. Or a hotel back when I'd been on assignment. Even better when I was on leave.

I slowed as I went down the stairs. As usual, my kitchen was in shambles. She had a tripod set up on some rickety version of a stand. She had it clamped to an apple box—God only knew where she'd found that—and a plastic bin full of my backup dog food from the closet for height.

Her hair was up in one of those fluffy knot things on top of her head. She'd stolen my Army sweatshirt again, but she'd gone at it with a pair of scissors, opening the neckline to slide off her shoulder.

A black tank peeked out as she leaned forward to put the finishing touches on something with a pile of berries.

My gaze tracked to the fact that she was missing her damn pants. My sweatshirt was big enough to cover all the vital parts, but still.

Jesus. All that damn leg was going to kill me.

Especially since they were encased in some sort of long...socks? Was that even the right word? They were nearly the same green as my sweatshirt and looked as soft as a cloud. They climbed up to her thighs, making her look like a cozy dream come true.

She looked up from her food masterpiece and smiled at me. The sun streaming onto the kitchen island made her glow, for fuck's sake.

"You're just in time to try my newest invention." She blew her hair out of her face and swiped confectioner's sugar onto her face with the back of her hand.

"You didn't wake me." Inwardly, I winced. Lovely. Now I sounded as if I was whining.

She shrugged. "You were out."

"You should have stayed with me."

Straightening up, she grinned widely, making my gut drop. She had no right being that damn beautiful. "Did you miss me?" Her laugh was bright and bawdy, but she didn't call me out any further. "I only uploaded enough videos until tomorrow. Wanted to get a few done before I went to see Rach for lunch."

I hit the bottom stair. "Hmm."

She rolled her eyes as she popped a raspberry into her mouth. "Wedding stuff is gonna be a thing. You can't cuff me to the bed."

"I can't?" I came closer and slid my arm around her waist.

Her eyes danced. "We can try it. Not that your headboard is set up for such things."

220

"I'm creative." I lifted her hand to snag one of the raspberries from her fingers, then I brushed her cheek with my thumb. "Got a little something."

"Oh, gosh." She wrinkled her nose. "Powdered sugar gets everywhere." She rubbed at her face with one of my oversized cotton towels. This time, she streaked raspberry juice on herself instead.

"You're a mess."

Instead of being embarrassed, she just laughed. "This is definitely going on my bloopers reel."

I pulled out another towel from my drawer and wet it to swipe at her cheek. "Bloopers?"

"Still rolling." I tried to back up, but she just dragged me closer. "I can delete it."

I glanced at the camera, not comfortable with the idea of being on her account. But it might come in handy to show I was more than just someone on the fringes of her life. To reiterate that she was mine.

For the cameras.

"You want me on your channel?"

She grinned. "You'll blow up my channel." She flicked a bit of sugar on my chest.

"Hey!"

She pressed her tongue behind her teeth as she flicked more at me. "Sugared abs and pecs for a thirst trap?"

"Me, a thirst trap? Unlikely." I used the towel to wipe away the sugar, thankful I wasn't overly hairy.

She maneuvered me in front of the camera. "Step on that little piece of tape on the floor."

"You kill my sweatshirt and now there's tape on my floor?"

"Like I was going to give back this sweatshirt."

I glanced over my shoulder. "I've had it since bootcamp."

"Then you shouldn't have given it to me. It's too soft to give back."

This was ridiculous. I should be out doing a perimeter check or contacting Aidan for an update. Anything but this. I shook my head, but I let her position me just the same.

"Now you get to try my sorbet."

"What? Am I supposed to drip it on myself?"

"No. Just taste it." She slid her arms around me from behind and teased her nails along my belly. "We can try it off your skin later. That's not for prying eyes." She peeked around me, speaking to the camera. "Or is it?"

I didn't know what to say to that one.

Her laugh was free and so very Chaos. "How to get a million followers in one day." She grabbed her phone off the counter and stood in front of me, lifting her phone in that familiar way of hers. "Want to make a debut on my stories?"

I folded my arms and leaned against the kitchen island, the icy treat forgotten. "Sure you want to go official?"

Her laughter trailed off. "Is that what we are? I mean, stories only last for twenty-four hours."

"And how many people watch them?"

"A lot."

"How many are your family?"

"I don't know." Her voice was a mere whisper.

I reached for her phone. "It's okay."

She shook her head and flicked something on her screen. "Try my food."

I scooped up a bit of the dark raspberry sorbet and held it out for her. This moment reminded me of our churro truck day, but this time, I knew what the end result would be.

Her under me.

Amused, her wide distractible mouth slid into a smirk. "Don't worry, everyone. He'll get this story thing eventually. People want to see *you* try it, stud."

I didn't look at her phone. Just her. Finally, she rolled her eyes and took a taste. When she licked her lips, I took the phone and tossed it on the counter.

"Ransom!" Her laugh filled the sunny room. "That's not how it works."

Then her cool lips were against mine with the sharpness of her recipe for sorbet as a chaser. As I hauled her in, the spoon clattered to the floor.

She slung her arms around my neck, making the sweatshirt inch higher. So, I cupped her delicious, made-for-my-hands ass. She'd stolen a pair of my boxers as well and the soft cotton felt better on her than it ever had on me.

I let myself fall into the kiss, not rushing to do anything else. No filling my time with my woodworking or the chores I created for myself to push away any emotions. I stayed right there in the moment and drowned in the lemon and raspberry scents she'd created.

A mess around us, but the perfect kind of chaos in my arms.

When I pulled back, her hazel eyes were fuzzy with desire and happiness.

"What was that for?"

"Do I need a reason?" I slipped my hands under the sweatshirt to lace my fingers at her lower back.

"No, I don't suppose so. Is this what you're like with a woman you're sleeping with?"

"Nope."

Her eyes narrowed.

"Just you."

"Oh." She pressed her lips together and broke our gaze. "Not sure what to think about that."

"Do we need to think?"

She frowned. "Who are you?"

I laughed. "For once, I don't want to plan things to death. Can't we just be? Get through the wedding and see what happens after that?"

And there was the truth of our involvement. It wasn't to push the case forward or for any other purpose. All I wanted was to be with her.

Which made me want to walk right out the door to my workshop or take a ten-mile hike. But I didn't.

The lines had blurred, and I didn't know what to do about that. The plan to make myself the target instead of her had seemed like a good idea at the time. Now I was afraid I'd be less effective as her bodyguard, but I still didn't back away.

I couldn't.

She lifted onto her toes and kissed me out of the deluge of dark thoughts. I crushed her into me and lifted her onto the counter. She yelped.

I pushed away the bowls and utensils she'd been using then wrapped her endless legs around me. "What are these things?" I snapped the long leg warmer-thing at the top of her thigh.

"Another one from the box. I get sent a lot of free stuff."

I raised one brow.

"To my PO Box."

"Hmm." I trailed my finger over the raised braid on the long sock that reminded me of a fisherman's sweater. "I like this box of yours."

"Is that right?"

"Guess you'll have to surprise me with something else later." I tugged the sweatshirt over her head.

"What about the video?"

I swirled my tongue along the length of her neck. "Later."

She tugged at the knot in my sweatpants. "Video is still rolling, stud."

I jerked back, searching her gaze to see if she was kidding.

She reached behind her and fumbled for something.

"Turning up the sound?"

She giggled and pointed something at the camera. "Now it's off."

"Thought we were making a movie." I smiled into the kiss as she drew me in.

"Definitely not the usual content for my channel." She played with my hair. "Now if you want to add something to my personal collection..."

"Yours?"

She wrinkled her nose. "Like I'd give it to you."

"How can I trust you with my bare ass?"

"That's true. It is a very fine ass. Definitely sharable."

The song changed to a bubbly Hozier song made for kitchen dancing. I pulled her down and twirled her around in the narrow space between the island and the other counter to the opposite side where we had much more room.

The bright smile on her face was worth the impulse.

"Who taught you to dance?"

"You wouldn't believe me." I spun her out, our fingertips tangling lightly before I dragged her close so her back was to my chest and our hips naturally fell into a rhythm. I took full advantage of her bare shoulder.

She slid her ass across the front of my sweatpants. "Tell me it was kindly barmaid on shore leave."

"I was not in the Navy, babe." I turned her around and lifted my arms into a classic ballroom dancing pose as she came back to me. She was all arms and legs and only about twenty percent grace, but she fit me. "My grandmother." I grinned down at her as I held her waist firmly and walked her into a simple box step.

She threw back her head with a laugh.

The song changed to a rough-hewn male voice offset by a heavy beat. "Once you know the basics, you can do just about anything." I pulled her in and slid my leg through hers to grind her along my thigh, *Dirty Dancing*-style. To her delight, I dipped her back in a wide arc.

When she straightened, there was only Chaos and sunlight and freckles.

I held her close as we moved in a slow, sexy sway. "How full is our day?"

She relaxed against me, pressing her cheek to my chest. "Very." Then she peered up at me. "*Our?*"

"Where you go, I go."

"I'll be perfectly fine with my sister. You definitely don't want to listen to us go over seating charts and favors."

"Favors?"

She blew out a breath. "Even a bougie rich dude wedding includes guest gifts, I guess." She toyed with my necklace, her usual signal she was about to say something important.

I rested my cheek against her head. She was just a touch too tall for me to tuck her under my chin. But somehow that meant she fit me better than anyone else ever had.

"Should I tell Rachel?"

"About us? Bet she figured it out."

"No. About the rest."

I didn't speak for a minute. I'd also wondered if we should bring them in on everything, but then I pictured my best friend doting on the woman who'd made him happier than I'd ever seen him and couldn't pull the trigger. "We don't really have much to tell them yet. But if you want to, I'll follow your lead."

She sighed. "I hate this."

"I know. I'm not a fan of it either."

And I'd do whatever needed to be done to make sure she was out of the line of fire. If this piece of human garbage came at me, all the better.

I ran my fingertip along the fluffy material at the top of her thigh. "Were these for me?"

Lightly, she swept her lips across my chest. "Maybe."

"Did I mention I really like this box of yours?"

She snorted against my skin. "You certainly do like my box."

"Dirty mind." I drew my fingers up her leg to the bottoms of the pilfered boxers. The soft crease of her thigh and the curve of her ass were the only thing underneath. Gently, I slipped my fingers a little deeper. She trembled at my touch, making me bolder. "But you are correct. And look how warm and wet you are for me."

I coasted around to the front of her and watched her face as I stroked along the slickness waiting for me. Her eyes dilated as I slipped one finger inside of her, rewarded with a shaky hiss. I already wanted to feel that clasping warmth around me again.

Her nipples beaded up under the thin cotton of her tank as she lightly undulated her hips in time to each dip and glide of my fingers. I turned my hand to get deeper, instinctively using the sultry upbeat song now playing to pick up the pace.

Her head fell back as I flicked my thumb along her tight clit. She was so goddamn wet and swollen for me. I held her tight, my other hand gripping her ass as I increased the pressure, scraping my teeth along her neck to get to her ear. "Come for me. Here in the sunshine."

Last night had been in the dark. Sighs and groans, sweat, and so much tension, I'd expected us to snap right in two. Today there was no darkness. Just her in the golden sunshine as she quaked around my hand. I was tempted to drop to my knees again.

Her taste was an addiction.

The bite of her nails in my shoulders as she surged against me was a high I'd ride daily. Hourly. Minute by minute. I'd give her every second of the day just to hear her come apart under me. She snaked a hand between us, her nails clawing at my wrist as I took more, demanded all.

"Feel how wet you are for me." I dragged her hand to her soaking slit. "For me."

Her head snapped up to meet my gaze. "Inside me."

I lifted my hand to tangle in her hair, our lips rough and tongues tangling to echo our fight for control. She pushed at my sweatpants with her other hand, finding her way under cotton to my cock.

I loved that she wasn't afraid to touch me. To stroke me hard and tight. I groaned against her neck. "Those condoms are still upstairs, Chaos."

"Bag," she said on a guttural cry. "On the floor."

"Prepared." I slipped my fingers out of her warmth. Drew my middle finger into my mouth.

"Good God." She pushed me back and grabbed her bag as we

stumbled into the living room.

She dumped her entire bag on my loveseat and grabbed a blue wrapper.

"What is *that*?"

"Blue raspberry, I think."

"For fuck's sake."

She shrugged and stripped off her boxers.

"Blue raspberry, it is."

She crowded into me and reached into my sweats. "Blue light saber?"

"Christ, it doesn't glow, does it?"

Her husky laugh made me harder if that was even possible. "Don't sound so horrified. Who's gonna see it?"

I tilted back my head and couldn't stop the groan as she fisted me.

"Tick-tock. How bad do you want it, Grumpasaurus?"

I snatched the condom out of her hand, tripping back onto the couch when she pantsed me. Those golden-green eyes were a little wild as she straddled me, then she plucked the condom out of my fingers.

Then it didn't really matter what color it was. She climbed on and angled me to take me all the way home in one warm, perfect glide.

I drove my fingers into her hair as she rode me slowly. I dragged her mouth to mine, swallowing all her soft sighs as I lifted my hips to meet her each time. Her lips spread into a smile as she took me again and again.

I lowered my hands to her hips, but there was no stopping the rhythm she'd set. Slow as a wave on the shore and punctuated with a heavenly sigh as she drew me in over and over. She reached above her head, stretching her long arms up and lifting her breasts high.

Right into my eyeline.

Leaning forward, I bit one tight tip through the cotton before pushing the tank up and off. I needed nothing between us. Her internal rhythm had my eyes crossing as I tried to keep up with her.

"Right there," she whispered, and I arrowed up to match her stroke for stroke.

Lazy movements tripped into hard slaps of skin on skin. My hands slid forward to tease her lower belly and both thumbs dipped down into the downy patch of hair above where we were joined.

She lowered her arms to rest on my shoulders, her hazy gaze zeroing in on my hands. Her lips parted and her breathing increased. I drew little circles on her flesh, but I didn't touch her clit just yet. I knew what she needed. Knew I could push her over in a blink.

I waited her out.

She grasped at her nipple, grinding against my dick as our game of wills grew more frantic.

When I opened my legs, she fell forward enough to grip the couch behind my head. "Ransom."

Her angle gave me complete access. I groaned, my thumbs drifting lower into the wet heat of her. Her thighs shook as we held each other on the pinnacle. I caught her mouth in a slow tangle of tongues as I lightly teased her clit.

She hummed into my mouth, her breath shuddering into me as she bounced against me harder, looking for that friction I knew she craved. I gripped the back of her head with one hand and held her there, our lips mere millimeters apart now.

Her eyes locked on mine.

Then I circled and stroked, chasing her when she tried to pull away.

She was shaking and I was fucking lost.

Her groan as she came was pure, agonizing beauty. She arched her back and my name streaked the air. I surged up into her, riding those shockwaves as she squeezed around my dick.

As if I had a choice but to follow her into the void.

My hands shook, but I held onto her as she collapsed against me, all unbound curls and sweaty skin.

My sunlit goddess who had no fucking idea just how gone I was for her.

Chapter 21

Willow

Temporary Clash of Skin

I lifted one fist in the air. "Blue condoms for the win."

He laughed underneath my now wrecked hair, which I couldn't even see through. He'd literally fucked the tie loose from my hair. That was a new one. As was the double decker orgasm that had just about killed me.

"I'm not sure I can move."

He drew his arms away, letting them flop onto the couch. "Make that two of us."

I giggled into his neck and somehow found some strength to straighten up. I was usually energized after sex, but nothing seemed ordinary about how we came together.

Literally.

The less joyous bits of our post sexual haze had us both wincing. He kissed me hard and fast before lifting me off him. Instantly, I felt like I was missing something.

Somehow he'd become the key to a lock inside me I hadn't even known existed.

I slumped onto the couch and prayed for a magical teleporter that could put me into his shower.

"Be right back."

Not gonna lie—it was pretty funny to watch him shuffle off to the bathroom with his sweatpants around his calves. I gave him a wolf whistle and he lifted a middle finger into the air.

Giggling, I hauled myself off the couch and found his—now mine —sweatshirt hanging off a lampshade. I'd never been the kind of woman who inspired flying clothes.

Personally, I was shocked just how fully in the moment Ransom was with me. I'd figured it would be a temporary clash of skin and wills and then he'd go off in a corner and be grumpy, not re-enact a Patrick Swayze moment in the kitchen. And I was definitely as awkward as Baby holding the watermelon.

I had *not* been prepared for that side of him. I was in so much freaking trouble. How was I supposed to hold out against him?

I was pulling on the sweatshirt as he came back from the bathroom.

"Damn. I was hoping to hide that."

I flipped my hair outside the ragged neckline, then I pulled up my sagging thigh-high tights. "It's mine, buddy."

He slid an arm around my back. "Was more for the naked thing."

I rested my hands on his chest. "I would prefer to stay naked all—"

"Sold."

Laughing, I shook my head. "Rachel."

He tipped his head back with a huff. "Wedding stuff."

"Wedding stuff. And I've been home for days and have barely spent any time with her."

Was that because secretly, I wondered if I should have even allowed myself to come here? Maybe it would be better for my family's sake to be the flighty sister and just disappear.

"Why don't you have her come over here? I can hide in my workshop and still keep an eye on you."

Was he rubbing off on me? That watchful worst case scenario mind of his had to be infecting me from our skin-to-skin contact.

I narrowed my eyes. "Just how will you do that?"

"Sure you want to know?"

"So, I'm not the only one with a camera?"

"I'm security-conscious."

I sighed because I understood. "Sucks that your life is to that level even without my...problem."

He kissed my forehead. "I'm not going to let anything happen to you."

I held onto him an extra minute. What if it wasn't only me in the crosshairs? My decision to come here had been made in haste, and maybe I hadn't considered the potential repercussions before. But I sure was now.

"I know. But I have to go over to the orchard. We're checking out the chapel and the Gala room where the reception is going to be."

"What's to check out? You've known the Ronsons since birth."

"Don't get snarky with me. We're setting up the decorations and the flowers will be coming in so we need to know where everything should go."

He let out a slow hiss of breath.

"Hey, you knew what was up when you took me on."

"I know."

I trailed my finger down his belly to tangle with the loose strings of his sweats. "Rewards will be yours later." I tied his sweatpants into a loopy bow.

"I'll hold you to that." Another hard kiss pushed me off balance with a barrage of emotions I was too wigged out to try to puzzle through. At least not while all this uncertainty surrounded us.

"Go shower and I'll finish posting a video." I headed into the kitchen and searched through the wreckage on the kitchen island to find my phone. I flicked it on to find the four clips ready for posting in my stories.

Ransom followed. "Are you doing that now?"

"I guess we'll see. I have to review our footage."

"Shower first." He turned me toward the stairs.

"Oh, I get to climb them myself?"

"You wrung me dry, Chaos."

I smiled at him over my shoulder. "Yeah?"

"You know you did." He snapped the elastic at the top of my tights. "Get going."

I started up the stairs and stopped when he didn't come up behind me. "You're not joining me?"

"I gotta check on some stuff. I'll be up in a minute."

Ahh, there was the Ransom I knew and I—whoa. Nope, that word wasn't coming out anywhere near me.

Damn weddings messed with even the most level-headed woman's mind. And I wasn't exactly level-headed most days.

I ran up the stairs and tried to ignore my racing heart. I was just in lust. Not the other l-word.

Absolutely not. Not that fast.

No freaking way.

I posted the short video clips to my stories without reviewing them. I didn't have the mental fortitude to see him grinning at me again.

By the time I got out of the shower, my notifications unfurled on my screen like a drugstore receipt full of coupons. *Holy crap.* I thumbed through a few, beyond overwhelmed as I towel-dried my curls.

I could feel my hair expanding exponentially. I still didn't have all of my things here—including my curly hair serums.

Another reason to leave his place. I needed to get my SUV. Ransom kept carting me around and distracting me, dammit.

I picked up my discarded clothes and padded into his bedroom to drape them on the chair. My box of goodies was full of social media fads, but I could probably find something to wear.

I dug through and found the butt-tacular yoga pants that had been in a wildfire meme for the ultimate work-from-home clothing that could drive your man wild. Hmm. I'd never wanted to show my legs and butt off for anyone before.

My claim to fame was my humor and tips and tricks, not my buns of steel.

Before I could overthink it, I tugged on the pants and found a fluffy raspberry-colored cropped sweater that I must've tossed in there by accident. I slipped it on and fussed with it in the mirror. "Not bad."

Hid the no bra thing and everything. Score.

I was braiding my hair when one of the boards in the hall squeaked.

"Jesus."

I turned at his voice and tried valiantly not to grin. "I'll just run downstairs while you get ready."

"You're not going anywhere."

"Don't look at me like that."

With several steps, he was in front of me. He looked deliciously ruffled as if he'd been outside. "Like what?" He tugged me against him, and I hissed at his cold skin. It was a windy spring day, and he obviously hadn't bothered with a shirt. "You should warm me up."

"Nuh-uh. We have to go to Rachel's."

"C'mon, she won't care if we're late."

I looped my arms around him, my fingers tracking up his back and instinctively finding all his scars. Almost immediately, his blue eyes lost their playful expression.

Inwardly, I cursed. "Sorry."

"No need to be sorry."

"Do they hurt?" My voice was little more than a whisper.

"Not right now."

"But they do sometimes?"

"Old man aches. That's all."

I stood on my tiptoes and brushed a kiss over his stern mouth. "Old man aches, my ass." I kissed him until I felt his lips bend into a smile then peppered his lips and face with more.

"Okay, okay." He cupped my face. The dark cloudy gray was

gone, and a sweet light had come back into his eyes. "You make me forget the aches."

"Yeah?"

"Yeah." He brushed his nose along mine. "You make me forget a lot of things."

Then I forgot that I was supposed to be teasing him out of the mood I'd brought on and drowned in the taste of him. A long, unhurried kiss spiraled into so much more.

It was always like this with us. No easy touches for very long.

He slipped his hands up and under my sweater. A groan vibrated into my mouth when he only found skin. Those big, calloused hands scraped over my flesh with equal parts need and tenderness. His firm touch ramped me up like no other in my life.

It was tempting to let him take me under. His lake-sized bed would be far more fun than listening to my sister list off a zillion plans for the Gala room and the chapel. But I'd been avoiding her for far too long.

His sigh stirred the hair against my neck. "I'm losing you."

My heart stuttered. That wasn't what he meant, but it did give me some pause. How would things change when all of this was over?

More importantly, would *we* still matter?

Right now, I was his responsibility. Add in a hint of danger, and everything became much more intense. Watching over me was a job. Sex was a handy side benefit.

"Rachel."

"Not the name I was looking for you to say."

I huffed out a tiny laugh. "We have to leave someday."

He straightened, but he didn't remove his hands from under my sweater. "Who says?" His touch gentled even more as his thumb traced the underside of my breast.

I tugged his arms away from me before he could do his best to convince me. "Get ready."

Neatly, I slipped out of his reach. I knew he could catch me if he really wanted to.

Fire replaced the sweetness and the sadness in his storm cloud gaze. Part of me wanted to run to see what he'd do.

Would he chase me, or would he let me go?

Which one did I want?

I walked backwards out of the room. He fisted his hands at his sides, but he stayed put. The spring sunlight gilded his dark hair, turning him into a handsome warrior full of battle scars.

His chest heaved as he watched me go. The predator to the prey.

My nipples beaded under my clothes, making me want to reach up and give myself some relief. But I just turned and ran down the stairs.

He didn't come after me.

I heard the shower go on as I neared the bottom of the stairs. The kitchen was neat as a pin. My camera was on top of my repacked bag.

As if the bit of wildness between us here had never even happened.

With a sigh, I checked the camera. Had he reviewed the footage and erased it? Maybe I'd do the same.

How much had I gotten of us before I turned off the recording?

I rewound and his gravelly laughter filled the frame. He hadn't looked into the camera once.

His gaze stayed solely on me.

My heartbeat roared in my ears as I rewound it again to watch him hold out the spoon for me to taste the sorbet first.

"Nope. Not going to think about that anymore."

I scrubbed back to the earlier footage of me making the sorbet without a machine. There was a new gadget on the scene. The company had reached out to me already, but I'd wanted to give it a go on my own before making people spend hundreds of dollars.

I'd need to use my laptop to edit the video and parse it down to the three-minute threshold for videos on the apps I used.

"Just do it."

I clipped out the piece with Ransom. Did I really want to fuel any more reactions by showing off the new man in my life?

I used the quick and dirty video editor on my phone and posted it.

The response to my smaller daily stories was outrageous. Along with getting tons of reshares, comments from people trying to figure out who Ransom was dominated my replies. People had even created edits to find the mystery man who made me laugh.

Had my impetuous move been a mistake?

You didn't want to bring any of this home to your family, so instead you bring it all back to Ransom's doorstep?

True, it had ultimately been his decision to protect me, but he'd been anonymous before. Not any longer, thanks to me.

My fingers shook as my gaze blurred on one of my direct messages. This one was from *willowsheart611*.

"What's wrong?'

I turned. Ransom was in full-on work mode—his face impassive, his eyes flat gray and emotionless. "Nothing."

"Don't give me that shit, Chaos. Your shoulders are so tight I could see it from the stairs."

I didn't even bother reading the message. The damage was done, anyway.

I handed him my phone then went to the fridge for the pitcher of water he kept at the ready. My hand only shook slightly as I pulled down a glass.

"Fuck." He pulled out his phone and typed something.

I heard the chimes from the chat program Poe had put on my phone. His fingers flew over my screen, his jaw tightening with every tap.

Slowly, I drank the water, hoping it would help my parched throat. Suddenly, Poe's voice came through the speaker, filling the kitchen.

"I've got him. But the IP address is rerouted through a dozen servers. I'm pretty sure this fucker isn't in Alaska or Germany. Dammit, I can't follow him."

"Isn't he live right now?" Ransom's voice was tight and harsh.

"He is, but he's a smart fucker. I'm smarter." Poe's voice lit with excitement.

My fingers tightened on the glass as they played cat and mouse with someone. I didn't even know if it was the same guy who was doing all of this. Maybe it was just one more person who thought it would be fun to get in my head.

It was working.

The glass rattled as I set it down. I fisted my hands and did the breathing trick Ransom had taught me when we were on the patio at Aidan's.

Before I could do two repetitions, he was at my back, his strong arm looped around my middle to drag me against his warm body.

"Is it him?"

"I don't know."

I covered his arm with my hand. "I'm okay."

"Glad one of us is. I want to rip his spine out through his nose."

A shaky laugh bubbled out. The dark and rather graphic violence should have scared me, but it was good to know I wasn't overreacting. Then again, Ransom was the king of the overkill mindset. "I know the internet is full of creeps. In my head, I know it." My eyes stung as I swallowed down the lump trying to strangle me. "All I want to do is help people." My voice was scarcely a whisper and I hated it.

Hated that I'd gone so quickly from playfulness to happy orgasm glow to worry to fear.

"Get angry, babe. Angry is better than scared."

I swallowed again. "You're right." I pushed his arm away to stalk to the kitchen island where my phone was. I could still hear Poe tapping away through the speaker. "Poe?"

"Yeah?" Her voice seemed distracted.

"What could I do to draw him out?"

"Absolutely fucking not." Ransom's voice was a shot.

"Hear me out."

"No."

Well, this was certainly more the Ransom I was used to.

I folded my arms and squared off in front of him. "I want this figured out before the wedding. We have ten days."

A vein throbbed visibly in his forehead.

"Poe?"

"Give me a few hours. I have an idea, but I want to run it by Aidan. Ta." The line went dead.

"You're not doing something stupid. I don't care what Poe cooks up."

"Isn't it better to, I don't know, flush him out?"

"That only works on TV, babe."

I rolled my eyes. "You know what I mean. Play the game better than him."

"Since he's an unknown variable, I'm not playing jack shit. Especially when it comes to your life."

I sighed and stepped in front of him. "Isn't it better to be on the offense than the defense?"

His eyebrow arched. "Are you seriously throwing game plays at me?"

"I'm not wrong." I pressed my hand against his chest. My heart was racing at the thought of pushing this guy, but maybe it was better to do it now. "You know I'm not."

"I'm not risking you."

My chest tightened and my belly flipped, but I knew I was right to push on this. Ransom would keep me hidden in this house forever. A tiny part of me wanted to let him take care of me. I was so tired of doing everything myself. "It's not your decision."

"You came to me."

"I did. I also told you I wouldn't live in fear again. Some faceless guy who gets off on looking at me is not going to rule my life. We don't even know if he wants to do anything more than follow me."

"That's the first stupid thing I've heard you say."

I jerked back. He'd narrowed his eyes and I literally watched a wall come down between us. "Yeah, well this stupid woman is going to go help her sister create her dream wedding. You can come or not."

Chapter 22

Ransom

Orchard Advice

This was the part that reminded me why I stayed in my own goddamn lane when it came to women. She didn't see reason and now it was my fault for pointing it out.

The ride to the orchard was a silent one. Well, except for the sound of Chaos aggressively swiping on her iPad. I didn't even know that was possible.

Then again, when it came to Chaos anything was. Including making me sex-stupid. The orgasms had obviously gone to my head. I had to remember that protecting her was the most important part. As well as turning the sniper scope back on me.

She was not going to become the target again.

I slapped the eco-option off on the Jeep and gunned the engine as we hit the hill just outside the tree farm. As we zipped by, I noticed a lone truck in the field. It was the off-season for the Christmas Tree Farm, which meant that Clay would have all his attention on the wedding as well.

Jim Townes handled the off-season time of planting and irrigation. For now, it was easily a one-man operation. Well, two, if you counted his feisty wife. Did Mary give Jim as much trouble as Chaos had given me in less than a week?

I doubted it. Mary Townes seemed pragmatic.

I glanced over at Chaos who was juggling a notebook, an iPad, and her phone. She also had her headphones on to make sure I knew not to talk to her.

As if I couldn't take the hint.

I wrapped my hands tightly around the steering wheel. I liked silence. Craved it even, but dammit, it felt like a wet horse blanket right now.

As we crested the hill, the orchard came into view. It butted up against the tree farm with a row of apple trees in full bloom. The sweet scent of the pink flowers infiltrated the truck even with the windows up.

Willow perked up and lowered her window, lifting her face to the breeze. She clutched her digital life to her chest and simply closed her eyes.

My chest tightened. There was something about her that could embrace the moment even when she was angry or scared. I'd witnessed the phenomenon a half dozen times in just a few days.

She must've felt my gaze because those big greenish-gold eyes opened. She gave me a cursory glance then went back to whatever it was that had consumed her throughout the ride.

I opened my own window and hoped that some of my shitty mood would go out with the stale air.

As we came up to the main entrance, I caught sight of Beckett Manning on his gray gelding, racing along with us. He tapped the brim of his black hat before disappearing into the thicket of trees.

I hadn't ridden a horse since I was a teen, but suddenly, I wished for a hard ride. Alone. Maybe then I could get her out of my head.

Then again, another kind of hard ride had effectively put her in my brain for the rest of my goddamn life.

A quick flash of her astride me in my bed and on my couch made me blow out a slow breath.

Finding someone who matched me and affected me so much at the same time was a first. My time in the military meant I'd enjoyed satisfying, sweaty, near-nameless sex for a good portion of my life. Scratch the itch, bring down the stress, move on.

Emphasis on the move on.

Chaos didn't fit the mold in any-damn-thing.

My tires hit a rut, jarring me out of my navel-gazing. Christ, she was turning me into a headcase.

I took a left to where the lodge and bakery cut a wide swath of open space. The sun was high in the sky and there were plenty of vehicles in the parking lot.

It left me feeling unsettled. More people meant more potential problems.

I reached under my seat for the holster I'd retrofitted for myself. I wasn't one to carry a gun all the time. I had a concealed carry permit, thanks to my work with Clay and some of the bodyguard assignments I'd had over the years.

I engaged the thumbprint lock to make sure everything was secure.

Chaos had already slid out and gathered her things. She stilled as she lifted her massive bucket bag. "What's that?"

"Now you're talking to me?"

"What's under your seat?"

"Exactly what you think it is." I hopped out and shut my door, engaging the locks.

She hurried around the front of the truck. "Why do you have it at the orchard?"

I turned her toward the lodge with a hand along her lower back. "After a drone popped out of one of the damn boxes here, I'm not taking chances. Let's not discuss this around people, huh?"

"Did you lock it away?"

"It's secure."

"That's not an answer."

"I'm not carrying it, all right? I just want it as a backup." I drew her closer to me, happy she was at least allowing that now. "I told you I'd keep you safe."

She didn't answer, just secured her bag tighter against herself.

I didn't like scaring her, but until I knew more about this guy, I'd rather be overcautious. She'd just have to get used to that.

Laverne peeked her head out of the bakery doors. "Do you guys want something to eat? Rachel's in the cafe."

I smiled at Laverne. "Sure. I could use some coffee."

She waved us forward, her smile widening when she saw how close we were. "We'll fix you right up. Rachel's taken over the big table in back near the windows."

"Great." *Not* great. Fuck. Of course, she had to be in front of the largest damn window in the place.

"Aunt Laverne, did I get any other packages?"

Her aunt tucked a wispy white lock of hair around her ear, tipping her head curiously. "Not today, sweetie. Were you expecting something?"

"No. Not at all. Just trying to get my mail situation under control." Chaos moved away from me to give her aunt a hug.

I stuffed my hands into my pockets. I couldn't glue her to my side, but the fact that there was about twenty people in here made my shoulder blades itch.

I studied each of them. There was a teacher type with a handful of tiny tags looped through her fingers was counting out treats in front of the bakery cabinet, a bored teenager stabbing his cup full of ice with a straw, half a dozen moms with strollers—great cover for a weapon, especially when the bonnet was tightly closed so you couldn't see in.

Years of being braced for the worst in humanity had left me perennially on edge for the first few months after I left the Army. Right now, it felt as if I was falling back on old habits. It remained to be seen if that was a good thing.

The old me hadn't minded working jobs off the books for a few of my teammates. After a few rescue missions, I'd learned that I didn't do well with hopping from adrenaline-fueled nights to restless quiet. It needed to be one or the other.

I'd tried personal security and that wasn't for me. Finally, I'd gone to find Clay and mend fences. At least our version of mending. The only kind I liked to do.

Don't fucking talk about it to death and hit the reset button.

I was pretty sure that would be a no-go for Chaos since she was actively ignoring me by giving me her full back. Those tight leggings were an added slap, and she knew it. My fingers fisted in my pockets.

"Love makes everyone a little crazy. It's okay."

"Laverne..."

"What?"

"Not the time."

She threaded her arm through mine and tugged me toward the counter. "She'll be fine." She patted my arm.

I let her lead me away, but I kept Chaos in my periphery.

"Care to tell me what's up with the packages?"

"She's just having a little trouble with where she's going to land. Roommate problems."

Laverne studied me with her faded denim eyes. "That's a partial truth."

I lifted a shoulder. "She'll get her bearings."

"But will you? Love is scary."

"Stop with the love sh—" I huffed out a breath. "Stuff. We barely know each other."

"Barely stop watching her, you mean." She stood in front of me. "And while I'd love to think you're watching her like that just because of the attraction deal, I wasn't born last week."

I grasped the back of my neck. "Ah, jeez."

"Remember I took the old CocoaBus on road trips. You think the open road didn't include hot, sexy flings?"

"I didn't think about it. Please stop talking about it."

She patted my cheek. "You're adorable. Just because I'm older and very married doesn't mean I've forgotten being young and wild."

"I'm not young."

She patted my chest. "I don't suppose you've been young for a long time. But maybe she makes you feel that way."

"I'm too old for her in the long term."

"I don't know about that. Willow is an old soul and she's been through a lot. She deserves someone—"

"Not like me?"

Laverne frowned at me. "Why would you think that?"

I shrugged again.

"Well, that's a coward's answer. Maybe that's your problem. Big Army guy can't handle falling in love with someone?"

"Can't fall in love with someone in four days."

"Bullshit."

My eyebrows shot up and I had to fight a smile. "Language."

"You've heard far worse, and I've said and thought even darker things. I work on a farm with idiot males, remember? Some I'm even related to."

I pressed my lips together against a laugh. I might've wished I could run for the hills when it came to figuring out whatever was going on between me and Chaos, but I did love this woman.

Impulsively, I pulled her in for a hug. She smelled like Chaos with an underlying earthy tone, as if she'd just put her hands in dirt.

She hugged me back. "This isn't going to stop the conversation. Even if I do like hugging on all these muscles."

I laughed and let her go. "There's nothing to talk about. We're still figuring out what we are. But here and now, it's all about the wedding. So, I'm going to get the largest cup of coffee and see what they're going to make me do."

"You don't have to hover. The girls will be fine together."

"I told Clay I'd make myself available." The lie flowed off my tongue. Well, half truth—I did tell Clay I'd help out. But hovering wasn't my style, so they would get suspicious if I did.

"Hmm."

"He's dealing with some merger or buyout or whatever it is he does."

She patted my chest one last time. "Okay, honey." She went around the counter and poured me a large coffee in one of the reusable cups she kept on hand for me, then put together a sweet cold coffee concoction in a sunny yellow cup with an eye-searing pink straw. "Willow will appreciate the coffee too."

"Sure hope hers is the Crayola explosion." I took both cups.

"Maybe a little sugar would do you good."

Not in this lifetime. "Thanks, Laverne."

The girls were giggling as I approached. The big book of doom—aka the wedding book—was back out along with a white board with an army of sticky notes. More seating chart fun, evidently.

I set the yellow cup next to Chaos. She took it with a muttered thanks and went back to rearranging post-its. "If you put these cousins together, there will be a conga line before the appetizers are done."

"And that's wrong?" Rachel's bluebell eyes twinkled.

"If that's what you're going for, you can add the Manning boys to the triangle."

"I'm not looking for drunken headlocks."

Chaos laughed and leapfrogged to one circle away, plunking the sticker with the number seven down. "Make it a little harder for them to get into trouble."

I leaned against the window, sipping my coffee. As I'd had a bar room brawl with two of the Manning brothers, I couldn't dispute her reasoning.

Rachel glanced up at me. "We'll probably be here for a while."

"Understood." I'd sat under camouflage in a jungle for eleven hours straight, I could handle wedding planning. At least I hoped I could. "I'm here for pack mule duty or whatever."

Rach straightened. "Well, maybe we should go to the lodge then. I can definitely use those muscles. Clay is supposed to be here in a bit."

"Good thing I'm here then."

She laughed. "Are you saying my future husband can't lift things?"

"If it's a Christmas tree, maybe."

Rachel shook her head and gathered up her papers. "He's quite handy to have around."

"I'm sure he's all about keeping you happy." Chaos gave me a tight smile before turning the megawatt brilliance at her sister. "You're very lucky, Rach."

"I am, aren't I?"

I resisted an eyeroll and took the pile from her. "I'm assuming you guys are using the bigger room?"

"We tried to keep the wedding list to a minimum, but between my family and Clay's, it was nearly impossible." She stacked up two more books and set them on top of my pile. "Look at that. You're already helpful."

"I live to serve."

Willow arched a brow at me and made me think of all the ways I could serve her without benefit of her clothes. Too bad we were fighting over her foolish female reasoning.

I was better off being Rachel's pack mule than thinking of what I was already missing like hell.

Chapter 23

Willow

An Apple For Your Thoughts

The lodge had two main event halls, the Gala and the Honeycrisp, that could be used for weddings or parties as well as a smaller business center for corporate retreat deals. My sister had taken the Gala room for her reception. It was massive and warm with faded wood post and beam details. It wasn't the typical golden toned wood—instead the Ronsons had gone with a dark walnut that elevated the hall into something a little more special.

White fairy lights had been installed along the beams to brighten up the space. Rachel had chosen to add more lantern-style lights throughout the room, which kept the cabin feel but classed it up.

Clear crystals hung down from the lanterns like diamonds. The tables were already set up in the winding circular pattern Rach had come up with. Fabric-covered gray chairs were tucked in tight until they were turned out with accessories and flowers.

Boxes were stacked in the corner with the tablecloths, dishware, and silverware labeled efficiently. A large pallet was piled high with boxes. A few had already been opened with stuffing exploding out of them.

249

Rachel rushed by me, skipping into the center of the room. "Isn't it great? I just gave my final approval on flowers, but we need to set up the urns near the head table and the large one over near the double doors."

She spun around, the skirt of her dress swinging around her calves. "We're going to come through those doors." She pointed to the ones on the far side of the room.

"Oh, right. That's smart. Right from the chapel."

"Exactly!" She clasped her hands under her chin. "I wasn't sure about what we should do for music. Ian tried to convince me and Zoe that he should play wedding singer."

I laughed. "I'm not sure Clay's family is ready for Ian rocking out at your wedding." Ian Kagan was engaged to our cousin Zoe. He was also pretty famous. "Oh, hey, is he coming to the wedding?"

Rach grinned at me. "Want to get him to do a video with you?"

I lifted my shoulder. "I wouldn't be opposed to it."

She linked her fingers with mine and dragged me over to the boxes. "Don't give him an in, or he'll never leave you alone."

"No?"

Rach shook her head. "Ian is like an exuberant puppy. He finds everything exciting. Zoe keeps trying to lose him in the orchard so she can get some painting done."

"Okay, now I need to see that one."

"Beckett is always rescuing him in the McIntosh orchard. You'd think he would catch on to her plans. Oh, and now Ian wants to learn how to ride a horse."

"The orchard is not ready for that."

Along with being a honest-to-God rockstar, Ian was insanely gorgeous, especially when he grew out his mane of dark curls. That kind of action on a horse would bring the ladies—and some men—to Happy Acres in droves.

Zoe would need an armed guard just to protect her husband.

Judging from how adorable their baby Elvis was, the same would go for her son one day too. The Elvis moniker wouldn't hurt if he decided to become a singer like his dad.

"No kidding." Rachel lifted out a beautiful marble planter. "We're going to have these on the floor beside the table at the doors."

"Man, you went with the rustic classy." I touched the cool surface. "That's gorgeous."

"Clay kept urging me to go bigger. Stupid man."

I laughed. "He loves you."

Her face softened. "Yeah, he does. Big love. More than I was ever expecting in my life."

I rubbed her arm. "You deserve it."

"I'm learning to believe that." She handed me the planter and dug out the other one. "Where did your bodyguard go?"

I jolted. "What?"

"He hovers like a bodyguard. At least he's hovering around you instead of Clay these days." She narrowed her eyes. "Which is a little weird."

"Just because he doesn't trust that I won't spill the beans for your present."

She scrunched her nose. "You're killing me with that." She hugged the planter to her and grabbed a frame from another box. "Let's go set this up."

I glanced over my shoulder. Sure enough, there was Ransom. He'd set the books and binders down on the podium just inside the door. His arms were crossed, his coffee propped on his forearm.

I didn't like fighting with anyone, but he was so damn hard-headed. Didn't he understand that the longer this went on, the more my family could get mixed up in my problems?

Not everything was black and white. I wasn't sure he understood that. Or even cared.

But today—and the next few days—wasn't about me. They were about ensuring Rachel was happy and making her wedding the best day ever.

And if I needed a weapon, one of these planters would do. Wowsers.

A shiver chased down my spine at the memory of another weapon. I wasn't sure why I was so shocked about Ransom having a gun, but the idea of it seemed like overkill.

We knew zero about this stalker guy. Maybe he really did just want to make money off me. Maybe I was even just a trial to him. Figure out how to do it with me, and then go for bigger fish.

Because I was seriously not important enough to warrant a freaking *drone.*

"Wil?"

I turned at my sister's voice. "Sorry." I grabbed another frame out of the second box and hurried after her. "What do you want Ransom to do while we work on this?" I squatted down and gently set down the planter.

She waved him over.

Ransom drank the last of his coffee and tucked his tumbler into the podium. "I'm at your disposal."

"All those boxes." She gave him a wide, sunny smile, the kind that got men to do anything for her. "Can you unwrap everything? I'll tell you where to put things."

"Roger that."

Just like that? He never let me get away with ordering him around. I flipped the easel of the frame out and set it down a little more forcefully than I meant to.

"Problem?"

"No."

"I can hear the pout in your voice, Wil."

"You don't live with Ransom Douglas."

Rach's lips twitched. "No, I sure don't. Is the house silent as a tomb?"

"No. He likes music." I shrugged. "Surprised me too."

She pulled a heavy piece of paper out of the manila envelope on the table. It was thick and fragile at the same time with little violets pressed into the soft paper. Layered on top was a thin piece of vellum with instructions to take a name card and bag from the table.

"So, what are these favors we're putting together? Tennis bracelets and pocket watches?"

"Shut up." Rachel bumped me.

"You're the one marrying a gazillionaire."

"Well, Clay worked with the boys to make a cider for the wedding. It's going to be on tap at the bar and there's going to be bottles as favors."

"Oh, that's fancy and cool at the same time."

"Then I had a local woman make up a batch of soaps for those who like that instead."

"You're so damn thoughtful, Rach." I hugged her. "And you know I'll be filming stuff to put up after the wedding."

"Wouldn't be you without it."

I laughed and stepped back. "So, let's set up everything we can."

"I'm so glad you came back early. I've really missed you."

My eyes stung and I fought back the sudden need to bury my face in my sister's neck. "I really missed you too. And the orchard. I'm surprised how much I missed the orchard actually."

"Well, you haven't been here since you got home."

"Yeah, getting all my stuff out of my old apartment has been a lot."

"I still can't believe Ransom volunteered. Then again, I'm shocked he's here too. He's not exactly the joining and volunteering type. We usually have to corner him."

"Believe me, he hasn't been happy about it." I took the back off of the picture frame to give myself something to do.

"And yet you're staying with him?"

"Not like we're making midnight margaritas and watching movies."

She laced her fingers under her chin. "I want to make midnight margaritas and watch movies. Can we do that?"

"Sure." Not certain how I'd get Ransom to allow that. Moreover, should I even come over to their house? *Ugh.* I hated overthinking every move I made and wondering if it would end in something awful. It wasn't as if this stalker dude truly *did* anything.

Maybe we were all overreacting.

I heard voices and turned to see Clay had come in. He went right to Ransom and they went into a huddle about something. Rachel frowned and kept glancing over at them.

Clay looked at us and gave her a bright smile.

"Oh, crap. Now what?" Rachel fiddled with the paper.

"Think something's up?"

"Whenever their heads are together, something is up."

"Maybe they're talking about the bachelor party deal. You know, we have yours this weekend too."

"I know. I don't want to really do anything wild."

"Oh, come on. I already got Jason Mamoa set to strip for you."

Rachel tipped her head back with a huge laugh. "Now I wouldn't say no to that. Pole and all?"

"I mean, why wouldn't I do it up?"

She slipped her arm through mine and dragged me toward the boys. "Oh, if it were only true. Maybe he'd take me away on his motorcycle."

Clay's head whipped around. "Who is stealing you away on a motorcycle?"

Rachel crossed to them and patted his chest. "Just a fantasy."

"I can get a motorcycle."

"Dear God, no." Ransom rocked back on his heels. "Disaster. Remember when you and Reid used to take the dirt bikes into the back of Ace?"

"I remember the broken arm."

"I rest my case."

Clay's voice went from light and fun to soft. "Reid's dad was not amused."

"Neither was your grandfather."

"What's Ace?" I asked to break the sudden tension between them.

"Ashley Academy." Ransom sliced open another box and pulled out a massive marble urn, setting it beside him.

My eyes widened. "You went to prep school?" I was trying to picture Ransom in the severe uniform. I wasn't really up on the whole private school set, but during my senior year, I'd messed around with a guy named Brant who went there. The mistake was going out with anyone named Brant, but I did remember the all-black uniform with the gold and green crest.

He gave me a lazy look. "Into guys in uniform?"

"Not generally."

Rachel narrowed her eyes and glanced from him to me.

Before she could ask a question I really didn't want to answer, I dragged her attention back to what we'd come over for. "What were you guys talking about?"

Clay moved to Rachel and took her hands. "Something happened. It's not a huge deal, and I checked with Hayes to make sure we can fix it."

Rachel's grip increased and I caught Clay flinching at her hold. "What happened?"

"Evidently, there was a break in last night."

"What? Here? At the orchard?" Rachel's voice rose.

"Calm down. It's not a big deal. Probably some stupid kids who were looking for some booze to party with."

"Booze?" She pressed her lips together. "Explain. And don't placate me."

My gaze tracked to Ransom. We didn't have break-ins at the orchard. And if kids wanted to get some alcohol, they'd go to the gas station at the edge of Turnbull, everyone knew that.

Well, *I'd* learned that during my summers at the orchard. Not that there had been a distillery on the property when I was younger, either. But where there was a will, there was a way. And traveling deep into the orchard wasn't exactly an easy grab.

Ransom shook his head as he opened another box.

I fisted my hands. "What happened?"

Clay sighed. "I'm getting there. Someone stole a dozen cases of the cider we were using for favors."

"What?" Rachel's voice pitched high enough to alert a dog.

"It's okay." Clay rubbed her arms up and down. "We just won't have a bunch for the reception. But Hayes said he had enough left-overs to do a few kegs for the bar instead. We'll just need to do the whole decorating deal again."

Rachel's eyes filled. "When are we supposed to have time to do that?"

"Ransom and I will do it."

Ransom straightened. "Excuse me?"

"We don't have as much to do. We can do it."

His jaw locked and his nostrils flared. "Sure. We can do it."

Besides, I wanted to get a look at the brewing room. And if that meant putting different labels on a bunch of cider, so be it. I'd just drink the crooked ones.

After the last few days, I could use some alcohol.

"We don't have any labels left." Rachel dabbed at the corners of her eyes. They were swimming in tears, but she was making a valiant effort not to let them fall.

"Easy peasy. We'll just use aunt Laverne's sticker machine. She has some of that fancy waterproof paper. I saw it when I was in the mail room." Not sure how I remembered anything other than the fact that more boxes were in there from my secret admirer, but I'd noticed a lot of office supplies.

"Yeah?" Rachel sniffed. "I didn't know she had that."

"Aunt Laverne has everything. Besides, she uses the sticker machine for the bakery. Not exactly your domain."

"How do you know that?"

I shrugged. "I annoy everyone by asking questions."

She rushed me and hugged me tight. "I'll never be annoyed by your questions ever again."

I patted her back. "We'll fix it," I said it to my sister, but I was staring at Ransom while I said it.

I didn't believe that this was a random break-in for one second.

"Are you sure you don't mind? I have to go meet with the florist and make sure we have all the flowers we need."

"Nope. You and Clay can do that. Ransom and I will finish in here."

Helplessly, Rach dabbed at the corners of her eyes with the back of her hands as she looked around.

I wasn't used to seeing my sister overwhelmed. She'd always been a type-A-plus-plus kind of person and super in control.

She blew out a slow breath and shook her hair back over her shoulders. "There's a diagram in my book. Let me get it for you."

Of course she had a diagram. That sounded more like my sister.

Clay raked his fingers through his hair. "Thanks, Wil. I can probably have someone at the gift shop help out. It's a slow time of year."

"We can handle it. If I need help, I'll SOS Taylor."

"Are you sure?"

"Definitely." I peered around Clay. "Right?"

Ransom just gave me an arched brow as he lifted another urn and brought it to the head table.

"He agrees."

Clay folded his arms. "You guys are..."

"We're helping our favorite people to have the best wedding ever." Quickly, I went onto my toes and kissed his scruffy cheek. "We'll make sure it's perfect."

"It's a small wedding, but it's still a dozen cases. We can make it a sticker party. Again."

I laughed at his deadpan voice. "I'm trying to picture you putting them on straight enough to suit Rach."

"Oh, I'm a pro—now."

"I heard that," Rachel called from near the doors.

"Love you," Clay called back.

He smiled down at me. "She keeps me humble." He lowered his

voice. "She wanted to be hands-on for this wedding. She's been doing really great even though this is the biggest thing she's done since... well, since."

Since Rach had a mini-breakdown.

I'd learned that the most put-together people could have a bad time. And Rachel had taken a long time to heal from her extreme burnout. My sister who thought perfection ruled everything had learned to go with the flow. Kinda. The CocaoBus and The Christmas Tree Farm had showed her a new path.

She was still the same Rachel. She was still a little high-strung with a list for everything, but she'd learned to let people in. Especially a certain tall, dark-haired man who could probably buy a state or two, but he only had eyes for Rachel. And they both had learned that slowing down meant more time for each other.

"I won't let her down."

"I didn't mean it like that."

I patted his arm. "I know. Mr. Stoic over there and his steady carpenter hands will help me get it done. Promise."

"I have to take Rachel into the city for her final fitting, and I have a meeting I can't do via teleconference."

"Oh, do you need me to go with her?"

Ransom stilled behind Clay, his arms full of heavy marble. I was certain he'd have a coronary if I wanted to go into the city with my sister. But she was only getting married once, dammit.

"She and your mom are making a day of it. Claire's been so upset that she hasn't been here for most of the details."

I was sure Clay preferred to believe that. My mother wasn't exactly the most demonstrative woman. She understood numbers and spreadsheets and accounting rules, but her creative daughters? Not so much. Our parents had probably given Clay their blessing to marry Rachel solely based on his bank account.

And I did have one hell of a portfolio.

"Okay. I'm glad she'll get to spend some time with our mom before the big day."

Ransom hulked the urn over to the head table with only a small grunt. I fought a smile and turned it toward my sister instead as she hurried over with a binder. "There's log-in details in here for my cloud account where all my files are to reprint the labels." She hugged it to her chest. "Did they take the gift bags too?"

"Afraid so."

Rachel shook her head. "Stupid kids. Why would they want them?"

Very good question. Kids wouldn't. They'd only want the cider and definitely wouldn't have a way to take a dozen freaking cases of it.

That required planning.

Clay moved beside her and rubbed her back. "I don't know."

"And there was nothing on the security videos? I know Beckett set it up when they built the cider mill."

Clay shook his head. "There was a malfunction. About ten minutes of feed was missing."

I just bet. I folded my arms, suddenly chilled. "You're sure it was kids?"

"Nothing else was taken. There is tons of expensive equipment in there. At least if you know what you're looking for. Manning Cider is starting to get a name in this area. They're still working on distribution. Not easy to do in New York."

Ransom came back to where we were. "I'll check it out when we go over there."

"Thanks. I'm sure Hayes and Beckett would appreciate it." Clay curved his hand up and over Rachel's shoulder, turning her into his chest. "We better get home to pack."

Rach groaned against his chest. "I forgot about the fitting."

"Good thing I didn't."

She peered up at him, her eyes shining for a different reason this time. "Always taking care of me."

"Always." He dropped a kiss on her head and pulled the binder out of her grip. "Time to pass the baton."

"If you lose that, I'll cut all your curls off."

I snorted as I took the binder. "Understood."

Clay tugged her even closer, giving Ransom a quick nod before steering her out of the lodge into the late afternoon sun.

I waited until they were outside before turning to Ransom. "You know it wasn't kids who stole that cider."

His eyes were the color of storm clouds. "We don't know anything yet."

"Now who's being stupid?"

"Dammit, Chaos. I didn't call you stupid."

"Yeah, well, I'm happy to give the moniker to you." I shoved the binder into his stomach. "Let's get this room finished. We have a lot of work to do."

Chapter 24

Ransom

Anything For Family

ackey was now my actual moniker.

For the next hour, she ordered me around the lodge. We used Rachel's diagram as a guide more than a template. Chaos changed the planters-slash-urns about thirteen times.

Thankfully, there wasn't an extra fifteen pounds of flowers in them yet.

She did have a good eye and had adjusted the room for a better flow from the head table to the dining tables and finally, to the wide dance floor. A glitzy chandelier somehow worked with the dark wood and lanterns scattered around the lodge.

We ended the afternoon climbing on ladders adding ivy around the lanterns to give the space a more natural feel. I wasn't sure how she pulled it all together, but then again, she was the queen of staging when it came to her job.

Normally, the silence would suit me. Instead, it ramped up my guilt. The light and airy romantic space highlighted exactly how different we were.

I couldn't give her this in the long term.

Maybe pretending we could actually *be* something was getting to me. Especially since I hadn't let her in on the game.

The worst part was it wasn't a game. Not anymore.

Sooner or later, she'd see through the façade, and I'd be back to my lonely house.

I snapped the ladder closed. It hadn't been lonely before her, dammit.

Enough of this. We could talk this out like reasonable adults. Or at least semi-reasonable.

I turned around, my gut tightening as I realized she wasn't there. "Chaos?" I waited a beat, and when she didn't answer, I let the ladder clatter to the floor.

I didn't want to worry her about the cider burglary, but she was too damn intuitive. The fact that this guy might have gotten on the orchard property had ramped up my protective instincts.

"Chaos?" I called out again.

I strode toward the double doors that led to the chapel and found her on the stone path, dragging a few of the extra urns to line the walkway.

Relief slammed into me and my heart rate stuttered at the sight of her in the late day sun. Her short sweater had rode up to show her freckled back as she bent herself into an impossible angle to drag the heavy marble exactly where she wanted it. Her hair was in one of her messy knots and a few untamable curls hung in her eyes.

"Let me help." My voice was low and strained.

She blew a curl out of her eyes. "I got it."

"Chaos."

She straightened up and I got a flash of her stomach before the fluffy sweater fell back into place. "I'm perfectly capable of doing this."

"I'm well-aware how capable you are."

"Could have fooled me." She pushed up her sleeves. "But if I have to do a million labels tonight, I'll let you help."

"One hundred and forty-four is not a million."

"I'll remind you of that in another hour."

I brushed a curl out of her face and she took a step back. "I think three will work on each side. Spaced out."

I fisted my hand. "Got it."

"Aunt Laverne finished printing out the labels for us. We can pick them up at the desk. She has a knitting club at the café so we won't have to socialize."

"I'm not a fucking ogre." I grunted as I lifted another planter. "Here?"

"Another foot toward the chapel."

At least she didn't say a smidge. A foot I could work with. Precise and no room for error. The exact opposite of us.

I caught on to what she was doing and moved the rest of them to match. I swiped the sweat off my brow and stood when the last urn was in place. My damn heart thundered in my head as she ran up to the doors of the chapel and spun around.

She clasped her hands together and looked out at what I'd put together for her. A light breeze kicked up and loose curls lifted around her freckled face. "It's perfect."

She damn well was.

Shit.

I swallowed the lump in my throat. I'd never imagined a woman staring down at me from the end of an aisle. Even a makeshift one.

Her eyes shone in the golden light, and Christ, she was so goddamn beautiful it hurt.

"Rachel is going to be so excited." She ran down the short steps and came right for me. Instead of opening her arms to embrace me, she shoved me back a few feet. "I gotta make sure it's the same for how people will see her. Move."

I stumbled aside and barely resisted the urge to bend at the waist and suck in oxygen. What the hell was wrong with me?

She whirled around and dropped into a cross-legged position, then she pulled out her phone from some sneaky pocket. She did a quick pan around the garden walkway and sighed before staring up at me. "Perfect."

I held my hand out for her.

She narrowed her eyes, but finally, she accepted it and popped up too fast. She fell into me, and my arm instantly went around her waist, my hand at her lower back. She tried to back up, but I wouldn't let her go.

"Let's go clean up the rest."

"I'm—"

"Save it." She slipped out of my arms.

I tipped my head back. Maybe it was better to let her be mad, even if it made me insane.

I followed her back into the lodge and locked the double doors behind me. It only took us a few minutes to gather all the packing materials and tuck them back into their boxes. I assumed the urns wouldn't be a permanent fixture.

We crossed to the front doors, gathering all of Rachel's wedding paraphernalia. Chaos paused at the door, looking back at all we'd done.

"So much more to do before the big day, but at least then we'll have the florist here to help."

"You did a good job, Chaos. Rachel will love it."

She glanced up at me, her gaze unreadable. "Thanks."

We shut off the lights and checked the locks one more time. A large atrium connected the rooms with a massive apple tree as the centerpiece. To guard from curious kids, or entitled idiots, there was a directory and history of Happy Acres on a trio of stands blocking access to the tree. A beautiful stained glass ceiling above the tree afforded light and left interesting patterns of color on the bleached wood floor.

I was the one who had to catch up to her long-legged gait this time. She was a woman on a mission.

"Chaos."

She whirled around. "Would you stop calling me that?"

"Willow, you need to stay with me."

Her eyes narrowed. "Never mind, use Chaos. My name sounds weird out of your mouth."

I moved into her, dragging her close. "Unless I'm inside you."

She licked her lips. "We're not talking about that right now."

"If you think a little fight is going to stop me from—"

"I'll be moving into the attic like we originally agreed." She backed away from me and headed down the hall to the front desk.

The foot traffic to the main desk of the lodge was lighter, so I could keep her in view and let her have some space. The conversation that had gone down earlier today wasn't even a fight. She was just too independent for her own damn good and she was flexing against our arrangement.

I *should* let her move into the attic.

Hell, I should rig the whole house with cameras and lock her in. Of course we had more wedding crap to deal with, so that plan was out the window.

And now we had a freaking break-in to investigate. Aidan had done a sweep for suspicious activity at the orchard, but I'd assumed this shithead would go for more watching.

The idea that this guy had come out of his cave made me very uneasy. Was he just showing off? Or was he getting more dangerous?

While Chaos was chitchatting with the front desk person, I checked in with Aidan.

Ransom: The Ronsons had a break-in at the cider distillery. It's out of the way and damn suspicious. Thoughts?

It didn't take him long to reply.

Aidan: Is there usually crime in Nowheresville?

Ransom: Funny. There's some, but usually of the petty variety. Twelve cases of cider earmarked for the wedding went missing.

Aidan: Anyone else likely to be problematic re: the wedding?

Ransom: Nah. Clay's family is thrilled with the turn of events. The Ronsons would serve apple pie to their enemies ffs.

Aidan: Okay. I'm assuming no video.

Ransom: Going to check with the manager here, but it seems like there's a blank spot in the video feed for the distillery.

Aidan: Great. I'm going to send you some extra small cameras to put around the orchard. They're bluetooth so you should be able to hide them easily.

Ransom: Thanks. I'm going to use the ones you already sent to set up around the venue. If this asshat is trying to mess with the wedding, Willow will be pissed.

Aidan: Let's hope that's all he's doing.

I cracked my knuckles because I'd been thinking the same.

I stuffed my phone in my pocket then headed for the desk. Chaos was straightening a stack of printed sheets. She was probably doing a quality check.

It was the off-season and no events were happening at the moment. But people were always staying at the Happy Acres Lodge. Laverne and Fred ran a nice place with good food and room for families to gather.

Things would be insane for the wedding and my head already hurt thinking about the logistics of it all. How the hell was I going to keep her under wraps with this guy actually coming out of his hole?

If he even was.

Was I overreacting? Was she?

The itch between my shoulder blades said no. And it had saved my life on more than one occasion.

She turned around as I approached. The emotions flitting across her face cut me off at the knees—awareness, disappointment, and then that goddamn backbone snapped tight and she straightened, her face full of resolve.

I nodded briefly at the woman behind the desk and ushered Chaos to the front doors. She still wasn't fully talking to me, and the silence between us was slowly driving me mad.

Fine, not that slowly. I was in a fast burn.

The ride out to the cider mill on the outskirts of the orchard was more of the same. The road was rutted from the spring rain, and the air was sweet and heavy in the late afternoon warmth. Chaos had her window down and her face tilted to the wind.

I tightened my hold on the steering wheel and took the road a little too fast. Instead of telling me to slow down, she held onto the handle above the window and let her hair down.

Lemons and the clean scent of her curls slapped me back in my seat. I was a professional, for fuck's sake. She should not affect me like this.

Futilely, I tugged at the leg of my jeans for some relief.

The blossoms on the trees changed as we passed another type of apple tree. They weren't as full of blooms and an earthy scent surrounded them.

Finally, the road opened up to a clearing with a rustic structure that was sneakily fortified with steel. Inviting and simple, the distillery was mostly used during the summer and fall months. A large wraparound porch which usually held small tables and comfortable seating was swept clean and bare. An outside bar was shuttered tight against the elements.

Spring was often unforgiving in Central New York, but the Mannings kept a tight ship. The grounds were kept up even on the off-season. They had added an outdoor fire pit and oversized swings off to the side.

Outdoor concerts were held on the edge of the orchard. Beckett had told me that before this, the rest of the property had been overgrown and unsuitable for more expansion. I called this a very good use of the land.

Chaos was leaning forward, her head swiveling back and forth as she took in everything. Before I even managed to park, she was out of the truck, leaving all her gear behind except for her phone.

Knowing she was going to do her Chaos thing, I gathered up the materials we'd need and left them on the porch. I kept her in my line of sight as I took a look around.

The locks were keyless, which was good in theory—unless you were a hacker like this dickwad. I spotted the first camera and the smaller one pointed at the bar area.

Great when they were in full operation, but they didn't help with a break-in. I pulled out my phone and took a few photos myself. Clay's security was as good as Aidan's, albeit simpler here with some cameras and a hub for the Mannings to oversee the orchard.

The galloping hooves in the distance got closer. Beckett shot forward from the back pasture, cutting through the trees, his striking gray gelding casting a tall shadow in the waning sunlight.

He'd swapped his black cowboy hat for his ratty baseball cap sometime between the time I'd seen him earlier and now. He waved at Chaos.

"You're going to up our marketing game right, Wil? Give us a bump on your show?"

Chaos rolled her eyes. "It's not a show—exactly."

Beckett stepped down, patting the gelding's neck before he dropped the reins to the ground. "Whatever. The girl Justin is seeing freaked out when she heard we were related."

I leaned on the porch rail. "Since when? He was hitting on a table full of girls when I saw him a few days ago."

Beckett shrugged. "I don't know. He's always juggling a few women."

"Typical," Chaos muttered. She started taking video again, moving toward the stage.

"Don't go far."

"Yes, Dad."

I shut my eyes. So much for keeping her safe being a noble occupation. I was now officially her pain in the ass.

I glanced up when Beckett's heavy booted feet hit the stairs. "I forgot to text you to come take a look."

"I saw you heading this way." He pulled off his baseball cap, releasing a mop of curls. He slapped the hat against his thigh and then scooped the mess back underneath. "Feel real bad that someone managed to get into the mill. I don't know who the hell would want to come all the way out here in the middle of the night."

That tickle between my shoulders turned into an ache. I wasn't sure how much to share since we were trying to keep things quiet. But it wasn't just about Chaos now. "Have you ever had any break-ins?"

Beckett shook his head. "Even the drunk and disorderly types are at a minimum during the concerts. Helps that we tend to have good security. Not that we use them in the off season."

"It's kind of out of the way and dark as hell at night out here."

"Exactly."

I glanced over to where Chaos was filming or doing whatever it was she did. Her shoulders were relaxed, unlike during most of the trip over.

"Is something going on?" Beckett leaned on the post.

"Will you have a problem keeping something I say between us?"

"Does it include my family?"

"It could." Chaos and her sister were extended family, but now that the orchard had been directly included in this mess, I couldn't be sure it wouldn't impact the Mannings and the Ronsons, as well.

Beckett hooked his thumb into his jeans pocket and tapped his leg. "I'll hear you out, but reserve the right to have a family meeting if needed."

Clearly, things were now getting real. "Fair enough."

"Go on then."

"Chaos—Willow—has a problematic fan."

Beckett's face stayed unreadable, but his eyes went very chilly. "Not like before."

Interesting. I hadn't thought her college stalker would be common knowledge. "Not like Grafton. More digital and a nuisance, but he figured out her address, which makes me wary. She's been careful about that since college."

"More than careful. We didn't even know her street address since she moved to the city. Aunt Laverne sends holiday stuff to her PO Box."

I crossed my arms. "No shit?"

"Think Wil was more worried about it being in our database. Family can be trusted, but..."

"You can vet employees, but nothing is infallible."

"Right."

I filed away that nugget of information to tell Aidan later. "He also knows the orchard's main address."

"Not that it's hard to find, but connecting it to her is harder." His jaw tightened. "Anything of interest?"

That was a roundabout way of asking. He definitely kept things closer to the vest than his brothers. "Just a few packages. One was a drone."

"That's what that was. Everyone at the barn was talking about some toy."

"It was intended to scare her. It worked. Damn sure wasn't a toy. Looked like a survey drone to me. The kind that real estate people use. Maybe even more high tech than that."

"Think he scanned the orchard?"

"The drone lit out pretty fast, but I wouldn't be shocked if it did a cursory scan of the property first. At least to tell where the buildings are."

"Can't say I'm thrilled with that, but Google does the same yearly from a truck, I suppose."

"Not quite the same."

Beckett pushed himself off the post. "Want to take a look inside?"

I checked where Chaos was again.

"Are you that worried about her?"

I met Beckett's gaze. Before I could say anything, he grinned at me.

"Like that, is it?"

"Shut up."

He chuckled and moved to the door to punch in the code.

"We're heading in," I called out.

She just waved and went back to whatever creative endeavor she was currently involved in.

The days were getting longer, and the sunlight gave me a small measure of comfort. Not that plenty of bad things didn't occur in broad daylight, but I couldn't be with her every second. Unfortunately.

As a compromise, I left Chaos to her own devices, but I left the door open to listen for her.

And I was *not* acting like her father.

Beckett hit the lights on the wall inside the door. "We use this mostly for storage in the off-season, but we keep an all-year production schedule for cider. This winter, we added our version of Apple Jack."

"Happy Apples?" I snorted when I saw the labeled crates.

Beckett grinned. "They'll make you happy after three or four of them."

"Let me guess. Justin's idea?"

"Oh, he'd prefer moonshine. That takes a whole different kind of permit to make. If the profits keep going like they are, we just might. Good to have backup for the leaner years."

The area was more spacious than I'd expected. There was a lump of something covered in tarp. Probably tables and chairs. A bar took up the back of the room with more coverings on the stools attached to a foot rail.

"Nice place."

"We expanded this past year. Having a few rockstars in the family has given us some good concert series options. Not just family but Ripper Records likes to use us for small concerts. It's worked out well."

"I've heard Donovan Lewis is a smart guy."

Beckett gave me a surprised look.

I shrugged. "I worked in New York City for a long time. I heard shit at the endless parties Clay used to go to."

"Now he's all about that slow life. He's seen the error of his ways."

"Can't say I mind it."

We chatted about security and I made some notes in my phone to get upgraded equipment for them. Even if they didn't have a lot of need for it out here, the distillery included a lot of expensive equipment.

"Oh, wow."

We turned toward Chaos in the doorway. She held up her phone as she immediately zoomed in on all the cases against the wall.

"Guess you'll be doing a video." Beckett's voice was amused.

Chaos flushed. "Sorry. Habit. I don't have to."

"Go ahead. Show off those Happy Apples. They're releasing soon."

"Oh, we'll have to bring a bottle of it with us for the bachelorette."

"Already earmarked two for you."

She gave him that gut-punch smile. "You're the best."

Immediately, she started chattering away. I felt more at ease with the sound of her voice behind me.

"Where did the thief hit?"

Beckett motioned to the far corner. "I can't believe they didn't take the Happy Apples. They're worth more than the cider. Not that anyone really knows about them yet. We're only just starting the marketing push. Found a distributor that was willing to work with us, finally. You'd think it would be easier to push booze."

Well, shit. "So, the wedding stuff was marked?"

"Yeah. We had them set up in apple boxes that Hayes had decorated for the wedding. Matching the whole," Beckett flicked his fingers, "la-di-dah kind of deal girls go wild for."

I laughed, partially to cover the darkness bubbling in my belly. "I get it. The whole rustic glam vibe I've been rearranging all day."

"What those women make us do." He shook his head with a rueful smile. "But it's good to see Rachel so happy. She was not in a good way when she came to us last year."

I jammed my hands in my pockets. I remembered the near-frail woman I'd met when Clay had dragged me to Turnbull in November. The Rachel I knew now seemed miles away from that woman.

"We had a few extra crates made, so we'll still have them for the favors table. The rest we just sprayed a matte black." He toed the pile to show which ones since there were various sizes stacked against the wall.

"Good thing, since we need twelve cases."

"That's my cousin. Ever the overachiever. We'd bottled extra to use at the open bar and for when we open the season on Memorial Day. We'll get more in production, but that dolly is full of unlabeled bottles for you guys."

I blew out a breath. "When you see twelve dozen in real life..."

"I'd send people over to help, but you guys seem to want to keep this quiet."

"I do. If it's this asshole that's bugging Chaos, I'd rather not let him know upset we are. He seems to get off on getting her riled up."

"I have blades to keep Storm's hooves clean. Could chop off an appendage if need be."

The deadpan delivery loosened a full laugh I didn't realize I was still capable of right now. "I'll take that under advisement."

"If you change your mind, Laverne will send a squad of people down here to help with the sticker madness."

"We'll manage."

"There are frozen pizzas in the back if you guys get hungry. The convection oven is still operational."

"Thanks." I hadn't even thought about food.

"Help me pull out a table and chairs for you, and I'll get out of your hair."

"Thanks, Beck. I appreciate the help."

"Anything for family, man."

I swallowed hard. My family seemed to be growing by the day. As did the need to keep them safe—if I could figure out what direction the damn threat was coming from.

Chapter 25

Willow

Just Let Go

Watching Ransom wrestle with a tarp should have put me in a better mood. I'd left the guys to talk, knowing that my cousin and Ransom were two peas in a pod.

Both were typically short on words, but they managed to find them when it was important.

As Ransom mopped off his forehead with the bottom of his T-shirt, I cursed my ever-present hormones. That tight abs situation was going to kill me. Especially when his jeans rode low because he'd forgotten his belt when we were rushing around earlier.

"Here okay?" Ransom called over to me.

I blinked out of the lust zone. "Works for me."

They'd dragged over a wide rectangular table that was better suited for a buffet than eating. It would be perfect for a label assembly line.

While they gathered supplies, I slipped outside to get stickers from the truck and check in with my sister. With the door open to Ransom's truck, I texted her that we were working on the cider bottles and that she could relax with Mom.

I also checked my notifications. My fingers shook as I scrolled through replies to my latest post. Luckily, it only included people excited to try my sorbet and questions about the mystery man.

Our playful morning seemed as if it had happened a million days ago. I watched the video again, my whole body tightening at the secret smile he wore. Intent bloomed in his eyes, making the blue more evident and calmer than the usual stormy gray.

A wash of memories of laughter and that intense look in his eyes as he fucked me senseless on his couch left me shakier than worrying about my faceless cyber-stalker.

Then I checked my direct messages and lost my breath.

A message from x_WillowsMine_x, a name I'd never seen before, was in my non-friend folder. "It's just a joke, it's just a joke," I mumbled to myself as I clicked it.

A photo with a table and two bottles of cider popped up. The picture was set in the distillery, a candle serving as the only light. The message had been sent with vanishing mode, but I quickly tapped the back of my phone twice to take a screenshot before the image disappeared.

I sagged against the seat. Well, that definitely answered the question about who had taken Rachel's favors.

I doublechecked that I'd managed to get the screen grab and shoved my phone in my pocket before grabbing the bags with the supplies.

A whinny made me jump. I laughed shakily and shook my head as I slammed the door. "Storm, you just took three months off my life."

The horse stomped and nodded his head as if he understood me. I crossed to him and petted his long nose. "Such a handsome boy." As he nudged my bag, I pushed him back. "Probably hungry, huh? I don't have any apples on me."

When he tried to eat my bag again, I laughed. "I only have some carrots. Can you smell them?" I dug into the front flap where I'd stashed some snacks. Before I could even get the carrot sticks fully out of the bag, Storm had his wet lips around my fingers. *"Ew."*

"Carrots are his favorite."

I smiled toward Beckett as he came down the stairs. "I can see that." I put the rest of them on the flat of my palm and let the horse hoover them up.

He nudged me for more and I gave him the all empty sign with my open hands. Instead of moving away, he just hung his big head over my shoulder.

My eyes stung. "Are you hugging me?"

"Damn flirt."

"Is that a yes?" I laughed and held onto Storm's neck.

Beckett patted the horse from the other side. "Storm's shameless with the ladies."

"I bet that works in your favor."

Beckett gave a light shrug. "Maybe. Not that I have much time for romancing anyone these days, horses or otherwise. If my brother comes up with one more way to *diversify*," he said with air quotes, "then I'm going dropkick him into the pumpkin patch."

"Which one?"

"It used to be just Hayes, but Justin is ganging up on me now too. That's how we ended up with the distillery."

"I'm shocked. Booze and Justin?"

"He's got a head for it. Not only the drinking part. I'm just glad he's finally looking into participating in the business." Beckett patted Storm one last time before he picked up the reins from the ground. "You sure you guys are going to be okay out here alone?"

"We'll be fine."

"You really should talk to Laverne and Rachel."

I gripped the strap of my bag. "What did Ransom tell you?"

He stepped toward me and gathered me into a hug. He smelled of earth and smoke. "Enough. And I'll wait until you're ready to tell people yourself. For now."

I gripped his plaid shirt and rested my head on his chest for a second. "Do you think I should go?"

"What?" He nudged me back to gaze at me, his mouth set in a hard line. "Why would you say that?"

My phone felt as if it was burning through my pocket. "I just don't want anything to happen to you and our family."

He narrowed his eyes. "What about you?"

"I'm not worried about me."

"You damn well should be."

I shook my head. "I don't mean that. Ransom isn't going to let anything happen to me. But he can't be everywhere."

"How bad is it, Wil?"

"I don't know."

He tipped his hat back and stared down at me.

"I mean it. It's all been petty annoyances. But the break-in?" I looked down at the ground before I did something stupid like cry. "That's different."

He tipped up my chin. "You're more important than a few cases of cider."

"I know." I gave him another hard hug. "I'm just being silly." But I was starting to wonder if maybe I shouldn't be here for the wedding. What if it only got worse?

If something happened to Rachel or Clay, how would I ever live with myself? My sister had dealt with so much to get to this place. Maybe my being here was just selfish and stupid to boot.

He rubbed my arms. "Rachel is so happy you're home. Don't forget that."

I nodded. "I know." But the last thing I wanted to do was become a regret for the people I loved. If my career would unintentionally cause that, I'd be better off going somewhere—anywhere—else. "And I missed everyone," I added quietly.

"Right back atcha. Ransom's a good man."

I felt the flush climb my neck. "Not you too."

"Matchmaking? No, that's Aunt Laverne's station. But if you wanted two cents, there they are." He stepped to the horse and hoisted himself up and over, resting his hand on the front of the saddle as if it was a part of him. "I'm just a call away. I've got some paperwork to work on at the main house."

"Okay. Thanks, Beck."

He pulled down his hat. "Talk to you later."

I took a few big steps back as man and horse turned and headed back into the trees. I felt someone's gaze on me, but it wasn't accompanied by a slick sense of dread.

Not this time.

When I turned, I wasn't surprised to see Ransom waiting on the porch, with his legs spread and his arms crossed.

I wasn't sure I had it in me to be mad at him anymore. Not after the photo I'd received.

He came down the steps, dropping his arms to his sides. "Everything okay?"

"I just got this." I unlocked my phone and handed it over.

He frowned as he took it, his fingers brushing mine and sending a jolt of warmth through me. Right then, I was grateful to have something else to focus on for a moment instead of the shitshow that was my life.

Even if the overpowering zing of attraction between us was just one more complication. At least it was a—mostly—welcome one.

"Where did you get this?" His eyes glittered in the last rays of sunlight.

"New screenname in my DMs."

"New?"

"Yeah. He sent me a vanishing message. There's an option in one of the main apps I use. I managed to screenshot it before it disappeared."

He gave me back my phone. "Forward it to Poe."

I nodded and shot off a quick message to her through the encrypted app she'd put on my phone. The fact that I had to be sneaky about everything sat heavy on my shoulders. My eyes filled and I tried to blink away the moisture before he noticed. The screen blurred as I dashed them away, determined to ignore them and brazen through.

"Dammit, Chaos." He pulled me into him.

I tried to fight it, to fight him, but his grip was unrelenting and gentle at the same time. When I couldn't hold back anymore, I looped my arms around his lower back. I hated to cry more than anything. It didn't solve anything and only ended up giving me a headache.

"Just let go." He cupped the back of my head and surrounded me, with his arms, scent, and warmth. Maybe I'd have been able to battle the tears back if he hadn't given me permission. The space he'd offered opened a gulf inside me, one I couldn't begin to breach on my own.

But he was there. Thank God he was there.

I slid my hands up his back to grip his shoulders and the tears flooded out like a summer storm. Wild and fierce until there was nothing left but Ransom's damp shirt. He didn't stop holding me or tell me to stop.

He just waited me out.

"We gotta stop having these crazy moments at sunset," I said against his shirt.

He stroked my hair. "At least you didn't make me sway like you do with the girls."

I laughed. "I think I need that Advil from your magic glovebox again."

"I'll get it." He set me back gently and thumbed away the last of the tears on my cheeks. Surprisingly, he kissed my forehead before heading to the truck.

I wasn't sure what to do with a caretaking Ransom. If someone had asked me yesterday what he would do in this situation, I would've said he'd slap my arm and tell me to buck up.

He jogged back to me with a package in his hand as well as a pill bottle. "Had some wet wipes too."

"Who are you?"

His eyebrow arched. "I like a neat car."

I took the wet wipes and was grateful to see they were for sensitive skin. "Now that I can believe." Ugh, I was *not* a pretty crier. I swiped the wipes over my cheeks and throat since the floodgates had been monsoon-worthy. "Thanks."

"Anytime."

I popped the pills into my mouth and dry-swallowed before tucking everything in my bag. "I expected you to run for the hills like most men."

"You don't have anything on my sisters. I've lived my whole life with rage-induced tears."

"Is that right?" I linked my arm through his and steered him toward the distillery. From the front, it looked like an old shack, but the Manning's operation was far more than it seemed. The porch was steel-fortified under the faded wood. "Tell me about them."

Internally, I winced. *Go, genius. Talk about his missing sister after he was just amazing with your shitstorm of tears.* "Sorry. I didn't mean to—"

"It's fine. My sister Marigold isn't lost or anything. She just wants to live her life on her own terms. Maple and I usually get a postcard once a year letting us know she's all right. I finally stopped searching for her to make her come home. I keep hoping she'll want to someday."

"What happened? I know some of the specifics, but it seems bigger than a breakup."

"You could say that." He opened the door, and he let me pass under his arm.

"Is that all I'm gonna get?"

He laughed. "Sit that gorgeous ass down and let's work."

"Does that mean no story?"

He pulled out a chair for me. As I sat down, he brushed his lips against my ear. "If you're good."

I didn't really want to be good. And I was supposed to be mad at him, dammit. "Oh, wow. You guys were busy." It looked as if half the dark brown bottles we needed to label were lined up on one end of the long table. Two chairs were set across from each other at the center with a pair of water bottles. Shockingly, the water wasn't in reusable bottles, but beggars couldn't be choosers since we were using someone else's space. On the other side of us, we had space for the completed bottles.

He went around the table and sat down. "Hopefully, we'll only be here half the night instead of all night."

I set my bag down at my side and slid out the folder containing the stickers "Guess we have hours for you to tell me a story."

"My family history is not that interesting."

"I beg to differ." I split the pile and passed half to him.

He rolled his eyes and pulled a bottle in front of him. "Flat or straight on?"

"Well, you're a carpenter, right?"

"Of sorts."

"Do you measure better—"

He stood up.

"Okay. Guess that's your answer." I cracked my water and took a sip. "Your back is going to hurt."

"Not a new thing."

And he hauled me around like I was nothing half the time. I set the bottle upright in front of me. "Too bad we didn't have a laser leveler."

"Now you tell me."

"You have one?"

He nodded. "Easier for some things when I build. And I like toys."

"Your kind of toys."

"Says the girl who probably has eleven cameras."

I ducked my head. "Twelve."

He shook his head.

"What? It's for work. And I didn't know what I liked until I tried them out."

"Same goes." He looked around the room. "This isn't going to work. Be right back."

I rolled my eyes and peeled off a sticker. He just didn't want to talk about himself—and had left me to do all the work like a typical male.

I studied the sweet logo my sister had made or commissioned with their initials and a pair of rings. As I was trying to hold the sticker straight, the clomp of his boots came closer.

"Wait up." He jogged to the table and held up four rolled-up towels and a sharpie.

"Where did you find those?"

"Storage." He crowded in next to me and set down two rolled-up towels. "You said level and..."

"You're such a smartie." He set the bottle between the towels like a bumper. "Okay, line up the sticker like you want it."

Carefully, I centered the sticker on the bottle. He uncapped the sharpie and made lines on the towels. I held up my hand. "Teamwork makes the dream work."

He slapped my hand then stole my towels.

"Jerk."

He grinned at me as he went around the table, his dimples making a rare appearance.

He would not win me over with dimples.

I made the marks on my towel, then I peeled off the leftover sticker paper to make sure the towels stayed in place.

"Now who's the smartie?" He did the same and laid a bottle down in his makeshift sticker bed, slapped on a sticker, and set it on the other side of the table. "Only one-hundred-forty-three left."

I set mine next to his. "One-hundred-forty-two."

Once we got into a rhythm, they piled up fairly quickly. We worked in silence for a bit, but I wasn't going to let him escape from story time.

I pulled out my phone and put on some Frank Turner.

"Tell me about your famous sister."

"Maple? Not much to tell. She left home at eighteen and made the modeling world her bitch."

"Not an easy thing to do."

"No. She's on the tall side like you, so that was one leg up. Her metabolism is one step away from needing medication, I swear. She can out-eat everyone, then take food off our plates when we are done."

"She doesn't look like a wire hanger like most models though."

"Nah. She never wanted to be that girl." He slid another bottle into the growing done pile. "She preferred doing the sexier Victoria's Secret line, which only made me slightly violent. I went out and taught her self-defense on one of my days off."

I sat back with a laugh. "I'm picturing you teaching a squad of models how to stomp and flip. Maybe gouge a few eyeballs."

"Just what I did. Lots of creeps backstage at the shows. They usually have a lot of amazing people to balance it, but she can handle things on her own. I just can't look at my baby sister in a push-up."

"I've seen her. Impressive."

"Stop."

I looked down at my own less than impressive set. "No pushup on this planet could make me have curves there."

He gave me a lazy grin. "A perfect mouthful."

"Get back stickering, Mr. Charm." But I couldn't stop a smile. "So, what really happened to make your other sister go on a world tour?"

"Mags got caught up in being the perfect socialite. She and Reid were the perfect golden couple the summer before we started college. She's only a year younger than me, but Mags was always a force. She wanted into our inner circle, so she got in there. Reid was so gone for her that it just seemed as if they would always be together."

He kept diligently slapping stickers on the bottles as he spoke. Which made me get back to work as well. His side of the table had more completed bottles than mine, and that couldn't stand.

"We all hung out during the summers in the Hamptons."

"The Hamptons. Really? Like *Revenge* Hamptons?"

He gave me a raised brow.

"Never mind. Television show, lots of drama."

"Well, they got the drama right. Rich kids with too much time on their hands. Add in the like-minded adults showing up and showing off and it was quite the scene."

I couldn't imagine that kind of wealth. My parents were well above the middle when it came to income, but they weren't jetsetters with a yacht. That was a whole other level.

"I keep forgetting you're wealthy."

"I enjoyed it when I was young and dumb. I enjoyed my fair share of parties until...well, until I didn't."

I paused with a sticker hovering over my bottle. "Wait, you weren't always grumpy?"

"Watch it."

"What? It's a fair question."

"No time to be young and dumb when you're in the Army, babe."

"No, I don't suppose so. Do you come from a military family?"

"God, no. My father is more worried about finding the next party than he is with fighting for his country."

I heard the derision in his voice and reached across the table to touch his hand. "I'm sorry."

He shrugged. "I might have become just like him if Mags and Reid hadn't imploded." A harsh laugh rolled out of his chest.

"And Clay?"

"Yeah. Only Clay and Mags really know what happened that night. We got stories, but I never believed all of it."

"And you didn't talk about it?" I leaned forward and took his hands before he could tear off another label. "Look at me."

He licked his lower lip in an annoyed gesture that shouldn't have gotten me revved. Too bad it did, anyway. I pushed that aside. Then his eyes locked with mine.

"You guys should talk."

"It's in the past. Where it should stay."

"Obviously not, as you're trying to dust your molars again."

"If they'd just had a grown-up discussion, then maybe my sisters would still be around."

"Who?"

"Can we stop talking about this?"

I blew out a breath and tightened my grip on him. "Maybe *you* need to talk about it."

"Do I look like I talk about emotional shit?"

"Don't get all grumpy about it. Maybe if you spit it out, some of the anger will go away." I narrowed my eyes. "Or are you mad at the wrong person?"

His hands fisted in my hold.

"You can't control everything, Ransom. We all make our own mistakes—and we have to deal with them. Your sister made her own choice."

"We were a unit. Clay, Reid, and me. Even Mags was part of us, and she blew it all apart."

There it was. I could taste the guilt in the air. "It's okay to be mad at her," I whispered.

"She's my sister," he said through clenched teeth.

"She's also a woman. I'm sure whatever happened killed her too. Enough that she left before her wedding."

Rach had told me Clay's side of things. That Marigold had come to him at the office late one night, distraught about something between her and Reid, and had tried to seduce Clay. She'd been afraid marrying Reid would be a mistake.

The problem was, Clay had kissed her back. Just for a moment, but that was enough. His friend had been hurting and Marigold was a massive personality. She had drama wrapped around her like a Chanel cloud from what I could gather. Including disappearing that night after the incident with Clay.

That was all my sister had given me.

"I love my sister. I also know her all too well. She never does anything halfway, but to pull that stunt was unthinkable. She did it on purpose."

I frowned. "What?"

Ransom's hands practically vibrated under mine. "She knew Reid wasn't going to let her go."

My eyes widened.

"Yeah. They were volatile. Looking back on things now, I can see it. But then? No. It was bad enough my best friend was into my sister. But then it felt as if I got lucky, since I would get to have him as my brother for real."

"Oh, Ransom."

His shoulders relaxed. "Also, we were hotheaded guys in our twenties who didn't know shit about life. We all came from families that had mapped out our futures from day one."

"Maybe Marigold didn't want to follow the map."

"Yeah, well, she made that abundantly clear. She used Clay to shatter Reid. But the joke was on her—it worked on all of us. The wedding of the decade was supposed to merge two of the biggest families in New York."

"That's a lot of pressure."

He flipped his hands and clasped mine. "It's rare for someone to take Marigold's side."

"Maybe that's why she left."

"I just wish she'd found a better way to do it." He sighed and slipped his hands away to peel a label off the sheet beside him.

"So, the band broke up?"

He laughed. "Pretty accurate. I bounced around from college to college without actually getting a degree in anything other than beer. I'd lost my two best friends and my sister. I had nothing left to lose."

"Army."

"Yeah. It gave me the family I'd lost. Until it didn't." He stood up. "I need another water. I'll be right back."

I watched him walk stiffly into the back and sighed. I had a feeling there were a lot more stories locked inside the vault of

Ransom. Did the fact that we'd shared our bigger secrets make us even? I wasn't quite sure.

My phone buzzed on the table with an update from Poe. She'd been looking into the account we'd given her to investigate, but before she could get anywhere, it was closed and deleted.

"Great," I muttered.

"What?" Ransom slid into his seat, his face still inscrutable.

"Just Poe. Nothing on the account who sent the picture. It's already deleted."

"Color me surprised. We've had no success following this piece of shit on your socials."

"No. I just don't know what he wants with me. For a fame grab, I'm not that exciting compared to some."

"It's a numbers game with people who get money from fandoms. I'm wondering if you're a test."

I frowned. "What kind of test?"

"At least you started out as one." He laid a bottle into our makeshift template. "You aren't exactly easy to get video for, right? Most of your work was done in your apartment and you only went out sometimes. If he can get footage of you, it shows he has skills."

I swallowed down the bump to my ego and tried to look at it from Ransom's point of view. "If he can do this with you, he can get a bigger celebrity." He glanced up at me. "Not that you're not—"

"No. I always wondered why he would go for me. I have a good social media following, but I'm not on *The Bachelorette* or whatever."

"Right. But if he can show this dark web forum what he can do, then he can make bank tracking others."

It was a good theory. And after what I'd seen on the dark web with Poe and Aidan, I could only imagine what else was out there.

"Problem is, I think this guy got fixated on you."

My hand trembled as I set down my phone. "Why?"

"That I don't know. I'm no profiler, but it's just a gut feeling. And my gut hasn't ever steered me wrong."

"Yeah, well I don't like your gut."

He huffed out a half-laugh and set a finished bottle near his rapidly growing collection. "You might not like it, but you aren't arguing with me."

"No." I sat up straighter and set myself to getting this project done. If I let myself spiral into possible theories, we'd be here all night. "Doesn't mean I like it."

Especially that intimate photo in candlelight at the distillery as if we were going to have dinner together. That part made me very uneasy.

But what bothered me most was that things kept escalating. What was next? And would we be able to figure out who the hell he was before he harmed my family in an even worse way?

Chapter 26

Ransom

Sunlight, Camera, Action

By the time we finished with the cases, it was well past midnight. And that was only with a quick pizza break in the kitchen. Both of us were beyond exhausted by the time I pulled my truck out of the dark parking lot.

The cases of cider were safely tucked into the back. I'd keep them in my garage until it was time to bring them over to the lodge.

Chaos was asleep before we'd even gotten out of the orchard.

I didn't mind the silence now. Talking with her had straightened things out in my own mind. I truly believed she'd been a project at the start of things. The messages she'd gotten from the various accounts could be just a bunch of different degenerates having a laugh, but I didn't think so.

He was escalating. Coming out of his cave was bold. He might be untouchable on the internet, but he was just a man the minute he walked into my world.

The ride to my place was a little slower with my precious cargo. I couldn't stop glancing over at her. I understood her spell. Even watching her videos, I'd felt the pull of the excitement she exuded. She made you feel as if she was in your living room talking to you.

What made her unique also made people think they were entitled to be in her space. I saw it in her comments and the demands people made on her time. As if she wasn't a person who had a life outside the realm of the internet.

I backed into my driveway, taking care against the pitted drive as I got closer to the garage instead of under my carport. The bumps stirred her beside me.

"Sorry," she said with a yawn. "I didn't mean to blink out."

"It was a long day."

She stretched her arms above her head, arching her back. I tried not to look at the sweet curve of her chest. She might think they were small by societal standards, but I loved every bit of her body.

Her body.

Not her.

I quickly got out and hustled to the back of the truck.

She slipped out, rubbing her eyes as she met me at the tailgate.

"You can go on in."

"No, I'll help." She lifted one of the cases before I could push her away.

Quickly, I unlocked the garage and disengaged the security before grabbing two cases of my own.

"So, this is the bat cave?" She set down the case beside her mattress and the end table still at the front of the garage. "Dammit, I still didn't go to Rachel's to get my stuff."

"We'll get it tomorrow."

"If I wasn't so tired, I'd make you bring up that mattress tonight too."

"Chaos, there's no chance you won't be sleeping next to me tonight."

"Do you really think it's a good idea we still do this...whatever it is?"

I set down the cases and turned her toward me. "Everything about us is a good idea."

I was shocked I actually believed that. Pretending to be in a relationship with her was no longer a job—if it ever was.

She frowned. "We're just in this weird limbo with the wedding. It's not real."

"Is that how you feel? For real?"

She pushed my arms away from her. "It's the smart thing." She tried to turn away from me. "We barely know each other."

I slipped an arm around her waist and pulled her back against me. Immediately, my body responded to her—and I didn't make any attempt to hide the fact.

She didn't try to wiggle away. Instead she leaned back against me and covered my arm with her hand. "That's just sex."

I nuzzled my nose along her neck. "Sex isn't what we have."

"Don't do this." Her voice was hardly more than a whisper.

I stopped. "Do what?"

"Don't make me love you if you don't mean it, Ransom."

I wasn't sure what to say to that. She was right. It was cruel to play with her emotions if I didn't intend on going all in.

All of this had happened so fast. But the idea of not having her around just made me hold on tighter.

"We're just beginning, Chaos."

Slowly, she turned in my arms. Her scent of lemons filled my head, making me dizzy. Her hazel eyes were wary, but she didn't back away.

Thank God.

I cupped her face and tipped it up to brush my lips over hers. Not the full on drag her to bed kind of kiss, but a softer one letting her know I wasn't going anywhere. And damn if that wasn't the actual truth.

"Let's get this stuff put away and we can collapse for a few hours."

She nodded. "Okay. I still need to get my stuff tomorrow."

"Tomorrow."

"Promise?"

I kissed her forehead. "I promise."

It only took a few minutes for us to finish up. I locked up and ushered her inside. I checked the front and found Midnight flopped on the porch. I dumped food in his bowl, but the big dog pushed me aside to go inside.

Chaos dropped to her knees and took all the affection Midnight would happily provide.

Evidently, we had a dog now too.

And we also now were a *we*. There was no denying that, either.

I brought both his dishes in and set them at the end of the kitchen island. Midnight happily went over to wolf down his kibble and slobbered water all over my floor.

He then proceeded to take his now empty water dish over to the couch and chew on it.

"You gotta get him some toys."

"He's not my—"

"He's definitely your dog, Ransom."

I sighed. "Yeah."

She pulled out her phone and took a quick snapshot of Midnight on my fawn-colored couch. "Welcome home, Midnight," she said as she typed.

Then she came over to me and took my hand to lead me up the stairs.

We took a shower together full of touches and soft sighs, ending with me wrapping those long, perfect legs around me as I took her against the stone wall.

The intimacy was almost too much—and exactly what I needed. Losing myself in her wet softness inside and out pushed back the doubts and fears that had crept in the closer we got home.

We tumbled into bed, and I finally shut off.

At least for a few hours, there was nothing to worry about but holding her close in the night.

I woke to her sitting in the sunshine beside me, the sheet shored up against her naked breasts. She didn't have her phone. Instead it was an actual camera.

She lowered it when I held out a hand. "Really?"

"You looked so peaceful. It's rare."

I pulled my pillow over my face. "Shut up."

"C'mon. This is just for me."

I lowered it. "Why?"

She shrugged and the sheet dipped. She tried to right it, but I pulled her hand away. "Hey."

"At least give me some incentive."

She narrowed her eyes at me and let the sheet puddle around her waist. "Happy?"

I reached out to trace her cinnamon-colored nipple until it tightened under my touch. "Happier."

She took a few more pictures and surprised me when she kept shooting as I tugged on her nipple. She licked her lips as I increased the pressure then moved to the other.

"What do you see?"

She swallowed. "How much you want me."

I shifted under the sheet. "Always."

The whir of the lens focusing was the only sound beyond her quiet gasp as the sheet lowered to see just how much I wanted her.

"Unless you're going for some more interesting pictures, put the camera down, Chaos."

She looked down at the camera's viewfinder, her pupils dilating at what she saw. When she didn't put down the camera, I let her have all the goods.

"Dear God, your body is some serious perfection."

"Battered and scarred. It ain't pretty, babe."

"Oh, but it is."

She trailed her fingers over the ridges of my abs to the lower lines that led to the base of my cock. There was a burn mark at my hip from some close call I couldn't even remember. There were so many marks on my body that had no names or times attached in my memory.

Each moment was just something I got through until I went to the next warzone they sent me to.

She crawled over me and sat on my thighs. With one hand, she cupped my shaft and gave me a long stroke. I hissed as I lifted my hips to seat her more firmly.

Her camera wasn't trained on my cock. No, she pressed the tip tight to her smooth, freckled belly, very out of frame. She rocked lightly as if she wanted me somewhere else.

God, I hoped she did.

I tucked my arm behind my head and let her do what she wanted, my jaw tight as she gripped me at the base.

She smiled as she changed the angle of the camera. "So stern and intense."

I gave her a toothy smile.

She laughed. "Now that's a shark smile. C'mon, just one for me." She inched forward until the base of my length was tucked against her pussy.

"That's one way to get a smile." I groaned at the wetness I could feel. Nothing between us. "And a dangerous move, Chaos."

She rose on her knees and stroked her way up my length. "It feels good." She tipped back her head for a second before she looked back down at me.

I heard the whir of the camera, but I didn't care anymore. I reached for her, grasping her hips to control the stroke.

Her breath hitched as I dragged the tip of my cock through her slick wetness. That damn camera never moved. The chase for control was on.

I never backed down from a dare or a fight. Not when it mattered. I tucked the flared head of my dick under the little hood that hid her clit from me. If I moved just a little, I could slide inside of her.

That warm clasp of her body never disappointed. And each time,

I got more addicted to the feel of her. But I wasn't a stupid man and I would never take that kind of chance with her.

Instead I lifted her and flipped her to the bottom of the bed. She yelped and her arm with the camera flew to the side, but she didn't drop it.

I hooked her leg over my shoulder and closed my mouth around her soft, swollen pussy. She arched up off the bed with a groan and my name rolled out into a rumbling sigh.

She soaked my face, and I knew I'd hold her with me today in my beard. One more excuse not to shave today.

I found her clit and sucked hard, driving her quickly up and over. Her thighs shook around my ears and she held me tight. I laughed as I heard the sound of her damn camera.

Biting the inside of her thigh, I gazed up at her. Instead of finishing up, I laced my fingers over her belly to hold her down. "Didn't think you'd be into a show."

"Neither did I." She was out of breath.

"Then let me provide."

"Oh, Jesus."

"No help from anyone up there right now, Chaos." I grinned at her then slowly destroyed her with my mouth.

I could live in her taste forever. Salty and sweet with the lightest peachy texture.

She bucked under me, her fingers gripping my hair as I relent-lessly demanded everything. I spread her wide and laughed when I heard the camera tumble to the floor.

"Ransom, please."

"One more."

"I can't—" She tried to inch away from me, her legs trembling as I lapped at her clit.

"I can't get enough." I jammed my hips into the mattress for some relief of my own. My dick was so rigid I was probably going to dent the goddamn bed.

But I wanted another.

I slid one arm up her belly to her chest, flicking my thumb over her tight nipple.

She covered my hand on her breast. "Harder."

I plucked and tugged as my tongue found the right combination that she needed. Her cry was intense enough to drag me out of the haze I was in.

"Willow." Guttural and almost agonized, I crawled up to cover her with my body and wrap myself around her as she shook under me.

"Inside," she said against my neck. "Please."

"I need to get—"

"No. I'm on the Pill. Inside. Inside."

I frowned down at her. "Willow."

"Please. It's been so long since anyone has been inside me like that. Just you." She gripped my ass, rocking me against her belly where I was tucked tight between us.

Sunlight striped us and her curls were twisted and jumbled against my light-colored blankets. I tucked a strand back from her sweaty face and shifted myself with my other hand.

There was no way I could deny her—or myself.

I groaned as her tight walls took me deep, clasping me with each inch I sank into her. I never looked away from her gold-green eyes, so steady on mine, until I finally was fully seated inside of her.

As I moved, they fluttered shut as a sigh gusted between us.

The pace was slow at first, both of us enamored with the first time skin to skin. She lifted her leg to curl around my hip as I levered myself up on my forearms and drove deeper and harder.

She met me stroke for stroke, her long body matching mine with an extra roll of her hips that made my eyes cross. I didn't want this to end.

For the world to intrude in on us again.

I buried my face in her neck as I pounded into her. In the back of my mind, I worried that it was too much, too harsh, but then she wrapped herself around me, her arms and legs accepting the raging power within the passion that had sneaked up on me when I wasn't paying attention.

It wasn't enough.

I leaned back up on my knees and dragged her up with me, surging up into her willing body.

Her legs were long enough to take the position and she pushed down on me with each upward cant of my hips. My stomach muscles flexed and burned and my back hated me, but I still drove inside of her, chasing something unnameable.

She curled her arms around me and cried out as she went over with the friction between us. I couldn't withstand the sweet clasp of her body or the punishing pace.

I held her waist to keep her tight to me as the burn scorched down my spine and I let go inside of her.

Mine.

Dear God, I hope I didn't chant it out loud.

She shook around me, dragging in gulps of air. "I'm sorry. I don't..."

"*Shh.*" I stroked her hair as she blew out slow breaths.

"Wow." She pressed her cheek to my shoulder, then she yelped as I crashed back to the middle of the bed. She flipped her hair out of both of our faces. "Sir."

"Don't start with the *sir* thing again."

She snuggled her face into my neck. "But it fits. If I was a cat, I'd purr." She nipped at my Adam's apple. "Maybe I just will anyway." She made a faux meow sound against my shoulder.

I laughed as I stroked my hand down her back and hip.

"Were you going for some record or something?"

"Or something." I kissed the top of her head.

I wasn't sure I wanted to dive into what *that* had been. It felt a lot like I was in trouble on about fifteen fronts.

She hooked a leg over mine and stroked my chest. "We need a shower again."

"Yep."

"And I need to bring my camera out more often if that's what I get."

"Didn't know you had a voyeuristic streak, Chaos."

"Me neither." She pressed a kiss to my chest then licked me lightly.

"You looking for round two?"

She skimmed her fingers down the middle of my belly to the trail of hair that led to my currently dead cock. "Maybe I just like touching you." She retraced the tip of her nail over each ridge of muscle.

I flexed because I knew it would make her laugh.

"How on earth do you get these? Like five million sit-ups?"

"Rings."

She propped herself up on her forearm. "Oh, those things I saw in the corner of your living room? I wondered what they were."

I shifted to get comfortable. When Chaos wanted to talk, there wasn't much use trying to deny her. "My last tour, I ended up in the hospital."

"What?"

"Yeah. Afterward, I needed physical therapy. The rings helped me with my upper body strength. Added bonus is a lot of core muscle work."

"I'll say." She used her two fingers to walk her way up my stomach to my chain. "I feel like there's still stuff you haven't told me."

"Have you told me everything?"

She shrugged. "Aidan opened up my past as if he was a can opener and tossed it up on a video screen."

"We all have stuff we keep close."

She drew a circle around the coin on my necklace. "Jason really fucked me up for a long time. Took me a good three years to even go on a date with a guy, let alone get naked with one."

"I prefer not to think about you naked with anyone else, thanks."

She leaned in and kissed my nose. "Ditto. And I'm sure there were a few."

I reached above me to drag a pillow under my head. "Not as many as you'd think. I was on a Blackhawk more than I was on land for a lot of years."

She laced her fingers on my chest to prop up her chin. "Is that what you did? Fly helicopters?"

"Mostly." Telling people who weren't in the thick of things about my job was hard to explain. "We pretty much were the guys who picked up and dropped off soldiers into some pretty hairy places."

"All the soldiers?"

I nodded. "A lot of times it was the SEALs but some others." I couldn't count the number of ops that had been in a very gray area for my own moral compass. "My last op was such a cluster I decided to get out. Parting gift was the bullet in my side."

Her eyes swam and one tear slipped out. I thumbed it away. "It's okay, Chaos."

She sniffled a little and wrinkled her nose. "Tough guy."

Today was definitely not the day to tell her about Jones. "Time to get going. I could stay in bed with you all day, but I'm pretty sure our to-do list makes that a negatory."

She flopped onto her back. "Lame."

I rolled over her, my hands on either side of her so I didn't crush her. I gave her a quick, hard kiss before hopping off the bed. "Shake your ass, Chaos."

"You first." She tossed a pillow at me, but she missed.

I turned back from the bathroom doorway. "Guess I gotta use up the hot water then."

"You wouldn't."

Probably not. I heard a bark and then Chaos's shriek.

"Midnight, no."

I peeked around the corner and saw the massive dog sitting on Willow's lap. I waved and shut the door behind me.

"Gee, thanks, buddy!"

Maybe I would be getting all the hot water, after all.

Chapter 27

Willow

The Truth Sucks

After removing a hundred and fifty pound dog from my lap, I did manage to get some of the hot water. Also, Ransom's version of washing my back was much better than my own.

We both had morning chores—taking care of the dog, letting him out, and checking in with Aidan. Apparently, they hadn't any more luck on the screen name or the photo, just that it had been definitely taken in the distillery.

He was getting more bold. It took a lot of balls to set up a damn table and put it back.

Plus, we couldn't figure out which one he'd used to try to get prints. Thirty tables were under those tarps and who knew how many chairs. But Aidan had agreed to send someone out to update the security so we didn't have to bother Clay right now.

Ransom was just as annoyed as I was and had disappeared into his workshop.

I cooked us breakfast and used the crustless quiche recipe I'd found in a magazine as a video for my channel. The magazine had been fancy as hell and no one had an hour to cook breakfast, thanks.

Unless you caramelized onions, that is. That pretty much was my only dealbreaker. Especially if you were making bacon jam.

I tried to put as much joy in my voice as possible, but I had a feeling I'd be doing a lot of editing after we ate.

With two plates in my hand, I knocked on the door with my foot, but Ransom's music was blaring. I juggled the plates and and opened the door. He must've been even more pissed than I'd realized, since he never blasted music at this level.

I couldn't blame him. This faceless coward was constantly a step —or more—ahead of us.

Sawdust was everywhere and it stuck to Ransom's hair as he sanded the top of the most stunning desk I'd ever seen. Delicate inlays had been carved into the corners and the fronts of the drawers, but the piece had clean, gorgeous lines.

The style itched at the back of my mind. What did this desk remind me of?

"Ransom," I called out over the sander.

He glanced over at me with his yellow protective glasses on. He was kinda cute all disheveled. Sawdust had even stuck to his rapidly growing beard.

Flicking off the machine, he pushed the glasses up on top of his head.

"Food."

"Oh, right. Sorry. I forgot about feeding you."

"Handily, I'm kinda good at that part."

He twisted around as if at a loss for the wreckage that surrounded us. "Maybe we should go back in the house."

"Nah. I want to see what you're working on." I held out a plate.

He brushed at his face before he pulled off his gloves and took it. "Thanks." Then he groaned. "Smells amazing."

"I raided your pantry. Sundried tomatoes and bacon seemed like a good combo to me."

He forked up a bite. "Bacon works for everything." Leaning on the workbench, he pointed to the desk with his fork. "Clay is having an office built for her while they're on their honeymoon as a surprise. She keeps telling him she doesn't need one, but..." He shrugged.

"She definitely needs one. I fear for their marriage if she doesn't have her own space soon."

He shoveled in another two bites and I tried not to laugh. For someone who liked to cook, he ate as if it was his job rather than for pleasure. "You get it." He swallowed with a sigh. "And so does he."

I popped in the last bit of my wedge of quiche in my mouth and set my plate on the end table tucked in the corner. "It's beautiful. You're a craftsman."

"Thanks." He set his plate down on his workbench and moved back to the desk to smooth his hand over the wood. "I'm just about done. I just need to stain and seal it."

I noticed the dark piece leaning against the back of the garage. "Like that?"

He nodded. "Goes with the built-ins Clay ordered for her. I knew the desk needed to be a little more special than prefab."

"Unless you're doing RID premades..." That was what it reminded me of. The uncomplicated style with clean lines and surprising details that you only noticed when you studied the piece for a while.

I turned to him and crowded close. "Tell me you aren't RID."

His face turned stony.

"Are you kidding me?"

He huffed out a breath. "It's not like it's a secret if you wanted to know."

"That is not the point. That you'd keep that from me is..." I pushed him back into the workbench. "I was babbling on about your work and you freaking designed everything?"

"Chaos..."

"Don't 'Chaos' me." I stabbed my finger into his chest. "I made a fool of myself about getting them as gifts."

305

"And I was flattered, but knowing I made them isn't important."

He was being deliberately obtuse. That his company was so much a part of him and he hadn't wanted to share it with me hurt in ways I couldn't catalog.

He covered my hand on his chest. "I tried to figure out who had bought the gifts, but he used a fake name there too and paid with a throwaway Mastercard available at any drugstore."

My heart was roaring in my ears. Why would he keep that from me? That this is who he was beyond the soldier and rich guy. Which he also didn't talk about. God, I was so stupid.

My shoulders ached from holding myself rigid and my throat was as dry as dust. "Why didn't you tell me? What else haven't you told me?" Before he could answer, I asked, "RID...your initials?"

He gave a curt nod in the affirmative. "Ransom Isaac Douglas."

"Unbelievable." I stalked away from him and paced from one end of the garage to the other. Then noticed another piece. "Is this something new?"

"Yeah."

It was a beautiful sideboard with a long tabletop and storage beneath, the kind used in a dining room for family meals. Making the piece a little more special, there were intricate spindles to hold platters or other larger pieces. This was so different from his other line and yet still the same. Instantly recognizable as his craftsmanship.

The fact that he hadn't even thought about sharing himself with me clanged in my ears like church bells.

"It wasn't exactly a lie," he said into the silence.

I pressed my lips together against the angry words I didn't want to let loose. The hurt just beneath was even worse. "An omission is just as bad and you know it."

"Then let's get it all out."

"There's more?" I fisted my hands, my voice raw.

"I was hoping that if I showed up on your channel or made myself seen, it would draw out this sniveling bastard."

I backed up a step, my hip dragging against the sharp edge of my sister's desk.

"Chaos..."

"So, you didn't want..." My mind whirled. How far did he take it? "You only were with me to—"

"No." His voice was a whip. "Don't go there."

"Go where? That this was all a lie for the cameras?" Us together. The day with the food trucks, kissing me in the rain. Kissing me outside my apartment in Brooklyn.

I bent at the waist. A vague memory of Aidan showing us a video of someone watching the front of my apartment.

"Chaos." He grabbed for my hand, but I twisted away.

"No. No. You don't get to touch me right now."

"It wasn't like that."

I straightened. "Oh, but that kiss outside my apartment was, right?"

He closed his eyes.

"Right. Just a means to an end right, Ransom?" Again, coming to Turnbull had just made everything worse. I'd drawn trouble right to my family.

"That's not how it was and you know it."

I didn't want to hear his half-baked explanations. He'd come up with a damn good plan and I'd fallen right in line. Give a girl a few orgasms and she'll follow you anywhere.

She'll even fall in love with you.

I stumbled back and pushed through the door to the house. Should I stay or leave?

Where would I even go?

Breathing hard, I pulled out my phone. I could call...who?

Rachel was out of town. I couldn't call Aunt Laverne or my cousins. I couldn't put my problems on any more people.

Couldn't risk causing anyone else harm, even inadvertently.

I didn't even have my car.

I grabbed my purse and ran for the door. Ransom, ever the organized one, put his keys right on the hook beside it. I snagged them and slammed out the door.

Before I could get to his truck, the house alarm went wild since I hadn't disengaged it. Midnight barked and chased after me. Tears streamed down my face, but I managed to get the door open to his vehicle.

"Stay, Midnight." I climbed in and shoved my bag into the passenger side.

"Willow!" My name was a roar.

I locked the doors and tore down the drive. I glanced in the rearview as Ransom shoved his hands through his hair. The cool April breeze lifted his plaid shirttails around him.

Sorrow wrapped around my sternum and squeezed. I didn't want to leave him. But how could I stay not knowing how much he'd faked with me?

Especially since everything on my side was all too real.

My phone blared out of my purse, but I ignored it. Before I got to the bottom of his property, the truck sputtered out. All the instrument lights on the dash came to life before blinking out as the engine went dead.

I slammed my hand on the steering wheel. "What the hell?" I scanned the nearby road, then I looked over my shoulder and saw nothing but trees.

I tried the ignition button, but it was still dead. The door also wouldn't open. My heart rate doubled. I pushed at the door, trying the handle.

Did he do this with of his fancy gadgets in his truck?

No, he wouldn't lock me in here. *Trap* me here. Would he?

I slammed my foot on the brake and hit the locks, hoping the brake to start the car would work the same for the locks. I was in luck. The unlock mechanism worked and I scrambled out.

What was I supposed to do? Go back up the damn driveway with my tail between my legs?

"If you make me chase you, Chaos, I swear to God." His voice was a deep baritone in the distance. Even that far away, the furious worry in his tone was enough to make me shiver.

At the sound of footsteps behind me, I reached in to grab my bag. Then a sharp pain against my skull robbed my breath just before everything went black.

Chapter 28

Ransom

Just Stay Put, Dammit

I booked it down the hill. Every gravelly punch to my knees made me angrier. I didn't care how much it cost to pave this drive, it would be done this year.

After I killed Willow.

I got around the break in the trees and all my muscles clenched tight. Why the hell had she stopped?

Glimpsing the open door caused me to pick up speed. What the hell was she thinking running from me? I shouldn't have freaking told her.

The itch between my shoulder blades burned. Not my lungs. I could run for days, but something was wrong.

"Willow!" My throat was on fire from yelling her name.

A glint of something came through the trees, then a swath of red hair on the ground seemed to glow in the darkness. I skidded down the steep incline at the bottom of my property, hopping over stones and old tree stumps.

A figure in a dark hoodie and dark jeans crouched over her.

"Hey!"

He looked up, the hood dipping low over his face. Something flashed in his hand just before he tried to lift her.

"Don't you fucking touch her!" I snarled.

I was no better than a rabid animal, ready to rip out this bastard's throat for even daring to step on my land.

As he scrambled back, whatever he held in his hand fell to the ground.

His head whipped between her and the weapon.

Jesus, a *weapon.*

"I'll fucking kill you." I got to the end of the truck and slapped on the metal back panel.

He snatched the weapon and sprinted for his car.

I ran right to Willow and carefully lifted her head to rest on my leg. "Chaos. Please, please." Flashbacks of Jones slammed into me, and for an instant, the blood from my friend transferred to her pale, freckled skin. *"Willow."*

The car fishtailed on its way off my property, and I managed to drag my attention away from her long enough to look up. A quick shake of my head dislodged my brain from the past, giving me enough clarity to finally focus and look for a tag.

The license plate was missing off the back of the car.

"Fuck." I crouched over her, protecting her with my body even if that was all I could give her right now. "Chaos," I whispered. "Come back to me."

She moaned, lifting her hand to weakly grip the back of my shirt.

"Thank God." I moved her hair and saw the burn mark at the back of her neck.

Taser. Thank God.

As awful as it was, I was so grateful it hadn't been a gun.

"Mmm. Ransom?" Her voice was groggy.

"It's okay. Take it slow."

"What the hell hit me?"

I hauled her into my lap and brushed away the gravel from her jaw. A small cut marred her cheek under a smear of dirt.

Just dirt, not blood.

Not like Jones.

I pulled her against my chest and cupped the back of her head. "Don't you ever run from me like that again."

She gripped my back. "You didn't want me."

"That's bullshit. Making myself a goddamn target instead of you isn't the same as faking my feelings for you." I hugged her even tighter, my arms straining with tension. "If anything had happened to you..." I laid my cheek against the top of her head.

"You're shaking."

"Some lunatic just tried to fucking *take* you. Of course, I am."

She peered up at me. "The truck went dead." She hissed and touched the back of her neck. "I couldn't even get out at first. God, what hit me?"

"A goddamn Taser."

"What?" She hissed again as she touched it. "I thought it was you."

"Me?"

She held onto me tighter. "Your truck is retrofitted with all kinds of tech. I figured you had an anti-theft thing or something."

I didn't know if I should shake her or just lock her in a room for not immediately realizing the threat had come from her stalker. "Smart about the anti-theft. I'll talk to R&D about working something out in an app. You leaving in my truck, however? *Fuck.*" I rocked her to chill myself out before I shouted. That was the last thing she needed right now. "What were you thinking?"

"Was..." She clutched the front of my shirt. "Was that him?"

"You know it was."

Her chest started heaving, a sure sign her panic and shock were about to collide.

"Chaos, take it easy. Slow breaths."

"He's here? Actually here? How did he find you? *Us?*"

"I don't know." I hauled her up to stand and rested her against the driver's door. "Just stay put for a second."

Still shaking, she looped her arm around my waist. But she stayed on her feet, so I had to give her credit. A Taser blast was a damn blow to the system.

I dug out my phone and dialed Aidan directly, putting the call on speaker.

"Roth." A lot of noise filled the line.

"Hey. Are those guys you sent out to the orchard more than just techs?"

"'Those techs' are me. I'm about thirty minutes from Happy Acres."

Even better. "Think you can reroute to my place first?"

"What happened?"

"I'm pretty sure he just tried to kidnap Willow."

The line went silent for a moment. "Are you sure?"

I crushed her to my chest, lifting the phone so the speaker wasn't muffled. "I don't think it was a well-thought-out plan. More like he took advantage of a situation."

She was shaken enough not to argue. She just held on to me.

"Well, shit. All right." His vehicle accelerated in the background.

"I'll send you a pin with my address." I texted him my location through maps, the easiest way.

"Appreciate it. See you in under an hour." He clicked off.

I shoved my phone into my pocket. "Step back for me."

She nodded and straightened, swaying a little before she took a step back. Steady enough for me not to call the cavalry, but not steady enough for a midnight stroll.

I hooked an arm under her legs and lifted her.

"Ransom!"

I went to the back of the truck. "Open the tailgate for me."

She pushed at me halfheartedly. "I'm not going to fall over."

"Tell that to your dissolving knees." I lifted her onto the tailgate. "Stay there. Don't move."

She gave me a snappy salute.

Clearly, she was starting to feel better. And I preferred her sarcasm to tears any day.

I put one foot in front of the other. I could fall apart after she was safe. My hand only shook slightly as I slid into the driver's seat. I tried the ignition and the truck roared to life.

She hopped off the tailgate and came around to the passenger side.

I disengaged the locks to let her in. "What did I say?"

"I'm still in the truck."

"This isn't a fucking game."

"I know it's not!" Her wide, still panicked eyes met mine. "He just tried to take me. I need to get out of here."

"We'll go to the hospital."

"No, just take me home," she whispered as she hugged herself. "Please."

I slammed my door and backed up then did a U-turn to head toward the house. Gravel sprayed under the tires, breaking the heavy silence between us.

If I hadn't been there...

If I hadn't chased after her, he could have taken her.

Maybe he'd already be gone with her. And I wouldn't have any way to find her.

Gone. Maybe forever.

The steering wheel squeaked under my grip.

The trip up the hill was blessedly quick. At the top, I shoved the truck into Park.

"Ransom—"

"Get in the house, Chaos."

"I'm fine. I promise. A little shaken up, but I'm fine."

"You scared the fuck out of me."

She touched my arm. "I'm okay. I'm here."

After wrenching open my door, I came around the truck to her side and dragged her out. Before her feet even hit the ground, I had her mouth under mine.

She gripped my shoulders, matching my desperation. The kiss was as wild and out of control as my feelings for her.

And maybe even her feelings for me.

"Chaos," I said against her mouth. "If you ever do something like that again—" I cupped the top of her head, making sure I didn't get near her wound. "I can't lose you too." I pressed a kiss to her forehead, holding her tight.

She readjusted to loop her arms around my lower back. "You're not going to lose me."

"You're damn right, because you're not going anywhere without me. I don't care how mad at me you get, you and me are in this until the end."

She nodded. "Right. Until we get this guy." She pressed her cheek to my chest. "I promise."

"I don't think you're getting it." I eased her back.

"I understand. I promise I do. That he could get so close to me, and I was too stupid to realize it was even him." She shivered.

Lightly, I shook her. "He's never getting near you again. You got that?"

She nodded.

"You're everything."

"What does that mean?" She gripped my shirt. "You can't keep playing with me about this. Pretending for the cameras without letting me in on it. Did you think I couldn't handle what needed to be done?"

"No." Frustration rose in me like a storm. It was fast. Too fast. Everything inside of me rebelled at it, but this felt right—even in the center of insanity.

"You hold on to me like it's more. I know it is. Or are you lying to yourself?"

"Not anymore."

She frowned at me.

I cupped her face. "You're it for me. End of the line. Believe it." I pressed my forehead to hers. "Please."

She gripped my wrists. "Ransom, I..."

"I love you, dammit."

Her greenish-gold eyes widened, but she said nothing. I wasn't even sure she was still breathing.

She wasn't the only one.

"I'm not kidding."

She shook her head. "You're just saying that because of the whole thing with the—the guy. He almost got me. You're just running on emotions."

"Do you know who you're talking to? When do I run on emotions?"

She shook her head and tried to push me away. "You can't say crazy stuff like that. Not if you don't mean it."

"I mean it." I grabbed her hands and brought them to my chest, holding them against my racing heart. "I swear it. Never in my life have I ever felt this way about another woman."

Her lower lip quivered.

"You don't have to say it back—"

She lifted on her toes to kiss me. This time, it wasn't a clash of wills and fear. It was solid and true and us.

As even as the ocean at dawn, but as always, there was a tempest just under the surface.

She slid her arms around my neck as she dragged her fingers through my hair to hold me right where I was. Not letting me move a millimeter. She murmured against my mouth. At first, it was a mere whisper, then it was a hum, and then it was my name.

"I love you, Ransom."

My lips stretched into a smile, making her laugh. I hadn't thought I still could, but that was just one of the gifts she gave me.

"There are my dimples." She brushed her finger along the dents hidden by my beard.

Or so I told myself.

She gave me one last quick kiss. "I'm still mad at you though." She reached into the truck for her bag.

"Typical. I tell you I love you and you can't let the other part go."

"Nope." She patted my cheek. "Now I need coffee before Aidan gets here."

She brushed by me, trailing lemons in her wake. Already, she had a new preoccupation, and it wasn't me.

"Midnight!"

I hung my head. Her laugh soothed some of the fear still crowding my chest. I wasn't sure it would ever leave me after what had happened tonight.

She crouched in front of my dog to give him all the scratches and rubs then they went in the house together.

Following at a slower pace, I made sure my security was engaged and checked my app on my phone to see if anything was caught on the various cameras on my property.

I should have thought to put some at the edges. That would be rectified before dinner.

He'd gotten to her because I hadn't been smart enough. Not thorough or careful enough.

It wouldn't happen again.

I ran up the porch stairs and followed her inside. Love crowded in and made things more complicated, but there was no putting that back in the box.

I wouldn't lose her. Period.

"Let's put some of your editing skills to the test, Chaos. We need to post a video."

"Just let me clean up."

I crossed to her, my fingers tightening into fists as her abrasions showed up even more in the light. Including some swelling. My hand wasn't steady as I touched the wound. "Let me get the first-aid kit."

"It's okay."

"It's not. It's starting to swell." I went into the kitchen and grabbed the bag of peas in the freezer I kept for just such a use. They worked better than the regular blue ice packs any day. Then I found my first-aid kit under the sink and put both on the kitchen island.

"Up you go."

"Ransom..." She blew out a breath when I plunked her on the counter. "I can take care of it."

"I know you can, but I want to. Let me do this."

She brushed my hair off my forehead. "Guess we have to add a haircut to the list of our chores this week."

"Who cares about my hair? We're going to be sitting here for the next week."

"Nope. We have things we have to do to make things easier on Clay and Rachel."

"Not when I don't know where that asshole will be."

"He already found us. I don't know how. Maybe I don't want to know. But we aren't going to let him get the upper hand again."

My fingers clenched around the first-aid wash.

She peeled them off the bottle and drew me between her legs. "You're the big bad soldier, not him."

"I wasn't enough today. He almost got to you." Fucking hacker had probably managed to hack my damn truck. Anything could have happened to her. Even if I was with her, what if he'd immobilized me?

"Ransom."

My gaze snapped to hers.

"I see all those what if scenarios whipping through your mind."

"I usually have a better poker face," I grumbled.

She set the first-aid spray on the island, then she cupped my face in her hands. "Don't worry. I just have made it a habit to study you more than most." She lightly stroked my beard. "I was stupid. This is the first and last time you'll probably ever hear that out of my mouth, but I was stupid. And I won't make that kind of mistake again."

"You're damn right you won't."

Her lips curved as she leaned down to kiss me. "We're better together. Don't leave me in the dark again."

I gripped her hips, my fingers tangling in the belt loops of her jeans. "It was never pretend. I need you to know that. The minute you were in my care, I knew that I was fucked."

"Because you feel responsible?"

"No. I mean some, of course. I have very few people I care about in this world. My family sucks, save for my sisters. And even then, I'm only close to one of them. But it's Clay and Rachel and now you. That's it."

"I know you have a crush on Aunt Laverne."

"Well, she might give you a run for your money."

She laughed before her expression turned serious again. "Don't put everything on your shoulders. We're a team."

I nodded because I knew it would appease her. But there was no way this didn't weigh on me. Now that I'd found her, there was nothing I wouldn't do to keep her safe.

"Let's get you cleaned up before Aidan shows up."

"Okay, Dr. Douglas."

I arched a brow at her. "Cameras and now roleplaying. What have I gotten myself into?"

She lifted her knees to wrap around my waist. "So much trouble."

I let myself take this moment with her. I had a feeling there wouldn't be much time for any for the next few days.

And they were too precious for me to miss any of them with her. I wouldn't lose sight of that again.

Chapter 29

Willow

Lock You Down

Ransom had barely gotten a butterfly bandage on me before the doorbell rang. I hopped down and followed him to the door.

"Chaos..."

I rolled my eyes and went back into the kitchen. If he needed to control the door, then I'd let him. I wasn't sure I'd ever seen Ransom so scared and angry at the same time.

Then he tossed that *forever* word at me like a damn dart. I had not been ready for it. It had been mere days, for God's sake.

Not nearly enough time for normal people to fall in love.

Then again, nothing in my life had been normal. From school to my career, I'd always been left of center. Why wouldn't I fall in love with a grumpy soldier turned wood crafter in the same amount of time it took me to perfect a quiche recipe?

Made total sense.

Hmm. Though it was interesting that we both were creatives in our own right. Ransom just preferred to stay in the shadows, and I was always looking for the light.

Midnight's nails scratched over the stairs and the kitchen floor as he flew into the room. The scruff of his neck stood up like spikes while he let out a series of menacing barks.

"Oh, hold on." The dog practically shoved me over a step as he crowded against me, standing just in front of me.

Ransom turned with a surprised look.

"Good guard dog," came the voice from the door.

"That was a new one." Ransom held the door open.

Aidan Roth took up space like no one I'd ever known. Ransom was muscular and tall, but Aidan was a whole different kind of bulky.

He stepped inside and the two men shook hands. Aidan carried a rather large box as well as a messenger bag bulging with some kind of equipment.

Looked like my life was about to get another level of locked down.

"How you doing, Willow?"

I shrugged as I stroked Midnight's coarse fur. "I can't say I expected him to get that bold."

"What happened?" Aidan set the box and bag on the island.

I gave him the specifics and then Ransom filled in the rest since I was freaking unconscious for some of it. Midnight seemed to notice my change in demeanor and he leaned harder against my leg.

I patted his massive neck and bent to give him a kiss on top of his head.

Aidan came forward. The dog was wary, but he'd stopped growling. The two males faced off and finally, Midnight's tail wagged. A minute later, Aidan crouched down and the two became best buds.

Typical.

I glanced at Ransom. "Treats and toys are on the list this week, buddy."

"We're going out as little as possible."

"Actually, I think going out and being seen is a good thing." Aidan stood and opened up the box. "I brought some gear. I have more in my truck for the orchard. As long as we have permission, I'll put some small cameras at the wedding venue, as well."

"We have to tell them." I stroked Midnight's flank then moved to the island to peer into the box. "They need to know I brought this to the orchard."

"You didn't know this was going to happen." Aidan opened the bag and pulled out a laptop. "We assumed he'd stick with the dark web. Coming out was a bold choice. But that also shows he's being irrational."

"That could make him dangerous." I crossed my arms, suddenly chilled.

"And that's why we shouldn't go anywhere." Ransom's voice was low and dangerous.

"I don't know if that course of action will achieve what you want. He might just wait you out. You can't be on her twenty-four-seven."

"Bet?"

I moved to Ransom and laced our fingers. "I won't live like this. I did it in college. No one is going to take my life from me again."

"It's like that, huh?" Aidan glanced between us. "I had a feeling, but it seems you've accelerated things since I saw you."

Ransom's grip tightened. "Then you better have more toys in there to keep her safe than a fucking camera."

"I do."

"Then let's figure it out." Ransom brushed a gentle kiss over my bandage and let me go.

Twenty minutes later, the kitchen island had been transformed into a command center. Even with all my tech understanding, I couldn't keep up with what they were putting together. Ransom seemed way more knowledgable than I'd initially believed.

I left the two of them to it and set up my own workstation on the couch with a pair of headphones to block their security speak. I was pretty sure they wouldn't want to hear my edits, either.

Midnight made himself at home beside me while I napped off a headache. Evidently, getting a few hundred jolts of electricity could take it out of a girl.

Ransom woke me before they went outside so I wouldn't worry if

I woke and they were gone. I used the solitary time to film a few short videos to cover me for the next few days.

By the time I realized how long I'd been working, dinner time had rolled around. Aidan and Ransom came in and gave me a heads up about the cameras outside, at the edges of his property, and in the house for good measure.

I wasn't sure what they were talking about when they discussed merging two softwares and was happy to stay in my own lane there.

My natural curiosity would normally have me hanging on every word, but I knew I needed to protect my space and psyche right now. I didn't know how I was going to tell my family about the mess I'd brought to their door.

Clay and Rachel would be coming home from the city tomorrow and that would be soon enough for me to figure out some way to gather them together.

We had a full week of wedding things starting this weekend—the bachelor and bachelorette parties, rehearsal, and I had to make sure my dress fit, as well. Picking up Ransom's tux was also on the list.

Ransom threw together a meal and Aidan stayed to eat. We'd talk to the Ronsons and Mannings tomorrow, as well as Clay and Rachel. Aidan would also set up the orchard and the distillery.

I helped clean up, finishing loading the dishwasher while Ransom walked Aidan out. Midnight followed them for his evening run outside.

Ransom came back in and leaned on the kitchen island. "How are you doing?"

I loaded the last plate and closed the door. "Today was a lot."

"I'm still certain you're handling this better than I am."

I went around the island and ducked under his arm. He straightened and gathered me in against his chest. "I hate all of this. I hate that I'm going to scare my sister again tomorrow, and I hate that I might be putting my family in danger."

Saying everything I'd been thinking for the last few days in a rush left me breathless and I was trying so hard not to start shaking again. I'd been so good all day.

Ransom drew me into the living room and sat down with me, our knees touching as he took my hands. "Look at me."

I stared at our joined hands.

"Chaos."

I pressed my lips together against the tremors that wanted to take over, and I made myself look at him. He instantly began to calm me, just by being there. Steady and strong.

"Hear me when I tell you this wasn't your fault."

I swallowed the lump in my throat. "I never should have come home."

"This is exactly where you should be."

"What if he hurts my family?"

"I won't let that happen. Aidan and I will make sure we are all smart about this. No more keeping them in the dark."

"What if he ruins the wedding?" A quick flash of waking up with my face in the gravel made me grip his hands harder. "I don't want Rachel to cancel the wedding for me. I know that will be her kneejerk reaction."

"It won't come to that."

"You don't know that." I let him go to rub my nose with the back of my hand. "I never thought he'd try to..." I trailed off.

I didn't even know what he looked like. He'd sneaked up on me and I had no fucking clue.

"He's never going to get to you like that again."

"You can't be with me all the time." His fierce eyes and locked jaw made me cup his cheek. "There has to be a better way."

"We'll figure it out together."

Shocked, I just laughed. "Did you just own up to teamwork?"

"Makes the dream work, babe."

I rested my forehead against his chest.

He rubbed my arms. "Let's go get some rest. I want to check those marks on your neck too."

I straightened. "You gonna play doctor?"

"Maybe." He stood and pulled me to my feet. "You seem fixated on that."

"What about Midnight?"

"I'll come get him when I do the last lock-up."

"Perimeter search for the win." I leaned against him. "What if he's out there while you are?"

"Then I'll probably kill him."

"Ransom." I stared at him. "No, you won't."

"I wouldn't bet against me."

"He's a sick individual, but—"

"I don't care. He's not getting near you again." He cupped my face and I leaned into him.

His sober expression and the lack of tension in his body unnerved me. It was as if making the decision to have no limits in dealing with this bastard had somehow eased him.

"I don't want you to have to do that. Ever."

"I've done things I'm not proud of, babe. This wouldn't be one I'd lose sleep over for even a minute. Him or you is no contest."

"But—" If anything happened to him or if he got in trouble because of me, I would never be able to live with that kind of guilt.

"I won't apologize for making you my priority." He took my hand and led me toward the stairs.

Well, there wasn't much I could say on that front. And the fact that I felt better knowing he had my back no matter what happened wasn't something I wanted to look at too closely.

Tomorrow would involve more talking and explaining than I wanted to think about. In fact, I needed to turn off my brain completely.

He seemed to understand that and took his time undressing me and checking me over for any other bruises or abrasions. I couldn't say I minded that his thorough checkup included his lips.

A shower followed by a surprisingly intense massage left me a limp noodle, and I passed out somewhere between the first application of lotion and when he got to my legs. I should have been ashamed, but when I woke up the next morning with my guy at my back and my dog leaning against my legs, I was just grateful.

I checked my phone and found a text from my sister.

Rachel: Dress is gorgeous and only needed a tiny bit fixed on the shoulder. They're delivering it on Monday. Can you believe it's almost time?

Willow: I really can't. Think we could get together today?

She started replying right away. I must've tensed up because Ransom sighed against my neck.

"Everything good?" His voice was scarcely more than a rumble, and I wished that I could melt back into him and enjoy our usual morning activities. Most of them included me screaming his name.

Pretty nice way to start the day as far as I was concerned.

"Just Rachel checking in."

"'Kay," he murmured against my shoulder, tightening his arm around my middle. "Does that mean we have to get up?"

I laughed and kept looking at the little dots going on my screen. Long text coming in, I'd bet.

Rachel: I have to meet with the catering staff at the lodge today to make sure everything is okay with food and all that. Then I have to meet with the florist. One of my flowers isn't having a good season. Crappy ones came in from her distributor. I have to figure out a different one. Do you want to come with me?

Oh, I did. But Ransom would have a meltdown about that one.

"I'm assuming going to the florist with Rachel is off the table?"

"You assume right."

I sighed. These were the things I should be doing with my sister, dammit. This fuckwad had ruined even that. "The florist is in the Cove, I think. Maybe we can get your suit at the same time?"

"Chaos..."

"I know, I know. But this would give me a minute to talk to Rachel alone. Before I have to tell the family. I owe her that, at least."

He flopped onto his back.

I rolled over to face him. Midnight gave a disgruntled moan and hopped off the bed. So much for my cuddly morning. "We'll make sure we stay in with the crowds. No going off alone where he could..." I didn't finish.

Would I be putting Rachel in danger just by talking to her?

"No, you're right." He sat up and shoved his hands through his hair. "We'll do all the wedding tasks today, then we can tell the family tonight."

"I hate this." I pulled a pillow under my cheek. "This was supposed to be the week I got to be with my sister and we could bond over all this wedding stuff."

"You can do it all again when we get married." He slid out of bed and headed into the bathroom.

"Excuse me?" I sat up and rolled onto my knees.

If I was a little lightheaded right now, who could blame me?

He obviously needed to do his business and I wasn't going to chase him in there. After a flush, the water started running. Then he moved into the doorway with his toothbrush in his mouth.

Completely naked, dear God.

"What?" he asked around a mouthful of foam.

"Married?"

He pulled his toothbrush out of his mouth. "Like I'm not going to lock you down after I told you I love you? Please." He disappeared back into the bathroom and I nearly fell off the bed in my rush to follow him.

I could *not* have this conversation naked. I opened the bedside drawer and found socks and underwear. Finally, in the bottom one, he had some undershirts. I slipped one on and followed him into the bathroom.

He was already in the shower.

I swung the door open. "You cannot just say 'when we get married' like that and just get in the shower, Ransom Isaac Douglas!"

He turned around, squinting his eyes against the shampoo in his hair. "I regret the fact that you now know my full name." He ducked his head under the rain shower hood and all the bubbles slid down his exceptional body.

Focus, Willow.

"In or out, Chaos."

I flipped the shirt off and stepped in. "You want to marry me? What if I don't want to marry you?"

He hooked his slippery arms around my waist and pulled me against his warm, still slightly soapy chest. I pushed my wet hair out of my eyes.

"You know you want to marry me."

I tipped back my head to get the rest of my hair wet before moving just outside the usually delicious deluge of water. "Maybe I want to be asked."

He grinned as he stood under the water. "Maybe I'll ask you later."

I launched myself at him and he laughed as he crowded me into the smooth stone wall. Then he went down on his knees with the water beating down behind him.

He lifted my leg over his shoulder as he kissed the inside of my thigh. "Willow Renee Doyle, will you," he kissed higher, "spend the rest," he lapped along my center, "of your life with me?"

I started laughing as I leaned back, then there was no laughing. Just his intense eyes looking up at me as he circled my clit and sucked hard, driving me crazy with that mouth of his. Then he stopped.

"I didn't hear a yes."

I pulled his hair. "You are the worst."

His eyes were full of light and the blue outmatched the gray as he dragged his softly bearded chin against me. "Say yes, Chaos."

"Yes."

"That's right." He nipped my inner thigh and stood to hook my legs around him, then drove up into me in one slick, perfect stroke. "Forever."

I wrapped myself around him, arms, legs, and heart. "Forever."

He moved inside of me with firm thrusts, leaning back to lock his gaze with mine. I wanted it to last for a little longer, but the way he filled me and the love in his eyes pushed me over.

His jaw locked as I scraped my nails down his neck to his shoulders. His groan set me off again, and I swore I could feel him coming inside me, the warmth and the love he gave more than I'd ever expected in my life.

We ended up in a pile on the shower floor. I couldn't help but laugh. "How are we going to tell our grandkids about this one?"

He laughed into my neck.

"Gram, how did Grandpa ask you to marry him?" I couldn't stop giggling.

"We'll figure it out."

"At least you dropped to one knee."

"Two. And I'm getting too old to do that." He got up and pulled me with him.

"Aww, you're not going to carry me?"

"I think you broke my back."

I looped my arm around his neck and pushed him back under the warm water. "Let's see if I can fix that."

Chapter 30

Willow

Truth and Punches

I hopped around the room trying to get my shoe on as I shoved my phone between my chin and shoulder. "I know, Rach. I didn't mean to leave you hanging. I got...interrupted."

"By who?"

"Let's talk about it when I see you. Ransom is going to pick you up, and we'll head into Crescent Cove."

"Why is he coming? Can't we just go?"

I glanced at Ransom, who was stuffing his chain under his shirt. "He has to get a haircut and his tux. It's just easier. And we don't have to worry about parking."

He rolled his eyes.

"Fine. We can walk everywhere. I swear my ass is spreading from all the meetings I've been going to. Let alone my regular business stuff."

"The CocoaBus will be waiting for you after the honeymoon."

"I know. And I'm excited to go to Greece. Can you believe that's where we're going? I've always wanted to go."

Another thing I'd missed discussing with her. We'd probably be shopping for fabulous clothes for her to wear. I stuffed down the sadness and brightened my voice. "Clay has been emailing me for a month, trying to hash out details for the trip."

"No hints?"

"Not a one."

"You guys are all terrible. You know I hate not knowing."

My type-A sister was going to enjoy herself, and I wasn't ruining any more of her wedding celebrations. It killed me that I would be putting a dark smudge on her perfect day.

Hurricane Willow strikes again.

"We'll see you in a half hour."

"Fine. At least you're coming with me for the flowers."

"And I'm excited."

"Probably want to film stuff, right?"

"Maybe." I had a whole series of videos I'd planned to gift her in the guise of making content for my channel.

"Well, bring a battery backup, it's going to be a busy one. Love you, bye."

And then she was gone. Rachel was always going at a million miles per hour, but the wedding had made her just that much more... Rachel.

Weddings did that to people. Would mine do that to me?

Not that I could even consider that right now. My sister's was my only priority at this stage of the game. I already felt hopelessly guilty for missing so much time with her. The last thing I was going to do was get caught up in thinking about my own future ceremony.

Even if I was just a bit *gah* about the whole thing. How was any of this my life?

I tugged at the one clean shirt I'd found at the bottom corner of my box of clothes. I looked in his mirror near the chair I'd commandeered for my wardrobe. The lilac shirt was a smidge too tight from probably eight million washes.

"Can we *please* get my stuff today?" I tried to keep the whine out of my voice, but my fun box was practically bare at this point. And I didn't want to flash any nipple action to anyone who wasn't my future husband.

Holy crap. Would I ever get used to that?

Survey said no.

He grinned into the mirror from behind me and twirled me around by the belt loops of my denim skirt. "I rather like this little number."

"I think the last time I wore this was in high school."

He cupped my butt. "And look at that, I bet your ass is just as perky as it was when you were eighteen."

"Perv."

He lowered his mouth to my neck. "For you, every day."

I wasn't sure what to do with this more cheerful Ransom. Especially when everything was still in limbo. Part of me wanted to grab onto the happy moments too. I deserved them even if my life was utter chaos.

But hey, that was also my nickname for a reason. I probably should just embrace my reality.

Minus being Tased. I shivered. I hoped like hell I never had to deal with that again.

I laughed as he brushed his beard over my neck. "I'm going to miss the beard."

"Yeah?" He itched his neck. "I don't usually let it go this long. Rach will definitely want me clean-shaven for pictures."

I tugged lightly at the longer bristles. "Well, maybe a little shadow."

His smile was a bright slash of teeth in the dark beard. "Deal." He kissed me hard, then he let me go. "Let's get this done."

When we got downstairs, we fed Midnight and let him go outside to roam. I don't know what he was doing in the trees behind Ransom's place, but he was always going over there.

Ransom checked the camera feeds from Aidan's crazy control center. They'd tucked the monitors and scary-looking board into the corner of the kitchen on one of Ransom's finished pieces.

"Anything?"

"I'll review the feed more closely when we get back, but it looks like it didn't pick up anything hinky overnight."

I wasn't sure if that was a good thing or not. Hopefully, it was, unless the camera just hadn't captured anything. This asshole sure seemed comfortable with being stealthy.

And I wasn't going to overanalyze that right now.

Ransom ushered me outside and locked up behind us. The truck was still parked in front of the garage instead of under the carport. He opened the driver's side door, but instead of getting in, he reached under the seat.

I swallowed as he pulled out his gun and tucked it in his waistband at his lower back.

"You're not taking that with us, are you?"

"Yep."

"Can you at least you leave it in the holster or whatever?"

"Nope." He slammed the door. "We're not taking the truck." He led me toward the back of his garage. A car was tucked under a cover.

"What's this?"

"Well, now that we know this jackass can kill the electrical components in my Gladiator, I'm not taking any chances." He whipped the cover off a gleaming muscle car in the darkest blue I'd ever seen.

"Whoa."

"Yeah. I haven't driven her for a while."

I arched a brow. *"Her?"* Not that I could say anything since my Santa Fe was named Lola, but it seemed like such a cheeky thing to do. Not like the Ransom I'd thought I knew.

"Chaos meet Veronica."

"Veronica?" I laughed. "Well, she's gorgeous."

"She's got a helluva engine. But there's no computer in this car, so we should be safe." He went around to the passenger side and opened it for me. The inside was black leather with a white stripe. "After you."

I slid inside and the leather was butter-soft under my legs. The only thing that told me the car had been under wraps was the stale air. As usual, the vehicle was as neat as a pin. Ransom closed my door and went around to the driver's side. He tucked the gun under the seat much as he did in the truck, but there was no little chirp from a thumbprint lock.

That just made everything more real.

"The safety's on."

"I know."

He leaned across the bench seat and kissed me soundly. "It's just a precaution. I'm sure I won't need it, but I'd rather have something than nothing."

"Right. Smart."

He flipped the visor down and a keyring dropped into his hand. "To Rachel we go."

"Are my things going to fit in this trunk?"

"You can fit two bodies in that trunk. We should be able to get most of your clothes and stuff. The rest we'll get after the wedding."

"Two bodies? There's a visual."

He laughed and turned the ignition. The engine literally growled in response. "There's a girl." He patted the dash. "Miss me?"

"You're adorable."

"Gotta treat my girls right." He pulled the shifter down into Drive.

I wasn't sure I'd ever been in a car that actually had one near the steering wheel. I'd definitely never seen such a big grin on Ransom's face.

Men. They were stupidly cute, at least when you didn't want to maim them with your bare hands.

It was a beautiful spring day and we rolled down the windows on the way to Rachel's.

When we pulled up Clay's driveway, Rach was waiting on the porch. She pushed her sunglasses up onto her head and smiled as she skipped down the stairs to meet us.

"Wow."

I climbed out and grinned at my sister. "Ransom has some fun toys."

"I'll say." She ran over to me, and I gave her a hug.

I held on a minute too long and the prick of tears surprised me. "What happened to the truck?"

"Only leather seats for your ass, Rach."

"Such a shit." She peeked inside. "How the heck do I get in there?"

"Good question." It was a bench seat. How the heck were we supposed to... Oh, there was a lever.

Ransom grunted as the whole bench seat bent forward.

"Oops."

He growled as I stuffed my sister into the back and followed her, clicking the seat back into place. Dammit, now I couldn't close the door.

He shook his head and leaned over to pull the door closed. "Where we headed, ladies?"

"I pretty much am doing everything in Crescent Cove. I found a sweet florist there."

"You got it."

Rachel adjusted the skirt of her pretty sundress. "I kinda like the chauffeur treatment."

I leaned against her. "How did the fitting go? More importantly, how was Mom?"

"You know Mom. She was more worried about what it cost versus return." She cleared her throat to imitate our mother's snooty tone. "'Rachel, the money you spent on this dress could have gone to your child's education.'"

I laughed. "Sounds just like her."

"She hasn't really caught on to the fact that Clay is worth a bazillion dollars."

"I'm shocked. Figured she would have had him reviewed by the IRS, for God's sake."

"Hush. Don't even speak that into existence."

I snorted. "Well, she's gonna bug you about a grandchild before me." Not by too much since I was only missing a ring to make my engagement official.

What kind of ring would I get from him? Would I even *get* a ring? The actual moment had been mid-orgasm denial, for God's sake.

I glanced at the rearview mirror and met Ransom's gaze. He gave me a half-grin and didn't say a word.

"What's going on between you two?"

I focused back on my sister. "What are you talking about?"

"There's a vibe."

I tugged on the strap of my purse. Now that it was time to spill the beans, my throat wanted to close up, and that was not an ordinary affliction for me. "The drive into Crescent Cove isn't long enough to tell that story, sis."

"So, there *is* a story?"

Um...

"I asked your sister to marry me." Ransom threw a quick smile over his shoulder. "Surprise."

So much for not knowing what to say.

"Jeez, Ransom. You don't just drop that on people."

Rachel twisted to face me. "What? I was only gone one day!"

"We have a lot to talk about."

"You think?" Her mouth dropped open as she looked from me to Ransom and back again. "How?"

"Short story? Or long one?"

"Abbreviated with option for expansion."

I laughed. "That project was a little more intense than we figured it would be."

"I'll say."

I'd hoped to tell her in like a café or something, with actual coffee maybe from Brewed Awakening since that stuff could put hair on your chest. But maybe in the car was actually better. No one could overhear us.

I gripped her hands.

"Oh, God. You're not dying or something?"

I hoped not. "I have a cyber stalker that turned into something more real life."

The brightness dimmed. "No. Not again." Her big bluebell eyes filled. "Why?"

"I don't know. I wish I understood it."

"Does Clay know?"

I shook my head. "We were trying to handle it quietly. I thought it was just a creep. Unfortunately, I've gotten used to them by doing the influencer thing."

"Aw, Wil. I could strangle you. Why didn't you come to us?"

"I didn't want to ruin the wedding."

"Who cares about my wedding, you're my sister." She threw her arms around me and knocked me back against the window.

I hugged her back. "I know. I had this guy in the front. And some help from his friends."

She shifted back to her side of the car as I explained about the trip to Manhattan and Aidan as well as Ransom's idiotic plan to put himself in the target zone instead of me.

Rachel slapped Ransom in the shoulder. "Why didn't you convince her that she could come to us?"

Ransom scrunched up his shoulders. "Hey, I agreed with her. You both finally deserved some happiness. And we thought it was just some random guy going over the line. It ended up being a hacker."

"What? We have to turn around the car and talk to Clay about this."

"We will." I covered her hand. "I'm calling a family meeting tonight. There's more."

"How could you not tell me? I'm not some fragile flower, dammit. Not anymore."

"Oh, honey. That wasn't why I didn't tell you. I didn't want to tell anyone. It felt like Jason all over again, only so much worse because there was no face to go with the creep factor."

I hadn't actually voiced that before and Ransom's gaze shot to the rearview mirror. A muscle throbbed visibly in his jaw and his hands were doing their grip-tear-off-the-wheel thing.

I leaned across the back of the seat and lightly drew my nails through his hair along the nape of his neck.

Rachel's eyebrows shot up. "So, this is really a thing?" She looked over her shoulder. "I keep expecting a camera to appear because I'm on reality television or something.

I snorted as I relaxed into my seat. "Yeah, I love the idiot."

"Thanks, babe." His voice was wry.

"The one good thing that came out of this."

"So, I guess you haven't been sleeping in the attic?" Rachel crossed her arms.

"No, mom. I definitely haven't been sleeping...in the attic."

"Gross." She punched me in the arm.

"Look who's talking."

She shrugged. "Maybe it's catchy. But why do I think you're still not telling me something?" She pushed some of her hair out of her face from the rolled down windows.

While I was in storytelling mode, I hadn't noticed we'd driven into Crescent Cove proper. Ransom turned into the parking lot for Brewed Awakening because he was a very smart and intuitive guy.

We piled out of the car. I wasn't sure if I should tell her about the incident yesterday or wait to tell the family all at once.

"Don't stop now. It's like a really big Band-aid." She looped her arm through mine.

Ransom glanced around the parking lot, his gaze cool and thorough enough to make me shiver.

"Wil."

"He was the one who broke into the distillery."

"Oh."

"Yeah." Ransom came up beside me and rested his hand protectively on my lower back. "And he tried to take her last night."

Rachel whirled to face me before socking me with yet another punch. "Don't you think you should have started with that?"

"Ow." I rubbed my arm.

She dragged me in for a tight hug. "I would have been so mad if something happened to you, and you'd never told us you were in danger."

I rubbed her back. "I know. It only happened last night. You guys were still in the city, and I didn't want to worry you while you couldn't get home."

"Thank God nothing bad happened."

I shook my head at Ransom. We definitely weren't telling her about the Taser.

"Ransom was there."

And he always would be. I'd just been too blind to realize it for a minute or three.

She moved from me to Ransom and wrapped her arms around his middle. "Thank you."

"It's okay, Rach. She's just as important to me." He awkwardly patted her back.

"Hug me back or I'll punch you too."

He rolled his eyes and looped his arms around her. "Can we get out of the parking lot now? It's making me itchy."

She peered up at him. "Is it that serious?"

"I'm pretty sure he went back into his hole, but I don't know how long it will last. So, let's make the best of this, ladies."

"Right." She straightened. "I'm glad you were there for her, Ransom."

"Me, too." He looked over Rachel's head and met my gaze. "Me, too."

I hugged my sister from the back and my long arms were able to take in most of Ransom too. "Group hug!"

Rachel laughed. "This isn't a laughing matter, Willow Renee."

"Man, two middle name mentions in the space of twenty-four hours." I eased back and looked at Ransom. "Hey, how did you know my middle name, anyway?"

Rachel glanced from me to him. "Do I want to know the context?"

"No."

"Yes." Ransom grinned. "I used it when I asked her to marry me. Naked." Then he turned Rachel around and pushed her toward the café. "Let's go, ladies. We're burning sunlight."

Chapter 31

Ransom

Shop 'Til You I Drop

I pinched the bridge of my nose as we headed into the fourth shop on Main Street. Luckily, foot traffic was fairly light since it was early in the workday for most normal people.

At least there was coffee.

"Ransom needs to stop at To Dye For. He needs to cut down on the poof action. I didn't know you had so many curls, sir." She ruffled my hair.

I frowned down at her. "I'm not getting my hair cut at a place named that."

"Oh, they're really good. I've been going to Paisley, and she makes my hair so soft." Rachel tugged on the end of her ponytail. "Not that it makes much difference since I always have it up for work."

"Me too."

"Shut up."

I rolled my eyes. "As long as they can hack off some of this, we're cool." I fisted my hands in the top of my hair. The boyish curls had been fun when I was trying to get ladies in my twenties.

Now? I felt ridiculous.

We were in some bookstore with art supplies and many small breakable things. This was not how I'd thought my day was gonna go. Flowers were bad enough.

I bit back a sigh when Willow crouched in front of a bookcase. This would probably be another thirty minutes I couldn't get back.

I'd probably be lucky if it was thirty.

A woman came around the corner with a stroller and hit her in the back of the foot. Instead of being perturbed, Chaos twisted around and grinned into the stroller. "Well, hello there."

"Oh my gosh, I'm so sorry." The woman with similar curls in a sunnier hue reached out to save a book tipping off the shelf and righted it. "This stroller is amazing on the sidewalk. Not so great in a store."

"It's okay." Willow reached into the stroller. "Oh, is it okay?"

The harried mother smiled. "Go for it. Maybe she'll be happier with you than me."

"What's your name, sweet thing?"

"Vivvie. Well, Vivian, but we call her Vivvie when she's being adorable." The woman pushed the bonnet back on the stroller.

"Oh, she's so beautiful." The little girl had a cap of curls with a bit more red than her mother.

My breath seized in my chest as Willow let the little girl curl her tiny fingers around her forefinger. I'd never even thought having kids would be in my future and right there—*shit*.

Willow glanced back at me and the smile on her face knocked me back a step.

"Did you just see your future flash before your eyes?" Rachel asked behind me.

I glanced down at her, but I couldn't get words to come out of my dry throat.

She patted my chest. "Yeah. You're adorable. I won't mind having you for a brother-in-law." She shook her head. "I can't believe you guys are together and getting married. Not that I should be surprised, Wil never does the expected."

"I definitely didn't expect her."

"Kinda her superpower." She nudged me. "She is really cute with a baby, though."

I still couldn't talk about that one.

"Hey, Wil. I'm ready to check out," Rachel called out.

Chaos stood and gave the baby a tiny wave before she joined us and poked me in the middle. "You're being a good sport."

I swallowed and gave her a tight smile. "All part of the service I provide."

She went on her toes and brushed my lips with hers. "Thanks for giving us this. I know you'd rather keep me home."

I kept my eyes open on hers.

She pulled back. "What?"

"Nothing."

"Weirdo." She slipped her hand in mine and dragged me to the registers.

A cheery woman with dark hair checked us out and we moved onto the next soul-sucking store. Finally, we were in the vicinity of Vintage December's shop where I could get my tux.

Rachel was more than happy to stop since she seemed convinced I hadn't actually done the fitting. As if I could fake having a sized tux.

"Ah, Mr. Douglas, it's nice to see you again." Em came around the desk to meet us as we walked in.

"This place is amazing." Rachel's voice was breathy as she glanced around.

I could see my day going down the drain. She'd be just like Chaos and find an armful of clothes. Then she'd have to try them on and model them and by then, my brain would be leaking out of my ear.

"I'm December. Are you the bride?"

"Yes. And I'm heading to Greece for my honeymoon. Look at all the dresses you have!"

"I can tailor anything you need."

"Even with the wedding being in just a few days?"

Em wiggled her fingers. "I'm magic."

I tipped my head back with a groan.

"Your tux is in." Em's amusement at my predicament was evident in her tone. "I have it hung up near the dressing room if you want to try it on one more time for me?"

"He sure will." Chaos pushed me farther into the store in the direction of the dressing rooms. "I'm still coming back in after the wedding, Em!"

"I'm counting on it. I'll just help your sister?"

"Sure thing." Willow planted her hands on my shoulders as she kept me moving forward. "We'll just make sure that jacket fits."

"I'm sure." Em pressed her lips together against a smile.

"Gonna help me with my tux, Chaos?"

"Maybe."

Okay, so maybe this wasn't going to be a completely boring trip, after all.

She pushed me along like a drunk bumblebee until we got to the dressing room doors. I knew she was tempted to stop and touch all the floofy, colorful things hanging on racks, but she clearly had a plan in mind.

The dressing room door was open and she went in with me, sans tux.

"Why, Chaos. Did you have an ulterior motive for coming in here?"

She jerked at my belt. "Damn right I did." She reached down into my jeans before I could get another breath.

"Oh, shit." I was hard in a second as her long fingers wrapped around me with intention. "Hang on."

"Shopping inspires a powerful thirst in me."

"Evidently." I groaned into her neck as she crowded me up against the wall and stroked me from root to tip. "Your sister is right out there."

"She's busy." She wiggled up her skirt.

My dick went from hard to aching. "I'm not complaining, but what brought this on?"

"Little reward for not rushing us along." She pushed my pants out of the way to get a better grip and my eyes crossed.

"I don't need a reward. I'm not a poodle."

"More like a massive German Shepherd."

That was a compliment I'd never received before. But I couldn't puzzle it out while she was swinging me around so she could face the wall.

"Jesus, Chaos."

She batted her eyes at me over her shoulder. "Maybe I'm the one who deserves the reward."

"Fuck."

After a quick fumble of clothes, I caged her against the wall from the back. I'd never been so glad to have a tall woman in my life as I slipped inside her with barely a hitch in my back.

"Fuck, you're so wet."

Her hands flattened on the wall. "I don't know if there's something about the air in this place or... Oh, God. Right there."

Her fingers crawled up the wall and I laced them with mine as I drove up inside her heat. "So fucking tight." Damn, quickies were definitely a new word in my vocabulary with her, but I was into it.

I slipped my other hand around her middle to slide down between her legs. My cock was slick with her wetness as I found her clit already stiff and swollen. I powered into her, trying desperately not to tell the whole store what we were doing, but she felt too fucking good.

She reached back to grip the back of my neck as she tried to stuff down the scream I could tell was brewing. I bit down on her neck, helpless against the same need to possess and hold.

"Willow." Her name was a promise.

Her legs shook and I knew she was with me. Our fingers flexed together as she shuddered under me and her breath hitched on a broken sigh as I emptied myself inside of her.

Christ, I wasn't sure I could ever stop. My spine was on fire as I surged up onto my toes to nail her to the wall.

The laugh that rolled up and out of her was a surprise, especially since it was more of a moan crossed with a chatter of teeth.

"Never stop wanting me like this," she whispered.

"Impossible."

She turned to find my lips. The kiss spun out, sweet and soft in direct opposition to the storm we'd created. Then she melted against me and I just held on, my arms locked around the best thing that had ever happened to me.

"I think you forgot the tux," Rachel said from outside.

"No, we didn't," I said against Chaos's neck.

Willow smothered a giggle against her shoulder. "Bad."

"You're the one who pushed me in here without even trying to pretend you weren't going to ravish me."

She shrugged. "Sorry?"

"Right." I slid out of her with a groan. I'd be wearing her for the rest of the day, just like she'd be doing the same. I opened the door a crack and a hanger landed in my hand.

"Pervs."

"You're just mad Clay isn't here."

"Maybe. Still pervs." She opened the dressing room next door. "And none of that business while I'm next to you."

Chaos just giggled and turned with a wince. "The whole sex in a dressing room is a good idea in theory." She waggled her eyebrows. "And in orgasm. But man." She picked up her panties, currently a fashion accessory around her ankles.

I snatched them from her and stuffed them in my jeans.

"Ransom."

I shrugged. "Not like you're going to put them back on. This is a nice place, but they were still on the floor."

She sighed. "No. Guess I'm just going to have to go out there and find something to wear. This skirt is a little too short to go commando."

"Damn."

She shook her head and kissed my cheek before slipping out of the room. "Uh, hi Em."

I winced behind the door as the two women talked about dresses. We'd acted like a bunch of horny teenagers.

Not the first time either.

I got myself back to rights and realized I'd let her go out there without freaking being next to her.

So stupid. I'd allowed myself to get lax for a goddamn orgasm. An incredible one, but still.

I didn't need to be in the dressing room to try on the jacket. I took the clothes and followed her. She glanced back at me, but she just smiled as she flicked through a rack of dresses.

I shrugged into the jacket, amazed that it fit since the last thing to mold to me that well was my dress uniform.

Chaos brushed by me with a little twirl, carrying a dress and a pair of very tiny panties.

I was *not* following her back into that room.

"Looks great." Em appeared again.

"I haven't been to a tailor in a few years. You did better than him." Of course, that suit had also contained Kevlar.

Maybe I should wrap Chaos in it. Then again, it wouldn't stop a fucking Taser.

"You sure? Your face and shoulders say maybe I should go back to my checkout desk."

I relaxed. "Sorry. Been a stressful week."

Em laughed. "I would have thought you would be relaxed for at least a few minutes."

My neck and ears burned. "About that—"

She waved me off. "This is the Cove. That kind of action seems to come with the territory. You two weren't even the first. Or the second. Apparently, tuxedos are very...stimulating."

"I don't even know how to reply to that."

She helped me out of the jacket. "I've learned to go with the flow. And I have very good clients." She smoothed the jacket over her arm.

"I'll wrap up your tux. I added a third shirt in the pile just because I had to send the order out again."

"Thanks."

"No problem. The ladies in your life make it more than worth it."

I laughed. "Clay going to get a bill like mine?"

"The bride has an armful, yes."

"Worth it."

"I'm glad. I'll just go get everything ready. I'm assuming I'll put Willow's dress on your account." Her lips twitched. "And her panties."

I tried manfully to keep my expression neutral. "Yes, please."

She started to walk away, but she stopped and looked over her shoulder. "She's a good one."

"Better than I deserve, but I'll do my best to keep her happy."

"That's what I like to hear." Em walked off, trailing a floral spice scent behind her.

When Chaos came out of the dressing room, my gut hit my shoes again. The dress was an off-white with the big red flowers and greenery. It had some sort of strap that went around her neck, leaving her shoulders bare.

"I should probably have a strappy pair of heels to match this gorgeous thing, but I'd prefer not to break my neck while we finish up today."

"You're gorgeous, Chaos."

She swung the skirt of the dress like a bell. "Em has a lot of magic in this shop."

Rachel came out with a pile in her arms. "Magic is right. I only need three of these altered."

"Hallelujah," I said and took a seat on the big hassock by the stage.

Em was efficient and had Rachel measured and the dresses and one pair of slacks all pinned and marked within half an hour. A haircut for me was next since the girls would have someone doing their hair the day of the wedding.

I kept the sisters in my eyeline as a bubbly woman named Ellie wet down my hair and gave me a quick cut.

Finally, we got to the florists. I waited outside while Rach and Chaos *oohed* and ahhed over silver roses to go with the massive peonies. Whatever those were. I only listened with half an ear as I checked in with Aidan and Beckett.

Aidan had outfitted Happy Acres Cider with a new set of cameras and Beckett would pick up the cases for the wedding the night of the rehearsal dinner.

Why anyone needed to rehearse a wedding, I did not know.

The wild cards were going to be the stag parties. I was hoping there wouldn't be too many tears when I convinced Clay and Rachel to cancel them.

There were far too many variables in that kind of situation. Originally, they were supposed to be at Lucky's with the girls using one side of the bar and the guys the other. Ruby hadn't closed it down to make it private party, though I was sure we probably could convince her.

I still didn't like it and I'd lobby hard to cancel.

Chaos mattered more than any one last night of freedom crap. I knew Clay was only interested in one thing. And it wasn't partying until dawn.

Aidan had the distillery locked down and he'd agreed to come back for the wedding if I wanted him to. I told him I'd reserve judgement and that I'd keep him updated.

Chaos came up behind me and wrapped her arms around my waist, resting her chin against my shoulder. "We should be done in a few minutes."

Automatically, I covered her hands. "Best news I've heard all day. Or is that only here?"

"Nope. All done."

"Thank fuck."

"Sir." She squeezed me.

"Sorry."

"You've been awesome."

"Special circumstances."

She laughed. "So, I shouldn't expect you to hold my purse while I shop?"

"Only if I get that kind of dressing room action each time."

"Depends. Not sure everyone is as cool as Em is about an interlude."

"Is that what you call it?" I twisted my neck and she met me in a quick kiss. "Pretty sure I rocked your world."

"Your groan proved I did the same, pal." She dug her fingers in my side, then she was gone.

My phone rang and I dragged it back out of my pocket. I picked up when I saw Beckett's name. He was even less of a phone guy than I was. "Hey."

"Hey. I corralled the troops. They aren't sure what's going on. How much do you want me to tell them?"

"Tell them it's important so everyone shows up."

"Got it. How's the shopping twins looking timewise?"

"Finishing up."

"Real talk?"

I laughed. He knew his cousins well. "We'll be at the lodge in an hour."

"Didn't take you for an optimistic sort."

"Just tell them to be ready."

"Will do."

I went into the flower shop to make sure I wasn't lying. Unfortunately, I was.

Ninety minutes later, we rolled up to the lodge. Beckett was waiting by the doors, his arms crossed as I herded the women inside.

"Shut up."

Beckett just roared with a rare belly laugh as he followed us in.

The low hum of voices told me where to go. Thankfully, Laverne had put everyone in one of the conference rooms. I didn't want to taint the Gala room with all of this if I could help it.

Rachel was being a rock as it was.

Clay was waiting with the rest of the family when we walked in. Rach rushed over to him and slipped her arm around his back. He looked down at her with a frown.

I felt like I was staring down the troops.

Laverne and her sister Sarah were sitting at the table with Fred and Christopher behind their wives. The Manning boys were leaning against the wall with their arms crossed. Beckett was slightly more at ease since he had some knowledge of what was going on.

Chaos and Rachel's parents weren't coming in until the day before the rehearsal dinner which I was glad about. I didn't really want to meet Chaos's parents for the first time by telling them she'd been attacked yesterday.

I reached beside me and found Chaos's hand.

The murmurs started right away at that. I cleared my throat. "Thanks for coming in to talk with us. We wanted to speak to all of you at once, so we only had to do it one time."

Laverne gripped Fred's hand at her shoulder. "What's going on?"

Clay glanced down at our linked hands and his eyebrow arched. I'd hoped to talk to Clay alone, but things hadn't worked out the way I'd planned since the day Willow Doyle had strolled into that bar less than a week ago.

It felt like a million years ago and a blink at the same time.

"As some of you may have noticed, I've been glued to Chaos's hip for the last few days."

"Do I need to find my shotgun, son?" Justin asked with a grin on his tanned face.

"Nope. I already asked her to marry me."

She slapped my arm. "Jeez. You have no tact, Ransom."

My lips tipped up at one corner as I glanced down at her. "Hit them with the good news first."

Laverne popped out of her chair and rushed over. "Oh my God. You don't waste time." She hugged both of us.

A half dozen voices started at once. I lifted my arm. "All right.

Yeah, it's quick, I know. But we aren't taking away from the happy festivities coming up. We just wanted to let you know."

"Not that I'm not happy to hear it," Fred's eyes crinkled with his wide smile, "but I'm assuming an emergency family meeting wasn't for that announcement."

I sighed. "Afraid not." I found Clay in the back of the room, our gazes connecting. "Sorry, man. I wanted to tell you before I did this, but something happened last night."

Laverne went back to her chair. "Nothing... I don't even want to speak the words."

Chaos rushed forward and crouched beside her chair. "No. No one is sick or anything, Aunt Laverne."

The older woman blew out a breath. "Okay. We can handle anything as a family, but I'm glad it's not that."

Chaos stood and came back to my side, then looked up at me.

I nodded. She should be the one to tell them.

"Most of you know about what happened to me in college."

Justin and Hayes straightened, their arms both lowering to their sides as they fisted their hands.

"Unfortunately, my job has a few downsides." She glanced up at me as she hooked her pinky with mine. "Ransom and his friend Aidan have been helping me deal with a fan who...well, he's gone from nuisance messages to a more active and in person role."

"Role?" Clay came forward. "What the hell does that mean?" He turned back to Rachel, and she rushed forward.

"Clay. Just let them finish."

I swiped a hand down Chaos's curls. "My friend is Aidan Roth."

Clay's jaw dropped open. "Roth Defense?"

"Yeah." I hated seeing my best friend's eyes shutter with hurt.

Hurt I'd inadvertently caused.

"Why didn't you come to me?"

"Aidan has a specialty in handling celebrity security. Chaos—sorry, Willow—has a unique background. It shouldn't have been easy for anyone to find her, let alone a stranger. Since her college problem

354

with a stalker, she was very careful to make sure none of her personal information was on the internet."

"That's why you were upset about the packages." Laverne's eyes teared up. "Oh, honey."

"I didn't want to worry anyone." Chaos closed her eyes, her throat rising and falling as she swallowed hard. "I didn't want to ruin the wedding or bring any of this home to you guys."

I wrapped my arm around her back and pulled her in against me. "The good news is that Aidan's team is incredible. He has a hacker who is just about as good as this guy who has fixated on Willow."

Chaos sniffed and opened her eyes to gaze at her family. "Poe is pretty amazing. She actually found out there is a whole forum of people who make money watching celebrities. I didn't realize I was a watch list-level celebrity."

"I don't pretend to understand this internet celebrity stuff, but what does that mean for Wil?" Beckett came forward.

I didn't want to confuse them with the dark web nor scare them unnecessarily. "At first, we just figured it was something we needed to monitor. She doesn't have a regular job and that amount of attention requires ample security."

"And I signed up for this when I put my face out there. I just didn't think it would come to this. Or that someone would involve the orchard."

"So, he has the address. What does that have to do with anything unlike any other idiot out there? We've dealt with annoying customers since we opened. It's just part of owning a business." Fred held on to the back of Laverne's chair. "I even have a list of people that aren't allowed on the property. Most of our customers are amazing, but there's always a bad apple, pardon the pun."

"I know, Uncle Fred. We were hoping that was all it was. Until someone broke into Happy Acres Cider."

Beckett tipped back his baseball hat, mirroring Fred as they took in the information. "So, it wasn't some random burglary." It wasn't even a question.

"No. He sent a photo to Willow with the distillery set up as if it was a date."

"Jesus." Christopher Manning shook his head. "What is wrong with people?"

"That's not all of it, is it?" Clay's jaw was tight.

"The guy came out from behind his keyboard yesterday. He tried to kidnap Chaos last night."

"I thought you were staying with her to prevent that," Clay shouted.

Rachel grabbed his arm, shaking him with surprising force. "Clay, don't. He was. Ransom being right there with her is probably why the guy didn't succeed."

Clay reached up to cover her hand with his own on his arm. "You're right. I'm sorry."

My chest tightened. "He's right. I fucked up." I glanced at the women. "Excuse my language."

"He's a fucking asshole," Laverne said darkly.

That seemed to break some of the tension in the room.

Chaos took my hand in both of hers. "Ransom isn't to blame. We had a fight, and I ran off to cool my head. I was just going to drive around until I didn't want to hit him with a hammer anymore."

"Thanks."

She shrugged. "I really wasn't leaving. I just..." She leaned her head on my upper arm for a moment. "We worked it out and then he told me he loved me."

"Is that all it takes, cuz?" Justin quipped.

"Shut up. At least he knows how to hold onto a woman longer than twenty-four hours."

"Burn," Hayes said with a cheery smile. "Yet truth."

"Yeah, he's up to a week so far, right? Go, Ransom."

"Children, hush." Their mom Sarah spoke up for the first time. "Do you have something you want us to do?"

I nodded. "I really don't want to, but I think we should cancel the bachelor and bachelorette parties."

"Done," Clay and Rachel said in unison.

"Oh, Rach, I'm sorry." Chaos's eyes filled. "I'm ruining everything."

Rachel rushed toward her sister and hugged her tight. "You're not. I just want you to be safe. If that means we won't have a hangover, then that's one less thing to give me wrinkles."

Chaos laughed and I let Rachel lead her away to sit down.

"Aidan has increased security here with Beckett's help. We just added a few more cameras to keep an eye on things. He was able to merge with Clay's existing software we put in over the winter."

"Glad I'm not totally obsolete," Clay said dryly.

"No. He has some smaller cameras that will work with what you already have. Military contacts come in handy sometimes. It will help for the summer concert stuff, as well."

"We appreciate it, son." Fred walked over to me and surprised me with a hug. "Welcome to the family."

I slapped his back. "Thank you, sir."

"No, sir here. Just Uncle Fred."

My eyes stung. "Uncle Fred sounds good to me."

Chaos was quickly surrounded by her family. I let them ask her questions and get some more specifics while I dealt with my own.

Clay nodded to me. The hour of reckoning was at hand.

Chapter 32

Ransom

Broments

I glanced at Chaos, and she waved me on. If I couldn't leave her in a room full of her family, then we really were in trouble.

Clay walked out into the atrium.

Beckett caught my attention as I wavered about joining him. Knowing Willow would be safe wasn't the same as being there myself to ensure it. "I'll keep an eye on her, Ransom."

"Thanks."

I followed my best friend into the sunshine. He went over to the tree and linked his hands behind his back. Hopefully, that would negate a swing for my head.

"I can't believe you kept this from me."

"I didn't exactly know how to tell you."

"I was literally at your house. You could have told me then."

"And what? You'd have to hold it back or tell Rachel and worry her before we knew anything?"

"Not your choice to make."

I sighed. "I did the best I could."

"And you'd still do the same thing," he said flatly.

"You and Rach have been through enough. We both wanted you to be able to enjoy your wedding stuff."

"Not your call, man."

"*She* is my call. Now."

"That's mighty quick." Clay folded his arms. "You were running for the hills whenever she was going to be around this winter."

"Yeah, well, I knew she was trouble."

He relaxed his shoulders a fraction. "Is that right? You really do love her."

"It doesn't make sense."

Clay laughed. "Then you really do. Because I was scared as fuck when it happened to me. Those Doyle women get under your skin."

"And then some."

"You sure it's not just the..." Clay cleared his throat. "Adrenaline?"

"Sex is great."

"Please, no. She's like my sister."

"Well, it's awesome with Chaos, but I mean, in general, sex is great."

"Duh."

I laughed. "But if it was just sex, we would have gotten out of our system and moved on."

"How do you know it's not your dick talking? And your overactive protective instincts."

I didn't answer him right away. They were both very good questions. I'd been hyper-vigilant since I'd left the army. Before everything had changed with Rachel, Clay had been ready to drop me off in the nearest lake and let me find my way home some days.

Maybe even the disgusting Hudson River a time or five.

"The idea of her not in my life sliced me in two. When that asshole almost got her," I fisted my hands, "I could have killed him." I met Clay's gaze. "I still might."

"Whoa, whoa."

"He fucking Tased her."

"What?"

"I didn't want to scare her family. He disarmed my truck. Hacked it or some such shit. She was a sitting duck. If I hadn't ran after her like a lunatic, he'd probably have her still."

"Jesus."

I took a deep breath against the black spots forming at the corners of my eyes.

"What happened?"

"We had it out. I fucked up and didn't tell her what I was doing."

"Gee, I don't know how that feels. You know you don't have to do everything on your own, Dougie."

"God, no. No Dougie crap."

Clay grinned. "But seriously. It's not your responsibility to carry everything."

"I tried to make myself the target instead of her."

"No wonder she was ready to kick your ass."

"Tell me about it. She ran. Says she only wanted to take the truck and drive, but I don't know, man. She was pissed. If I hadn't been—"

"Yourself? You probably ran after her like Forrest Gump." Clay cupped his hands around his mouth. "Run, Forrest, run."

"You're such a dick." But the nerves rolled back into their dark hole located at the back of my mind.

"Good thing you did. I'm forever grateful, Ransom. Rachel would be lost without her now that they've reconnected. Hell, even before."

"This guy's far bolder than I'd given him credit for. I thought he was just going to stay behind his keyboard." Maybe a small part of me had known it would get worse and hadn't wanted to believe it.

"What about the security stuff with Roth?"

"Evidently, there's a dark web full of pieces of shit like this guy. They sell videos to the highest bidder."

"Like paparazzi?"

"Worse. But yeah, there are a ton of people who will pay good money to find out everything about celebrities. Aidan found some hits on his own clients, as well. He's going to have a mess to clean up and look into beyond what's going on with Chaos."

"That's terrifying." Clay shook his head.

I didn't blame him. I was giving him a shit ton of information.

"So, what are you guys going to do now?"

"I just don't know. Aidan's agreed to run point at the wedding if I need him to. There will be a helluva lot of people there even with the intimate tone of the wedding."

"Whatever you need."

"Thanks." I scrubbed my hands over my face. "I am so sorry to have this going on during your wedding."

"It's not like you could ask this freak to wait for a better day."

"I know. Last night really messed me up. I know she's fine with your soon-to-be cousins—"

"Soon to be yours too."

"Yeah. That's just weird." I blew out a breath. "Anyway, I know she's fine in there, but my shoulder blades are on fire because I can't see her."

"Controlling everything still wouldn't make things perfect, Ran."

Surprised, I chuckled. "Man, you haven't called me that since we were in school."

"Fit you though. All you did was run."

"I was a scrappy short idiot until I was seventeen. Better to be able to outrun the guys who wanted to pound on me than to stand up to them."

"You and Reid were..." Clay scraped his fingers through his short dark hair. "That was a long time ago."

"Speaking of Reid. I was surprised to hear he was coming."

"Yeah. He and Helena are seeing each other."

"Well, that's fucked up."

"Yeah. I don't want her to get hurt. He's not the same guy we used to know."

"Think he can still land that right hook?"

Clay winced. "I don't want to find out. I remember it well."

My gut churned. This was the perfect time to tell him about Mags, but the thought of hashing that out now made me want to do some of that prep school running.

I looked around. We were still semi-alone.

"Something you want to say? Or are you looking for Wil?"

"I talked to Chaos about Mags."

"Oh." Clay swallowed. "Thought we pretty much were never going to mention that again."

"We've both been carrying a lot of shit about that night for a long time. I know I'd rather bury it."

"I'm fine with it."

I clasped his shoulder. "Believe me. You know I hate talking about my goddamn feelings."

"Ditto."

"But I blamed everyone when there was really only one person to blame."

"Me."

"No, man. Mags."

Clay's dark eyes looked stricken. "She didn't know what she was doing. I was the one who messed up. I never should have kissed her back."

"About that." I huffed out a breath. "It took me a long time to figure it out. Trying to find her for years gave me a lot of time to put stuff together. You know she and Reid weren't right. She made him crazy—and not in the good way like Chaos does to me."

Clay exhaled. "I mean, yeah, they were volatile. Marigold liked to push buttons."

"Yeah." I swallowed hard. The acid in my gut warning me to run instead of talk. "This is just speculation. The only thing I know about my sister is that she's still out there somewhere. But she made sure Reid came after her that night. She knew he wouldn't let her go."

Clay frowned. "She said she wanted to leave him. Not that she'd done it already." He gripped the back of his neck, the muscles in his arm rigid.

"I didn't want to face the fact that my sister split us all up. Maybe that wasn't her intention, but the only way Reid would let her go was if she burned the two of them to the ground."

"With me." Clay looked shattered, but his shoulders finally relaxed. "I knew she liked to make him jealous sometimes. Mostly to get something she wanted because he'd get all possessive." Clay pinched the bridge of his nose. "God, I feel so stupid."

"Guilt sucks." I was relieved to have it off my chest. Damn woman always knew the right thing to open up all my many locks. "I'm just sorry we lost so many years because of this bullshit."

"You really think that's what she did? Used me?"

"It makes the most sense."

Clay hauled me in for a hard hug. "I'm just glad you're back and actually here. Present instead of a shadow."

I'd hugged more people today than in the last six goddamn months. "All right. Can we stop with the mushy stuff now?"

He gripped both my arms and set me away from him as he flashed me a shit-eating grin. "We got a whole wedding to do, man."

"Great."

"And another one in the wings. What a life, man. Who'd've thought either one of us would get hitched, let alone to sisters."

"That just sounds inappropriate."

He slapped my back with a chuckle. "Let's go get the girls. I'm starving."

Maybe it was stupid to think that anything could be resolved this easily. But he was my family, one vital piece of it Marigold hadn't damaged irreparably.

And sometimes, things really were that simple.

"I could eat."

Chapter 33

Willow

Meet the Parents

The next few days were insane.

If I wasn't at my sister's house working on the last of the favors, I was helping her pick out clothes for her honeymoon. In between, I helped Ransom with the desk, and he helped me with a few videos.

I wasn't sure if he was taunting my stalker, or if he was just trying to keep my mind off of things. Either way, my channel was on fire. People were begging me to make a YouTube channel where I could make longer videos.

Ransom was officially a hit in the Wil's Way sphere. I was also more creative than I'd ever been. Scribbling notebooks full of notes. And yes, that was plural. Thank God for Amazon overnight deliveries to the orchard.

I commandeered most of the living room, which I knew was driving him crazy even if he didn't say anything. If I was marrying him, we'd have to find some way to add me to his house.

Maybe that attic would be mine, after all. And that possible redesign became another notebook with an accompanying Pinterest board.

The nights were amazing even if I kept waiting for the next shoe...or Taser to drop. Every night, we loved each other as if it was our last time.

I didn't want to think too closely if that was even a possibility.

Finally, the night of the rehearsal dinner was upon us. Thankfully, it was a small affair with only our family.

Of course, that also included my parents. They knew absolutely nothing about Ransom or my stalker. The fact that I hadn't once considered including them made my heart ache.

We hadn't been close since college. They'd gone from being worried about me to abject confusion about my decision to go off on my own. I wanted to try and mend fences with them, but I wasn't sure if this was the way to do it.

I fussed with my dress in the mirror. I'd managed to tame my curls into an artful mess on top of my head. Lots of pins had been involved.

"Are you trying to murder me?"

I turned toward his voice. "Maybe."

"You can't wear that dress and expect me to be on my game tonight. And meet your parents for the first time."

I laughed as I crossed the room to him. He had on his dress pants and nothing else. What was it about a man and bare feet and denim or dress pants?

It just didn't make sense.

"I'm sure you can control yourself."

He slipped his finger under the strap at my shoulder. "Maybe get it out of my system now?"

"Nope. We have no time for that. Maybe we can have a quickie in the chapel if we're feeling frisky."

"I'm going to go to hell now that you put that in my brain. Dammit, Chaos."

"Are you going to call me Chaos when we say our vows?"

He grinned at me. "Probably."

I shook my head. "Hurry up and put all of that away." I made a circle with my finger. He had far too many delicious muscles going on there. "My sister will freak if we're late."

"We have ten minutes."

Laughing, I slapped his hands away. "Don't be proud of that number."

"I seem to remember you enjoying my three minutes in the dressing room, woman."

I grabbed my heels and hurried out before I changed my mind. He was a menace.

While I was downstairs waiting for him, I made sure my software was still doing the last pass on Rachel's wedding present. It took ages even with Poe's added memory. Then again, I was used to doing three-minute videos.

Guess I'd have to upgrade my gear if—when—I started making longer form videos.

I was tempted to check my social media accounts, but I didn't want anything to ruin my mood. My sister was getting married tomorrow. I was not going to let some asshole ruin every part of it.

Midnight popped off the floor, making me jump.

"Wow." Ransom came down the stairs wearing black-on-black and my whole system shivered. For good reason. "You clean up nice, Grumpasaurus."

"Thanks. I hate wearing a suit."

"Well, it really likes you." I patted Midnight on the head. "Ready to go?"

"If you are."

I grabbed my navy clutch and tucked my phone away as well as my lipstick and my tiny black fold-up shoes that were the best invention in the history of inventions. That was about all that fit in the stupid little thing, but this dress didn't have pockets.

We took Veronica because he was still wary of the whole hacker aspect. I didn't mind so much, especially since the night air was warm enough that I could skip a jacket.

The lodge was lit up and the parking lot held about a dozen cars.

A few topiaries had replaced the usual greeneries in the front of the bed and breakfast entrance.

We headed inside, chatting like any other normal-ish couple.

Until Ransom slowed as he spotted Reid in the atrium. "What's he doing here? I thought this was family only."

"I don't know. Oh, Helena."

He glanced at me. "Helena?"

"Yeah, one of Rachel's bridesmaids had to bow out. Her mom got sick. I think Helena jumped in to help out."

His shoulders tightened, and I touched his cheek. Sure enough, he was grinding like crazy. "Dusty molars, sir."

It was enough to make him relax and laugh. "Come on, let's get inside. Best man and maid of honor need to be on time."

The room was full of everyone I loved and when I saw Rachel and Clay laughing in the center of everything, my heart expanded.

This was the important part.

I dragged Ransom over to my parents first. Might as well get that over with. He was all tightened up again, but this time, it was for regular boyfriend—er, fiancé reasons.

I hugged my mom and then my dad. My dad's peppermint and Old Spice scent instantly eased some of my nerves.

"Mom, Dad, this is Ransom." I smiled brightly. "Ransom, Patrick and Claire Doyle."

"Sir. Ma'am." Ransom was stiff as he shook my dad's hand and gentle with my mom. "Pleased to meet you."

I clutched Ransom's hand. "So...things happened a little fast, but I wanted you to know before—"

"You're getting married?" My mother's mouth was a thin line. "Yes, your aunt told me."

I winced. Dammit, Laverne.

I hadn't thought of that part. *Crap.*

"Sorry."

"It's my fault, ma'am—Mrs. Doyle." Ransom cleared his throat. "I swept her off her feet. Well, she sort of did it to me instead. I'm just along for the ride. I do love her very much, though."

"Hmm."

"Excuse me, everyone!" Rachel stood up on the small dais that held the head table. "Can we go over to the chapel? We'll do a quick run through and then dinner. Sounds good?"

Saved by the bride.

I followed everyone out, clutching Ransom's hand. "See, that wasn't so bad."

"Oh, yeah. That was a dream."

"We'll figure stuff out. We have a lot to figure out." I bumped him with my arm. "By the way, we're going to make the attic my space, right?"

"Dear God, yes. I already started measuring."

"We're already in sync. Look at that."

He rolled his eyes and ushered me forward. "I just want my living room back."

"You're the one who asked me to marry you, pal. And you nick-named me Chaos."

"Oh, I remember." He kissed my shoulder. "It's worth it."

And cue the melting. I was going to be a puddle of goo by the end of this wedding.

The actual rehearsal didn't take long. Rachel and Clay were keeping things simple. The chapel was non-denominational and had a whole different feel at night.

The stained glass glowed, and the pews gleamed. Walking up the aisle made my heart race and trip in ways I hadn't dreamed. Most girls usually role-played being a bride when they were younger. I'd been playing reporter or stealing my dad's old camera to take pictures.

But this was something else.

I looked over at Ransom as he walked with me down the aisle. I could see that it affected him just as much.

I'd be doing this with *him*.

Three weeks ago, I wouldn't have believed it was possible to be this happy.

As we turned to look out at the pews, I noticed Clay's parents were quiet and fit in with mine. His were studious academics and matched my stuffy accountants. Somehow it all worked out.

Clay gave Rachel a dramatic dip after he kissed her. They looked deliriously happy.

The actual wedding was going to be one for the books.

I pulled out my phone to take a quick video of the altar with the pink poinsettias and mini Christmas trees that Rachel had incorporated into the peonies and Sterling roses. Christmas was how they'd fallen in love, after all.

It really was all so beautiful.

I double-checked that I'd actually taken video in between all my personal swooning, then I ran after my family as they all filed out. Ransom was waiting for me at the door to go back over to the lodge. We were having dinner in the bed and breakfast portion of the building.

A few people were setting up tables. I waved at the ones I remembered. Most people stayed working at the orchard for years after they found Happy Acres. Laughter rang out from every direction.

Though I wasn't normally a fanciful sort, I could feel the love and the sense of family and community between each and every person in the room. Even my stuffy parents lit up when they spent time with my aunts and uncles.

I lifted a glass of something pink and bubbly from a tray, murmuring my thanks as I gratefully took a seat.

"Is it all right if I sit with you?"

I looked up at a gorgeous woman with dark blond hair standing alone. "Helena." I kicked out a chair. "Absolutely."

"Thanks." She sank into the seat. "I just feel weird here. People are probably staring at me. I don't know what I was thinking when I said yes to Rachel."

I patted her hand. "You said yes because you're sweet and understand they love each other."

She sighed. "I do. Clay and I always ran in the same circles. It was just easier to attach myself to him, so I didn't have to go to those blasted work parties alone."

"I can't say I get it, but I'm glad you guys could remain friends."

"I only want the best for him. There were never any fireworks with us. He was just safe." She glanced over at the tall, handsome man with light hair she'd attended this shindig with.

Wait, was his hair silver? Wasn't he Ransom's age?

Helena sighed. "Now I've gone full circle with one who's anything but safe."

I gave him the once-over. I was pretty sure his dove gray suit could buy me four laptops—top grade. He had that hot patrician thing going on, though I preferred my guys more ruggedly handsome. "Is that a good thing?"

She laughed lightly. "I'm not sure."

"Been there, girl." I waved down the waiter and took another glass of bubbly off the tray and handed it to her. "Why there's alcohol."

She clinked her glass with mine. "Today, I'm all about it."

Ransom brushed his knuckles over my shoulder. "Sure you don't want to go over and sit with Laverne?"

"I need a second. Helena and I are gonna hang."

"Don't go any— What is she doing here?"

I looked up. "Who?"

"I'll be right back." He was distracted, but my feet hurt too much to get up.

I craned my neck. "What is he talking about?"

"I'm not sure."

"Do you want me to call over your guy? Reid, right?" I glanced over at him standing alone near the mini bar.

"He won't come over here. He's a solitary sort. I'm not sure how to get a read on him."

"Ahh, the mysterious type."

There was a commotion near the kitchen. Two of the waiters seemed very distracted, talking amongst themselves before one of them approached me with a strained smile.

"Miss. Ransom asked me to bring you over to him."

"I can manage on my own." Lightly, I touched Helena's shoulder. "Sorry, I have to see what's going on."

"Don't worry about me."

I stood up and the room tilted.

"Let me help you." The waiter tucked his hand under my arm. "This way."

Dimly, I realized the waiter was leading me away from the room. What the hell? "Wait." My tongue suddenly felt too big for my mouth. My head was pounding, and my ears were full of static.

What was happening?

"Shortcut around the people."

"No, I don't think I should..." I wasn't sure if the words were actually coming out of my mouth. There was a disconnect between my throat and my head.

Was I floating? It seemed as if I was.

"Ransom isn't going to want me to leave," I whispered. God, my limbs were so heavy. Walking was too hard, but the waiter was dragging me now, even as I stumbled.

"Don't worry about him."

As the world went black, one word was in my head.

Ransom.

Chapter 34

Ransom

Freaking Tasers

"I know, I know. I wasn't sure I could make it, so I didn't want to say yes to the wedding." Maple hugged me tight. She was tanned, probably wearing something couture, and creating a stir in the room as usual. Famous super model and all.

"Weren't you in Madrid or something?"

"Milan."

"La-di-da."

My sister launched herself at me again. She smelled of something expensive and heady. It was so her and so foreign at the same time. It had been at least three years since we'd seen each other face to face. "I miss your dry humor, grumpy."

"I want you to meet someone."

"Oh? A girl someone? Or a guy. I don't judge."

"Good to know. No, it's a woman." I led her through the small group of people who had congregated around the chafing dishes full of food.

Everyone was hungry, including me. But I wanted Maple to meet Chaos first. I was certain they'd get along well.

I didn't see her near the icy blond by the door. I looked around, my gaze bouncing from Laverne to Rachel to their parents. My heart kicked and the skin between my shoulder blades burned.

"Chaos?" I called out. I didn't care if she thought I was over-reacting.

Nothing.

Reid crossed to me. "What's wrong?"

I didn't know what to say to him and he tossed a hot, shocked look toward Maple before the frozen blue of his eyes turned emotionless once again. "Where's Chaos—Willow?"

Reid slid his hand out of his pocket, suddenly more alert. "I think I saw her get up to go to the restroom."

"Where?"

Reid frowned. "What's wrong?" he repeated.

"Where. Did. She. Go?"

"Through there."

I left my sister there and started running. The hallway was dark since we were the only party in the B&B right now. I called her name, my heart pounding in my ears.

"Chaos!"

"What the fuck is going on?" Reid followed me.

"Too much to get into."

"This isn't just you being a possessive freak, is it?" Reid jogged after me.

"No." I glanced right and left. "Chaos?" My voice carried, but there was no answer.

I heard the click of a door and took a left. It was a side exit out into the orchard.

Reid ran after me, and we both crashed through the door hard enough that it bounced against the hinges and slammed into my hip before I could get clear.

I swore, but I kept running. My hands shook, but my breathing evened out as I suddenly became very cold. Everything went stone silent in my head as I searched the dark.

There were tiny white lights strung across the courtyard, but it barely cut the darkness. Briefly, I caught a flash of light skin. I took off, instinct overriding any sense.

I could hear Reid's footsteps thundering behind me, but I zeroed in on the flash of pale flesh in the low light. Her skin was a beacon, drawing me to her. Thank God she was wearing that goddamn dress.

I was going to have it bronzed when I got her back. Because there was no other option.

A branch cracked and I veered right, hiding by one of the craggy trees that were in full bloom.

"Get up, get up." The voice was just above a whisper, but it wasn't Chaos.

I ran into the darkness. I didn't know if he had a weapon, but it didn't matter.

Only *she* mattered.

I dove for the dark figure, pushing Willow to the ground in the process. She collapsed onto her side, flowers scattering around her in the dim light. Distantly, I heard her slurred words. Maybe my name.

She was alive. That was the only thing I needed to know. I drove the man to the ground, my fists plowing into anything I could find. Ribs, a knee, a shoulder. And finally, his face. Sharp, rat-like features were skewed in pain.

The man tried to curl into himself, but I was incensed.

"Ransom!" Reid roared from behind me.

I didn't stop. I couldn't stop.

He'd dared to try and take her from me again. I felt the jolt in my side, the searing pain of the Taser, but my adrenaline was too fueled to feel it.

Just the blood under my fists as the man choked out pained sobs.

"Ransom. Enough!" Reid dragged me off him as I struggled and swung.

Reid ducked from my hammering blows. "Stop!" He shoved his shoulder into my belly and took me down to the ground in a tackle. "He's down. He's not going anywhere. I promise."

"Chaos?" I looked around wildly, but I couldn't get free of Reid.

Voices in the distance were calling both of our names.

"Get off me," I managed.

"All right, all right." Reid rolled off and laid spread out on the grass. "Whatever. Kill him if you want to go to jail."

I stood over the man who'd done this to her. His face was a mess of blood and swelling already. He was barely conscious and still curled into himself.

Clay and Rachel were running toward us, but I only had eyes for Willow.

I stumbled to her. My side was singing, and the ground came at me way too fast, but I pulled her onto my lap. "Chaos?"

"We gotta stop doing this," she said against my shoulder. Her eyes were heavy, but she was valiantly trying to keep them open.

"Never again." I wrapped my arms around her. The pain didn't even register at this point. I was surrounded by lemons and apple blossoms and earth, but the most important part was in my arms.

"I didn't want to go with him." She touched her forehead and shook her head. "I think something was in my drink."

I pressed her cheek to my chest. "He won't be bothering you again."

Sirens in the distance allowed me to relax a fraction more. I looked up and Reid and Clay were on either side of the man on the ground. He wasn't going anywhere.

Laverne and Claire, Chaos's mom, ran over to us. Hands tried to take her from me even as I fought to hold on.

"It's okay. She's okay," Laverne said softly. "You can let go, Ransom."

I didn't want to ever let go, but I knew she would be safe with them.

There was a flurry of activity. Cops and paramedics came in. I tried to wave the paramedic away. "Go to her. To Chaos."

"Sir, that's okay. We're taking care of her."

"Not that piece of shit over there. Let him bleed." I held my side. "Fuck."

"Can I please see?" the paramedic said. His face was affable and annoyingly cheerful. "Real quick."

I groaned. Now that the adrenaline was slipping away, I felt every bit of pain in my side.

The paramedic was a hulking man, but he gently lifted my shirt. "Well, that's gonna hurt."

"Ya think?" I glanced at the tag on his uniform. "Thanks, Ben."

"No problem. I can take you in if you want. Nasty Taser burn, maybe a bruised rib. My chief would say bring you in."

"Not in this life."

"Kinda figured." Ben grinned. "Marine?"

"Army," I said with only a small groan.

He lubed up a large square piece of gauze. "I put pain gel on this. Should help a little."

I hissed as he pressed it on and sighed at the pain medication seeping into my burn. "Thanks. Where's Willow?"

"Arguing with my partner over there. Something about a wedding."

"Her sister is getting married tomorrow."

"You guys sure know how to party."

I laughed even though it hurt.

Ben tossed some stuff back in his kit and snapped it closed. "She'll be fine. Not sure about that guy."

The cops lifted the man. Now that there wasn't a red haze over my vision, he looked small and pathetic.

Even after all the chaos and pain he'd caused. Not good chaos like my girl. I needed her.

I tried to struggle to my feet and Ben helped me up.

"Sure you're good?"

"Yeah, man. Thanks."

Clay rushed over, passing Ben who was heading back to where his partner was. "Shouldn't you be going in the ambulance?"

"I've been Tased before. I'll live. Just another scar to add to the collection."

Clay steadied me. "You certain about that?"

"I'm going to go check on Chaos."

"She's with Rachel. They're fine."

I limped over, determined to go under my own steam. Rachel was on one side of Chaos and my sister on the other.

"You guys are wild." Maple grinned at me. "I like your girl."

"Yeah. I like her too. Gonna marry her."

"No shit?"

"No shit." I bent to kiss Chaos. "I love you."

"I love you too." Her eyes were still glassy. "Did you kill him?"

"Nope."

She smiled and my heart flipped. I was definitely gonna marry her.

"Good."

"Good?" I stroked her hair.

"I just want him to get help, not be dead."

"You're too good for this world, Chaos." I pressed another kiss to her forehead.

"If you two won't go to the hospital, you're going upstairs. I have a bedroom all set up," Laverne announced.

"Not the baby room again." Rachel sighed.

I shook my head. There would be no babies being made tonight. We were safe there.

Holy shit, weddings were dangerous business.

Epilogue

A Great Day For A Wedding

Willow

The sky was impossibly blue, and I was pretty sure all the birds were chirping for my sister on her big day. It was a perfect 65 degrees with the slightest breeze.

Last night's insanity was in our rearview, even if I'd awakened with a monster headache from whatever drug that awful person had given me.

Aidan had given us a report this morning. And a photo since I had a bit of a black mark in my memory from him trying to take me again. I kind of wished I hadn't seen the photo of the guy with sharp, weaselly features.

Mark Luther Charles.

A serial killer name. Wasn't that a lovely thing? But he was officially behind bars. I sure as hell was going to make sure I did whatever was necessary to keep him him there too. Especially since he had a record for stalking two other women before. He'd escalated to kidnapping. Wasn't I the lucky one?

Now he was facing *two* kidnapping charges. Federal jail was definitely in his future.

But I didn't give two craps about that man today. It was my sister's wedding day. I could focus on her and my family without any black clouds, thank God.

My mom came up behind me to straighten my dress. "Are you sure you're okay?"

"I'm fine, Mom. I promise."

She cupped my cheek. "You scared me."

"I know." I covered her hand. "I definitely won't be doing that again."

She looked over at Ransom, standing so straight and tall in his tux. Mercy, he was a sight. You couldn't even tell he'd beaten the holy crap out of a man last night. Or that he had a Taser mark on his side that I'd kissed this morning.

He'd also helped get rid of that pesky headache too. He was a multi-talented individual.

Ransom must've been reading my mind because his dimples popped out. They were on full display now that he'd had to trim his beard down to scruff.

My sister was so glad we were alive, she didn't even make him go for a full shave.

"That young man will keep you on your toes, Willow Renee."

Middle names again. *Oy.* "Yes, he sure will. I'm excited to see just how much."

"You really do love him? It's not just...hormones."

I laughed. "All the way love."

"All right. If you're sure."

"More than sure."

She patted my cheek lightly. "Shall we get your sister married then?"

"Definitely."

I moved into the lineup. It was a small wedding party, just Helena and Taylor from the gift shop who had become my sister's best friend. Oh, and me. We all decided on the same pretty pink gowns that dipped off our shoulders. Thank God my sister hadn't picked something horrifying. Even if pink wasn't exactly my color.

Ransom came up next to me and held out his arm. "Ready?"

"Ready."

We walked down the aisle in the small chapel in the middle of the most beautiful orchard in all the world. At least in my eyes.

And when Rachel came down that aisle, there wasn't a dry eye in the whole place. She and Clay pledged their love with simple words and a few tears of their own.

My eyes were on Ransom's the whole time. Okay, and on my sister too.

I was good at multi-tasking.

Cheers rang out around us as the new Mr. and Mrs. Clay Winslow kissed. And in a blink, the chapel emptied out and we all moved across the stone path to the Gala room as if the horror of last night didn't exist.

They'd found happiness. And for that moment, we got to share in it with them.

The speeches were hilarious. Ransom roasted Clay, of course, and I sang my sister's praises with a little extra sibling salt for good measure. Afterward, the day was so beautiful that we ended up outside for part of the reception.

The cider was a hit and Beckett even brought out his horse to show off to the ladies in attendance. My cousin made quite the picture in his dress jeans, button-down shirt, and navy vest. That was about as dressed up as Beckett Manning ever got.

I was standing with Ransom under the arbor, both of us exhausted. But we knew we had to stay a little bit longer.

Suddenly, there was murmuring.

"Oh, man. I don't have it in me for anything else," Ransom said with a sigh.

I stood and peered over most of the guests. That super eyesight and height thing really came in handy when I wanted to be nosy. "Ransom, I think that's your sister."

Ransom stood up, shielding his eyes from the sun with his hand. "What the hell is she doing with Reid?"

My eyebrows went up. They were standing a little too close together for, uh, friends. I noticed Helena on the sidelines, her face in her hands as her shoulders shook.

That was *not* a good sign.

"Maple?" Ransom pushed his way through the crowd.

"Ransom, back off. This isn't about you." Maple stabbed her finger into Reid's chest. "You're a fucking rude bastard."

"You enjoyed my rudeness for that long weekend, didn't you?"

Helena pushed through the crowd, and I tried to go after her.

Beckett was still on his horse, and she ran right for him. He didn't seem to know what was going on, but he held his arm down for her and he swung her up behind him.

I heard her yell, "Just please go."

When I turned back, Ransom's arm was flying once again. Reid took the punch squarely. He didn't even try to avoid it.

"Holy crap." I ran back to Ransom. "What are you doing?"

"He fucking slept with my sister." His face was red and his jaw iron. "Both of them."

"Dammit." I pulled Ransom back. "Come on. That's enough."

Clay pushed through the crowd to stand in front of Reid. "I think it's time you go."

"Fine." He looked around. "Where's Helena?"

"Not your concern." Justin came up beside Clay. "Leave."

I dragged Ransom back to the reception and sat him down, then ran to the bar and grabbed some ice for his hand.

"I can't believe you."

"I can't believe he insulted my sister here at Clay's wedding." He hissed as I put the ice on his knuckles.

"You can't keep hitting people."

Maple sat down beside us. "You didn't need to defend my honor, jackass. I'm quite capable of kicking his ass all on my own."

"Yeah, well, then why didn't you?" Ransom demanded.

Her face crumpled. "It's complicated."

"Complicated? What part of that is complicated? He was engaged to our sister."

"Yeah, that we haven't seen in ten years."

"And that makes it okay?"

Holy *Days of Our Lives.* I resisted the urge to prop my head up on my hand and watch them like a tennis match.

And this woman was going to be my new sister-in-law. Along with the missing drama llama.

"It doesn't matter. I'm done with him. I swear." She got up and disappeared through the doorway leading to the atrium.

I had an odd feeling that was not the truth. Or even close.

Ransom tried to get up, but I pushed him back down. "Easy there, Rocky. I think she needs a minute."

"I don't believe this."

"Not really your business, pal."

He shot a hot look at me.

"What? She's a grown woman."

"But Reid?"

"Well, that part isn't awesome. I bet there's quite the story there."

"I don't want to hear it."

I did. But I'd get it out of Maple later. Probably. If she didn't pull a Douglas sister special and disappear.

"I'm really worried about Helena."

Ransom sighed and pulled my chair closer to him before tossing the makeshift ice pack on the table. "Did I mention you're too good for this world?"

"Maybe." I cupped his face and stroked my thumb down his bristly cheek. "She really looked shattered."

"Reid has that effect on women. Why do you think I don't want Maple anywhere near him?"

I sighed. "Can we not worry about anyone else for a little while?"

He touched his forehead to mine. "We could make use of that bedroom of ours."

"Here?" Aunt Laverne liked calling it the baby room a little too much for my taste.

"God, no. The one at my house."

I laughed as I leaned in and kissed him. "That sounds like a very good plan."

We appreciate our readers so much!
If you loved the book please let your friends know. If you're extra awesome, we'd love a review on your favorite book site.

Turn the page for a special sneak peek of CEO DADDY, a standalone novel in our Crescent Cove series.

And if you missed Fiancée By Christmas, we included that too! Happy Reading.

CEO Daddy

Hannah

I might be single and alone on New Year's Eve. But I'm not woe is me. No, ma'am. I'm looking at this moment as an opportunity to cherish my solitude.

With a sigh, I set down my pen and picked up my water glass. I should be drinking alcohol at least. Maybe I still would. I wasn't much of a wine fan, but I could use tonight to broaden my horizons. A cocktail sounded nice. Very adult.

A drink I could enjoy happily on my own.

Okay, cut the crap. In my diary, I should be honest. The diary I was writing in while I ate my dinner of consommé—fancy soup essentially—and garlic breadsticks, because who was I going to kiss at midnight? No one.

Joyfully solo, that was me.

In reality, I was fresh off another broken Tinder date. Broken by *me,* no less. I could never quite close the deal. Probably because a date with me held more weight than the usual hookup.

I'd been adult about that too. Virginity was a burden, so I'd just rid myself of it quickly and quietly. No fuss. Until the time came to actually meet Joe Blow in the flesh—yes, that was his name on the site —and I'd balked. I'd made up an excuse about getting together with an ex and that had been that.

As if I had any exes. Just a few high school boyfriends who hadn't amounted to much.

Since then, I'd stuck close to home, the dutiful older sister who raised her younger siblings after our parents had died in a plane crash. Now that the twins, Emma and Rachel, had turned nineteen and gone off to college, that left me at loose ends.

Alone for real.

"Can I get you anything else? Maybe you'd like a look-see at the dessert menu? The lemon bars are my favorite. They're my mama's recipe."

I blinked up at the grinning blond waitress. At least I thought she was a waitress, though she had a more commanding air about her despite her small town friendliness. "Your mama works here too?"

"Not anymore. She used to own the joint. Then she retired and sold it out from under me with no warning, but I got it back because of my lovable pain-in-the-ass baby daddy. Well, husband too. So, lemon bars?"

I rubbed my temple. Whoa, information overload. "You have a husband? You look...youthful."

Luckily, I'd managed not to say she looked twelve, which was a misstatement in any case. She looked at least sixteen. But not old enough to be married, at least in New York.

She laughed and sat down opposite me at the table. "Sure do."

"And a baby."

"Yeah, she's not even a year old yet. Star's the light of my life. Want to see?" She was already tugging a folding wallet of pictures— many, many pictures—out of her apron pocket.

"Um, sure?"

She showed me an array of photos of a chubby baby with bright green eyes and a drooly smile.

"She's beautiful. Her hair is so dark."

"Like Oliver's. Unless it changes. I hope it doesn't. It's my ace in the hole I wasn't impregnated by the milkman."

Unsure if she was serious, I smiled faintly. "I think I'll try those lemon bars, please."

She nodded enthusiastically and bustled off to the kitchen. She seemed sweet.

Everyone in Crescent Cove was sweet. It was a picturesque village, nestled against the long curve of Crescent Lake. At the holidays, the place really shone.

The big formal banquet room I was seated in was jammed with guests. Most were families, along with a good amount of couples and solo businessmen passing through the area due to the proximity to Syracuse. I lived in between Crescent Cove and Syracuse, in a town so tiny you could miss it if you shut your eyes.

Which you shouldn't do while driving, especially in the fall and winter. We were in deer and wild turkey country.

Spending New Year's Eve in Crescent Cove was a luxury. I didn't have the funds to spare on such things, but I'd asked for money for Christmas from my sisters and my bestie just so I could splurge.

Now I was wondering if it was a huge mistake.

I'd thought I would feel less on my own in a crowd.

Wrong.

I'd had to wait a half hour for this table. There was holiday music playing, and cheerful lights twinkling, and every surface seemed to be decked out with candles and poinsettias and big satin red ribbons. People were laughing and enjoying time with their loved ones.

And I was scribbling lies in my diary about how I didn't mind that my sisters had chosen to return to campus early rather than hang out with their big sister. That I wasn't at all jealous my bestie had a date for New Year's with a guy she worked with.

Worst of all? The prospect of homemade lemon bars excited me more than the gorgeous fireplace suite I'd reserved to spend the evening—you guessed it—alone.

"Here you go. I gave you an extra one. On holidays, calories don't count." The blond proprietress smiled and set the plate in front of me. "Can I get you anything else?"

"Yes, actually, you can. I'd like some champagne, please."

"Oh, sure." She nodded as if it wasn't weird at all I was ordering champagne with lemon bars after drinking water since I'd sat down. "Flute or bottle for the table?"

Did she know something I didn't? Was it usual for women dining alone to drink a whole bottle of bubbly? Maybe on New Year's Eve, anything went.

"Bottle for the table, please." The deep voice barely registered. In fact, I didn't even look to see the owner. He couldn't be speaking for my table. I definitely didn't know anyone who sounded like *that*.

Hello, man, not a boy.

The blond shifted away from me and I dazedly followed her gaze to where one of the businessmen I'd noticed earlier stood beside the chair opposite me. I hadn't seen his face, just the tidy queue of dark hair on his neck as he was seated. A solo diner, just like me.

Unlike me, he hadn't been writing in a journal with flowers on the tattered cover. No, he'd been flipping through a thick sheaf of paperwork, and he'd barely looked up long enough to order.

I hadn't seen his face, but he'd seen mine. Or else he was in the habit of joining strangers once the alcohol was served. Judging by his well-cut pinstriped dark suit and fancy Italian leather briefcase, he wasn't hurting for money. I preferred looking at those things rather than his features. If his looks matched up with his voice—

Well, let's just say I wasn't in any shape to handle that level of disappointment once he rethought his decision. Because, seriously? Why did he want to sit with *me*?

"Oh." The blond smiled. "Are you joining her?" She glanced at me. "Dinner date?"

Normally, the blond's presumptuousness might have irritated me, but it felt as if she was on my side. Like she was making sure I wanted this guy to sit at my table. I must be giving off vibes that I did *not* know this dude. No matter how handsome he was and how important he seemed, a woman had to be careful.

"Two people eating alone on New Year's Eve should eat together." His deep voice caused a tingle low in my belly. "Sage, you know I'm harmless." His smile was anything but.

The blond—Sage—raised an eyebrow. "So said Ted Bundy." She smiled sweetly and shifted to glance at me. "Your call."

He switched his briefcase to the other hand, allowing me to see the bundle of winter tulips he also held, wrapped with a burlap bow and with pine greenery overflowing the colorful tissue paper. Tulips were a weakness of mine, and I'd never seen a winter bouquet of them before.

As if he'd noticed me staring at them, he held them out as additional incentive. "For you."

I borrowed a page from Sage's book and lifted an eyebrow, saying nothing. But I accepted the flowers. I was no dummy, and the tulips were gorgeous. I could already imagine them in the center of my table at home, cheering me up as I experimented in the kitchen. The pale reds, pinks, and yellows were perfect.

"He can sit."

Sage nodded. "Would you like anything else besides the bottle of champagne?"

"A cup of coffee for me, please." His smile was easy and self-assured, and he never looked away from me as he took the seat opposite me at the table.

Sage left us alone with a waggle of her brows.

"Friend of yours?" I set the bouquet of tulips in my lap and drew a nail through the powdered sugar beneath the lemon bars on my plate. I rued not redoing my nail polish for tonight. The silver was chipped at the edges. Surely, a man like him would notice.

"Oh, Sage? No, not exactly, although we've met a few times. I make it a point to eat here when I'm in town. Something I'll be doing a lot more soon."

He paused as Sage brought over the bottle of champagne and two glasses. She popped the cork and poured for us both, then left us alone again. A moment later, she brought his coffee, which he largely ignored.

I picked up my glass, clinked with my new dinner guest, and sipped. The bubbly went straight to my head as it always did, so I set the glass down.

He was still watching me, his lips curved ever so slightly. He hadn't taken a drink yet.

"I'm Asher," he said as the silence extended uncomfortably. Somehow our personal silence was much more noticeable because of all the excited chatter around us.

"Hannah."

"Nice to meet you. What brings you here tonight of all nights?"

"I didn't want to sit alone at home." *Nice one, Hannah. Can you sound any more pathetic?* "It's a night for parties and fun." I saluted him with my champagne and drank.

Heat flowed out from my belly through my limbs. I couldn't decide if I liked the sensation or not. Or maybe the heat was from Asher's gaze. His eyes weren't as dark as I'd originally believed. With the candle flickering between us, I'd guess now they were a warm hazel, perhaps varying depending on his clothing.

Apparently, his black pinstriped suit didn't offer any appreciable change to them. But whoa nelly, that suit was working wonders on me.

Maybe three-piece suits really were the equivalent to lingerie for a woman. His was definitely revving my motor.

Revving everything.

"So, do you have plans after this? A party perhaps, or some other kind of fun?" He ran his fingertip along the rim of his glass.

"How old are you?" I blurted.

His dark brows drew together. "Thirty-two in March."

"Hmm."

"Is that a good *hmm* or a bad *hmm*?"

"I'm twenty-three. I've never..." I took a deep breath. *Try not to embarrass yourself again.* "Well, this is just sharing some lemon bars and champagne, right?"

"That's up to you. Why don't we start with some conversation and go from there?" His slow smile only served to stir me up even more.

Relax in this gorgeous, commanding man's presence? Not likely.

"Sure. Let's begin with why you came over to my table." I picked up my dessert fork and cut off the corner of one of my lemon bars, belatedly remembering he didn't have one. Sage hadn't brought over another plate.

By accident or design? Even without knowing her well, I could easily see her as the matchmaking type.

"Sorry, it's rude of me to eat when you don't have anything. Here." I set down the fork and lifted the plate toward him, swallowing deeply as he pushed aside the vase and the flickering candle to make room for the plate between us.

"We can share." His fingers brushed mine as he broke off a corner and lifted it to his mouth.

His perfect mouth. His lips were neither too full or too sparse. Just right.

As everything he possessed seemed to be. And I hadn't even gotten a look at him beneath the waist.

Probably good. I didn't need to be any more intimidated, especially by pinstriped thirty-two-year-old cocks. I was already freaked out enough.

Hello, out of my league.

"No fork?" I asked a little breathlessly. He seemed the fork-and-knife-at-all-times type to me.

"Nah. Fingers are better. See?" He broke off another piece and lifted it across the table to me, not dropping so much as a crumb. "Lean forward."

I obliged him and his fingertips brushed my lips as he fed me the treat. His voice was entrancing. I was afraid to imagine all the things he could make me do with just one of those husky commands.

His eyes held me in his thrall so completely that I barely noticed the burst of lemon as I swallowed. The bars were a delicious mix of sweet and tart, but I probably wouldn't have noticed if the dessert had been undercooked and bland.

"Good?"

I nodded and he repeated the move several more times. He wasn't even eating himself, just feeding me. He had long, elegant fingers with a surprising bit of ink swirling down his hands. The bold Roman numerals and heavy, old typeface of a latin phrase were mixed with a bit of artistry.

So incongruous to the buttoned-up businessman. It somehow made him even hotter.

Once, out of the corner of my eye, I noticed Sage start to approach with the bill in hand. She took in what was occurring at our shadowy table, widened her eyes, and sped off in the opposite direction.

I would've laughed had I not been so turned on that I could barely think.

What was happening here? We weren't even talking. Was this what occurred when under the influence of a lonely holiday meant for couples and some expensive champagne? I'd had a couple more sips in between rounds of Asher feeding me. Big, bolstering sips. The kind that made a normally shy, awkward woman feel bold.

"No ring," I said casually—or so I hoped. I'd had plenty of time to see his hand as it came closer to my mouth. "You're single?"

"Very. The kind of single that means I'm alone on New Year's Eve, just as you are." He lifted his thumb to his lips and licked off a stray crumb from the piece he'd just fed me. The movement was far more sensual than it had any right to be. "You are alone tonight, aren't you, Hannah?"

Something about the question and his use of my name made my

throat tighten to the point that if I hadn't gulped more champagne, I might've choked. This time, I didn't mind the floaty feeling that overtook my body, or the resulting wave of warmth.

"I'm alone far too much these days. But right now? No. Neither of us is alone."

He nodded, lowering his head for an instant while his jaw locked. He finally took a few sips of coffee before he met my gaze once again. "I have a room upstairs. Just for tonight."

Questions flitted through my mind.

Who are you, Asher?

Why did you pick me to talk to?

Was it just that I looked lonely, so I must be an easy target for sexual advances?

In the end, I didn't really care. We were both alone, and no one was waiting for me at home. What did it matter if I chose this handsome man to spend the evening with? No one would be hurt. And I would finally be able to cross one thing off my bucket list.

Sex with a gorgeous man, check.

Sex, period.

But that didn't mean I'd make it easy on him.

"Who were the flowers for?" I stroked the downy soft petals of the pink tulip on top of the bouquet in my lap.

"My grandmother." He smiled wryly. "She thinks I need to get out more, so she'll approve that I gave them to the most beautiful woman I've seen since..." He trailed off, looking uncharacteristically unsure. Even with only knowing him a very short while, I was quite certain Asher rarely faltered. "Ever."

"I believe you don't get out much after that statement." I rested my cheek on my fist. "My hair isn't really blond, by the way. I put in a rinse today. Truth in advertising and all that."

"It doesn't look blond. Not exactly. More like the color of honey." His voice deepened. "Rich and luxurious."

"Glorious Tones hair color thanks you for your appreciation of their product." I toyed with the stem of my now nearly empty champagne glass. "When is the last time you approached a woman with that line about having a room upstairs?"

"Never. I've never had a room upstairs here before." His lips twitched. "And to be honest, I don't have one now. I wasn't planning on staying until I saw you. Writing so furiously in that." He nodded to my abandoned journal. "What were you writing?"

"Where were you going after this?" I countered.

"To my grandmother's. She was going to be who I counted down to midnight with." He finally reached for his champagne and took a single sip. Easing back in his chair, he licked his lips, slowly and surely. "I'd much rather kiss you once the ball drops."

"Which balls are we referring to?"

I didn't know if he'd find me funny or crude. It was usually half and half, depending on my company. But his laughter was quick and appreciative. "You're different than I expected."

"Oh, really? What did you expect? A meek little mouse who'd trot after you and hop right into bed?" Okay, this had to be the champagne talking, because this was next level, even for me.

"No. I wasn't even thinking about bed when I came over here. I just wanted to hear your voice. To see if you ever smiled. You still haven't, you know. Not at me."

"Smiles are earned. Keep trying. You might get there."

"Luckily, I don't give up easily. Why are you alone tonight? No family?"

"No." The lie came easily, and sometimes seemed far too true when my sisters were busy with school and out of touch. My family was a fraction of what it had once been. "Let's just say I live an isolated existence."

It wasn't that far from reality. I was alone too often.

I couldn't stand another moment of it.

"No lover." The word dripped off his tongue, laced with a sensuality that was far beyond my realm of experience.

"No." I tilted my head. "So, what's your story?"

His lips lifted on one side. "I'm a man who works far too much and spends New Year's Eve with his grandmother. What more do you need to know?"

Indeed.

I nodded at the bottle of champagne. "Think we can get that to go?"

NOW AVAILABLE in all formats!

Fiancée by Christmas
Don't Call Me Shirley

I tapped the secret panel I'd had put into my office. It definitely wasn't sanctioned by my personal security.

But right now, I didn't give a crap.

I needed to hear the water.

I needed to *breathe*.

I dragged in a deep lungful of briny, sharp air. November had come in with a bite. And okay, the Hudson River wouldn't be anyone's idea of fresh air. Even me most of the time. However, sometimes the sterile, perfect air pumping through the building got to me.

Sure I could take a walk outside. We had an eatery, outside work stations, and a million dollar promenade I'd let an architect convince me to build. It was stunning and had only elevated the Winslow name across the country.

The only problem with the exquisite campus was the reaction from some of my employees. Either people tried to avoid me—which I actually didn't mind—or I had to deal with the suck-ups who came flying at me like a swarm.

I didn't have that in me today.

Instead I made do with a 360° view of the river and the vast coastline of buildings spiring up into the sky. It felt like a new one was magically appearing every time I took a moment to look. Then again, I didn't have much time to enjoy my view.

My perpetual slate of meetings seemed to take all my time.

When all I wanted to do was escape to my helipad and get the hell out of the city. I didn't even need to look at the calendar—it was as if my body was attuned to the day November hit. But this year, I felt even itchier. Enough that I contemplated doing a no show to three parties I had scheduled this weekend.

One included a date with Helena Danbury.

The perfect socialite and my grandfather's vote for the future Mrs. Clay Winslow. Too bad we had about as much chemistry as flat seltzer water. We made a very pretty picture, but the taste was bland and slightly off-putting.

A discreet chime reminded me that again, my time wasn't my own for another twelve hours, and I definitely needed to put aside wedding thoughts. Nothing good came from that line of thinking, even with my grandfather's constant lectures about adding to the Winslow family tree.

With a sigh, I slid the panel closed. It had been built to hide within the endless windows that made up my office. The canned air and dry meetings waiting for me ramped up the unsettled undercurrent that sat on me like slushy city snow.

Twelve hours until I could escape.

I glanced down at my watch with a frown. Make that thirteen, dammit. I stroked my hand down my tie to make sure it sat flat under my vest. I buttoned the gray wool Burberry suit jacket I was expected to wear just as Ransom Douglas strode through my door without a knock.

Part of the perks of being my bodyguard as well as my best friend since boarding school. He also wore a perfectly tailored suit, but instead of soft winter wool, his was made of a specialized material that let him have a free range of motion.

It made him feel better. I appreciated that it made him look slightly less threatening—just barely.

I wasn't sure why he and my board of directors thought I needed a near ninja-level bodyguard. Being one of the billionaire elite in Manhattan required a certain level of security regardless of the endless boredom of the bulk of my meetings. I was pretty sure I didn't need a Special Forces dropout, but I was glad to have Ransom back in my life in whatever capacity he allowed.

He frowned and sniffed the air, then he pulled his phone out of his pocket.

"What are you doing?"

One eyebrow spiked and he gave me a flat wintry stare, then went back to typing something before slipping his phone back into his pocket. Another thing I'd had to get used to since my best friend had come back into my life. The carefree Dougie was long gone. I was pretty sure I wasn't the only reason for that.

I resisted the urge to rebutton my jacket. Especially now that he'd told me it was one of my tells—nope. I wasn't giving him any reason to think I was guilty.

Ransom was like a dog with a bone. His brow furrowing even further as he scanned the room. He'd probably find the panel by next week, then I'd have to hire another crew to come in and save me from abject mania.

Ransom checked his jet black watch which matched his suit, shirt, and tie. "We have to be in midtown in an hour. We need to get going."

I grabbed my leather satchel full of hard copies of contracts that should be digital only at this point. "Someday old man Jennings will get with the times, and I won't have to drag my ass over there for meetings."

"The day you get George Jennings to do a video call is the day I run down the bike path naked."

"Deal."

Ransom shook his head, but as usual, a smile didn't dent his face. "Let's move."

"Not sure how many times I have to remind you I'm not in your unit." But I strode through my spacious penthouse office to the double doors.

"Former unit," he reminded me and hustled to pass me and open the door for me. I was slightly taller than him, but he had me in muscle and fear factor. I could have used intimidation lessons from him my first few years in the boardroom.

Luckily, my quick brain gave me some advantage against those who thought I'd only earned my spot because of nepotism. And people like Ransom who didn't treat me like the prince of New York.

I let him go first through the doors to make sure my admin didn't kill me. Some days that was hit or miss too.

"Shirley, could you send flowers to Miss Danbury?"

My admin turned to face me. She was a striking Black woman of indeterminate age. I only knew she was in her late fifties because I'd hired her. Anyone else wouldn't have a clue. She wore a ruby colored head wrap which matched her tailored suit. Tasteful gold jewelry wreathed her wrist, fingers, and neck. She commanded a wide U-shaped glass desk with a trio of screens set up with a terrifying number of windows. Shirley Hunt ran my life from her magical keystroked kingdom.

She lifted one of her elegant fountain pens and jotted a note. "Of course. Would these be regretful roses or perhaps something more cheerful?"

I resisted the urge to sigh. She knew me too well.

"See if you can find Sterling roses. She appreciates those."

Shirley gave me an almost imperceptible shake of her head, but wrote down the information in her neat handwriting. "I'll take care of it."

"Thank you." I nodded to Ransom and we strode toward the bank of elevators.

He swiped his key card over the sensor. It would override the elevator so it wouldn't stop on any other floors as we left. "Don't you have a date with Danbury?"

"I think I'm heading to Turnbull this weekend."

He gripped the elevator doors to keep them from closing on us. "You mean *we're* heading for Turnbull. Isn't it too early for that?"

I shrugged. "I need to check the trees."

"You have three other employees who take care of that."

"Just down to two now."

"What, because you can't afford it?"

I stood against the back of the elevator and gripped my hands together in front of me. "Was that a joke?"

Ransom gave a huffed growl, strode in and stood in front of the doors, his back to me. I knew he didn't like enclosed spaces, but thankfully, he'd stopped making me take all nine flights of stairs. Running into a threesome on the third floor stairwell had cured him of that way of thinking. The game development branch of my company was always an interesting visit.

I'd been so impressed with the choreography I hadn't fired them. Especially since Felicity Baskins was among the trio and had earned me a cool ten million at the last gaming convention with her new adventure series.

"Don't change the subject."

"Toby had to retire. His grandson and new wife can handle most of the details. I just want to have a look."

"Control freak," he muttered under his breath and stepped out of the car.

I was. It was how I'd doubled the worth of the Winslow name in the last ten years, but I also was more than happy to use it as a reason to get out of the city.

Winslow Industries was the most advanced tech campus in New York City's Hudson Park area. Hell, I was pretty sure the only one who could compete with my company's largesse was Google.

And maybe Pierce International, not that I'd ever own up to that in mixed company.

But that success also felt like a jail cell some days.

A stunning cell, but a cell nonetheless.

I strode out behind him, only rolling my eyes in my mind as Ransom scanned the lobby. The central hub of the visitor's center was already decked out for Christmas. Two stately trees flanked the information desk, both in a trendy muted palette of aged gold and burgundy.

People rushed in and out of eateries and cafés. Being out by the piers meant it was easier for my company to have facilities on site than to have my employees have to go off campus.

There was a large glass enclosed business center with internet and charging stations for visiting executives. Above us was a stained glass ceiling in moody ocean colors. Each of the nine floors were represented with balconies tastefully decorated to match the main lobby. In the summer, it was dripping with plants voted on by each department.

It made Ransom twitchy to have so many vantage points for someone to attack. That concern was mostly based on his own obsessive tendencies, but I appreciated that he looked out for me. The tech industry did have its fair share of imbalanced people, but I tried to mitigate that by hiring carefully and by paying my people what they were worth.

"I wish you had built a parking garage into the base of this building." Ransom's biting tone had me swallowing a grin.

"Next time I build a two hundred million dollar campus by a body of water, I'll remember that."

"That number is disgusting. And should include parking."

"It does. At the back of the building. We could take the subway."

Ransom gave me a side-eyed stare.

I shrugged. "I've ridden the subway plenty of times."

"Not since you hired me. First of all, germs, and second, there's no way to protect yourself in a tube underground."

"But you want me to have below-street parking?"

"Shut up. It's just not safe enough."

"Well, if you want to get particular—and if you'd ever watch a movie—tons of shit happens in parking garages. This way, I keep my employees safe."

Ransom gritted his teeth together and didn't reply. He nodded to the security guards as we made our way through the doors to the executive parking structure around the side of the building. Another checkpoint and flash of a keycard brought us to the dozen cars I made available for my employees who had to have off-site meetings.

A brisk wind sliced through my suit, reminding me that soon enough I'd have to bundle up. As usual, the weather didn't seem to faze my bodyguard.

He opened the door for me. Not to be galant or even deferential, just so he could make sure there wasn't anything hiding in the car to kill us both. Being in the tech industry included a few too many unknown variables for Ransom's peace of mind. When hundreds of millions were on the line for a project, it wasn't unheard of for there to be danger waiting in the wings. The fact that I had at least seven high stakes deals in various levels of completion at any given time gave my best friend indigestion.

He slammed the door and rounded to the driver's side of the sleek BMW sedan. It was outfitted with a dozen extras, including bullet-proof glass. Overkill as far as I was concerned, but when my CFO had been carjacked last spring, Ransom had made some modifications to all the cars.

He was a competent, if slightly terrifying, driver. He weaved in and out of traffic like a seasoned cabbie. I took the time to review my notes on my phone while he fought his way up to the upper west side.

Jennings took great pride in his offices overlooking Central Park. I was also pretty sure he enjoyed making people come to him. He was all about the power plays. He might be a dinosaur when it came to meetings and contracts, but he was as paranoid as Ransom about security.

Any digital footprint could be hacked and the old man believed in a handshake as much as a signature. So, I'd do the damn meeting. And then I was getting the hell out of the city.

I sent off an email to my admin.

The rest of the day could go hang.

Now Available

For more information go to www.tarynquinn.com

Fiancée by Christmas
Bodyguard by Night

Coming in 2023
Forever by Morning

More by Taryn Quinn

About Taryn Quinn

USA Today bestselling author, ***Taryn Quinn,*** is the sexy and funny alter ego of bestselling authors Taryn Elliott & Cari Quinn. We've been writing together for years, but we have decided to pull the trigger on a combo name just for fun.

And so...Taryn Quinn was born!

Do you like ultra sexy small town romance full of shenanigans? Quirky office romances full of steam? Okay, look...we pretty much just love writing steamy stories. If you're all about that, we're your girls!

For more information about us...
tarynquinn.com
tq@tarynquinn.com

Quinn and Elliott

We also write more serious, longer, and sexier books as Cari Quinn & Taryn Elliott. Our topics include mostly rockstars, but mobsters, MMA, and a little suspense gets tossed in there too.

Rockers' Series Reading Order

Lost in Oblivion

Winchester Falls

Found in Oblivion

Hammered

Rock Revenge

Brooklyn Dawn

OTHER SERIES

Tapped Out

Love Required

Boys of Fall

If you'd like more information about us please visit

www.quinnandelliott.com